Conten

Dedication

This book is dedicated to my children, Jessica, and Max, who warm my soul and whom I am immensely proud, and to my departed wife, Carol Lee Gonzales. She passed away much too young.

4

I thank my friends who made suggestions and helped in the editing. Also, I thank The Lucky Llama coffee shop, and the Market Garden Cafe, where I wrote. I especially thank my friend, Ali, proprietor, of SADE, A Turkish coffee shop hidden away near the railroad tracks in the scenic beach town of Carpinteria, California (Santa Barbara County), for his excellent service, and kindness, even plying me with Turkish cuisine, while I write in peace.

By Linda Ulmer: Thumbprint

As you tip back the chair for distance

Arms folded

Head tilted

Were you aware

When you study me

Your soft dark eyes change to the color of a cold grey mist

Your lids eclipse half-mast as your dark pupils shrink to the size of a small black dot

What are you thinking?

Book Cover by Zara Danyal

-

Copyright Notice

Disclaimer

The main characters in this tale are largely fictional and have no relationship to persons living or dead. The strike events are actual, as are the geography and localities, such as the Ferry Building, Nob Hill, Cow Hollow, Sutra Baths, and the streets and history. Characters such as the governor, the mayor, the Chief of Police, and the Mafia boss, were borrowed for the story. Others may or may not have existed and are left to the reader to decide.

Texas Oil Fields, 1906

A single amber streak of cloud crossed the dessert moon. A cool crisp breeze kissed the cool clean crisp air. It was the dead of night, yet it looked like early morning with a clear sky and bright countless stars. The only sounds in the surrounding desert were of crickets and crunching boots on dirt.

Lost in thought, David Elder was striding to Ramona's brothel to exact revenge for the killing of his friend, PeeWee Stanton.

He thought of violent death following him from an early age and exacting what he considered justice. He thought of his once-loving father becoming a degenerate drunk following the death of his wife, Ella Grace. He thought of his twin sister, Kathy, who had run away from the abuse of their father. She was a teenager. He thought of his last awful fight with their father. He questioned his own path, and wondered if he were cursed. Well, one thing he knew, he was in this God-awful, dirty, dusty, three-block, no-name oil town in Texas, in the middle of nowhere, intent on killing the sons of bitches who had murdered the finest fellow anyone could know.

David Elder, Abe Jackson, GeeGee Popindinski, and PeeWee Stanton had pooled their money for a faro game. Elder played and won land so distant from the working oil fields that they might have left it alone. But no, after convincing Ramona, the only person in the town who had big money, to join their partnership, they hit it big. Humble Oil Inc., contracted with them, and they were off and running, except now for PeeWee.

Rory and his crew, hearing about their good luck, couldn't stop grumbling. They were cheated, they said--the land and oil rights rightfully belonged to them.

The news spread like wildfire. PeeWee Stanton (Pea) was stomped to death in a muddy alley between Jack's Boarding House and Jack's Bar.

On each side of Elder were Abe and GeeGee, each in their thoughts. Elder contemplated the events: Even though it was late at night, PeeWee got it into his head to go next door to Jack's bar to pay their tab. Rory and his crew of roustabouts were there drinking themselves into oblivion. A young roustabout, Vincent, sitting alone, watched PeeWee enter. He watched Rory's reaction; shortly thereafter, Vincent awoke in the alley, battered—and PeeWee next to him dead, face down in the mud.

7

Vincent went back into the bar and told Jack. Together, they carried Pea's body next door to Jack's Boarding House and laid him on a table. Jack went upstairs to inform PeeWee's buddies. Not wanting to believe their ears, they ran downstairs. It was true. Pea lay on the table, muddy, battered, and dead. Touching his body in horror and rage, swearing revenge, they stood bewildered. About an hour before, he was full of life.

GeeGee, Pea's life-long buddy since infancy, with tears streaking his face, delicately plucked mud from Pea's hair and face. Over and over, he exclaimed, "Oh, God, why wasn't I with him?"

Almost absently, Abe had said, "They must have stood on his head."

Elder, looking intently at the ruined body, muttered, "Vincent?"

Vincent, standing behind him replied, "I'm here."

Elder took in the bruises and puffiness on Vincent's cheekbones, and his puffy cut lip, and asked, "Vince, who did this?"

"It was Rory, his brother, Otis, Ben, Black Billy, Cap, and Ratty. Pea came in and gave Jack some money. He was straight away leaving, but Rory, smiling real big, blocked his way. Pea tried to walk around him, but Rory moved in front of him. He insisted that he have a whisky, on him. But it wasn't just one. They were glad-handing and patting him on the back congratulating him for your oil strike. They forced him to drink one after another. I told them he had enough. Otis told me to shut up and held a glass up to Pea's lips to pour it down his throat. You know Pea, he didn't like to offend. Rory insisted on more, always just one more. They thought it was real funny, poor guy. When they thought he was good and drunk, they turned him around a couple of times, and pointed him to the door. He was wobbling, bad. I got up to steady him to the door. Then Rory said, 'Alright, let's go.' I had a bad feeling and followed them out.

"I hoped Pea made it home. It was dark. We heard a noise. He was in the alley pissing with one hand on the wall. Anyway, real quick Rory came up and hit him with his brass knuckles. Pea went down like a sack of corn. I tried to stop it. I pushed Ratty and Black Billy aside and got between them and Pea. The last thing I remember is Rory's face coming at me."

"Were all in on it?" Elder asked.

"Yeh, even Ben. I thought they were friends."

"Do you know where they went?"

"Before Pea arrived, they were talking about going to Ramona's."

"How old are you?" Elder asked.

"Sixteen, from Rochester, New York. I can't take it anymore. Bad things happen here. I'm going back. My parents live there. There's a college. I'm going to be a doctor."

"Here's $50. Go home. I don't want any witnesses."

Somehow the word had spread. Men stepped outside to see what was going on. They saw the murderous looks of three men walking, looking through them, like death, and backtracked.

Elder, Abe, and GeeGee stood at the entrance door to Ramona's, girding for revenge. Swaying by the door was a hanging, dim, flickering red kerosene lamp.

It was 1:00 a.m. Two women lounged on plush red velvet settees. Two played cards; another slumped in a chair, sleeping. It was the middle of the week, not payday. There were no customers, at least not downstairs. Although it was late, Ramona, as usual, was dressed elegantly in a long velvet lavender gown. She looked apprehensive. She knew they'd be coming.

"Well, well, Elder and Abe. And you brought in GeeGee. What would be your pleasure?"

"Did you hear about Pea?" Elder asked.

Apprehensively, she replied, "Yes. They've done their business, but they're still here, upstairs drinking. They're so high and so liquored up with what they done they can't stop talking."

"What room are they in?"

"Are you going to kill them?"

GeeGee, shifted his feet. Pacing, standing tall above the others, angry and frustrated, he roared, "Damn woman, hell, yes, we'll kill those murdering, mother-fucking-sons-of bitches. Everyone in town knows what they done; if they don't, they were just born."

Even at that moment of high tension, everyone stopped in amazement. GeeGee had grown up with PeeWee. They were lifelong buddies and traveled together to various oil fields. GeeGee was beyond mad. His usual cuss words were gosh darn it, shucks, dang it, dag nab it, gee whizz, gosh almighty, and hell almighty. But coming from a man at 300 pounds and 6 feet, 7 inches tall, people took notice.

Recovering from GeeGee's profanity, Elder put his hand on his shoulder and said, "Partner, Hang on."

Ramona thought of the repercussions. She tried to talk them out of it. "Leave it to the sheriff. They'll get their just deserts and be hung."

Ramona delayed and argued. This was a harsh world in which these men lived, but murder to avenge a murder was wrong.

"No," Elder exclaimed, "We're doing this now. We'll burn down this building with them in it. But you listen! You nor any of your girls saw us anywhere near this place. If you don't like it, the way I feel right now maybe I'll kill you too. You hear me?" Seeing the horror on her face, he softened. "Ramona, I don't mean it. But we got to do this. You gotta get out of the way."

Ramona liked these young men and didn't want to see them taken away in chains. She protested, but they were unmoved. She asked, "What about my business? Where will we go? This building alone cost me $600. I'll be out of business."

"Ramona, Humble Oil will pay your royalties. You'll be fine."

Elder pulled his Colt revolver from his belt from his cowboying days in New Mexico and tucked it under his armpit. Digging down again, he pulled out a wrinkled envelope. "Here," he said. "Here's a $10,000 check from Humble Oil. There'll be more. Start over somewhere else."

Ramona's eyes widened at the amount. A fortune. But resisted, "It's not enough. Anyway, I'm one-fifth partner, and with all the money I've invested, most of that is mine." She persisted, saying the girls would lose $20 to $30 a week and couldn't be expected to return to clerking at Woolworth's, earning pennies an hour, nor could she. And the destruction of the furniture should also be considered.

This dickering was much to GeeGee's annoyance. Impatient, he was about to bolt for the stairs. Guessing his intention, Abe blocked his way. No mean feat, considering GeeGee's size. "GeeGee," he said, "we're doing it together."

"Abe," Elder asked, "how much do you have?"

Abe pulled out an envelope. $215. After counting it, he changed his mind. Shaking his head, he said, "No, Elder, we'll need it."

GeeGee pulled crumpled bills from his pocket totaling $53. Ramona waved it away. Adding to their agitation, a man half-drunk burst through the front door, interrupting their dickering.

"Henry, we're closed," Ramona exclaimed.

"But I have money."

Grabbing him by the arm, Ramona pulled him to the door.

"Henry, come back tomorrow."

Looking over his shoulder, Henry saw three men facing away, cowboy hats pulled low, and called out, "Hey, GeeGee, is that you?"

11

Ramona repeated, "I said, come back tomorrow and mind your own business."

"All right, Ramona," Elder said. "We gave you everything we have. What's their room?"

"Fourteen, but Otis already left."

"What about Rory?"

"I don't know. One of the girls told me Otis left. She didn't say anything about Rory. I asked, but she didn't know."

"Okay, let's go," Elder said.

"Hold it; I have a couple of Johns upstairs. They're innocent, and two girls."

"Get them out. If you have to, give them back their money." Nodding, she ran for the stairs. Taking two at a time, dress flouncing, she called sideways to Betsy, "Betsy, put a note on the door. We're closed."

In a whining tone, Betsy exclaimed, "But we're never closed." Someone laughed.

"Betsy, do it!" Ramona snapped, "And go out the back door. Now! Everyone!"

At room 14, boisterous, drunken laughter blasted from within. Elder, revolver in hand, stepped aside and nodded to GeeGee. GeeGee exploded through, shattering the pine door. His forward momentum almost landed him on the bed. Two men were half-reclining, two revolvers at their feet, their backs against the headboard, drinking, shirtless, shoeless, sockless, wearing only Levis. Another roustabout, looking shocked, was sitting in a chair. A fourth, Ben, was passed out on the floor. In quick succession, GeeGee slapped the revolvers toward Elder and Abe, and effortlessly snatched up the closest man to whom he rendered a horrific blow to the shoulder.

12

Elder and Abe cried out, "No, no, wait," but GeeGee knew what he was doing. If he had struck the man in the face, it would have killed him. Although the man was struggling in pain and close to passing out, he could talk.

Just as Ramona had said, Rory was not there. Elder demanded to know Rory's whereabouts and that of Otis. The men didn't know or didn't want to say, only that Rory had left.

Elder held his own revolver. The two from the bed were in the hands of GeeGee and Abe. Nodding in unspoken agreement, they opened fire. Despite the explosive shots, the man on the floor, whom they knew, but they knew them all, had not stirred. It was Ben, the one they had considered to be PeeWee's friend.

Abe crouched down and laid his gun by his knee. Saying, "It's not right killing a sleeping man," he shook and slapped Ben and poured whisky on his face. That did it. Rubbing his face and squinting, Ben looked around. Seeing his friends bloody and dead, he was rendered instantly sober and, quick as a wink, scuttled backward on his butt to a wall. Abe followed.

Abe asked, "Ben, do you know why we're here?" Ben opened his eyes wide with fear. His mouth dropped open. Abe turned away from the putrid breath. Ben nodded. "Ben, this is for PeeWee," Abe pulled the trigger and hit an empty chamber. GeeGee handed him another revolver.

Desperately pleading, Ben said, "Abe, you know me. I got a wife and kids. I'm sorry. Can't you let me go?"

"Gosh darn it, Ben, I'm sorry too. You shouldn't (h)ave done it."

To Ben's pleading, Abe lowered the barrel to fire. But unexpectedly the gun was snatched from his fingers. Ben's head exploded. GeeGee, hate coursing through his body for the loss of his life-long buddy, had impatiently snatched the weapon from Abe, and fired. Blood and bone spattered, speckling the clothing and faces. Stepping away, Abe ran his

13

fingers through his hair, smearing blood. Looking away, feeling nauseous, he put his hand over his mouth and gagged. Recovering, he spat bile.

The three stood shock still and saw the grisly horror of what they had done, like a Godawful dream. The acrid smell of cordite from the bullets floated in the air, mingling with the sickening, sweet, cloying metallic scent of blood. The bodies on the bed, seated and slumped, had multiple chest holes. Blood, fat, and gristle leaked out. And behind them, blood from exit wounds spattered the wall. Blood soaked the bedding and dripped to the floor. Ratty had a finger blown off in a protective move before the slug struck his clavicle. Black Billy, the man in the chair, had a gaping hole where his chin used to be. Another bullet had neatly parted his thick, black wavy hair down the middle taking more than hair and skin.

A vein in Abe's temple visibly pulsed, and his heart was thumping so hard he thought it would jump out and run down the hall. He expected killings, but this was grotesque, beyond his imagination. Shuddering, he mumbled, "Gawwwd almighty." He was the first to recover and yelled, "Come on, get moving." Grabbing kerosene lamps and liquor bottles, they wildly splashed their contents over the bodies and bed. The others sprang into action, running from room to room, gathering flammable liquid to spray wildly on the walls, beds, everywhere. Matches were lit, and with demonic whooshes, flames erupted.

Flames snaked up walls and slithered across the ceilings, swoosh, whoomph. With the rooms and hallway burning and window glass exploding, they ran for the stairs. They had misjudged the rapidity of the fire's spread. Looking deranged, full of adrenaline, whooping, they ran. Flames at their heels, their faces flushed red hot, they ran, wildly caroming off walls, patting sparks on hair and clothing, reeling, breathing smoke, coughing, and reaching out to balance one another.

14

Rory had been sitting on the brass toilet at the end of the hall, installed at considerable expense by Ramona. Hearing the door shatter and the shots, he muttered, "Shit, fuck." Quickly standing, he pulled the hanging chain to flush—a needless move and pulled up his pants. He had left his revolver, the one used to blow out Ben's brain, behind in the room. Panicked, he looked for an exit. None. No window. The only way out was through the door, but he would be seen and killed. Panicked, coughing, and burning up with heat, he waited. Smoke licked under the door. Forcing himself, he waited. Flames cracked through the middle of the door and spread. Gasping for breath, flush with heat, desperate, he made his move. Crashing through the door onto the burning floor, he scrambled to his feet--hair and clothes on fire--and ran screaming for a window.

Abe took the stairs two and three at a time, and slipped, perhaps from blood on his boots or urgency. Falling on his hip, he bounced down three. GeeGee swooped him up and carried him outside.

Despite the moist night, Ramona's pine building burned mightily, like kindling. There was no fire department, and no attempt was made to put it out. Crackling, in flames, it collapsed and spread next door to Jack's Livery, taking Jack's corral and stables and causing a scramble to set the horses free.

Three days later, Bexar County Deputy Sheriff Isaac from the nearby town of Conroy arrived. He was a tall, lanky old codger with creased leather for skin and a man of few words. Taking in the no-name town, he was impressed that such a small town could survive.

Before the fire, there were only four buildings, Jack's Boarding House, Jack's Bar, Ramona's Whore House, and Lucy's Boarding House, all serving oil roustabouts. Lucy's was also owned by Jack. How Jack picked the name, no one knew.

The deputy had heard the bare-bones story of PeeWee's death and the names of his friends. His curiosity was piqued. Smoking his stubby cigar, he walked carefully through the charred ruins. Fairly quickly, he found corpses and two revolvers. Shifting through the debris to find melted lead slugs took considerably more effort. Finally, rising stiffly, he went in search of witnesses.

The deputy walked Elder and Abe to Jack's Bar. Jack placed three shot glasses on the table and poured his finest whiskey. Before questioning, they sat drinking leisurely jawing about the weather and work—and the deputy took their measure. Jack watched. The deputy had already talked to Ramona and the girls. They all lied. The deputy didn't press. GeeGee could not be found. He was in hiding, too emotional, and might confess.

The deputy had never previously met David Elder or Abraham Jackson, but he felt an instant liking. After talking, he walked them outside to wait and returned to the bar to mull over the events. Jack, just in case he was asked a question, was ready to serve up a lie or lies as necessary. The deputy had already been lied to—told that Abe, Elder, and GeeGee couldn't have done it because they had been drinking with him at his bar. Jack, seeing the deputy's doubtful looks served him another shot.

The deputy, putting the glass to his lips, considered that the men killed at Ramona's were heard bragging about their dastardly deed. Tapping his glass, Jack gave him a refill. The deputy dropped his eyes to the glass and thought of the dead. He had the witness statement from Vincent, who went home to Rochester, New York. PeeWee was well-liked. The dead, nobody would miss. Oh, he strongly suspected revenge and found it mighty interesting that PeeWee's killers were dead almost within an hour. Two revolvers were found, but four dead. Swift justice, he mused. Coughing and kneeling on his aching knees, he had filtered through the ashes. Melted lead slugs were scattered near and under the charred bodies—more than enough for the killing, especially since they were supposedly shooting each other.

After glancing at Jack, hovering, the deputy leaned over, spat into the spittoon, and again glanced sideways at Jack. After running his arthritic fingers through his white, thinning hair, and keeping his eyes on Jack, he thoughtfully sipped whisky. Then, with a clatter, he brought his left hand up and dropped a handful of melted slugs on Jack's bar, and said, "Interesting. All from two revolvers. To have this many, they had to reload."

Meeting the deputy's steely gaze, Jack agreed and topped off the shot glass. "Yes, interesting. What are you going to do?"

The deputy snorted, rolled the makings for a smoke, and with a crooked wry smile, said, "I'm thinkin,'" and tapped his forefinger on his glass for another shot. Jack complied.

Two more shots of Jack's fine whisky and the deputy tapped again. "All right, ah, where was I? Oh yeah, here's what I think. Those jackasses were drunk, got into a fight, and killed each other. Liquor bottles and kerosene lamps got knocked over. The fire started." Swaying slightly, he asked, "Well, Jack what do you think?"

Filling the deputy's shot glass and wondering how much he could drink of his fine whisky, Jack said, "It's good."

"Yeah, well, the deputy continued. . . ." Words trailed off, words that Jack couldn't hear. Then, "By the way, them gals at Ramona's ain't good liars. You ain't neither, but you're a good man, and your whisky's mighty fine." Jack poured another. The deputy had seen and heard enough. He couldn't care less and wanted to go home. Anyway, the dead were known as mean, unsavory characters, and the sole suspects in the murder of PeeWee Stanton.

"No, Jack, the dead didn't kill themselves, but I don't care and don't want to know." Hearing this, Jack was surprised but said nothing. "In my day," the deputy added, "I would have done the same. Actually, I did but never by fire."

After another free shot of whisky and a fit of coughing, the deputy asked Jack to call in Elder and Abe. Slurring and leaning heavily on Jack, he told them flat out that it was time for them to move on, perhaps to California. "San Francisco, I hear, has great opportunities, Go there, go anywhere, the sooner, the better before there's more killings."

"Now, Jack, I think you've gone and got me drunk. Find me a place to sleep."

Rory and Otis had disappeared. Elder, Abe, and GeeGee tried to find them without success. Thinking Rory and Otis weren't finished, they waited.

After fruitless nights, Otis came at 3:00 a.m. Stealthy, slowly, he ascended the stairs like a crab, with all four limbs spread wide and barefoot.

Abe was sitting on a narrow box at the end of the dark hall when he heard him coming. Every stair painfully creaked, but Otis was two sheets to the wind, drunk and too dumb to notice.

Otis's head of unwashed, red unruly hair peeked over the top step, then his bushy unshaved, scarred, pockmarked face, just like his brother's. His hands and upper body came next. His eyes blazing, grinning crazily, and looking demented, he cast his eyes about. Standing upright, he inched himself flat against the wall. A revolver was in his waistband. In his left hand was a sawed-off shotgun.

Although Abe had Elder's revolver, he felt stabs of apprehension. His heart quickened. Otis was a pitiless, ruthless man with thick hairy wrists and fingers, and considerably heavier than Abe. Abe waited to see if Rory

18

was following. No. "Cowardly son-of-a-bitch," Abe whispered. For a second, he wondered if a bullet could actually penetrate Otis' thick body.

Standing outside the door, Otis tucked the shotgun between his arm and chest and daintily reached out with his right thumb and two fingers. Locked. He stepped back as if he might kick it open. Instead, he leaned the shotgun against the wall and pulled out a set of skeleton keys, keys that would open virtually any door. Concentrating on his actions, he didn't hear movement behind him.

With a quick forceful plunge, cleanly, in and up, Abe's blade passed smoothly through the scapula to the heart. Had Otis's chest not been so large, and the blade longer, the knife might have exited to the left of the sternum. Gasping, Otis leaned back, stiffly stretched taller, and turned in herky-jerky motions. With eyes wide in astonishment, he looked at Abe— and died.

Abe muscled the body to the wall and helped its slide to the floor. "No need to wake Elder or GeeGee," he murmured. Laying Otis on a threadbare rug, he rolled him up. That completed, he struggled to heft him to his shoulder. Too heavy. Abe and the body fell against the wall; the body slipped and, with a resounding thud, crashed to the floor. In dismay, Abe said, "Shit, sorry Otis."

GeeGee came out, shirtless and buttoning his pants, followed by Elder. Doors opened. Men in long johns quickly backed up and closed their doors. GeeGee gingerly nudged the rug with his foot and asked,

"Rory or Otis?"

"Otis."

GeeGee hefted Otis to his shoulder and began descending the stairs. Each step painfully creaked. At the bottom was Jack, barefoot in his nightshirt, knobby knees showing, and holding a big cocked single-action Colt .45. Dog, his gray and white mongrel, half-German shepherd, half

19

retriever, stood by his side, its tongue hanging out, furiously wagging its entire body.

"Taking out the trash," GeeGee said.

"Let's see." After uncovering Otis' face, Jack offered, "Sure, let me help."

Jack brought up a hitched two-horse buckboard and two saddled horses from his stables. The horses were for Elder and Abe. GeeGee and Jack sat on the buckboard seat. Dog sat between them. Brilliant stars filled the sky. The air was clean and crisp. Distant lightning flashed, reminding Elder of New Mexico. No sign of humanity. Only Dog seemed happy. Leaning heavily against GeeGee, he occasionally barked at things only he could see. Following Jack's lead, they traveled until the morning sun peeked its head.

Abe rode up next to the buckboard and asked, "Jack, what is this place?"

"Pulgas Gulch, Fleas Gulch. Lots of ravines. Hangman's gulch is a bit farther and might be more fittin' but this will do."

GeeGee pulled the body from the flatbed and let it fall to the ground like garbage. Startling air escaped Otis's hissing lips. GeeGee dismissively waved the others aside, picked up the body, walked to the ravine's edge, and tossed it out. Silence, then noises of breaking twigs, branches, and a thud.

Abe hefted the shotgun and looked toward his partners to see if they wanted it. Nope. He tossed it in, followed by Otis's revolver and wallet. He kept the money. "Here you go, Otis," he said, "Here's a buck to see you into hell." The bill fluttered away. He handed the rest, three silver dollars and $200 in paper bills to Jack, enough to rebuild the corral and stables.

Having caught the mood, Dog walked near the edge, sniffed, and shit.

20

Lifting his oak-handled Colt six-shooter, a beautiful revolver, Elder walked to the edge and looked down. It had seen him through some tough times. He was fond of it.

"Don't do it," Abe said.

"Yeh, I will. I'm done with killing." Thumbing the cylinder twice, he listened to the smooth, revolving sound, snapped it open, snapped it shut, and threw it far out.

Although each believed the killings were justified, each handled it in his own way. GeeGee was heartsick over the loss of PeeWee, and it would take a long time to dissipate. If he could, he would kill those bastards all over again. Elder took walks alone and reflected on why it seemed violence always found him. But it wasn't like he hadn't killed before and wondered if killing ran in the family. Abe considered the killings horrible and prayed for forgiveness.

On the fifth day, Elder and Abe tried to persuade GeeGee to go with them to San Francisco. Rory had disappeared. The word was that he had fled to Oregon.

"Nah," GeeGee responded. "I'm taking PeeWee's money and the papers of his one-fifth interest to his wife and little girls in Kansas."

All three traveled together to Corcoran, Texas. From there, GeeGee would travel to Topeka, Kansas, and Elder with Abe to San Francisco. Before saying their goodbyes, they went into a two-bit diner for breakfast. Seeing that it had one of those new-fangled bathrooms, a water closet, one like Ramona's, GeeGee and Abe left Elder seated alone.

The waitress asked Elder to move to the white section. He declined with a simple "No, I'm fine."

"Suit yourself." But seven cowboys walked in, eager to have breakfast. A greeting was called out, "Mornin' Karla." She smiled, nodded toward

Elder, and shrugged. One separated himself from the group and approached Elder.

"Mister, you're at a colored table. The white section," he gestured, "is over there." To his surprise, Elder leaned back and said, "Yeh, I know."

"Then move!" Elder didn't reply.

A little uneasy, the cowboy hooked his thumbs in his belt and tried again, "Are you hard of hearing?"

"I'm fine here."

The other cowpokes heard and moved to the table. Now, they demanded he move. A big one with a bushy beard said, "Mister if you don't move, we'll do it for you." But to their amazement, GeeGee and Abe walked out of the water closet, pulled out their chairs, and sat. Their surprise derived from seeing the largest man they had ever seen, and a colored man, Abe, using the white bathroom instead of the outhouse. Looking back and forth from Abe to GeeGee, and then to Elder, they were speechless.

Guessing the situation, GeeGee shifted on his chair; he lifted his big right fist and brought it down hard on the table. "Thud," and said, "Say it, or get moving." Someone muttered, "Not good." These were large, fit men hovering over them, but looking at GeeGee, they rightly hesitated. His body dwarfed his chair; his shoulders were broad and full of muscle. His arms and chest strained the material of his shirt, and his hands and wrist were large. Damn, he was massive, and if he was agile and fast, which he was, it could be bad. Abe and Elder looked amused. The cowhands shifted uncomfortably but moved closer.

In a cowboy drawl, a fellow in the back with a healthy head of white hair spoke up, "Hold on, boys. Son, move aside; lemme see." As they parted respectfully, he moved to the table and stood above Elder.

Elder and Abe, having been cowboys themselves, missing each other by months, in New Mexico, knew that these men would not back down. They scooted their chairs back, ready to rise. It could erupt at any moment.

Standing over them was a weathered, fine-looking, neatly sculpted cowboy—flat stomach, broad shoulders, deep chest, and a fresh haircut, somewhere between 50 and 70. Holding his black hat and decked out in a well-worn but neat cowboy dress, white shirt, black boots, Levi's, wide belt, and silver buckle, he stood, evaluating. Seeing that Elder, Abe, and GeeGee were tense and ready to rise, he said, with a downward motion of his hands, and a half grin, "Easy boys, nuthin' is happenin'---not yet." Turning his eyes to his men, he included them in his meaning. His cheek creases deepened when he smiled, friendly enough. "Well," he drawled, "let's start over. Howdy. It appears you boys are used to trouble." He hesitated for a few beats to see their reaction, and then said, "What we got here is a Mexican standoff. Well, this morning I got up real peaceful." Casting an appraising eye at GeeGee, he added in his slow, easy way, "I do believe I would like to go to bed the same way. And I'm sure not going to muss my clothes for the like of you. Sit your ass's here if you like. It don't bother me. Consider yourselves lucky. Now, I'm having breakfast."

The comment about being lucky did not sit well with Elder. He started to rise, to say something, but Abe put his hand on his fist and shook his head.

"Smart fellow, there," the cowpoke said. And with a flick of his fingers, he turned and motioned for the others to follow. Without a peep or backward glance, they did.

"Hmmm, I guess he's the head honcho," Elder quipped.

Abe asked, "Was that about me?"

23

"In a way, but this time, we whities are in the wrong section. Abe, when you came out of the water closet, and they saw you, that was a surprise in itself. But the double-take when they saw GeeGee was priceless. GeeGee, you're so burnt from the sun, and with your curly hair, they might have thought you were a giant Negro. Yeah, two giant Negros using the water closet. Damn, we almost had a fight. Someday, my stubborn pride is going to be my ruination."

"Well," Abe said, "You can be mighty crusty. You don't like being pushed. But let me say—now, don't get me wrong, I'm with you, but you weren't thinking about how it might have turned out for me, not being known and colored and this being Texas. They could kick me to death in a cell. I'm glad that honcho was calm and rational because you weren't. It would have been a mess of trouble and surely would have ended our trip to San Francisco."

"Hell, I'm sorry, Abe. I forget. GeeGee, what do you think?"

"Except for what Abe said, it didn't bother me at all. Once, I took on 17 in a hell of a fight in a run-down honky-tonk bar in Memphis. Pea didn't lift a finger—just drank his beer and watched. I threw men out windows, women too, and a couple of midgets, broke arms, and cracked heads, turned over pool tables, and even took a beer break. Man, did I tear up that place!"

"Really?" Abe asked.

"Hell no, but it makes a better story than if I fought one or two. I'm not crazy. The only thing true is that I did have beers with Pea in Memphis." Mournfully, he added, "Yeah, with my buddy. You know, he was five feet in his boots. But he was big. Someone once called me Poopindinski and Pooper. That little guy lit into him. I had to pull him off. God, I loved him."

24

After silence, they joshed a bit, and talked about the lying whopper stories they told each other for entertainment. After working off adrenaline, GeeGee said, "My appetite's back, let's eat."

Leaving the café, the white-haired foreman looked up and gave them a friendly half-grin and wave. The others conspicuously looked down at their food.

Elder and Abe boarded the train and traveled in separate cars. As depicted by a sign, there was a separate car for the "Colored." They had not anticipated so much prejudice. And while waiting to board, Abe was not allowed in the waiting room. Elder made such a fuss that the station master was called. Abe was advised to calm down his friend or else there would be an arrest. Otherwise, the man was civil enough, saying, "Listen, if it were up to me, I wouldn't care, but I'm an employee. I would surely appreciate your kind cooperation." There was no recourse. They couldn't walk to San Francisco. To add insult, the cars were not equally furnished or equipped. The coloreds went without bathrooms, a drinking fountain, and a dining car.

Later, Elder said, "I'm so sorry."

"Not your fault; I pissed out the window. Too bad the train rocked so bad. Must hit inside."

Chapter Two: San Francisco

On April 17, 1906, at 5:00 p.m., Elder and Abe stepped off the Southern Pacific. Looking around, they were awed by the largest city they had ever seen--grand homes on steep hills, cable cars, paved streets, and buildings everywhere as far as the eye could see. At Fisherman's Wharf, they ate an unfamiliar meal called "shrimp cocktail." Afterward, they walked in twilight to the ritzy neighborhood of Nob Hill and joked about splurging for a suite costing upwards of $6.00. Upon entering the most prestigious hotel in town, the luxurious seven-story Palace Hotel with an interior courtyard, they noticed they were drawing attention. People were staring. Perhaps it was because of their rough clothing. But it wasn't. It was because of Abe. He was a Negro. Negroes in San Francisco, a huge city of about 400,000 to 460,000 made up only about one percent of the population, or about 4000 to 4600. They asked for a room and were rejected. They'd heard wrong about San Francisco. It was not the liberal open city where all were welcome.

Angry and solemn after their experience at the Palace Hotel, they walked through Chinatown, a crowded, seedy slum area of approximately five square blocks populated chiefly by single men. Lodging was found in a clean, modest two-story hotel in the adjacent neighborhood of North Beach, primarily occupied by Italians, Russians, Germans, and Eastern Europeans.

Having awakened at the break of dawn on Wednesday, the 18th of April, Elder and Abe explored the city. The business section of Polk Street hummed with shopkeepers preparing for the day.

A friendly couple sweeping the sidewalk outside their café allowed them in early for coffee. Raising their cups, Abe said, "Here's to luck in San Francisco."

It was 5:12 a.m. Elder exclaimed, "What's that?" The floor rumbled. The table skittered away. The coffee pot and cups tipped off and shattered. Elder grabbed Abe's arm to hold him steady. A teenage boy and the couple ran out of the kitchen, yelling, "Get out."

Outside, the earth undulated, buckled, and sawed back and forth, knocking them off their feet. Sounds assailed their ears like a powerful locomotive bearing down on them. The two-story building where they had sat moments before buckled, leaned, and crumbled. With a great racket, it

26

crashed into the next building. Like dominos, buildings tottered and fell. Panicked rats erupted into the street, scurrying in all directions.

Bricks bounced and tumbled, miraculously missing all but the woman from the café, painfully hit by a tumbling brick to the thigh.

A gloomy, murky pall, settled on the city, blotting out the sun. For four days fires would rage. Ninety percent of San Francisco was made of wood and burned fiercely. If owners had no earthquake insurance, but did for fire, the owners set it on fire, and the fire department looked the other way. That night, and continuing to the next, light gray ash settled on the streets.

Streets filled with noise and confusion. Terrified humanity streamed toward the Ferry Building and the railroad depot to evacuate. Wagons laden with belongings were pulled by children, adults, dogs, and horses.

Competing for space were horse-drawn carriages, Fords, Buick Roadsters, Pontiacs, and elegant Duesenbergs. Two expensively dressed women in a one-seat buggy, looking dressed to go to church, called out warnings. Their horse, its eyes wide and terrified, nostrils flaring, tossed its head and reared, rocking the carriage. Neighing loudly, it was out of control. Grabbing the leather harness, Abe spoke soothingly and stroked its massive neck. Shaking, the horse set its large round chocolate eyes on Abe and with heavy breathes calmed under his hands. After a few minutes, like a new animal, it cantered ahead. The woman called, "Young man, thank you."

Hearing cries for help, Abe, Elder, and passer-byes lifted debris off one man. Uncovered, he reached up for a helping hand. A mean gash on his forehead seeped blood—but he was smiling, holding a small dog, grinning, coughing, and thankful.

Assailing them were discordant sounds: clanging of fire bells, honking horns, the crackling of burning buildings, the clatter of horse-drawn

27

carriages, and shouts of refugees calling to one another. Smoke and turbulent twisting flames rose, snaking high into the sky.

After hours of helping survivors, and irritating coughing from foul air, Elder and Abe quit throwing aside debris searching for survivors. If they hadn't their hands would be too damaged to work. As it was, Abe suffered a nasty cut to his hand. Walking back to their lodging, something hit Elder in the legs. "Oomph," he exclaimed. A golden German Shepherd puppy with a black snout, its back fur smoking, looked soulfully up at him. Abe quickly smothered the smoking hair with a jacket. They continued walking. The dog followed.

Impressed, and dismayed, Elder and Abe stood across the street from their flaming hotel. Also burning fiercely were sidewalk tables, and trees. With faces and ears already flush from the heat, Abe shouted, "Watch out!" Creaking, crackling, and groaning, the building collapsed. Clouds of dust, smoke, and flames shot out. Flames flashed out and snapped back as fast as they had come. "Whoa," Abe exclaimed, "that scared the hell out of me." Turning to Elder, he burst out laughing. Elder's finely white/gray ash-dusted face had a look of wonder. "Elder," Abe exclaimed, "you're a mess, and your eyebrows are gone." Turning his attention back to their ruined hotel, he asked, "Do you have money on you? Because everything we had in there is gone."

"Yeh, in my money belt."

Retreating to nearby Washington Square, a small neighborhood park, they moved among milling families, children, dogs and cats, a parrot, singles, friends, the old and the young. All races and ethnicities together with the intent to survive. Camps were made. Food, water, and blankets were shared. Children were settled.

At one end of the park, a small group prayed. Elder sarcastically thought, "A lot of good that'll do, God knows everything doesn't he? He

28

doesn't care." Elder chuckled over his humor. "Maybe he's busy somewhere else--perhaps strolling around in France or Italy looking after things there or sitting in a sidewalk cafe with a glass of wine and looking at the pretty gals." Elder had a beef with God. Such thoughts were not generally shared with Abe. Abe, he thought, might mosey over to join the prayer group, and lead them in the best prayers they've ever heard.

Men rested before venturing out again, their hands wrapped in cloth— or wearing gloves if available.

"Come on, Bradley," Elder said.

"Is that his name?"

"It is now."

Bradley tagged along in the fire-lit sky and watched as they assisted wherever they could. In Chinatown, Abe stopped in front of a burned-out store. Neatly stacked in front were boxes of Mason jars. A sign said, "Peaches." Each contained 24 jars. He took one box, put $2.00 in an empty jar, and wondered if it and the jars would be stolen. The peaches were in liquid. Drinking water was a precious commodity, and folks were already scavenging for it and food. Quickly, the city arranged for water to be delivered to the city in barrels from remote areas for five days.

Floating ash congested the lungs. Elder, Abe, and thousands of others, worked without time in mind. Horse soldiers arrived with food and water. Wagons followed with shovels and gloves.

Water pipes ruptured, power lines fell, and stoves, candles, and kerosene lamps overturned, setting infernos. Firefighters on horse-drawn fire engines arrived at locations only to find the pipes and hydrants were broken and had not a dribble. Dynamite was used to create firebreaks but often caused unintended results. To aid the population, the National Guard and U.S. Army set up hundreds of neat rows of small portable shacks,

29

many at the military presidio, and thousands of rows of tents for approximately 250,000 homeless, comprising 26 tent cities.

On the third day, Elder and Abe were assigned a tent in Golden Gate Park and given directions to the communal showers, restrooms, infirmary, mortuary, and the closest kitchen. Near the kitchen, they dusted off their filthy clothes. An amused young lady, a kitchen volunteer, observing their joshing banter, chalky faces, and healthy toothy grins, smiled. Seeing that she was evaluating them, Elder approached and apologized, "I guess we look frightful, but we're harmless." She smiled warmly. Elder, thinking she was cute, asked for her name. Serving a hefty portion of mashed potatoes, she replied, "It's Georgia Sandbourne."

After eating they went directly to the makeshift communal shower. Abe quipped, "Elder, I think you would have made a better impression with that pretty gal if you didn't smell so bad. Maybe we should have cleaned up before eating." Elder smiled wryly, and replied, "I think she likes me."

The showers were cold and felt great. The filth sloughed off. They were content. Bradley rolled around their feet, and vigorously shook off the water, only to get soaked again.

Robust singing erupted from an adjacent shower. Elder and Abe joined in. What they didn't know, they ad-libbed. Others in the shower and adjoining ones joined in with full-throated, uninhibited exuberant voices. They were alive and singing, "In The Sweet By and By" with joy and optimism.

> "Down Lover's Lane we'll wander
> Sweetheart, you and I. . . . . .
> Oh, say
> Things are gonna be okay
> In the sweet, a-sweet, a-sweet, goodbye and by . . ."

When the verses died down for lack of remembering, someone would recall words and pick it up. Suddenly, close by, a full throated chorus of women's voices joined in.

"Wait till the sun shines, Nellie

When the clouds go drifting by

We will be so happy, Nellie

Don't let me hear a sigh

Way down in Lover's Lane we'll wander

Sweetheart, you and I. . . . ."

Despite their situation, they were full of youthful enthusiasm.

Looking at Bradley, Elder said," Well look-it here, this is a fine-looking dog. Tell me, Abe. Are we rich, or aren't we?"

"Don't tell anyone. They wouldn't believe us."

"I didn't mean that."

"Right. I didn't think you did, but we do look like bums."

"Hopefully, like good, respectable bums. Abe, I like that girl, Georgia. Black hair, blue eyes, and beautiful skin. I had a Mexican gal like her in Santa Fe, but I was too callow to know when I had a good one."

In the tent city, adults looked for friends, and loved ones attended funerals, and fretted about the future. Children made friends, played hide and seek, and ran in and around the tents. Barbers opened shop, and so did seamstresses and cobblers. To the dismay of many and the pleasure of others, prostitutes continued to sneak in and out of tents.

Men cleared rubble, repaired the water system, and found survivors and the dead. A particularly onerous task was the removal of carcasses of bloated horses whose stomachs had burst from flies, maggots, and rot. This assignment fell to Elder and Abe more times than they cared. This task was saved for the end of the day, so they could go directly to shower.

31

Railroad tracks were laid directly into the city to facilitate debris removal. Eventually, a man came around and told them they were earning $3.00 a day.

Working daily in the commercial areas, signs popped up, "For Sale." Whether damaged or undamaged, properties presented excellent speculative opportunities. Their first was purchased for a price they considered ridiculously low and more followed. Years later, Elder asked, "Abe, were we fair?"

The catastrophe had inadvertently been good for them. He referred to their purchases from distressed and desperate owners who thought San Francisco would never rise again. Those who believed the city was through were wrong.

"Were we fair?" Abe replied. "Were they? No! They thought us fools for what we paid. They were glad to get out of a dying city."

Chapter Three: Georgia

It was Georgia's first day volunteering, serving the refugees in the camp kitchen. Two men, one black, one white, approached. Almost there, they dusted themselves off, throwing off small clouds of dust and some crusted mud. Although filthy, they struck her as interesting. Elder, she noticed, was missing his eyebrows. Yet, his filthy button-down shirt nicely draped his torso and trim waist, and the robust smile on his dirty face was charming.

Elder took in her crisp white uniform, her height, 5 feet 7 inches, taller than average, her lithe figure, blue eyes, and long lustrous black hair. Young, and pretty, she had an aura of education and sophistication. Thereafter, he flirted with her. She, in turn, liked his masculine voice and thought him bold at his continued efforts to date him. He allowed others to pass him in line to extend their visit, however short. He persisted and she began to look forward to seeing him.

One afternoon she felt an emptiness when he didn't come. Her replacement arrived. She stayed, waiting, disturbed, feeling a loss. She wondered, "Where is he?" She didn't want to leave without seeing him. Holding her long hair from falling in her face, she leaned over the counter and scanned the long walkway between hundreds of rows of tents.

Elder approached in the opposite direction, tired from shoveling debris into trucks. Carrying a red rose, he stopped and observed her behavior. She had continually rebuffed him. But now, just maybe, she was warming up and looking for him. Even though he was standing next to her, she was so concentrated, she didn't notice. He took a tray. She lowered her head, and her sad, downcast eyes said she was unhappy. Clanking the tin tray, her eyes lifted. The smile from her lips to her eyes was wide and pure. She blushed. Elder, going for casual, said, "Hi."

Responding with a grin and "Hi," she looked away and back. Reaching out, she touched his forearm. His heart leaped. If there was any doubt, with that small gesture it was gone. Wholly smitten, he handed her the rose. After a pleasant moment gazing into each other's eyes, he asked if she would take a walk with him and Bradley, his dog, that is after he showered and ate. She nodded. After that, she waited until his workday was done, had eaten, and showered. They walked close together, brushing, and conversed about things they cared about or didn't. It was enough to be together. They observed the activity of adults, some tending to projects, while others contentedly lazed about on chairs, smoking. Children played without worry, trusting that the adults had everything under control. They walked beyond the tents into undisturbed areas of the great park to find privacy.

Elder was slow to offer his hand. Georgia grew impatient and reached for his. Tentatively, he placed his arm around her shoulders. She smiled with her eyes and lips. She moved closer and lifted her face for a kiss. His heart leaped.

Georgia's home was in the exclusive area of Nob Hill, a place of stately mansions destroyed by the earthquake. The houses were Victorian, Gothic, and Italianate styles of stone and oak, with turrets, dormers, and columns. Turkish bedrooms and bathrooms of ivory and marble were the fashion.

Georgia's father was a medical doctor who devoted little time to his practice but relished the title of "doctor." Most of his wealth was derived from his wife, Georgia's mother, Olivia. Olivia was a descendant of early Spanish settlers and ranchers in Santa Barbara, California. Not spoiled, she did her share of work. Her family questioned her reasons for marrying an emotionally stiff, rigid man. To add to his stature, Dr. Sandbourne was a deacon of the nearby Lutheran church. Olivia was active in charities and social events.

On Elder's first visit to Georgia's home, he hitched a ride with a young couple in a Model A Ford on their way north to the coastal logging town of Fort Bragg. Employment waited at the Mendocino Lumber Company. Elder was dropped off at Mason Street near the fire-damaged Fairmont Hotel. When the earthquake hit, it was under construction and nearly completed.

He was early. To calm himself for the impending introduction to Georgia's parents, he cut through Huntington Park, small, desolate, and burned out, and stopped to talk with one solemn couple. They had returned to the neighborhood to look at their burned-out home. Upon exiting the park, he crossed the street to the Gothic-styled Episcopal Grace Cathedral. He climbed the steps to its huge artistically carved front doors. The charred skeleton of the structure remained, as well as the stone floor, pillars, and sections of walls.

After blocks of ghostly ravaged homes, with nothing but stark, black charred frameworks or less, and an occasional home seemingly unscathed, he arrived at the Sandbourne's. His impression: "Wow, ugly." It was a two-story mansion, part English manor, part imitation castle, painted rust brown. A good third was destroyed at the eastern wing. Four workmen tossed debris onto a flatbed wagon. Two draft horses grazed on sparse vegetation. Elder pulled a short chain on the door. A tinkling bell sounded from within. A uniformed Negro servant opened the door and asked for his name. Behind him, eagerly waiting, was Georgia. A painting of the family crest hung in the entry.

Georgia apprehensively worried that her father would judge Elder unfavorably and common. He did indeed. Doctor Sandbourne, informed of the impending visit, had already pre-judged. Elder, he noted, worked as a laborer clearing rubble, owned nothing, and had no more than an elementary education. Therefore, he was lower class and undeserving.

Georgia teased Elder about his new look. To make a good impression, he had cut his ponytail, shaved away his daily stubble, and wore his first suit and tie. Her mother graciously shook his hand and escorted him to a family room. Doctor Sandbourne entered, paused for effect, and contemptuously stared at Elder from a distance. Then, approaching warily, wearing a formal black three-piece suit, and gold cufflinks, scowling, he stopped five feet from Elder. Elder stepped forward and offered his hand and almost withdrew it. To send a message, not missed, Doctor Sandbourne was intentionally slow to offer his. Also, Elder made the mistake of calling him Mr. Sandbourne instead of "Doctor" and was brusquely corrected.

35

They retired to a room the doctor called his library. Although bookshelves lined the wall, the shelves were empty except for books on accounting and business. Chairs were distantly placed. Georgia conspicuously physically moved hers next to Elder's. A maid served tea.

While Georgia unabashedly smiled at Elder, her father shifted uncomfortably. Making a show of it, he scrutinized Elder, from his shoes to his head, deliberately communicating his dislike. Elder tried to break through the frostiness without success. The doctor preferred to stare and scowl. After unsuccessful starts and stops and dead silence, Elder brought up the subjects of money and the economy. Despite the doctor's intention to remain frosty, he was interested in money. A short but lively discussion followed regarding the future of San Francisco. Georgia listened and hoped her father would be impressed. After all, Elder was starting his own construction company, investing in real estate, and earning oil royalties.

Elder left after an uncomfortable 90 minutes, thinking, "He doesn't like me." He was correct. Sandbourne begrudgingly called him tolerably intelligent but lower class, uneducated--an outsider trying to advance through his daughter. And he hoped and prayed that his lovely daughter would come to her senses. He liked Elder even less after being introduced to his associate, Abe Jackson, a Negro.

Abe came to the Sandbourne house with Elder, once. That was enough. Invited in, they were met by Doctor Sandbourne. Clearly surprised and displeased, he stiffly forced himself to be civil for the briefest seconds and excused himself, claiming illness. As he climbed the stairs, unable to contain himself, he looked back, fixed his eyes on Abe, and shouted. "Tell the boy to leave!"

Georgia stood by helplessly, thinking she should somehow intervene, but she also loved her father. Conflicted and young, she remained silent, except for saying, "No, no." He did hear, but his prejudices were so great that he couldn't control himself.

Upstairs, seething with anger, Sandbourne mused that if it were the old days, he'd beat "the Boy" within an inch of his life. Muttering about status and social class, he gingerly washed his hands and cleaned his fingernails. Straightening his fingers, he turned his hand, checking for germs as if he could see them. Momentarily, he had been disarmed by the tall patrician bearing of the man, his gracious manners, perfect diction, with a touch of southern accent, and hypnotic green eyes. Before he could catch himself, he had shaken the "Boy's" hand. "For gosh sake," he cursed. Disgust flowered his face. That he had colored servants did not dent his prejudices. There was no way that he would sit in the same room with the "Boy," even for tea—and any utensil he touched would be sanitized, and the bathroom downstairs too, just in case. The irony of having colored help to sanitize things used by another man of color escaped him. "The 'Boy' is arrogant," he thought. "Absurd for him to come to the house and enter by the front door."

Downstairs, Elder and Abe excused themselves and left. Georgia, appalled at her father's abhorrent behavior, didn't know what to do. But her mother did. Hugging her distraught daughter, she sent her after them with apologies.

Georgia was shaken, ashamed for having thought that her father would be civil and for subjecting Elder and Abe to her father's hate. Her thoughts of both were positive; to her, both were charismatic, endearing, intelligent, humorous, and attractive. She never had a Negro friend but found that Abe was no different and more interesting than others in her society. After their first meeting, she commented to Elder, "He's awesome." She felt good in their company, and when the occasion arose, she could banter and exchange joking barbs just as well as them. She considered Elder to be a diamond in the rough. He made mistakes in English grammar, didn't know ballet, opera, which fork to use, or how to spoon soup properly. That didn't matter. He was kind, attentive, and learning. And he kissed wonderfully.

Dr. Sandbourne detested Elder so much that he found pleasure in badmouthing him whenever he had the chance. To his dismay, Georgia did see Elder, frequently. To stop this "disastrous" relationship, he threatened to put her out on the street, but his wife prevailed. She convinced him that their society friends, would be horrified both at his behavior and at Georgia's. Indeed, although they would find some support, unbridled gossip would spread, and some might scorn them, even at church.

Sandbourne yelled, paced about, waved his arms, and harangued his daughter for rejecting her social standing. She didn't argue. She embroidered with her mother while he stood over them, hectoring and lecturing. Aside from this, the only sounds were the crackling fireplace and quiet words between mother and daughter. They would look up at him, smile, and nod, until, frustrated, he stormed off. He implored his wife to talk to their daughter. She said she would but did not. Reluctantly, he relented. Georgia would do as she pleased, and it pleased her to see Elder.

They took a weekend trip north to Mendocino Village, a small beach town populated by loggers, wine growers, laid-back craftsmen who liked to try strange mushrooms and, and artists living their dreams. A few miles further north was the bustling logging town of Fort Bragg, population about 2,700, with large Victorian homes, ocean views, and noisy cutting barns. On the other side of the highway, inland were mostly simple wooden homes.

Logging wagons pulled by teams of horses clogged the streets. They came and went, full and empty. And in the five-block center of town, including side streets, folks enjoyed cafés, general stores, and artisan

38

shops. Elder and Georgia went in and out of the shops: art, leather, woodworking, pottery. Intriguing to Georgia was a glass-blowing studio operated by a willowy, pretty, young lady blowing wine bottles.

For fun they took the smelly, swaying, gasoline-fueled lumber train, the Skunk Train, 10 miles inland to the town of Willits.

Sitting next to each other in the sole passenger car rubbing shoulders they gazed at the lush passing scenery of the forest of redwoods, spruce, and fir. Passing the Pudding Creek Estuary, they marveled at an herd of mule deer grazing in a lush green meadow of ferns. They disembarked at Willits. Three hours later, they resumed their round trip to Fort Bragg. In thought, Georgia absent-mindedly stared off into space.

Gently, Elder asked, "Sweetheart what are you thinking?"

"I wonder if you'll always love me like you do now?"

"Georgia, I'm not good at this. But I will say, I love you because you love me despite my shortcomings. You've taught me the difference between clams and mussels, which fork to use, and to walk on the curb side with you on the inside. You never beat me up with your culture and intelligence. I love you because, because I do. You make me happy, and of course you're beautiful. I can't imagine a day without you. I'll love you until I die."

Upon return to Fort Bragg, walking to their lodging, they stopped at a low, white-painted fence to listen to skillful fingering of guitars and singers. Inside the yard, Mexican families were having a cookout. A slim, fine-featured, bronzed middle-aged man, Julio Garcia, called out playfully, "Hey, Gringo! You and your señorita, come in. Join us."

It was a delightful evening of laughter, conversation, food, drink, and singing. Children played, mothers held babies, and stories were told. Their hosts spoke of their lives in the vineyards. Generally uncomplaining, their outlooks on life were positive. Julio was rich, he said, as long as he had his

39

health, his lovely wife, and three daughters. After a mouthful of food and a thoughtful pause, he added his mother, father, two brothers, three sisters, and grandparents. Chuckling again, he said, "And my dog and my best friend, Hector, and food: beans, chile, barbecued pork, enchiladas, tamales, and tacos. After a sip of a drink called a margarita, he added chili rellenos, a fluffy batter of eggs stuffed with green chilies and cheese, fried in fat. "But I also like gringo food like meatloaf."

Elder spoke passable Spanish from his early cowboying days in New Mexico, but it wasn't needed, except with the elderly grandparents. Georgia was fluent from school and her mother's family.

As the evening wore on, the party grew larger, and there were more musicians and neighbors. Elder and Georgia joined in the dancing. They twirled, robustly stamped their feet, and danced slowly swaying, cheek to cheek—two gringos among the Latinas and Latinos having a wonderful time.

It was late. Walking under a full moon, drunk with alcohol and love, they clumsily entered their room. Laughing and kissing, they half undressed and fell on the bed. Cuddling, and kissing, bodies entwined, they fell asleep. Lovemaking waited until morning.

Chapter Four: Getting Married

Georgia's mother accepted Elder. Her father did not. He was upset with their premarital activities but eventually realized that he could do nothing except relent; otherwise, the family might be tarred by the scandal of an out-of-wedlock pregnancy. However, controversy couldn't be avoided such as a Negro being the best man in a white church—and "the horror" of having colored folks sitting in the pews with whites. There would be no reception. This was decided after Georgia's father refused to have whites and blacks dining together.

Georgia's parents announced the engagement of their daughter. It was on the celebrity pages of the Chronicle and the San Francisco Times. Elder was described as a businessman from Texas.

Although plans for the wedding were made, Sandbourne made a last-ditch effort of sabotage. He invited Elder to a meeting with two prominent businessmen. Elder was advised that it would be casual and that he should come directly from work. Sandbourne lied. It was to be with seven, including Sandboune, and the dress was formal suits and ties. Dinner was to follow. Georgia forewarned Elder, but he was undaunted. He would attend, just as invited.

Sandbourne's associates were to confront Elder dismissively, to make him feel that he was out of his element, that he did not belong. Elder arrived wearing well-worn, scuffed black work boots, Levi's, an old off-color white canvas shirt, and a weathered black leather jacket.

The butler escorted Elder into the spacious, sparsely furnished, high-ceiling library. Surveying the room and the men waiting, he thought, "Seven, my lucky number." Approaching them, his footsteps resounded on the hardwood floor. They were puzzled. He wasn't what they had expected. He radiated confidence; he looked strong, formidable, and taller than everyone. Without hesitation, he introduced himself. Taken aback, the suits shook his hand, recovered, and went to their task. To cheap laughter, one asked where he got his raggedy shirt. "Oh, oh!" With a steely withering gaze, he fixed his eyes on his questioner. He replied, "I hope you're not trying to offend me. I wouldn't like that. Neither would you." The man squirmed. But after a heartbeat, Elder broadly smiled, and said, "It's from Santa Fe, New Mexico. I was a cowboy. Try picturing me on a black stallion wearing this shirt and Levis. Add slick leather chaps, boots, jingling spurs, a Colt Peacemaker .45 revolver on my hip, a razor-sharp knife on my belt, and a Winchester rifle by my right leg."

41

The suits became still. Elder was a combative man, and wouldn't take guff. He was suddenly a formidable man with broad shoulders, a trim waist, and a deadly six-shooter on his hip—possibly a fast-draw gunfighter, certainly not a man to mess with. Seeing them standing very still, looking small, he smiled warmly. In a kind and pleasant manner, he began regaling with stories of his cowboy days, campfires under endless shining stars, strong, rough, cowhands, cattle drives, and cattle rustlers. Gathered around Elder, these businessmen and politicians were intrigued.

One asked, "Where did you sleep?"

"Why, on the ground, on bedrolls," he replied, "under the stars."

He told the story about a stampede: "It was sunset. We were hit with deep, rolling thunder and lightning strikes, one after the other. It was a dry storm with no rain. Now imagine 3000 stampeding beasts weighing upwards of 2000 pounds. And I was in the middle of it. Me and my horse were pushed one way and the other. I was in a thick of it. I couldn't breathe. I couldn't see. I thought my life was over. I was going to be ground into the earth. It was hell. I held on to the saddle horn for dear life. I'd be dead if it wasn't for my horse and foreman, Big Hat Sam. He yelled advice. I couldn't hear most, but I must have heard some because I'm still here. Then hard pelting rain came. All night. We couldn't start a fire. It was miserable, sleeping in soaked clothes." His listeners asked for more.

"Now," he continued, "imagine after a long cattle drive, cowboys, Indians, and big, handsome Mexican vaqueros, all crowded together, drinking in a tiny adobe bar with a dirt floor, horny as hell trying to make time with the women."

"What were they like?"

"The men were rough, and scary. They smelled, and needed a shave and haircut, but if you mean the women, they were beautiful. Some were gals from wealthy ranches without their daddies but with their vaqueros to

42

watch over them. And there were gorgeous señoritas with long black hair, colorful shawls draped over their shoulders, smooth skin, beautiful soulful brown eyes, some with green, some with blue, women you'd die for.

"No guns were allowed. Old Juan Diego Torres Serrano, the owner, took them at the door." Elder was enjoying his own story. "That didn't stop one huge fight over the prettiest woman there."

As expected, he was asked, "Were you there?"

"There? I started it! A huge vaquero, good looking but huge, actually her brother, took offense to me flirting with his sister. He said something. She slapped him; he slapped her back. I knocked him windmilling across the room."

The suits leaned in, careful to hear every word.

"He came back at me with a wicked smile. Of course, his men jumped in, and so did mine. All hell broke loose. Best damn brawl ever. Everyone was going at it, even the women. To stop it, old Juan Diego, wrinkled and ancient but far from senile, set his two mongrel dogs on us. Their sharp teeth ripped our clothes.

"Now, imagine over two dozen drunken Indians, cowhands, vaqueros, and the most gorgeous women this side of the Mississippi stampeding for the door. One vaquero had his pants ripped clean open, and part of his long johns. He hopped away holding his gun belt and a sombrero over his ass. What a sight. We were bloodied and laughing like hell."

"Did you finish the fight with the vaquero?"

"Hell no. We were drunk. We were friends blowing off steam."

"Were you ever in a gunfight?"

Elder was enjoying himself. These men wanted adventure, and he wouldn't disappoint. "A gunfight? Well, maybe someday, I'll tell you a hair-raising story about a blazing gunfight. For all I know, maybe I'm a wanted man. It was me and my partner against seven. Every shot hit its mark." Elder was talking nonsense, but his listeners were enthralled. Cowboy shootouts were ancient history.

Elder moved on and told of striking oil and an embellished tale of Ramona's brothel burnt down with drunken killers upstairs. "The Sheriff suspected me of murder. Can you imagine (smiling)? Me! He told me to get out of town." With their mouths hanging open, he turned to the destruction caused by the earthquake and the fantastic financial opportunities for those brave enough to take risks.

As an example, he spoke of Chinatown, virtually wiped out. "The last building to go was Saint Mary's Cathedral. It survived the first day but the next day it burned to the ground. Even the bells melted. Developers wanted the prime land and attempted to have the Chinese relocated to the mudflats. But the Chinese resisted, and the city leaders feared losing Chinese trade and tourist dollars. Also, the Empress of China promised that their embassy would only be rebuilt in the center of Chinatown.

"They know," Elder said, "that San Francisco will rise from the ashes, that it will be bigger and better than before. You know it. I know it. And if anyone wants to sell, I'm buying, maybe not in Chinatown, but I'm buying all I can."

Fascinated, the suits stared at Elder. In their eyes, he was a rugged hombre riding the range, romancing beautiful women, wrangling cattle, a gunfighter fighting off rustlers, a wildcat oil driller, and a businessman. They asked where he could be reached? Sandbourne's plan had backfired. To his dismay, Elder was someone to know.

Chapter Five: In The Shadow of Death

In San Francisco, there was prejudice against people of color and laws outlawing marriage between the races. Abe was a Negro. He married a nurse, and although she was light-skinned, she was mulatto.

Nonetheless, Abe did exceptionally well in life. He had his society of friends and made inroads into business with and without Elder. As his enterprises grew, so did a coterie of loyal employees of the highest rank, managers, accountants, and lawyers. And woe to those who offended him or would disparage him to Elder or to anyone, and it got back to them.

In 1907, one year after the earthquake, Elder and Abe innocently made offers to purchase homes. It was in the elite, high-status Nob Hill area. Elder's bid was accepted. Not Abe's. They tried again. Generous cash buyouts were offered. Again, Abe was refused. As courteously as he could, the agent disabused him of the notion that he could buy or build in Nob Hill. He was told, "Go to Oakland or Berkley where there are more of your kind."

They found Cow Hollow, an area of rolling hills, clean water ponds, a small lagoon, considerable acreage, and, on the edges, some desolate-looking apartment buildings, houses, and businesses. Eventually, their homes and those that followed rivaled Nob Hill. Outsiders came to admire the changes.

Cow Hollow, formerly an area of thriving dairies and small Mexican and Asian farms, had been converted. Cows that polluted the water and the farms were gone. The large city sewer pipe, spewing foul waste like a small waterfall, was rerouted. Close by were two hospitals, Saint Mary's and Saint Joseph's, and a small boat harbor.

Their homes were magnificent examples of two-story stone and lumber built on the same property. Mediterranean style with balconies, separated by a large expanse of yard and gardens, Elder's house had six bedrooms. Abe's had five, with a more modest kitchen and family room.

Abe and Maia planned to add more rooms with children but had difficulty conceiving. Eventually, after two miscarriages, Michael, little "Mikey," was born. Mikey, whom they adored and read stories to every night, snuggling close, brought tender love, inner peace, and joy. Tragically, the little guy fell sick with influenza—so easily curable by an antibiotic, but penicillin, although discovered in 1928, did not reach practical use until the 1940s. A candle service was held, and prayer vigils until he passed away. He was four years of age. At his funeral, the minister prayed over the casket, saying that the Lord had called the little boy home to heaven, infuriating Elder.

The sorrow of Abe and Maia was so great that it sorely tested their marriage. They went inward, grew quiet, and often were separate in private grief. Maia left to be with her parents in Puerto Rico. With her gone, Abe's suffering was compounded. On the day of her departure, Elder looked for Abe and found him sitting, forlorn, in a secluded corner of the vast yard. No words would suffice. Elder draped his arm around his friend's shoulders and offered a cigar. There they sat quietly, two lifelong friends, late into the evening until Georgia insisted they come out of the cold.

In contrast, at 18, Georgia gave birth to Samuel and, two years later, to Jessica, lifting them to levels of contentment from which they felt they would not descend.

As life would have it, Georgia began suffering severe debilitating headaches. Doctors, suspecting a tumor, suggested exploratory surgery. She refused. Maybe someday, they said, there might be better technology, some way to look through the bone into the brain. X-rays were available for soft tissue but were not adequate to penetrate bones.

There was a slow decline until Georgia could not leave the house and then her room. Nurses were hired. Days passed. Sometimes, she did not recognize her children as her own. She yelled at them, called them imposters, and denied David Elder as being her husband. Inexplicably, there were moments when she would lucidly converse with Jessica and,

46

the next, lash out, screaming that she was not her actual daughter, an imposter. The children were confused and asked if she were crazy.

Elder said, "Let's just say that she's colorful and sick." Brandy and laudanum were prescribed. Laudanum, a mixture of alcohol, opium, and traces of morphine and codeine, also called tincture of opium, was calming but highly addictive. Its use was initially at Georgia's discretion, but after finding her in a stupor too many times, it was put under the nurses' control. Visits by her mother and father became less frequent. It was too painful.

Georgia's spacious room accommodated an oversized bed of exotic Brazilian cherrywood, two padded Georgian-style armchairs, a writing desk, and Italian lamps with colorful lead glass shades. French doors opened to a spacious deck overlooking the gardens. The bathroom boasted a double-wall-boat style oval copper bathtub on lions' legs, a separate shower room, a toilet with a bidet, and a vanity desk.

While bathing, he washed her body, starting with her back. They talked. He washed her hair and brushed it. This was a favorite routine, giving her respite from discomfort and pain. Her mind and health were on a slippery slope. Days and moments dwindled when she could converse. Under strict orders, the nurses were to inform the household whenever lucid moments occurred, and they would visit. In pain, she made efforts to seem normal, asked pertinent questions regarding events of the day, the children, and David's life. She listened to the news on the radio and read newspapers until she could no longer concentrate. One afternoon, as Elder sat with her, she had a lucid moment, "David, I'm leaving soon. Be good to yourself and love the children. I love them so much. They don't deserve this, nor do you. I don't know why the good Lord has given me this, but he has."

Elder bent and kissed her lips, and whispered, "Georgia, I love you. I will until I die. She reached up, ran her fingers through his hair, and smiled with weariness, and love. When they talked, he was attuned to when she was reaching her limit. Words stopped in mid-sentence. Gripping his hand, she'd say, "It hurts, it hurts," until the pain subsided, or didn't. Her mind wandered and became confused. She grimaced. Her face fell. She stared off into space. Demons and angels spoke to her, giving her conflicting thoughts and directions. They argued amongst themselves for control. Tormented, she'd shout, "Shut up. Leave me alone." Eventually, she managed a détente. The voices arbitrated and made compromises giving her some peace.

Their sexual relationship ended. Elder felt impotent and wondered if he had entirely lost his libido. In embarrassment, he recalled the day when her mind appeared clear. Laughing and flirting, she wanted to love him, to hold and kiss him as they had in the past. Looking at him lovingly, she said, "Honey, get in bed." It was disastrous. Amid their intimacy, she lost her mind. She screamed in his ear. She didn't know him. It was a shame that would be with him forever.

Elder was affluent, had friends, lived in a mansion that few would ever have, and was respected and envied. Yet, he was unhappy. He missed the ebulliently healthy Georgia and hoped that she might miraculously recover. He went against his belief in non-belief in a God and prayed as he had before in his youth, beseeching the Lord God for help. Falling to his knees, he prayed, "Lord, I haven't prayed for a while, and I'm sorry. Please, Georgia needs your help." Then, he became angry when it failed, failed just like before when he had prayed for his sister, mother, and father. Remaining faithful to Georgia was not a problem, but the loneliness, sadness, and remorse were. If it were not for his children and Abe, he wondered if he would care to live.

Max and Jessica suspected their mother was so miserable that she might take her own life. She did not. But two days short of her 40th birthday, she

48

awakened clear-headed and without pain. She told the nurses to dress her in something gay and to help her to the balcony.

She waved to two employees walking across the lawn, Matteo and his son, Xavier. They returned the gesture. Scrub Jays at the far end swooped low. A wispy breeze rustled the leaves and branches of the tall apricot tree abundant with blossoms touching the balcony. Lamenting that this might be the last time she would see another day, she reached out to an occasional visitor, Señor, a big, fluffy calico cat grooming on the balustrade. Purring, it rubbed its face on her hand, and arched his back to be petted.

"Hello, Señor. Did you come to say goodbye?" Taking in the brilliantly blue sky, tinged with whites and grays, and the scent of jasmine from the shrubbery below, she thought, "A beautiful day to die." She looked for the dogs but couldn't find them. She summoned Sam and Jessica. Entering the room, they found her sitting in a straight-backed chair. Instead of her usual robe, she wore a light summer dress, a floral front button-down cotton with padded shoulders. But she was a shadow of her former self, frail and gaunt with sunken cheeks. Her once thick, lustrous, long hair was no more. It was dull white and wispy. And her once proud breasts were flaccid sacks on a bony frame. Weakly but determined, she weakly mustered, "Sam, Jessica, my sweet children, I love you so much. I'm sorry, I'm leaving soon. I won't see your weddings or your children. I won't be here when you need me. I'll miss you."

"Mom don't say that," Jessica said.

"Honey, I don't want to, but I think my life is ending. I want to say goodbye and tell you how much I love you before it's too late, while I still can."

Tears welled. Jessica spoke in sorrow, "Mom, maybe you'll get well."

"Honey, you know I won't. I don't want to leave, but I will, soon. Tell my parents that I love them. You're the only one they talk to. Now, get your father."

With Jessica rushing out, Sam feeling pity and love, leaned to his mother and kissed her. She was skeletal, like a living corpse. Shaken, he asked, "Mom, do you want to pray?"

Georgia woefully shook her head. "No, I'm prayed out; cried out too. He knows."

With emotions so raw, barely able to speak, Sam said, "Mom, I'll miss you so much."

Georgia smiled weakly and reached for his cheek. "Sweet Sam, be nice to your father. Help him and remember me."

Elder was found in the kitchen with his sleeves rolled up, making rhubarb apple pies with Maia. Abe was seated offering ignored bits of advice and drinking coffee. They came running.

Seeing them enter, Georgia weakly looked up and smiled. But as Elder approached, her eyes widened, her chest heaved, once, twice, and convulsed. With her eyes half-lidded, she stiffened and passed into unconsciousness. Kneeling, Elder took Georgia's hand and called her name, "Georgia, Georgia; I'm here."

Abe felt himself tearing up. Through clouded eyes, he took in the room: Sam and Jessica, Maia, Elder, the two nurses against the wall, and a cat jumping from the balcony onto a tree. Forcing a look of composure, he put his hand on his friend's shoulder and said, "David, she's gone."

"Dad," Jessica said, "she tried to stay for you."

Indeed, she had made the effort. Keening weeping filled the room.

Kneeling, Elder nestled his head in his wife's lap and wept.

Sam stood by stiffly, shaken to the core. He had never experienced death, not like this, up close, personal, and horrible.

50

Maia checked Georgia's pulse. She was alive. Dimming the lights, they put her to bed.

The day went into the night. Elder sat by her bedside and held her hand. Once he thought she might have returned his grip. Reminiscing, he spoke of their life together, when they had laughed, danced, sat in hot springs with friends, shared wine, and camped and hiked in the redwoods. He spoke of their adventurous times in Italy and Paris and their walks on the clear starry nights, just the two of them kissing and in love.

Bending, he put his nostrils to hers and synchronized their breathing, taking in her life force, her breath to remember. "Georgia," he said, "thank you for being in my life." Tears welled at her closed eyelids. Gently, dabbing her eyes and kissing her lips, he whispered, "Dear heart, I'm so sorry. I should have loved you more. Now, you're going away without me. I'll miss you." At 3:00 a.m., those waiting in the hall heard a long, deep wail, "Noooooo." Cradling her emaciated body, he kissed her forehead and cheeks, and sobbed his heart out.

David Elder thought he was ready for Georgia's passing. He was wrong. Hearing his wails, his children pacing outside the door sent in Maia. His grief and remorse were unbearable. He wondered if there was something more he could have done. Perhaps he should have sought a doctor from Europe. He had tried the ancient oriental arts of herbs, potions, teas, diets, and something new, acupuncture. Nothing worked.

With Elder's permission, a partial autopsy revealed that Georgia had a malignant brain tumor growing into her spine.

With her passing, Sam and Jessica wondered if they should feel ashamed but eventually reluctantly admitted that their lives were easier. Her suffering had been profound and affected everyone. Of this, she had been all too aware and hated it. When she sensed her end was near, she told them to be wise, to be happy, and to have good lives.

Depressed and hollow, Elder went about his days listlessly and automatically: eating, dressing, speaking, and working mechanically. Thoughts of what he could have done differently possessed him. Sorrow overflowed into self-criticism. Broken, mulling over real and imagined shortcomings, mistakes he had made in life, and people he had harmed, even Georgia, he lost control of his mind. In despair, in the silence of his room, he wept with abject sadness. Tears racked his body and soul. Outside, with her hand on the door, his beloved daughter, Jessica, listening, scratched on the door to let him know he was not alone. She called out, "Daddy, I love you."

Suicide came to mind. If it were not for the love and attention of the family, perhaps Elder would have done it. Every night, he went to bed hoping he would not wake. In the morning, he was disappointed. He went to the gun cabinet. Empty. Together, Sam and Jessica had moved them.

Sitting on the leather couch in the shadows of the study, Elder didn't know if it was day or night. He was in a deep hole and didn't care to crawl out. Someone had set a fire in the hearth. A played-out log broke and settled. Sparks flew—another sip of brandy. A slight sound alerted him to the fact that he was not alone. Abe was sitting across the room looking at him. Maia poured coffee, looked at Elder, shook her head, and left the room.

Abe took a sip and raised his eyes to Elder's.

"Hi, Fact," Elder said, making Abe chuckle. Elder had used his old nickname of years past. In the oil fields, in discussions, Abe often asked, "Is that a fact?" Then, roustabouts teased, saying, "Hey Fact, is that a fact, Fact?"

Abe nodded, grinning, and returned the greeting, "Hi, David." Elder felt a movement. Softly, a body bumped him. Jessica was sitting next to him. "Hi, honey; how long have you been here?"

52

"Does it matter?"

"I don't know."

"Dad, come on. This has to stop. We need you. Can you try?" Seeing her father so adrift and weak was frightening and destabilizing. He had always been the steady backbone of the family, their leader.

Looking at his sweet daughter, so worried, his eyes misted. "How long has it been?"

"Three months."

"All right, enough."

Jessica's concern had revived memories of the funeral of Elder's mother, Ella Grace. Standing at the gravesite, his father had glared at him and his sister, Kathy, as if they were the cause of their mother's death. Hoping he was mistaken, he tried to hug him but was roughly pushed away. After that, their father stayed physically but went away emotionally and mentally, as if replaced by an imposter.

David Elder's paternal grandfather was an alcoholic, a falling down drunk, and died young. Following the funeral of Ella Grace, Elder's father became the same and worse. David had vowed it would never happen to him. Yet here he was wallowing in grief, thinking only of himself, and drinking himself into a stupor just like him.

To regain his sanity, he took long walks, jogged with Bradley, and walked in the rain and sunshine, sometimes unaware of the sounds of other voices or someone by his side. He looked at his reflection in the mirror and practiced smiling and laughing. He made toothy grins, slapped his face silly, told himself to snap out of it, and laughed and cried at his antics. He noted the good things he was involved in: support of the Salvation Army food kitchen, the preservation of the Old Spanish Mission, and contributions to the Catholic and Presbyterian orphanages. It wasn't about religion. It was for the children. He thought of friends and family who warmed his soul and loved him. And he knew he wasn't the only one suffering.

Chapter Six: New Friends

Sam picked up his cup of coffee and took in the rhythm of the street: workmen in a four-foot-wide trench repairing sewer pipes, and passing stout, thin, short, tall, shapely, and not so shapely pretty girls and handsome boys carrying books, a woman pushing a baby carriage. Savoring his coffee, he put it down to take a bite of a ham sandwich. He was at Arnoldi's Café, popular with students for its comfortable ambiance, good food and low prices. Formerly a residence, it had seating inside and out, and from his vantage seat on the porch, he had an open view. Although already a graduate of the University of Standard, with a degree in economics, he was enrolled in a master's class in investing. Now, he was relaxed, relishing the day.

A sharply dressed gentleman with neatly trimmed thinning graying hair, scanned the menu. Finished, he tipped it down to the table. Tilting his head upward to the warm sun, he reflected on his life. A widower, he was lonely. His three children resided out of state. Keeping in touch with him had low priority. His life had been as a boxer, sparring partner, trainer, and, most recently, the owner of a boxing gym. He wanted to retire but couldn't afford it. Budgeting his income, the gym was his business and his home. The large walk-in closet was originally for storage. Now, it was for clothes, storage, and a sleeping cot. Cooking and bathroom functions were performed in the locker room. Stale, that's what his life was. Gus surmised that the young man, sitting at the next table checking out a young lady, was probably still living at home with his family. "Yes," he mused, "his future is open."

The waiter, a young man, refilled Sam's coffee. Gus, the older gentleman, had been served. Nearby sat the neatly dressed young woman with auburn hair and dark brown eyes, reading.

Sam glanced at the young lady. She was wearing a knee-length dress. Her legs were crossed. While his eyes took her in, he considered another coffee refill. He had nothing pressing except to study. "She's cute," he thought and tried to catch her eyes. If she noticed, she didn't show it. She turned the page of the book, "Cup of Gold" by John Steinbeck. He had read it. While observing her graceful fingers (with red nail polish), her auburn hair, brown eyes, throat, and face, he began a low humming. For Sam, like his father, such humming usually indicated attraction, deep thought, or impending retaliation if in conflict. Lifting her coffee cup, she cocked her wrist to bring it to her lips. "Nice lips," he thought. His eyes went to her shoes, moved to finely turned ankles, and to her crossed legs. Humming continued while his eyes worked their way to her slim waist and other attributes.

Sounds of distress intruded. A pretty, Asian student was pleading with three men to leave her alone. Touching her arm, they flirted and mimicked her accent. Jerking her arm away, almost in tears, desperate, she looked around for help. In a cultured British accent, she pleaded, "Please, Sirs, please leave me alone." With a beseeching look, she turned to the deck, at Gus and Sam. Sam stood. So did Gus.

Gus judged the mettle of the men. Despite his age, he trained every day. Trim and fit, he'd easily dispose of the leader and the others would back off. Upon rising, he was in the process of removing his coffee-colored corduroy blazer but stopped. The waiter had stepped down to the sidewalk. Clearly not afraid, he invited the woman into the café. She moved to enter, but the senior of the three molesters, grinning, widely amused, moved to block her way.

Looking desperate, the young lady grabbed the waiter's left bicep and pulled him closer.

Addressing her tormenter, the waiter said, "Sir, she is not interested. Please be kind and move along."

One of the men was young, perhaps 15 or 16. The other two were in their late 20s or early 30s and well-dressed. They didn't like this interruption. The girl moved to enter. But the eldest and largest rudely grabbed her arm, causing her to drop her books.

She moved tightly to the waiter.

The man positioned himself for confrontation.

He barked. "Mind your own business." Then with his eyes on the waiter, challenging him, he stroked the young lady's arm, and whispered something in her ear. Her response was a disgusted look. Perhaps it was an obscene proposition.

"All right, sir," the waiter said, "that's enough. Please step away." The tranquility of the café had evaporated, replaced by tension.

Gus, observing, could see that this ill-mannered individual was taken aback, perhaps by the waiter's calm manner. Or perhaps, he was surprised that a waiter had the audacity to act in a manner of authority.

Aggressively, the man snarled, "Get lost, you Wop."

Wop, originally from the Italian guappo meaning good-looking, in America, had taken on the meaning of stud or swaggering dandy and worthless, a derogatory term for an Italian. The word itself did not disturb

56

the waiter. He wasn't even Italian. He was, despite his first name, Irish—Caesar O'Sullivan.

Calmly, but also with a tight hint of aggression, the waiter, said, "My name is Caesar. Now sir, for your health, you should leave." For his gallantry, he was arrogantly poked in the chest. A second poke missed. Moving gracefully like a matador, Caesar grabbed the hand, pivoted, and pulled. As the aggressor's body passed, Caesar helped its forward movement by placing his hand on the back of the man's shoulder. He pushed, and it was over. The man was sent sprawling. He tried again and received a lightning slap. Dazed, he stood dumbly, muddle-headed, staring at Caesar with his hand on his cheek.

Gus thought, "Ooooh, ouch," a slap, but what a slap and all done effortlessly, even with the young lady hanging onto his arm.

The proprietor was watching. To the three men, he said, "Please, gentlemen, that's enough. Please go." He was ignored.

Upon seeing his friend's condition, another man rushed Caesar. Caesar dodged, and the man hit air. After evading the charge, Caesar gripped the man's shirt and whipped him to and fro like a helpless tap-dancing rag doll. Caesar shifted his feet and body one way and the other. The young lady gracefully moved with him. The addled man couldn't find his footing. This was enough. They took their dazed friend, still holding his cheek, and walked away.

The young lady left in the opposite direction. In her genteel voice, she called, "Thank you." Caesar waved and turned back to the departing tormenters. Curiously, the youngest, the one who had stayed out of the fray, waggled one hand behind his back as if saying a pleasant goodbye. Whistles, a scatter of applause, and shouts of "Well done" came from the workers in the trench.

57

Gus was impressed. So was Sam and the proprietor. Clapping Caesar on the back, he whispered, "Good job, now get back to work."

Gus reasoned that Caesar was perhaps 5 feet, 10 inches, and a light heavyweight, at about 175 pounds. He was well-proportioned, and his balance and coordination were impressive.

The pretty young lady sitting nearby gasped at the quick exchange. To Sam, she said, "I saw you get up when that creep grabbed that girl. Were you going to help?"

"I was, but the waiter handled it. I wasn't needed."
Thinking she was through, Sam returned to his table. Without being invited, she followed. She introduced herself as Rachael and asked if he would be kind enough to treat her to a bowl of soup. Guessing she had little or no money, he replied, "Sure, my name is Sam. I'll treat you to soup and a sandwich, that is if you give me a little conversation." She ordered both.

Time passed quickly. Rachael's words were spoken with warm pleasing sounds. She had dropped out of college and was looking for work. She was at the café to apply but was rejected. "Well, Rachael," Sam replied, "I'm the assistant manager at a speakeasy. If you're interested come by and apply. Prohibition is ending, and we're turning the place into a restaurant. We're calling it the Palace Station Cafe, down by the waterfront, not far from the Ferry Building."

She asked if the doorman at the speakeasy would let her in. "Do I need a password like Blackie sent me?"

Rachael had never been in a speakeasy, not for lack of desire, but for lack of money. Speakeasies were illegal but tolerated. They sold liqueur, had gambling, and, she imagined, were frequented by rakish men smoking cigars, with sexy, loose women hanging on their arms. They also had lively jazz and stayed open all night. She would like to visit at least once so she could dance the Charleston and jitterbug.

Sam told Rachael the story of one notable raid by The Bureau of Prohibition, and local police. It was the agency formed to enforce the National Prohibition Act of 1919, outlawing the sale and manufacture of alcoholic beverages, except by medical prescription. Rushing through the doors of the infamous, colorful Palace speakeasy, they found 25 peaceful diners, eating, drinking tea, and listening to a pianist. There was a total absence of gambling tables and alcohol. An informant in the police department had forewarned Sam. All evidence of illicit activity had been removed, and the homeless were invited to be his guests.

Sam almost gave her his full name, but no. Their father was well known in certain circles, and if Sam was to work at the cafe, he did not want to be known as the son of a prominent man. He would use another surname.

Sam gave her the address and instructed, "If it's still the speakeasy, knock and say Sam sent you. That's all, just Sam. If you come, I'll treat you to a steak dinner." A smile played around her lips. Looking at him, up and down, and with new interest, she replied with a flirtatious smile. She said, "We'll see."

"How bold," he mused, and inwardly chuckled.

Feeling regretful that he hadn't asked for her number, Sam watched her walk away. Would he see her again? Returning his attention to the cafe, he saw Gus conversing with Caesar. But the owner, irritated by the earlier trouble, barked at Caesar to get back to work. Curious, Sam asked Gus if he could join him. Gus motioned to the empty chair. Soon, Sam learned from Gus that Caesar worked full time and was the sole support of his two pre-teen sisters. Gus had convinced him he could earn much more boxing than as a waiter. Sam asked if he could come by to watch. "Sure," Gus replied. "And if you're interested, I'll get you into shape."

As a fit athlete who had run track and pole vaulted, this comment amused Sam. He wondered what made Gus think he needed conditioning. He soon found out. After a few days of boxing, he arrived home with puffy cheeks and a sore body.

Gus believed that with his youth and talents, Caesar could be a champion. But he wasn't aggressive, preferring to win by points, not by a knockout.

Within five months, Caesar had seven fights, all won on points. Gus was both pleased and exasperated. Caesar was too considerate. He softened his punches, especially if he and his opponent were friendly outside the ring. Simply put, he didn't want to injure anyone. There were heckling catcalls of "fixed fight," but Caesar's attitude was that fighting was temporary, for money.

A fight was scheduled for two days before Christmas. It was a preliminary bout at the Civic Auditorium. Jake Tanner, "The Bull," another Irishman, was Caesar's opponent. Jake was prepping to be a contender for the light heavyweight title. But his real goal was to move up to the heavyweight division to become the Champion of the world.

The flamboyant Jake entered the arena to loud cheers, whistles, and applause. Looking good, he danced, pranced, and waved his arms. Caesar received lackluster clapping and boos. Touching gloves, they went to their corners. At the bell, Tanner was the aggressor, always moving forward, eager to showcase his skills as "The Bull."

Caesar scored points for skill, maneuvering gracefully, connecting punches, and slipping away. In the second round, Tanner picked up the pace. He moved in. They clenched, pulled, and pushed, body to body, and exchanged blows. Tanner had the weight advantage and pushed Caesar into a corner. There, he pummeled Caesar with fast, repeated blows.

Caesar retaliated. With feet shuffling, there was an exciting back-and-forth exchange. Caesar slipped and fell. It was counted as a knockdown.

In the third round, a flurry of punches connected on Caesar's arms and one low blow that should have been called a foul. None worried Caesar, but it was clear that Jake was the crowd pleaser.

Gus barked instructions, urging Caesar to get aggressive. If he wanted fights, he had to put on better show. He tried, but it was against his nature. There were times when he knocked opponents down, but not out. To see if he was listening, Gus shouted, "Hit him in the nards." With a sly, crooked smile, Caesar let Gus know he had everything under control. Picking up the pace, he rocked Tanner, only to back off. The crowd alternately cheered and booed. Engaging again, the fighters punched. Tanner missed with a fierce sweeping uppercut. Tanner wanted more aggression from Caesar, wanting him to look formidable to show the crowd that, when he beat him, he was indeed the 'Great Bull," the next heavyweight champion of the world.

Even though Caesar was fighting, he was also slipping away, frustrating Tanner's desire for a quick win. Tanner decided to antagonize Caesar.

Meanwhile, Caesar decided that he would pick up the pace. In the next round, he'd knock Tanner down without killing him. His blows became more precise and more robust but so did Tanner's. Tanner hit him with a solid left to the ribs and a grazing right to the face. Thinking Caesar was through, the crowd roared.

Julie, Caesar's pretty, teenage sister, sitting with Sam and Jessica at ringside, called out, "Caesar hit him," ruining Caesar's plan.

Tanner, pleased that the spectators had reached a high level of excitement, pulled Caesar in, and with a smirk, whispered, "Nice piece of quim."

61

The last thing Tanner heard was, "Asshole, she's my sister!" Caesar feinted with a left, shifted, and delivered a thunderous right to the heart, another lighting right to the midsection, and a left to the chin. Tanner flew back. Like a stiff plank of wood, he hit the canvas. The crowd's roar stopped for the briefest seconds, stunned, and then erupted.

Tanner awoke, on a metal platform surrounded by attendants, a doctor's stethoscope to his chest, and his ringside assistant saying, "Bucko, you should have kept your mouth shut."

Jessica had sat in rapt attention following Caesar's every move, cheering when she thought he did something good and cringing when he was hit. When Tanner hit the canvas, astonished, she exclaimed, "Oh my gosh!"

"I've offered him a job," Sam said. "Dad wants another employee at home. Maybe we'll also have him work at our new restaurant. What do you think?"

To Sam's amusement, she said, "I'll take him," making him grin.

"He's not going to be your exclusive employee." But he was pleased to see his sister's hands clasped to her chest, smiling and blushing. "Well, well," he thought, "Jessica, who never finds any man to her satisfaction, likes him." With Sam's, "Okay," she burst forth with a lusty laugh. It was contagious.

In the locker room, Caesar showered, dressed, picked up his bag, and walked out the side exit with Gus. Midnight. Standing on the dim cobblestone street, an unpleasant surprise awaited. Five paunchy, middle-aged men and older waited. Bunched under a flickering streetlamp, 30 feet away, full of beer, and drunk, they swayed. After a group sway, they moved forward. They had bet on the wrong man.

"Oh, nuts," Caesar said. "Gus, go ahead; I'll be with you in a moment. Look at them. They're delusional."

62

Excitedly, Gus said, "Hey, let's take them on. Let's do it." In his youth, Gus was quite a scrapper. Even though the body was older, his mind told him they could lick these fellows. Also, he still had quite a bit of adrenaline coursing through his body, on a high, from Caesar's fight.

Caesar gave him an amused half-grin and said, "Are you serious? Gus, you stay out of it unless I get into trouble." However, as the men moved toward them, a beautiful, two-tone, black, and gold, four-door Chrysler drove up. The door opened. It was Sam and Jessica. "Come on, get in!" she ordered.

Sam stepped out of the car. He looked at the five, swaying and drunk, and asked, "What do you think?" The three looked at the five. Sam had reached a level where he sparred with Caesar and was up to the challenge.

Jessica grabbed Sam's arm, and said, "Oh, no, you don't. Let's go. Get in. All of you."

But Sam couldn't resist. Taking bold striding steps toward the men and shouting, "Come on!" they retreated. Two tripped over their own feet and fell. Good sense had returned to their drunken brains.

Jessica quipped, "Well, Sam, you've had your fun."

On the drive home, they spoke of employment. Gus was to manage the new restaurant, the Palace Station Café. Caesar was to be a combination driver, bouncer, bartender, and waiter, as needed. And, as he was told in private, to keep a protective eye on Jessica. Also, they would live in the big house with the Elder family. Although a small family of three were also employees, that is, Matteo, his wife, Aida, and their son, Xavier. They had their own quarters.

Jessica sat in the rear seat between Caesar and Caesar's sister, Julie. Gus was in front. Sam drove. Turning a corner, the car swayed. Never known to be timid, she leaned heavily into Caesar, felt his warmth, and glanced at his face for his reaction. Seeing an endearing grin, she impulsively ran her fingers over his knuckles. She liked this fine specimen of a man and squiggled a little closer.

The next morning, Sam sent Matteo to transport Caesar and his sisters to the mansion. Once there, inside, they were presented with an unobstructed view from the stone lobby to the tall glass doors at the far end. Beyond the doors were the gardens and manicured lawn. Overhead was the high barrel ceiling running the length

Matteo asked, "What do you think?"

Julie said, "It's nice." Lilith, her little sister, age 10, tugged on her sleeve and in her innocence whispered, "Gosh, are we going to live here?"

Maia had long been the house manager, the volunteer majordomo. Her choice. She enjoyed her role and was quite efficient. Upon seeing the girls, her heart quickened. After she and Abe lost their little boy, a hole was left in her heart. When the girls walked in, the hope of having children was revived.

Maia welcomed the newcomers and gave them a tour, including the large kitchen, the gathering place where they would eat with the family. Upstairs, the girls were offered a bedroom for each but chose to be together in the same room, a room larger than their previous apartment. This was Elder's instructions. He liked to be surrounded by family, friends, and employees. If they didn't fit, they were dismissed.

At 5:00 p.m., with the setting sun, everyone gathered in the kitchen for dinner. Caesar and his sisters were introduced. Jessica was usually the first to enter, drank coffee, and waited for the others. But not today. This evening, she was the last. She looked over the seating and asked Sam to move. This was so she could sit next to Caesar. "I want him to feel welcome," she said. Seating completed, grinning, she playfully bumped Caesar. After that, she was the first to arrive, sat as close to him as possible, and attempted to start a new tradition, that is hugging in greetings. Evident to all was that she would embrace Caesar. It was awkward. As much as she tried, casually, it didn't last.

Chapter Seven: North Beach, 1934

Almost three years had passed since Georgia's passing. David Elder was back to living. Not content, but back. On a crisp spring morning, he put four Cuban Arturo Fuente cigars in his pocket and went to the garage. There, he examined his Model 101 Indian Scout motorcycle. After two kick-starts, it rumbled to life. He circled the driveway. With the motor purring, he rode out of the wrought iron gates, rode a few miles past the small boat harbor, returned, and thought of driving headlong into the garage's rear wall. Since Georgia's death, he was adrift, without meaning. He was making deals and interacting with the kids, but life wasn't the same. If something new did not come into his life, something to make him look forward to the next day, he would wither away. Abe and his children couldn't be at his side every moment to give him company. He thought again of his gnawing hunger for a woman he could love. Distracting him from his depressing thoughts were the sounds of colorful tinkling.

In one corner of the garage, Georgia had hung chimes to add a little personality to the white sharp lines of the building. His eyes went to the cars, two Duesenberg's, and the Chrysler. Sweeping his eyes over the expansive yard and mansion, he mused, "Oh, misery, wealthy, but unhappy."

Ruefully, Elder smiled. Old Lobo was looking at him; if a dog could smile, he was smiling. Watching Lobo thumping his tail, he turned the motorcycle to an idling rumble, sat a few seconds, and put the kickstand down. He turned it off. A year prior, on a whim, it was purchased for a road trip to the Mendocino wine country and to Fort Bragg, California. It was an attempt to recreate memories with Georgia. He returned home with a sore ass, dissatisfied.

Using the garage telephone, he summoned Caesar, his new employee. Listless, he wanted to take a ride with the dogs, Bradley the third, and Lobo, his sire. They would go to North Beach for breakfast. Then he would decide whether to return home to do nothing or to go somewhere else. The waiter at Tucci's saw them coming and placed them at a preferred table. Steaming coffee with heavy cream was placed on the table, and a water bowl on the floor for the dogs.

Across the street, Washington Square, the park where he and Abe had retreated during the 1906 earthquake was alive like an old friend. A man raked leaves. Folks threw balls for their dogs. Lovers held hands and kissed. Chinese women performed graceful dances of Tai Chi, snapping fans open and closed in unison. A man played the saxophone, a tin cup for coins at his feet. The unemployed sat on benches, leaned against trees, and lounged in the sun. Others slept under Canary Island pine trees with newspapers over their faces.

A tall, handsome young priest walking around the park passed a group of longshoremen airing grievances. They interrupted their arguments to acknowledge him. Elder commented, "That priest looks sad."

"Yes," Caesar replied, "that's Father Raffael. He's a priest at St. Mark's. The story is that he fell in love and gave her up. Now he walks the park looking for her."

"Poor man," Elder said.

Taking his eyes from the priest, Elder clipped the ends of two cigars and handed one to Caesar. Caesar didn't smoke but accepted. Then Elder asked, "Caesar, have you met anyone special?"

"Yes, but she doesn't know."

Elder blew out smoke. "Caesar, tell me about yourself."

Caesar began: His family were corn and wheat farmers in Cimarron County, Oklahoma. But the long drought without rain and the resulting infamous dust bowl storms of the 1930s took the rich topsoil. The land turned into a dry wasteland. ents went to New York wasteland, breaking the farmers, and worsening the Great Depression. "I was 19, and Lilith and Julie were seven and nine.

"It didn't work. After a few months, my grandmother made a special dinner for a special talk. Our poor old grandparents. They had given up. There was no water. No rain, just dry fields. It was no use staying on. So, we could either go with them to live with Grandpa's sister in Tulsa or go out on our own. The emphasis was to go on our own. As nicely as they could, they let us know there wasn't room for us. Also, well, they couldn't afford more mouths to feed. It was sad. But as it turned out, Grandma died. My grandfather gave us some money; he went to live with his sister, and we came to San Francisco. As for mom and dad, the last I heard was that my dad was a driver for a bootlegger selling rot-gut gin, and my mom had moved in with a cousin near Yankee Stadium."

On the way to California, "I worked on a ranch in Santa Fe, New Mexico. I'll tell you about it later."

"Tell me now. I was a cowhand in Sana Fe, years ago."

"I'll get to it."

"We traveled on the Greyhound Bus. In Los Angeles, a stop was made in Los Angeles, called the City of Angles by the Mexicans."

67

"We got off almost next to of the city's oldest street--Olivera Street. We filled our bellies with Mexican food." Nearby, in close walking distance was Chinatown. Los Angeles was impressive by its size and teeming population, but they found it distasteful, noisy, and crowded.

Caesar paused in his story, blew out little "0's" from the cigar, and picked up his coffee cup.

He continued: They passed restaurants with finely dressed customers dining on white tablecloths, with fine chinaware and silver utensils. Chauffeurs smoked and leaned on expensive cars exchanging gossip. One block further was a food line of over a hundred at a Presbyterian church, waiting for the doors to open. To save money, they ate free food at the Salvation Army soup kitchen and at Olivera Street. Two days walking about Los Angeles and two nights lodging at the Presbyterian Hall was enough. They continued to San Francisco.

"Why did you give up boxing? Gus says you could have been a champ."

"I never told Gus, but a new kid came to school. I was a senior in high school. He was a bully. Eventually, he got to me. I felt sorry for him, figuring maybe he had it bad at home. Anyway, he wanted my lunch. I gave it up. But then he wanted my money. I refused and jammed my hands in my pockets. I only had a few pennies, but I was stubborn. He hit me in the stomach, and I fell. He pulled on my hands, but I wouldn't give in. A bunch of kids were watching. They started laughing."

"Then?" Elder asked.

"When I got my breath back, we fought. He must have thought I was a pushover. He was bigger and older, but he missed most of his punches. I hit him with a few good ones, but he wouldn't quit. So, I hit him in the face with all I had. It started from the bottom of my toes, up through my body and to my fist. It felt good, and maybe that scared me—that I could

68

feel that way. That was it. The kid cried. I felt rotten. He never picked on anybody again, and I had a new reputation.

Now, I'll tell you about Santa Fe, and a message from a guy called Big Hat Sam."

"What?" Surprised, Elder leaned forward.

"Big Hat Sam, Samuel Torres, told me to look you up and to say he was still alive. And if you ever went back, he'd give you a job."

Elder chuckled, "I heard he went to Mexico to fight with Pancho Villa, in the Mexican Revolution. They lost."

"Yeah, he escaped back to Santa Fe. I worked for him for a few months as a cook."

"Well, I'll be. What is it about life? I don't believe in fate, but it's quite a coincidence that Max met you, and here you are, someone who also knew Big Hat Sam."

"Yeaaah, he put me right to work. It was rough, but I enjoyed every second. Even the first day when a cowhand kicked my butt. I was carrying cooking water, and almost fell into a bonfire. I knew it. I was being tested. We fought. I won, easily, but I stretched it out a bit while betting was going on. Big Hat won a bundle."

"Why do you think he bet on you? He didn't know you."

"He saw my sisters climb up on a buckboard for a better view. They were smiling."

"So, they know you can fight."

"Yeh, but I won't do it unless I'm forced. Anyway, Big Hat arranged for me to fight another forehand from another spread. His name was Ricardo Santana; he had the reputation as being the best in the State.

"Yeah, I knew him."

"Anyway, they were friends, and because of that he warned him that I was good. One thing he didn't tell him."

69

"What was that?"

"That he was betting on me."

"How did it go?"

"The only rules were no wrestling and no kicking. It was in the plaza. The whole town turned out, families, children, cowhands, Indians, the blacksmith, everyone. There was a huge barbeque, tortillas, beans, rice, red chili. We drank mezcal (alcohol made from Aloe plant), beer, whatever. I even had a couple, which wasn't too smart. Ricardo was big, bigger than you. He hit me a few times, and they hurt. One punch to my arm turned it numb. I made a mistake thinking he was slow, and old. He was about 45, and he wasn't slow or old. He could hit like a mule. I had to dance around a bit, to get the circulation going again. While I ducked and danced, everyone was booing and laughing. I had to end it—I couldn't take a chance. But he rushed in and knocked me to my knees. He kicked me over and tried to stomp me. The two refs pushed him away. I got up and hit him in the heart with all I had. He doubled over, and I hit him in the temple. The shock went through my arm and down my body. He was out, and I was relieved. You should have heard the crowd."

"Were they loud."

Chuckling, "No, there was dead silence. Not even a dog barked."

Breakfast completed, Elder directed Caesar to drop him and the dogs off at the northern end of Russian Hill, at the corners of Broadway and Mason. Caesar was to wait at the other side, at the downside of Russian Hill at the Lucky Llama Cafe on Polk Street.

Before beginning his trek up the steep rise of Broadway, Elder's eyes roamed over the buildings and the folks on the street. He had good memories here. Three passing young ladies pleasantly nodded. He smiled. It was said that the women of San Francisco had such nice legs and were

70

so fit was because of the hills. Midway, feeling his glutes and leg muscles flexing and tested, he felt good.

Chapter Eight: Caesar

While waiting for his employer at the downside of Broadway, Caesar ate a beef sandwich, and leaned against the Cadillac, waiting, and thinking. Thinking of his life, he reminisced how he had come to this point in his life:

Two years prior, he and his little sisters, Julie and Lilith were waiting in the sad, desolate Greyhound bus station. It was Tulsa, Oklahoma. Fine sand whipped by dry wind whipped their clothes and made them cover their nose and mouths. Caesar looked up at the sky to see if another rolling dust cloud was coming. The last one had convinced him to leave Oklahoma, and their grandparents' farm.

On that day, they were outside, harvesting the last of their skimpy corn crop. The land was parched, dry, and cracked, and the stalks were dry and wilted. Julie, his sister cried out in alarm, "Caesar, look." A huge rolling dirty gray cloud, hundreds of feet high, without visible boundary, left or right, rolled toward them. Although it was at least a mile away, it ominously rolled toward them, pushed by wind, and picking up and adding dry, dust topsoil.

Caesar sprinted for Julie, picked her up and ran for the square little boxy farmhouse, yelling for those inside to close and shutter the windows. Inside, all, his elderly grandparents, Julie, and his other sister, Lilith, crowded into the panty room, closed the door behind them, and covered their faces and mouths with cloth. The dust cloud rolled over them. Coughing violently, they struggled to breathe. The girls especially suffered. Julie fought a chronic cough for months.

In the darkness of the crowded space, Grandma Betsy, bore the storm stoically, comforting the others, advising prayer and patience. But the storm, and lesser ones undid her emotionally. Within a month she passed away. It was no use staying with farming. It hadn't rained for months; even their well was virtually dry, barely giving them barely enough for their own subsistence. Their livestock fared worse, became weak, and died.

Caesar was 19. His sisters, Lilith, and Julie were seven and nine. It had been a hard time in the 1930's. Prospects for a decent future were dim. The nation was hit hard. There was the Great Depression, the stock market crash in October 1929, and the Great Dust Bowl in Oklahoma, and other states. No rain, winds, huge rolling, choking dust storms, and erosion turned previously fertile soil to dry, cracked, unproductive farmland.

Hobos, men, and women, walked desultorily around the square bus terminal, asking for food or money. Caesar reached into his pocket for a few coins to give to a woman with a small child. As he handed it to the thankful woman, he felt a pang of guilt. It was for himself and his sisters. They needed every cent they had for their long overland trip to San Francisco, the promised land, where unemployment was considered lower than the rest of the nation, variously described as ranging from 22% to 28%.

Caesar's parents had been wheat and corn farmers, on 100 acres. But it had turned worthless. Oklahoma, Colorado, New Mexico, Texas, and Kansas were all part of the Dust Bowl. In the panhandle of Oklahoma, no rain, high temperatures, and high winds, and insect infestations, had devastated the land and spirits of anyone who was still hanging on. Caesar's parents abandoned their farm and left their children in the care of their maternal grandparents, also farmers. It didn't work.

On the bus station platform, Caesar ran his hand over his sweaty brow and gave a scathing look to a hobo eyeing the girls. Caesar shook his head. Embarrassed, or chastised, the man backed away, and went around the corner.

Lilith took his hand and said, "Caesar, here comes the bus.

"Yea, that's it," he replied. They had waited in the barren, dry, barren landscape, the only building for miles, in suffocating heat over an hour.

The waiting passengers crowded the gray and white Greyhound bus crowded waiting platform, as the bus, with a cloud of dust, braked to a stop. Caesar's sisters held close to their elder brother as they boarded, along with the others, mothers with children, men somber with anticipation, hoping for employment in California.

During the day, they gazed out the windows at the passing scenery—cacti, sage bushes, distant hills, and at the remote trading posts. Native Indians sat in front of woven blankets selling silver jewelry. Thousands of grazing cattle were passed, watched over by cowhands and their dogs. A large chuck wagon tended by a Chinese family. A young fellow appeared to be the head of the family. He was broad, good-looking, about 5 feet, five inches tall, and had a youngster on his shoulders.

In Santa Fe, New Mexico, Caesar turned to his sisters. "We've getting off here. I have to get a job."

First, they fed their rumbling stomachs at the closest cantina. It was the first time they had tried Mexican food—handmade flat corn tortillas topped with melted cheese, chopped onions, a side of beans, strips of beef, and over easy eggs—delicious, cheap, and satisfying. He asked the owner, for possible employment, and lodging. "Try Santos Cantina at the end of the road," he was told. "Ask for Big Hat Samuel Torres. He's the foreman of the largest ranch in the state."

73

Wondering how he could apply, and his responsibility for the girls, he nonetheless felt he should try. At the cantina, he had the girls wait outside. Inside, drinking at a stand-up bar, no stools, were two men, one with long, wavy, pure white hair, with a ponytail. The other was a lean vaquero, chaps, black, worn cowboy hat, and spurs. Guessing that the larger, broad-shouldered man wearing a big hat was Big Hat Sam, Caesar approached.

"Excuse me sir, if you are Mr. Samuel Torres, I'm looking for work."

Big Hat looked him up and down. He glanced at the two girls peeking in from the front door. Julie, impulsively gave him a little impish wave, making him grin. "With a Spanish accent, Big Hat asked said, "Can you cook? My man needs a helper.

"Yes," I can," Caesar replied.

"The pay is the same as for the cowhands, $20 a month, and maybe $40 for a drive. And it's not payable until the end of a drive. You can have it if you want, but these young girls are your problem. Talk to Sonny, he run's the chuck wagon."

As it turned out, Sonny was as agreeable as he was cheerful. The girls could walk or ride along. They would sleep on the ground on bedrolls like everyone else. Quickly, amid thousands of milling cattle, Caesar and the girls were put to work. Their days began at break of dawn, amid a great din of mewing, shuffling cattle, and cowhands on horses. Occasionally, they were herded to new grazing areas. If on a long drive, the chuck wagon started out the day before. Caesar received curious stares, some not friendly. He and the girls stood out as different. They didn't look like cowhands. They wore clothes fit for farmers or city folk, and in the opinion of the cowhands, they looked soft. The only concession Caesar had made was to outfit the girls and himself with canvas shirts, Levi's, and boots.

74

The first evening, Caesar helped Sonny with the cooking of a large kettle of beans, onions, and chopped pork. Going through the line, the cowhands gave Caesar and the girls flat, expressionless looks. They were rough looking men, wiry, strong, resilient, and resolute in their vocation— white, black, and Mexican vaqueros, often working 20 hours a day with four hours sleep.

Throughout the day, Caesar toiled, cooked, cleaned, and disposed of garbage. His sisters, helped. Sonny told them to go off to play. On the third day, as men sat around a blazing fire, jawing about their day, Curly, a taciturn, wiry cowpoke, had his eyes on Caesar carrying dirty wash water. As he passed, he put a boot on Caesars rump, and pushed. Caesar fell forward, heavily onto the pot, splashing contents. After a scattering of laughter, Caesar stood and cleaned himself off. Then, he kicked the bottom of the outstretched boot of the cowpoke. Silence. A dog sitting on its haunches barked. "Oh, oh, muttered a few. Grinning, Curly stood. "Ah shit, another muttered, "He's picking on the greenhorn."

Silently, Curly approached. Caesar didn't move—didn't back up, didn't look worried, and didn't say a word, just waited. Amused, Curley walked around Caesar, grinning and looking him up and down.

The cowhands took notice of Caesar's behavior, his size, the absence of fear, and Caesar waggling his hands at his sides. The cowhands began taking bets. Curley flicked out a left punch to Caesar's face. Caesar slapped it aside. The betting increased.

Big Hat Sam leaning on a buckboard, smoking a cigar, curiously watched. Glancing at Caesar's sisters, he told them, "Climb up on the buckboard for a better look." Big Hat, seeing them unconcerned, queried, "You don't seem worried!"

Julie shook her head, "Uh, uh."

"Himmm," rumbled in Big Hat's throat. He looked back at the combatants and bet on Caesar.

Curley, circled Caesar cautiously, and lunged, attempting to grab him. To his embarrassment, Caesar deftly moved aside, and in so doing, reached out and yanked Curleys right ear. Cowpokes tried to take back their bets. Curley tried again. Caesar shoved him into the burning embers of the fire. The man jumped out, howling and swatting his clothing. Still, he tried once more, but Caesar tapped his knuckles on the side of Curly's jaw. Not enough to knock him down, but it hurt. The cowhands were impressed.

"Okay," Curly said, "Sorry, I'm done," and offered his hand.

Big Hat was pleased. He had just won a fistful of money.

Hopping down from the wagon, Julie looked at Big Hat and said, "I told you."

What was not immediately apparent to folks was that Caesar, although appearing peaceful, even docile, if riled, could erupt into a mean, tough, son-of-a bitch. He could be pushed only so far and was especially protective of his little sisters.

Big Hat Sam arranged for a fight between Caesar and another foreman. Caesar was convinced. Big Hat would bet for him and even give him some of his winnings.

On the appointed day, in the late afternoon, a festive spirit pervaded in the pueblo of Santa Fe. Families, children, cowhands, merchants, landowners came the square to watch. Senoritas with colorful shawls, and other young ladies came with their chaperones and cattle baron fathers.

Ricardo Santana, the foreman of another huge ranch, was Caesars opponent. Ricardo and Big Hat were good friends. So good that he even warned him about not underestimating Caesar, and that he was betting on him. On the other hand, Caesar was warned that Ricardo had a knockout punch in both hands. Ricardo stood at six feet, two inches taller than Caesar, and about 30 pounds heavier.

The spectators watched intently as the combatants met in the middle of the plaza in the dry air. The rules were simple—no wrestling, and no kicking. There would be no breaks.

Chapter Nine: Reminiscing

Midway on Broadway, Elder stopped and ran his hand over a wrought iron outer security gate, the gate to his old apartment. Beyond it, three steps up, painted sage by him and Georgia was the front door. The bedroom was tiny--10 feet by 12. Ruefully smiling, he recalled that he and Abe had folded a mattress almost double to get it through the door. Pushing forcefully, it suddenly cleared, and they fell through together, laughing.

The floor of the living room and entry was so uneven that a marble could roll from one wall to another. Hours were spent on hands and knees leveling, sanding, refinishing, and replacing boards. To his chagrin, the landlord liked the improvements so much that within six months he raised the rent.

The bathroom shower stall was so narrow that if the soap was dropped, it was easier to step out to retrieve it than to retrieve it in the stall. He and Georgia tried showering together and barely fit. Laughing, they wiggled and waggled about, body to body. She was soaping his chest when he said, "Gosh, Georgia, I love you."

With a sly smile, water spraying, circling her fingers on his chest, she asked, "And? Come on, David. Say it—come on, I'm waiting."

Looking at her, he asked with a wry smile, "Give me a hint."

Pressed against him, smiling broadly, and feeling his arousal, she pressed her hands to his chest. Unable to contain himself, he said, "Oh, my gosh. You lovely woman, will you marry me?" Those were happy, youthful days with Georgia. They were in love, optimistic, and healthy.

Weariness from memories filled him. Sighing, he whispered, "Dear sweet Georgia, I miss you." He wasn't religious but hated the thought of death and nothing after.

Two months before her passing, Elder found Georgia sitting outside on one of the cushioned benches. Her head was inclined backward, eyes closed to the warm setting sun, her hand on Lobo's body cradling his head on her lap. Bradley was at her feet. She smiled at her husband, and for moment, her life essence bloomed forth. She looked young.

She leaned into his shoulder. His hand went to her hair, stroking, careful not to pull away weak wispy strands. Seeing them through a window, Maia brought them hot tea and a blanket.

Before drifting off to sleep, Georgia said, "Sweetheart, I'm sorry I never met your sister." Fifteen minutes later, Elder gently lifted his beloved wife and carried her to her room.

From a window, Maia, Sam, and Jessica watched, aware that Georgia's time was near. Now, almost four years later, Elder was reminiscing in front of their old apartment. He recalled their wonderful courting days. They took weekend trips along the coast to Mendocino, and to Fort Bragg. They walked in the shallows of the Pacific Ocean kicking up water without a care. Brilliant starlit nights were their companions, and in the evening, a cozy little room overlooking the ocean wrapped them in its arms. They lay talking late into the night, cuddling and kissing. He loved to stroke her hair, and, in making love, explored the hollows and curves of her smooth skin. Together, they blocked out the worries of life.

Under his breath, he whispered, "Georgia, I miss you. Remember that night with the Mexican family in Fort Bragg? When the grandma took your hand, she said, 'Que lindisima!' Was it so long ago? You were

78

beautiful. We got drunk. Your dad never forgave me for taking you away from him. We knew he wouldn't. He never liked me. I tried."

Grimly, recalling memories, Elder continued up Broadway. At Taylor Street, he took in the sweeping views of the buildings and homes of Chinatown below, then of North Beach, and further away, the Embarcadero with its shipping docks and the bay. Had he walked a little higher to Vallejo Street, turned right, and up the incline, he would have had different views of the bay including the 22 acre Alcatraz Island Military Prison, affectionately called "The Rock." In this portion of Russian Hill, a long, steep, narrow strip park was squeezed between apartment buildings and elegant homes. Pedestrians could ascend, descend, or rest under shady trees on the grass and benches. Occasionally, a tree-lined and bush-decorated walkway led to the door of a home. Talking softly, as if she were there, he said, "Georgia, San Francisco is beautiful. What do you think? If only this hill to my left was sliced off, we might be able to see the construction of the Golden Gate Bridge." Reaching out with his forefinger, and thinking of Georgia, he traced the skyline, and murmured, "Lady, where are you?"

On Broadway, Bradley sniffed the scant bushes, found a deserving spot, raised his leg, and peed. Lobo sat on his haunches and watched. After Bradley, Lobo ambled over, sniffed, and added his own. Waiting patiently, Elder looked around. Directly in front of him, a house bearing the nameplate "Ramona's Gentlemen's Club" caught his attention. "Could it be?" He wondered. "Is it Ramona from Texas? Come on, boys," he said, tugging gently on the leashes, "Let's see if they kick us out."

When Elder left Texas, he was lean, rugged, and young, and no longer frequented "sporting houses," not after meeting Georgia. At 45, he was strong, vigorous, affluent, and bored. Following her passing, he had no interest in a new relationship; however, loneliness and encouragement

79

from the household, or pestering, as he called it, motivated him enough to date.

There was one liaison he particularly regretted. They mingled in the same circles. It was with a debutante, the daughter of a business acquaintance. Short-lived, the result of her embarrassment at the difference in ages, they sneaked around. Playful to her—not to him.

On a weekend trip to Monterey, California, they ascended the long, steep red staircase to the colorful and elegant Sardine Factory restaurant in Cannery Row. Flower beds with blooming flowers graced each side of the stairway built into the hillside. A distinctive red canvas canopy covered the entrance. Inside were various dining rooms, each differently furnished and decorated. Each had high ceilings, glass globe chandeliers, plush carpets, and white tablecloths. His table reservation was for the exquisite room with a glass ceiling.

Elegantly dressed men in black suits and ties and women with low décolletages looked up as they entered. He had expected a pleasant evening, just the two of them. But inside, they found four of her young friends, two couples, waiting for a table. Elder's date introduced him as her uncle David. Since he had a reservation, he was compelled to invite them to dine with them. One of the young men annoyingly pestered him suspiciously with questions about his age and how exactly he was an uncle to their friend. Finally, after an awkward and tedious evening of not fitting in with young people, and his date calling him "uncle," he was handed the bill. After hugs and kisses from her friends, they retired to their hotel. She initiated sex and appeared to enjoy every moment. He did not.

Elder dropped the news. He was through. Remorseful, she attempted to convince him otherwise, saying she would announce their love. But he was not in love. There was no loss, no regret, just relief. Grousing, he determined that he would not play the fool nor have sex with anyone

80

unless they were at least good friends. Hopefully, there would be chemistry, probably with someone younger. Some would call him shallow for preferring someone younger, yet he could not force himself to go against his nature.

There were others, but whereas they formed an attachment, he did not. Loathing the pain he caused, he quit his efforts to meet someone new. And now, he was on Broadway, standing in front of a "cat house," thinking about fate and going in.

Broadway and Sacramento streets were the places to go for prostitution. Although illegal, they operated openly. One only had to grease the palm of the proper city official with about $700 or $800, and they could open. Graft and corruption were rampant, and the houses paid "protection money" to police and politicians. They were popular, and all were welcome, including respected city leaders and police. Restaurants were usually attached.

He tried the door—not locked. He didn't have to push a doorbell. Inside, he took in the spacious, generously furnished living room: dense wool pile carpet, small, comfortable beige and white settees, round-topped oak tables, vases of roses, floral cloth wallpaper, and oil paintings of San Francisco adorning the walls. At the far end, Ramona, looking robustly healthy and dressed in a long sleeve lavender gown, was speaking to two women.

Grinning ear to ear, enormously pleased to see her, he raised his hand. She looked at him appraisingly, up and down, fluffed her thick black hair, and turned back to the women. His heart dropped. There was no recognition. "Ah, well, after all," he told himself, "it has been a long time." Sighing and sorely disappointed, he said to the dogs, "Come on, boys, It's not my day. She doesn't remember." Turning to walk out, he felt a tug at the hem of his jacket.

"Mister," Ramona said, with a mischievous grin, "hold on. What's your pleasure? For you, free, today and every day." Laughing heartily, she hugged and kissed him and said, "You rascal, I'm playing with you."

Holding her at arm's length to look at her, he asked, "Is this the Ramona from that shitty two-bit, no-name dirt town in Texas, the same Ramona who risked her money on me to find oil?"

"None other," she replied.

For the second time that day, Elder was to receive personal information from a friend. Ramona took his hand and practically pranced, pulling this fine-looking man to a table. Coffee was served, and they talked.

Natchez, Mississippi, is where Ramona was born and raised. There, she met a tobacco trader from London. Thinking he loved her, she got pregnant and was abandoned. After her religiously strict parents cast her out, she fled to Houston, Texas. While clerking at the Magnolia Hotel in Houston, one of the finest, she observed two women plying their trade. After calculating their earnings and informing them they were barred from the premises, she offered to teach them reading, writing, and (a)rithmetic, and to be their madam. From Houston, they moved to the bustling oil fields of Texas, rife with men and no women. "And where," she said, "I met you."

Oil royalties were more than adequate to provide a comfortable way of life. She retired. But bored, she invested in commercial properties, and did so well that she moved up in society---well enough to be sought after in her community of Palo Alto near Stanford University. She returned to her birth name, Adele Eastworth. But at her house of prostitution, she used the name, Ramona Sofia Carrasco. That she did not have an olive complexion, spoke with a southern accent, and did not speak Spanish was not a concern. She wanted something colorful. The name rolled off the tongue and seemed exotic. She knew she was different in a good way, more

82

intelligent and cannier than most men; and her hair was black, she was statuesque, her eyebrows were thick and dark, and her eyes were brown.

"So, Elder," she quipped, "here I am, and you walk in the door. I always wondered what happened to you. Well, anyway, when this building came up for sale, I decided I'd have a high-class parlor catering to the wealthy. Of course, I do have cops and others who are willing to pay all they have to be with a beautiful woman. With unemployment being what it is, it's easy to recruit my girls. They're mannerly and sophisticated. I pay well. I provide a doctor and save a percentage for them. It's not the norm." Abruptly, she stopped talking and fixed Elder with a questioning look. "Say," she asked, "Can you fix it so I don't have to pay off the cops to stay in business?"

Elder nodded.

Ramona continued. They now had a daughter whom they adored. Elder asked if she loved Travis, the storekeeper from Natchez, Tennessee, where she grew up. She replied, "He hired me when I was a teenager, just 16. But he wasn't much older, just a few years. He was running the store for his grandfather. Now, I'll tell you a story.

"After you burned down my building in Texas, I convinced Travis to move with me to Prescott, Arizona. After a time there, we came to San Francisco. We were having drinks in a place I owned, the Pink Lady. We were minding our own business when a wrangler came to our table and propositioned me right in front of Travis.

"This wrangler was a tough hombre. He looked evil and had a mean reputation. You know, Elder, I've been in the sex business all my life, and I've only been intimate with two men, and here this cowboy propositioned me. Travis told him to apologize or to step outside. I tried to talk him out of it, but they took it out back. Right off, Travis was hit with a blow that could kill a moose. My heart jumped into my throat. I about died. But a special feeling came over me. Seeing him defending my honor, hurt, and struggling to his feet in that dirt lot, a switch went on. I tingled. Something inside erupted into a hot flame, and it's been burning brightly ever since. He gave a good accounting and landed some pretty good licks. He bloodied the guy, but he isn't a fighter. Every hit he took was a stab to my heart, and I loved him. I tell you. I swear.

"A bunch of cowboys had followed us outside. They stood around, serious, mostly quiet, just watching. A vaquero told me not to worry. I looked at him and realized that those boys were watching out for Travis. You see, everyone liked him. He went down again—about to be stomped. I've never seen men move so fast. Before you could say Jack Daniel's, they shoved that wrangler aside so hard he landed on his backside and skidded a good two feet. You should have seen his face. Then, they picked up Travis, dusted him off, and clapped him on the back like he was the winner; he was, to me.

"I could hardly wait to get him home. I proposed. We went to Mexico City and got married. So, yes, I love him, crazy in love, and now we have a daughter. And Jacob, my son, from the British guy who said he loved me but didn't is living in England and working as an engineer."

The following week, Elder visited again. He took the dogs. While in the parlor with Ramona, he looked up to see the source of sweet laughter. At the base of the stairs, a slim woman, with strawberry blond hair, with her back to him, barefoot and kneeling, was stroking and talking to the dogs. Lobo rolled over to have his belly rubbed. Bradley followed. Feeling a presence, she turned and caught Elder's stare. He estimated that the woman was about 5 feet 4 inches tall, and 20 years younger than he, but it was 11. She was 34. Entranced with her laughter and how the simple cotton dress clung to her body, he stared. Her skin was pale. Her eyes were, "Wow, emerald green, ummm." Her lips were young and inviting.

84

Her eyebrows matched her hair. Watching him watch her, she did a little toss of the head and pulled a ribbon loose. Beautiful, long full hair tumbled free. Something inside Elder turned, something unused and rusted. Low-throat humming began. With a playful heart, his eyes twinkling, smiling, he winked. Being stared at was not unusual for her, and usually ignored. But with this ruggedly handsome man, with thick dark hair in need of combing, dark eyes, a noticeable scar over his cheekbone, and a rakish smile, her heart jumped. Surprised, then amused, her lips opened; her cheeks lifted into a wide smile, and she winked back.

"Oh, my," he sighed.

Sitting across from him, Ramona said, "Yes, I know, she's rare. Have you ever seen anyone like her?"

"Not quite."

"She's Jewish, a refugee From Hitler's Nazi Germany. Her English is good. She speaks German, French, Russian, and English. In Germany, she was a professor. Her mother was a doctor, and her father owned a steel mill and a machine shop. She's my highest-paid and most in demand, but only to a few. From the start, she demanded to have the right of refusal. Otherwise, she'd move on. If she doesn't like someone, forget it. Elder, if she likes you, you can have her, no charge. Thanks to you, I'm set up better than I ever imagined, maybe better than you," she joked.

"Do you believe her about her education?"

"Why, yes, I believe I do. I speak some French, and hers is excellent. Wait until you hear her voice. It's soft and dusty. Come on; I'll introduce you."

"Don't you mean smokey, not dusty?"

"You'll see."

Stephanie Rosen, her actual name, was going by the name of Stephanie Robin. She frankly examined Elder's eyes, face, and clothes. Reaching for his hands, she turned them over and ran her fingers over the rough skin. Returning her gaze to his face, she gently touched a finger to a scar, then returned to his hands and touched another scar.

Submitting to the examination, he thought, "Yes, my skin is scarred and calloused after all these years."

Still holding his hand, she tapped the glass crystal of his Cartier wristwatch with a red polished fingernail, "Tap, tap, tap." Then smiling, in accented perfect English, she said, "My father has one like this. Let's sit. Talk to me. Tell me a little."

Stephanie's careful elocution and accented, dusty, smoky voice drew him in. Ramona looked on, amused, and wandered off. So entranced was Elder, he didn't notice when pastries, tea, and coffee magically appeared. Ninety minutes flew by, and not once did he lose interest. Her knowledge of world politics and economics was impressive, particularly her first-hand familiarity with the economic depression in Germany and the rise of Adolph Hitler. And he didn't mind just looking at her.

During the visit, a good-looking, very large, broad, big-chested policeman entered and asked for Stephanie. She excused herself. A loud distasteful dispute erupted. She motioned toward Elder. The man shot Elder an ugly, stony-faced scowl and tried for a staring contest. Elder, not in the least disturbed, returned the stare with curiosity. To the policeman, Elder was unfazed. It made him uneasy. There was no nervousness, nothing, no concern—and a huge insult to be dismissed so casually. After a few more words, Stephanie returned to Elder. In explanation, she said, "His name is Lugo. He's a wretched, terrible man. I took him when I first arrived. A mistake. Now, I refuse to see him. He persists."

Stephanie spoke quite frankly of her home country and its devastation following the end of the War to end all Wars from 1914 to 1918. "Its depression is worse than in the United States. It's aggravated by the

86

monetary reparations it pays the allies for the war. The Government doesn't have the income. So, they print money. Now it has almost no value. Barter of goods and services is common. And now we have Hitler, that evil, stupid man. He promises a German rebirth, a return to greatness, and is believed. The people are like sheep. They shout 'Heil Hitler' like he's a God. He has put people back to work, but it's war production. He's demonized, Jews. To him, I'm subhuman. He's cancer, and people don't see it. He hates us. We're losing our businesses and freedom. We're arrested for nothing and disappear. My Christian friends were afraid to be seen with me. It is terrible. I fear for the country I love."

Shuddering, she recalled the day a group of women cursed and spat at her and her mother for being Jewish. "I told my parents to emigrate to Australia with me. They wouldn't listen, even after my mother was fired for being Jewish and their licenses were taken away. They were convinced the German people would come to their senses and rid themselves of Hitler. Now, I don't even know where they are."

Her voice quaked and she stopped talking, obviously emotional. She looked down. Then, raising her green eyes to Elder's, she continued, "And no, they don't know what I am doing here. They think I'm using my degrees and working in the tourist industry. My education means nothing, not in Germany and not here. Even in San Francisco, we're disliked.

"Enough," she said.

"Am I dismissed?" he asked.

Seeing his confusion, she took his hand and pulled him toward the stairs.

"I'm sorry," he said, "I have my dogs, and someone is waiting. I'll come back tomorrow."

Intently, she looked into his dark brown eyes.

"Will you?"

"Yes. At 10:00. Dress for a day out. The entire day."

Elder was of an age where he was neither young nor old but interesting and distinguished. He radiated energy and moved and spoke with a certain elan. Although attractive in many ways, and desired by many, he believed that he had loved once and that it would never come again. But now, having met Stephanie, he looked forward to a new day. Since Georgia's death, his zest for life had been flagging. An old refrain kept running through his mind, "What will I do when the well runs dry?" meaning the loss of something dear to one's heart but could apply to any concern, youth, money, hope, or love. After meeting Stephanie, the well didn't look so dry. But he cautioned himself to keep in mind, "She's a prostitute."

Stubbornly, off at some distance, Lugo waited. His impulse was to go for a confrontation. "Maybe," he thought, "I can push the guy around or kick the shit out of him." But he couldn't. He was a cop, and the guy was well-dressed. "He might be somebody important," he mused. And he looked like someone who would not be intimidated. Also, the dogs gave him caution. Instead, Lugo followed well back. Meanwhile, Elder was preoccupied with thoughts of Stephanie and not alert.

Broadway Street at Russian Hill was steep, with 165 steps conveniently put in by the city. So steep that it was an arduous hike. Almost to the top, Lobo stopped and sat. "What's the matter, old fellow," Elder asked, "Are you tired?" He picked him up, no easy feat, for Lobo weighed 110 pounds. Lobo licked Elder's face and draped his head over Elder's shoulder. Seeing Lugo, he emitted a throaty growl. After 20 more steps to the top, Elder put him down and said, "Now, you walk!" Upon their descent to Polk Street, Caesar was waiting by the Cadillac. Old Lobo looked back at Lugo. Following Lobo's gaze, Elder said, "Good dog, Lobo."

Polk Street provided ample free entertainment, popular for its lively cafés, convenience stores, hardware, and drug stores. Family markets provided outside shelves of fruits and vegetables. Not rushed by the gregarious talkative proprietor, Elder and Caesar sat at a sidewalk table, and ordered iced tea. Caesar told stories of his time as a waiter. There they sat, enjoying the company of each other, and whiled away the time watching the activity on the street. And Bradley was always happy on Polk Street, but he was always happy if he was with family. Other dogs were greeted with considerable sniffing of rear ends and exaggerated wagging of bodies and tails. Bradley was always eager to meet a new girlfriend or buddy. Lobo, at 14, watched.

Meanwhile, Lugo retraced his steps to Ramona's, and reflected on Elder and the man waiting for him. He had seen him fight, and he was good. At Ramona's he asked for Stephanie. Ramona advised, "Lugo, I'll say it again, Stephanie is permanently closed to you. Choose someone else." His temper flared. His eyes took on a wild, crazed look, and he moved closer, too close. Ramona, thinking, "He's going to hit me," put her hand in her dress pocket to the double barrel derringer. It took him a sudden second to realize that the gun was touching his testicles. Jumping back, decidedly dour, he turned and left.

As for Elder, he returned home and prepared for dinner with a friend, Sondra Walker. Maia had convinced him to try dating again and suggested Sondra, a lovely widow with gorgeous black hair, elegantly pretty and close to his age. They had been meeting casually, but she was often so busy with charitable and business affairs that she was usually late and often canceled. To make amends, she invited him to a late dinner and cocktails.

Her two-story mansion, with a deep front yard and wide impressive sitting porch, was in the fashionable district of Nob Hill—sometimes called Snob Hill. The butler ushered him in.

89

After waiting a good while, Sondra appeared at the top of a wide curved staircase. With a twinkle in her eyes, and looking ravishing, with a low décolletage, she descended slowly and carefully carrying a bottle of vodka, totally snockered. Elder was amused and amazed by her ability to carry on a lucid conversation. After a meal of slow-cooked maple candied duck, asparagus, and a robust red Italian Barolo wine, they retired to her expansive, high-ceiled living room. They sat together on a well-padded settee and tried exploratory kisses. Between kisses and her questioning looks, she sipped a sweet liquor, and he the Barolo. When the time came for him to stay or leave, they decided that if they had to talk about it, they would pass. She didn't mind. She was more interested in having another drink. Elder didn't care. His mind was on Stephanie.

Chapter Ten: First Date

Elder arrived promptly in his sporty two-door Duesenberg at 10:00 a.m., nervous, and anticipating the day. He wondered if she would like him, and perplexed that he should even care. After all, she was a prostitute, yes, a lovely one, and cultured and intelligent, but still.

Stephanie had awakened early. She scrupulously cleaned her room and placed newly purchased sheets on the bed. Then she sat in her one chair, fretting, wondering if she was dressed appropriately, and wondering if he would like her. Since yesterday, when they met, she thought of him constantly.

She extended her hands to him. He led her to the car past the women of the house, and Ramona--- smiling broadly. Their day started with breakfast, then they walked through the gardens and lakes of Golden Gate

Park, conversing--getting to know each other. Late lunch was in a little café in Chinatown, and to extend their time together, they took in a movie starring Ginger Rogers and Fred Astaire, in 'The Gay Divorcee.' He reached for her hand. She took it and placed her other hand over both. They were more aware of each other than the movie. Afterward, they had dinner at a restaurant owned by Abe, frequented by both blacks and whites (unusual for the times), and received excellent attention and a fine meal. He took note that she was completely comfortable. She didn't even notice that the waiter was black. He was glad. After dinner, he returned her to Ramona's. Elder walked her past the envious looks of gentlemen waiting, including 'pillers of the community.' There was only one other in the House who rivaled Stephanie, a fine, tall, southern belle by the name of Sarah. Her accent alone enchanted.

In Stephanie's room, she felt a pang in her heart, and sad as Elder hesitated, and looked over the room. Weakly, she said, "The sheets are new, and I washed the blanket."

Elder awoke at 3:00 a.m. Suffused with feelings, he quietly dressed. Then he sat in the chair for an indeterminate time taking in Stephanie's tousled hair, her face, her lips, throat. He wondered what had come over him, consorting again, after all these years, with a prostitute. Frowning, he stood, carefully adjusted the blanket to her shoulders, and silently left the room.

Stephanie turned her head and cried. She had been aware of Elder's scrutiny. She was not immune to hardship, sadness, pain, and loss. And he really didn't know her. "Well, I guess that's it," she thought.

But it wasn't. As she sat in her room, turning away appointments, she sat, unmoving, gazing outside at the jays chirping on a green, leafy tree. A soft knock on the door startled her from her reverie. It was Elder, holding roses. Her eyes became moist.

91

He noticed. "Ah, God," he thought.

Chapter Eleven: The Policeman

Earlier that day, while Elder was entering Ramona's, Lugo, in full uniform, stepped out of a brownstone apartment building into the clear morning sun. He paused on the top step of the porch, happy, anticipating his visit to Ramona's for a romp with Stephanie. He counted the money in his wallet and took in the pedestrian traffic. Across the street, a boy wiped tables. Feeling good, his eyes met the lovely eyes of passing young ladies casting appreciative glances.

Lugo knew he cut a fine figure. He was tall, had a chiseled face and jaw, good cheekbones, blue eyes, and a strong, tapered body. Nordic-looking, he thought. He returned their smiles, and for dramatic effect, like an imagined movie star, turned his face to offer a perfect, profile. He lit a cigarette, took a couple of deep drags, blew out smoke, and with thumb and forefinger flicked it away. Under his breath, he murmured, "Ladies, another time."

Lugo had spent a good night at Muriel's, a typist at the police department. He wanted to get going, to Ramona's, to see Stephanie, but Muriel had arisen early and made breakfast. Trying for affection, she massaged his shoulders and asked, "Honey, when will I see you again?" Irritated at her words and touch, but counting her as one of two friends, he said nothing. But finally, losing patience, he snapped, "I've told you to get someone else," and stood, knocking over the chair. "Muriel, I like you, that's it. I don't love anyone." Seeing her crestfallen look, he relented and snapped, "Maybe, I'll come back tonight."

Outside, watching the passing young women, he thought of his comment. He had loved, once, his sister Josie. That part of his life he kept to himself.

When Lugo first heard of the exceptionally lovely woman at Ramona's, Stephanie Robin, he was not impressed. It was just one more beautiful woman, that is until he saw her. Then he was enthralled. After their first time together, he left elated and feeling special. To afford her, he increased his income from petty graft and extortion.

Lugo was one of Stephanie's first customers. When he applied for her favors, she was impressed by his handsome face, wavy black hair, practiced polite manners, and winsome smile. She didn't know that his politeness and smile did not come naturally.

Upon seeing him naked, she was impressed with his sculpted body but astonished by the size of his genitalia. And concerned that she might suffer pain. On his next visit, the other girls were curious and waiting.

Lugo lay smug, the center of attention, mentally strutting and posturing himself on the bed, offering views. The women giggled and joked. A latecomer crowded in, saying, "Let me see that naughty rascally wang!" eliciting peals of laughter. Lugo was immensely pleased. He puffed his chest and propped his body on an elbow. Repositioning himself, he provided views of his semi-erect penis laying over on his thigh.

Stephanie thought, "Oh, he is truly a snake, dirty, revolting, and vain." In the accent he liked to hear, Stephanie instructed, "Ladies, that's enough. All out."

Filing out, tittering in amusement, the women made off-color remarks. One said she wanted to try him. Another noted that he was built like a horse. One woman, Sarah, Lugo, did not hear. "It was too much, not normal," she said. "I want a regular man, a decent working guy I want a boy and a girl and an honest life."

"Dream on, Sarah," commented another, "You'll stay here until you're all used up. You'll be selling yourself for a dime in one of those filthy rat-filled cribs in some dark alley in Chinatown, not like this fine parlor." The comment hit Sarah hard.

Chapter Twelve: Lugo, Background

Lugo was born and raised in San Francisco. His parents, Jeff and Cassie Spaak were good people, friendly, good-natured, kind, honest, and pleasing to the eye, but by his standards, small-boned and puny. From the beginning, he believed there must have been a mix-up at birth, that he was given to the wrong parents. He figured his real birth parents were somewhere out there, stuck with a puny son. Intellectually, he knew that his parents were nice and made efforts to connect, but he couldn't care less.

His father, an accountant for a well-known mercantile company, provided well. They resided in a Craftsman style, four-bedroom home with front and rear sitting porches. The depression had been advantageous for them. It allowed them to purchase the house at an exceedingly low price. Jeff and Cassie could easily have put Lugo through college, but he was always in rebellion. At 11, towering over mother and father, he tested for dominance. After a fatherly attempt to discipline, he pushed his dad to the wall, and with a contemptuous "Sure," that was the end of discipline.

Shaving at 13, big unruly, sullen, and ill-tempered, Lugo didn't care for rules and the teachers' droning voices. However, although unpleasant and lacking in social graces, he was exceptionally bright, and devoured history, geography, and math on his own. Grades fluctuated from A's to F's, depending on interest. Behavior was aloof, cold, and indifferent. He had acquaintances. No friends.

A second child, Josie, was born when he was five. She was small and delicate, like their parents. The unexpected happened. Lugo loved her. Initially, he found her presence and crying irksome, but one day she crawled to him, put her head on his lap, and fell asleep. He put his hands on her shoulders to push her off, but curious, he touched her delicate fingers and hands. He sniffed her head and played with her hair. Something came over him and took root. He didn't move until she awoke. After that, he displayed affection just for her. Since Lugo dispensed rudeness without care, when Josie reached the age of 15 months, she surprised him by crying whenever he raised his voice to their mother. That stopped him. He paid attention.

Lugo adored his sister, and she him. Beginning as a child, she became his mentor. In time, she explained good and bad behavior and humor. In her youthful but precocious ways, she attempted to explain the importance of civility and manners and how he could benefit. Although typically flat in emotions, he was intelligent and an apt pupil.

One day, Lugo was presented with an object lesson. Walking Josie home from middle school, they passed two boys holding down a boy he knew. Leon was flat on the ground, on his back, and they were demanding money. Leon, a Negro, had once given Lugo a thin paper pad and pencil. But Lugo was not one to understand gratitude and the return of kindness. He stopped only out of curiosity. Holding Josie's 11-year-old hand, he started to move on, but Leon cried out.

"Lugo, help me."

"Why should I?"

"I'll treat you to something."

"Josie," he asked, "would you like something?"

That day confirmed Lugo's belief that his size could be a positive factor in being treated special. He told the two boys to get lost. Seeing doubt, he said, "If you don't, I'll break off your fingers and stuff them in your mouths." Quickly, Leon was released. True to his word, Leon treated them to sodas at Thrifty Drugstore. Leon and Josie told Lugo he had done a good thing by chasing away the bullies. Both were careful in explaining the dynamics of good and bad behavior, good and bad results, and the effects on others.

For an occasional treat or coin Lugo became Leon's protector. That Leon was a Negro was unimportant. Both understood the plight of being treated as if they didn't exist, as someone to be ignored and not fitting in.

Leon said, "Look, I like me just fine, but just be glad you were born white." This, Lugo did not fully understand until he was an adult.

Lugo's prime emotions were anger, pain, and pleasure, particularly sexual and food. Classmates thought him strange, even retarded, and disliked being near him. He didn't understand humor and giving of himself, but he never considered himself dull-witted. Quite the opposite. He believed himself to be superior in intellect, strength, and handsome, and after he rescued Leon, he became a curiosity. Others sought his protection, including girls. Sometimes, after rumors about the size of his genitalia went around, a few girls, in exchange to see, allowed him to see their breasts, nothing more.

Sadly, Josie passed away when she was 13 from an illness he did not understand. She often had a cough and was sickly, but he didn't think she would die. He suffered, but to his parents, he was his usual withdrawn self. He had not shed a tear at her passing or funeral, nor did he commiserate with them. Avoiding them as much as possible, he stayed outside late into the evenings and disappeared on weekends. Josie had been the buffer. Now, he and his parents never spoke unless necessary. When Jeff or Cassie addressed him, he gazed at them blankly and might or might not reply. Unable to stand him any longer, Cassie found relief by getting a job at the same company as her husband.

Two weeks after Josie's funeral, walking home from school, Lugo was waylaid. A large boy, he knew, and two of his friends intended to take over his little protection racket. Deep in thought, thinking of Josie, he hadn't taken notice of their presence. A fist came out of nowhere. The boy might as well have hit a tree.

Lugo's reaction was a look disbelief, and "Why the heck did you do that?" Then rage. Yanking the boy forward by his checkered flannel shirt, he knocked him senseless. Holding the body upright, he struck twice more. Letting go, the body fell in a heap, straight down. The boy's friends didn't move, not to help, not to run, only to stare in disbelief.

Lugo grabbed the unconscious boy by his heels, dragged him to the curb, and positioned his teeth on the concrete edge. It was clear. He would stomp down on the back of the head, shattering teeth, and jaw.

Balancing, he put one shoe tentatively on the boy's head, positioned himself, and raised his foot. The spectators, realizing it was to be murder or close to it, cried out for mercy, "No, no, don't do it." A small female voice cut through the others, "No, don't. Please." A little shy voice and image popped into his mind. It was Josie. Thinking of her, his eyes teared. She wouldn't like this savage behavior. He bent, gently turned his assailant over, propped him against a fence, and brushed the dirt off his shirt. When he walked away, one of the spectators incredulously asked, "Is he crying?"

They didn't hear it, but Lugo quietly said, "All right, Josie, that was for you."

Two months later, without bothering to tell his parents or attend his high school graduation, Lugo left home. He found a small apartment in the sleazy nine-block area of the Barbary Coast, an area of streetwalkers, bars, hawkers outside trying to pull in suckers, strip joints, derelicts, drug addicts, and drunks.

Employment began as a longshoreman at the San Francisco docks. Every day he showed up at 7:00 a.m., no matter the weather or sickness.

At the docks bunching up with others for the "shape-up." Elbowing aside the weakest, Lugo waited to be picked to work for the day by one of many private contractors. Men jostled, hoping to be chosen by the agent, the "walking man," a man they might beg and give a kickback. Heavy, brutal labor awaited—pushing, pulling, and hauling with rudimentary pulleys, winches, screws, and ramps, often working all night and continuous days without sleep. It was the "slave market," where men dropped dead on the job from exhaustion, but Lugo excelled, able to do the work of two men.

Relishing the sweaty days of hard work his body filled out. Muscles grew; he became known as the gorilla. Five years later, at 23, he applied to be a policeman at the San Francisco Police Department and was accepted. With a steady income, he moved from the infamous Barbary Coast to a quieter apartment in Chinatown. The only thing he missed was the dilapidated piano left behind that had come with the apartment. Listening to the boogie-woogie music blasting from the street bars below, he had learned to play by ear. When he played, he was happy.

Chapter Thirteen: Befuddled

When it pleased Lugo, he spoke intelligently and with manners. But perhaps thinking it added to his manhood, he found pleasure in being crude, and vulgar. Stephanie wondered what Sigmund Freud, the renowned Jewish psychoanalyst, would think of him. Lugo vacillated in behavior from being kind to brusque, rough, and foul-mouthed. The third and last time he came to Stephanie, he had a soggy cigarette dangling from his lips and smelled of beer and urine. She told him to leave, but he slapped her and threw her on the bed. Too fearful to protest, she submitted, detested every second, and counted it as the worst day of her life.

Two days later, he returned. As was his custom, he brazenly parked his police car at the curb, at the front door. Inside, Ramona blocked his way. "Lugo, she won't see you."

Pulling out a wad of money, he snapped, "I'll pay more."

"I've told you," Ramona exclaimed, "She doesn't want anything to do with you. Now leave, and don't come back."

"Leave?" he muttered, insulted, "leave?" His face flushed. Uncontrollable rage welled up. "Fuck that," he spat. Shoving Ramona aside, he bounded up the stairs. Ramona called for Adam, the bouncer, and followed.

Without knocking and intending to throw out any "John" Stephanie was entertaining, he threw open her door and barged into her room. Beyond that, he had no coherent plan except to fuck her and convince her not to drop him. But she was alone, peacefully reclining on her bed, reading. Seeing his murderous look, she tossed the book aside and leapt to her feet.

Ramona urgently called the other women. Doors banged, opened, and closed. Leaving their "Johns," they came running. With six others, Ramona stood in the doorway of Stephanie's room, including Adam, who, with a light hand, she stopped from entering. Three men behind them hurried down the stairs.

Lugo held Stephanie by her hair and yanked her head back and forth. A red mark was on her cheek.

Ramona asked, "Lugo, what are you going to do, kidnap her—or rape her?"

A woman behind Ramona shouted, "Get out, Lugo! Get out!" The others took up the chant, "Get out, get out, Lugo, get out, get out," on and on, in an insistent rising crescendo. Stephanie struggled against Lugo's grip. Annoyed, he smacked her with the back of his hand, sending her to the floor. Befuddled at the developments, he faced Ramona and stupidly patted his badge---as if that would subdue them.

Groggily, with a throbbing headache, Lugo regained consciousness. Stephanie, with a lead sap, had cold-cocked him from behind. He had been manhandled, bouncing down the stairs, dragged through the lobby, and down the entry steps. Once outside, in full police uniform, he was carefully propped like a bum against the red brick building. In his cap were two dimes and 15 pennies totaling 35 cents. His revolver, wallet, belt, one sock, and shoes, and inexplicable his underwear, were missing. Cursing and holding up his pants, struggling to his feet he rushed to the nearest police call box to report an assault and battery on a police officer--and theft. He also called for a raid on a house of prostitution.

Pacing angrily, he waited. Within 35 minutes, two police vans arrived, plus three police cars, two officers in each. Lieutenant Jamie Anderson and Sergeant Richard Frank led the raid. Crowding the lobby, the officers looked around, eager to see their favorites—except for Sgt. Frank. He and Lugo shared a secret both meant to keep.

Ramona elegantly rose from her chair. "Hello, Jamie," she said, and handed him the telephone. "Someone wants to speak to you." Hesitantly, he took the proffered phone. Faint yelling could be heard at the other end. Holding it slightly away from his ear, he uttered, "Yes sir, yes sir. Yes, yes, right away, sir." Angry and red-faced, Jamie returned the telephone to Ramona and turned to his men. To Lugo's bewilderment, he shouted, "All right, everyone out. False alarm."

The lieutenant forcefully grabbed Lugo's arm. To him and everyone else who could hear, he said, louder than necessary, "Lugo, you're lucky you aren't fired. Thanks to you, Ramona's is off-limits for a month, to all of us. Not only that," he shouted, waving his arm, "there are no more freebies, no payments, and you Lugo, you are barred permanently. And get some shoes." Officers groaned. Lugo was ridiculed.

Throughout the exchanges, tall, reedy Sgt. Frank remained off to the side and said not a word. One of the girls quietly handed him Lugo's revolver, badge, nightstick, and wallet.

Ramona had called Elder, and he had taken care of everything. Lugo was the butt of jokes, especially for losing his belt, shoes, and sock; items never recovered. Humiliated, he swore to find the son-of-a-bitch who had protected Ramona. He deduced that it was probably that rich guy, Elder.

Furious and jealous, Lugo stalked Ramona's, and Elder's homes, often with the help of a fellow policeman, Mack. They also stalked the Palace Station Cafe, where he knew Sam and Jessica, Elder's children, worked. It was mainly from a distance, but he wasn't averse to going in for a drink, not giving a damn that he was considered rude, unpleasant and not welcome. At Ramona's, he stood across the street, waiting and watching.

Lugo's attitude about women was "Once I fuck them, they're mine." Sometimes it was until they found someone else with a nicer deposition or someone to marry. Stephanie detested him as a supreme narcissist, whereas he was under the delusion that she saw him as a fine specimen of a man—an exciting and valuable individual with a toned, muscular physique and a big penis. He reasoned, "She wants me but is settling for someone with money." He couldn't forget how wonderful he felt after each sexual encounter and longed for more. He thought, "I'm going to get her back." And then, sarcastically, "Yeah, sure. She won't even talk to me."

Chapter Fourteen: Chinatown

The Chinese were generally restricted to their district. According to the Chinese Exclusion Act, immigrants carried certificates of residence showing legality in the U.S., and any Caucasian could challenge them for their papers. The Chinese traveled throughout the city to work, usually as domestics. In the mornings and afternoons, they crowded the cable cars returning home. The whites traveled as they pleased, like Lugo.

In Chinatown, the Tong gangs terrorized merchants and extorted money.

Lugo detested any disturbance to his peace, including the unease it caused in his neighbors. He only cared about his block. After each visit by the Tongs, the merchants loudly, incessantly chattered, disturbing his peace. He put out the word for the Tongs to stay away. They didn't like it. Knowing he was home, six came and deliberately caused a loud disturbance with a merchant below. Awakened from slumber, Lugo angrily went downstairs, barreled into the store, grabbed the leader by the neck, and threw him into the street. There he stood, bristling, like a giant bear, six against one. But his steely, contemptuous, uncaring behavior was unsettling, and he was a cop. They couldn't attack him in public, not in broad daylight.

Two nights later, Tong thugs were so bold as to creep up his stairs in the dead of night, 3:30 a.m. Four in their short black jackets, black pants, and black slippers. The leader, holding a sawed-off short-barrel shotgun, ascended the stairs. He was the one Lugo had thrown into the street. The others followed. The top step creaked, and Lugo's door flew open. He stepped out crazily grinning and holding a revolver. Shouting, "Kon'nichiwa." he lashed out with his booted foot and kicked the leader's chest, sending him flying backward onto the next in line. The second hit the third, and the third hit the fourth, ending in a tangled sprawl.

In haste, Lugo had mistakenly shouted hello in Japanese. He meant to shout the Chinese "Ni hao." Pointing his short-barreled revolver, Lugo

102

took one step down. Frantically, they scrambled away, leaving the shotgun midway.

Anticipating they would strike again, Lugo struck first. It was done with what he considered a sense of humor, humor at the expense of others. In Little Tokyo, he purchased a red classical Japanese dance-drama Kabuki costume with stiffened shoulder extensions. Also purchased were white and red paints for the face, a long, wild, brilliant red wig, a wide-brimmed peasant hat, and wooden platform shoes.

In Chinatown, in a littered, dark, narrow alley, he donned his costume over his street clothes. He crudely painted his face. It was 11 p.m. He waited. He had concealed himself there before, and they had passed without noticing.

A clear view of Cora's Whore House made it easy. Fifty-five minutes later, the intended victims walked out, paused to light cigarettes, and as expected, walked toward the dirty, littered alley, joking, and playfully shoving each other.

Screaming like a lunatic and flailing his arms, Lugo jumped out and threw the leader flying to the opposite wall. The other three ran screaming in terror. Straddling his stunned victim, Lugo ripped his shirt open and plunged down with his six-inch knife, searching for the heart. Messy, still pulsing, he dropped it and turned his attention to the terrified boys at the end of the alley. Fearing they'd be next, they ran for their lives.

Noisily, clumping through the dimly lit empty streets on his wooden platform shoes, doors slammed shut, lights were extinguished, and wooden shutters were closed and locked. The friends, breathing in frantic gulps, waited in ambush. Shots rang out. One clipped Lugo's oversize shoulder pad. Returning fire, the shooter was hit in the face. The others had enough. Whimpering like dogs, they frantically ran fearing he would catch them like magic.

Striding along, smiling widely, shucking pieces of costume, Lugo felt invincible, indestructible, and his heart beat with happiness. With the dawn, residents marveled at the trail of discarded pieces of costume. They spoke of that night for years, of the lone Japanese apparition, who came to kill the Tongs. They did wonder why it was a Japanese Kabuki dancer and a not a Samurai warrior, and why he had to be Japanese. But no matter. They were glad he had come to the neighborhood to rid themselves of particularly onerous members of the Tongs.

Chapter Fifteen: Indifference

Lugo had no interest whatsoever in maintaining contact with his parents. In fact, at mid-day on the previous Sunday, at the Southeast corner of the Ferry Building, a waitress had just served Lugo and Mack coffee and apple pie with ice-cream Looking past her, he saw his parents across the street, strolling along, holding hands, probably on their way home from church. Both were suitably dressed, his father in a dark suit and tie, and his mother in a dark gingham dress and hat. She waved. Lugo met her eyes but didn't return the gesture. Staring, he thought, "Strange." He felt nothing. To add to his puzzlement, with a flourish, his father doffed his Homburg hat, put his fingers to his lips, blew him a kiss, and walked on.

Mack asked, "Do you know them?"

"No, not really."

"You're a strange guy, Lugo. A lot of folks know who you are, but I'm your only friend. Most think you're, well, ah, different. Yeah, me too, but we get along. But sometimes, you puzzle me."

"What do you mean?"

"First off, it looks like that fine old man knows you. But I think he just tossed you a kiss my ass, fuck-you-kiss-off kiss."

Lugo exploded with roaring laughter, startling Mack. Mack had never seen Lugo laugh so hard, nor so genuinely, nor had he ever, except once. When he was a minor, refusing discipline, he pushed his father to the wall. Seeing his father's look of sorrow, he burst out laughing. But today, for once, he respected his father for his gesture.

"All right," Mack continued, "take that day at the bus depot. That little teenager, about 15, black hair, brown eyes, like you, real cute looking to do tricks. She was a runaway from Spokane. She said she was trying to return home. Anyway, that's what she said. You scolded her like you were her father. You bought her a ticket. You gave her money, and we waited until the bus left to make sure she got on."

"Oh, that, yeah. Lucky for her, I was in a good mood."
But his heart tightened. That girl reminded him of his sweet little sister, Josie.

"Mack, things are going my way. There's a lady I'm seeing, a lady from Germany. She's going to move in. We'll get a larger place and get married."

Mack didn't believe him. But Lugo persisted and described her beauty, her sophistication, and made up a story of her working as an office worker. Eventually, Mack congratulated him and added, "I had the feeling you would remain a horn dog until you died. I guess I'm wrong."

Lugo wondered about love. Intellectually, he recognized it in others but had never personally experienced it, except for his sister. He didn't think it was needed, that is until he met Stephanie.

Chapter Sixteen: Urgent Call

Confused with his increasing attraction to Stephanie, David Elder stopped seeing her. His thoughts about her were clouded. He stepped back to consider what he wanted out of life, and what he wanted from her.

Although he was infatuated, he missed Georgia. While confiding his thoughts to Abe, Abe asked him if he was in love. Elder shrugged, sipped coffee, and said, "I don't know."

Abe commented, "You'll never forget Georgia. She'll always be with you, just like my little Mikey is always with me. I loved him--still do. I have my memories. He was full of life—so happy to see his mom and dad each day. He'd hug me and call me 'Dad.' Yes, I remember. I'll never hold my little boy again, my little loving boy. Maia was broken. I found her holding him, rocking his small body. I'll never forget, not until I die. She was heartbroken, and I couldn't help her. Hell, I couldn't help myself. She went to Puerto Rico, to her parents. I was afraid I had lost her. But I've recovered—well, somewhat. Elder, you must go on living. Live your life. You have Jessica and Sam. They love you. Maia loves you, and I'm here. Now, let's go inside."

Fifteen minutes later, Elder, Jessica, Maia, and Abe chatted and drank iced tea in the cozy kitchen. A maid wearing a brown apron cleaned. A carafe of iced tea was on the table. She stopped to serve herself. Seeing her intention, Elder filled a glass for her. At the kitchen island, a cook cut meat and vegetables for the evening meal. The telephone rang. Trailing a long, straight, black cord, Maia handed Elder the phone. It was Ramona asking if he was done with Stephanie because she had quit and was packing. Elder was stunned. "When you stopped coming, she put on a good face, but she's been crying. Now, she's leaving." Elder hung up, and immediately had Matteo bring the Chrysler around.

Bounding up the porch steps and then the stairs, Elder knocked on Stephanie's door. Stephanie opened the door and stepped aside, indicating he could enter. But she was expressionless, as if his visit was of no importance. There was no hug. No smile. But she allowed, since he was there, that he could visit while she packed. Two suitcases were on the bed,

106

one filled and closed and the other open with neatly folded clothes. Taken aback by her cold demeanor, he asked if she was leaving.

"Ja," she replied. "I'm going to New York. I'll rest and move on."

"Is it because of me?" he asked. No reply except a look and, a shrug of the shoulders.

"Don't go, Stephanie. I've missed you. We can start over."
He had wrestled with his emotions and conscience, vacillating. And now, here he was, and all he could do was lamely say that he would resume his visits. She shook her head. He tried again.

"Stephanie, I've been miserable but stayed away because I got nervous. Frankly, I'm confused. I've been working it out, thinking about you, my life, yours, my children, and where we're going with this, this, whatever it is. I don't know. But I've missed you. Please, Stephanie, if I hurt you, if I made you sad, if I made you cry, I'm sorry. Don't go. Is there anything I can do to make you stay? Tell me!"

She closed the suitcase, leaned on it with both palms flat, and shrugged. They were speaking mere words, but something palpable, indescribable, was in the room, like crackling electromagnets pulling them together. They resisted even though they wanted to touch, to blend, to be one. Pride was in the room holding them back.

Prefacing her words in a way he had grown accustomed to and thought charming, she said, "David, here's my point. Do you know what you want?"

Wanting her to stay, yet to be honest, he equivocated and said, "Try me for a week. If it's good, we'll do another. Or I'll travel with you until you decide. You can return to San Francisco or go on, on your own. But I don't want you to go." He was holding a part of himself in reserve. He honestly didn't know what he wanted, but he knew he didn't want her to go, not yet.

107

Stephanie considered. He had said nothing about love, nor could he, not at this time, maybe never. "Nein," she thought. "He can't even say he likes me." Yet, he had come. They had not met at a social event or in genteel society but at a house of prostitution where she slept with different men. Could he, she wondered, forgive her? Was he worth the risk of emotional pain? It was obvious. He had come in a panic but was vacillating. Staring off into space and sniffling, she put her hand to her nose. She thought she was finished crying but wasn't. She didn't want to leave, to miss him. She liked his intelligence, his humor, his hands, and how he enveloped her with his arms. She even liked when he was stared, evaluating her when he thought she wouldn't notice. She raised an eyebrow and gave him a side glance. Fighting with rational thought and emotions, her emotions won. She flew into his arms, hugging him as if he had returned from the dead.

"How," he wondered, "can a woman appear so cold and indifferent one moment and the next melt my heart?" Although his entreaties to have her stay were weak, they were enough. Stephanie said, "David, will you take me away from here?" He found himself nodding.

"Yes, when?"

Before he could change his mind, she replied, "Now, today. I'm packed."

"I'll talk to Ramona." Wondering if he was crazy, he went downstairs. Adam directed him to a side door leading to the restaurant.

Sitting at a round table for four, Ramona looked up, set her ledger and dip ink pen aside, and invited him to sit. A waitress approached with two boiled eggs, strips of thick bacon, and two cups of steaming coffee, one for Ramona and one for him.

Without preamble, he asked, "Ramona, how much do you want for her?"

108

Ramona frowned. "Elder, my friend, you are a dunce. The girls here are not slaves like the girls on Cora Street. They're free to go whenever they please."

Apologizing, he rephrased, saying, "I could pay you for lost earnings."

"No, it's up to her. Have you asked her?"

"Yes, she's ready."

"So, you're in love. Well, let me tell you, after you met, she canceled all her appointments. You fascinate her. There is no one else. Her earnings to the house stopped. I know she's never asked you for money. I thought her behavior ill-advised, unbelievable since you had just met. I thought of firing her. I considered taking her directly to the station to get her away from you. But I knew. I knew it wouldn't work, not after seeing the look on your face when you met. And I like you. I like her. I've been watching. I owe you. She looks forward to your visits, always asking when you're coming and going to her room, and disappointed when you don't. You're tall, tough, intelligent, and somehow look elegant no matter what you wear. And Abe is your partner. She likes him. You have bodyguards and a chauffeur. When you stopped coming, you broke her heart. But it is the right thing for her to leave."

He asked for an explanation.

"As you know, she's Jewish, and Hitler hates Jews. They're despised. Her mother was a doctor at a hospital in Berlin. She was sacked because she's Jewish. Her father protested and was arrested. Then, the family business was taken over by the Nazis. Her father, grandfather, and brother are missing, probably in jail, and the last she heard from her mother, they were in hiding. She cries in her room and drinks. Before you met, she had sips of wine all day and vodka in the evening. When you walked in, she stopped. So, I'm glad about that, but be careful. She appears strong, but it's a veneer. She's vulnerable. She needs someone to lean on, to take care of

109

her—to be an ally. Elder, when she walked in two months ago, from the beginning, I had the feeling she was passing through, that she wouldn't last. I guess you've decided her to stay."

"Hmmm," he asked, "Is she a sloppy drunk?"

"No, not at all. Somehow, she never appears intoxicated, but I still don't like it."

"I don't think I have anything to worry about. I'll take her. I'll help her, but I'm not going to marry her." Then joking, he asked, "Can I return her if it doesn't work out?"

"You're not buying her, and she's never coming back; she'll go back to Germany first and die. Anyway, Mr. David Elder, I took a huge chance on you once before, and I was right. You didn't know, but I was going broke giving you money for our little oil venture in Texas. And I'm right about you and her. You'll do good by each other. Invite me to the wedding." Seeing his alarm, she said, "Honey, you don't know your own mind. You're younger since you met. I like to spread happiness. It makes me feel good, and I might earn some credits with the good Lord above. I don't know if He'll let me in, but I'll take my chances. Anyway, I don't believe in hell. I'll go into the void and be surprised. Just treat her right."

Chapter Seventeen: Reconsidering

While Elder talked to Ramona downstairs, Stephanie reflected on Elder's words, his anguish, his pleas for her to stay, and the emotional toll of their relationship. Feeling deflated, she reasoned that if they were to continue it would not be without peril. Doing self-talk, she considered that she had to be prudent to win his heart. "I cannot force him. Above all, I must avoid demands. Patience," she told herself. "I must allow him room to breathe, to sort out his thoughts until he realizes that he loves me—or not."

Never had she been in such a situation. Her beauty and personality had always given her the upper hand. Men always fell in love with her, yet here she was longing for Elder, and he had ignored her. A few minutes earlier, when he entered her room, her heart swelled with joy, but angry and hurt, she pretended she didn't care.

She was one of the lucky ones blessed by nature. Even in childhood, she had received favorable treatment. She thought it unfair, especially when encountering resentment from other girls. She tried disguising her beauty, but it didn't work. Her parents had been her buffer from unwanted advances—from strangers, uncles, her father's business associates--even a female relative. This situation with Elder was different. To be rejected was unfamiliar.

She wanted him but had to overcome the distaste that must lurk in his mind for her being a prostitute. She thought of the evening at the opera. Elder greeted two men and their wives in the mezzanine. One, she knew as a former "John." Nothing was said to give her away, but somehow Elder discerned their connection. Perhaps, it was in the eyes or the straighter way the man stood, preened his hair, and the exaggerated attention he gave to his wife. Or the way she looked away. Elder appeared unruffled, except for a split second when he shot a scathing look. Quickly, the man excused himself and walked away. The other couple stayed, exchanging small talk.

"Clearly, to keep his interest," she mused, "I must be more than his sexual partner. Deep down, he must know that he's a catch. He can easily have another woman. If there is one thing he lacks, it's humility." She corrected herself; "It's confidence he has, not humility." She continued her musing thinking that others sought his attention. He wasn't arrogant or haughty, although he might be misjudged as being aloof and bossy to strangers. She considered that he was not mean but kind and tender, and she loved his humor, generous smiles, banter, confident voice, and the little humming rumble in his throat when aroused. "He is easy on the eyes. Can I succeed?" she wondered, "In a moment of sobriety or anger, he'll despise me, leave me, and I'll be heartbroken. It's too late to cut off sex— to start over. I have to win him somehow. What if his family doesn't like me? Even if he suffers, they come first. And he still loves his deceased wife." Once in the throes of lovemaking, he had called her 'Georgia.' "What can I do?"

Her mind raced, but her thinking was circular, with no conclusion. If their meeting had been another day, another time, she would have withheld her prostitution from his knowing. She thought of Ezra, the only other man she had loved. He would be disappointed that she had stooped so low. But she had to survive and hadn't known she would meet another love so far away from Germany—and not even Jewish. "He is mesmerizing," she thought, and she felt wonderful and safe in his presence. She wondered, "Will Mama accept him?"

Thinking of her attraction to Elder, Stephanie recalled their day at the Sutra Baths, a series of swimming pools at the seashore filled with ocean water. She was standing in front of him toweling herself dry. He was seated, watching. His hands went to her shapely thighs and roamed over the contours. Looking him in the eyes and down at his hands, he stroked and massaged almost to the nether regions. She wondered if, in that public place, she would stop him. Almost subconsciously, she helped by moving closer. Aroused, she held her breath. But he wasn't trying to arouse. He was admiring the well-defined musculature of her legs and thinking she could have been a competitive athlete.

Although Stephanie did not know the term, she recognized Elder as an alpha male, confident and dominant. And she was an alpha female, perhaps more emotional, intelligent, more educated, and sufficiently rational with everyone else except him. He would provide good genes for their children and easily support them. "Yes," she thought, "we are a match." In effect, she had hit the jackpot.

Before their meeting, Stephanie had rationalized that she would be a prostitute only until the people of Germany came to their senses and Hitler was overthrown. But now, she was caught in her a web of her own making. She had envisioned returning to Germany and meeting a proper suitor, someone ignorant of her past. Little did she know that Hitler would bring on a world war and that his regime would not end until years later, in 1945, when the Allies conquered Germany.

Sighing, she reached a decision. "It won't work. Nein. I have to leave. I'm being absurd. I can't escape what I've done. He won't forgive me. He'll become revolted. He'll tire of me, and one-day mein herz writ gerbrochen (I'll be heartbroken). Ja, I can't live in a fantasy. I'll tell him I've changed my mind." Returning to Stephanie's room, Elder found her sitting at the edge of the bed looking solemn, bags at the door.

"Are you ready?"

"Ya, Ich bin den prostituierte, I'll be your prostitute." She finished by looking away and whispering, "Und ich liebe dich (and I'll love you)." She took his hand and said, "But we can't live together." So much for my resolve, she mused.

The comment, "Be your prostitute" squeezed Elder's heart. At a loss for words, he could only weakly say,

"Are you sure?"

Disappointed, she replied, "Oh, David, I've been packing and unpacking, waiting for you."

"Should I ask why?"

113

Sighing and deeply exasperated with this back and forth, she raised her eyes, appraising, until he felt she saw into his innermost being. Her reply was slow, making him think, "The tough one is back. She's got me, and I'm squirming."

"If you have to ask, you're not as smart as I thought." Calmly, knowing what she was risking, she said, "I do want you, I can love you dearly, but I'll get someone else if you don't want me. If you're not serious, please be kind enough to drive me to Union Station. I'll go to New York. I'll decide where to go from there."

The words were harsh, but she was a survivor; she wanted this man and wanted to know if he wanted her. She had no time to waste with this silly vacillation. She had to get on with her life, and it wasn't going to be at Ramona's, maybe in Canada, Australia, or Portugal, places she had considered, or the south of Mexico.

Seeing that he was wrestling with his demons, she said, "David, if it doesn't work for both of us, I'll go away. Don't worry; I'll be fine. Why not treat this as an arrangement?" And maybe, she thought, "We can pretend we didn't meet at Ramona's."

Elder thought, "Yes, like a business arrangement. I can deal with that. I'll have my bookkeeper set up an account for her." Never had he been challenged so frankly, so directly, by a woman, nor did he have so much conflicting doubt and hope. Picking up her bags, he asked himself, "What am I doing?"

Outside, Matteo was waiting. Not surprisingly, Lugo was standing across the street, watching angry, and astonished. It never occurred to him that Elder would take a prostitute to his home, to his family. He had reasoned that Stephanie would stay at Ramona's; Elder would come and go using her until eventually his interest petered out and dropped her.

Rushing to his car, he followed Elder's car for a few blocks and turned away. He knew where Elder lived.

At the mansion, Stephanie was introduced as a friend who would stay temporarily, but they were not fooled, not in the least. He fumbled with his words, treated her gently, and if eyes talked, they were with love. They watched her eyes follow his every move and how she keenly listened when he spoke. They noticed the interplay of their fingers as he covered her hand with his, and her glowing face raised to his.

Sam and Jessica had loved their mother. Fond memories of her in their early years would be with them forever, but with her illness, they had grown careful and fearful, not only for themselves but for her. They knew before her passing that she would never recover. Now, they were happy to be introduced to someone new, someone who would revive their father's zest for life.

Stephanie was not intimidated by the splendid house and grounds. Growing up, her family had lived on an estate passed down from generation to generation, with horses, stables, and all the accouterments and costs that went with it. As stewards of the land, they worked hard and valued education. She mused, "He has a lot to learn about me and my family."

Maia cast a disapproving look. She knew that Elder had been consorting with a prostitute but never had she considered that he would bring one home. When he had, the meaning of appalled was a weak expression. Of course, it was his house, and he could invite anyone he wished but questioned his thinking. The woman was attractive, mannerly, and seemingly intelligent, but there was more to life than sex. As far as she was concerned, prostitutes were dirty no matter how often they bathed. They were morally corrupt, promiscuous, carriers of disease, ass-benders, and going to hell. If Elder persisted in having one around, she would be

115

civil but an infrequent visitor. "The woman," she mused, "is clever in getting Elder to bring her home; she knows a good thing and is after his money."

After Elder escorted Stephanie upstairs to their room, Maia cornered her husband. Maia was disappointed and scolded him.

"Abe, Elder has jumped from having a cultured wife to a prostitute, and it's your fault."

Lamely, he replied, "I think she's cultured."

She shot him a scowl.

"What did I do?" he asked.

"Abraham." She never called him Abraham unless she was angry. "He listens to you, but you looked the other way. That's the problem. You didn't protect him. This will ruin his life and his reputation. If it were my house, I would throw that worthless piece of grime into the street. If you don't talk some sense into him, I'm leaving for Puerto Rico until I calm down."

Abe was torn but agreed. Maia was serious, and she wasn't joking about Puerto Rico. He crossed the lawn to speak to Elder. But Elder lifted his hand and explained. It was not his intention to move Stephanie into the house permanently, and it was obvious that Maia was upset. Stephanie also felt the animosity and did not want to cause disharmony. Her stay would be brief until he got a place for her.

So instead of the counseling Maia had requested, Abe only commiserated with Elder. "Abe," Elder said, "she occupies my mind. Maybe it's wishful thinking. Maybe she's a great actress, and she's using me. Is she after my money? Maybe? It's fair. I'm using her. She makes me happy. Am I deluding myself? Probably. Maybe? I don't know. But I look forward to each day. I feel alive again. This is my life, and I'm glad our paths crossed, even if it was at Ramona's. I don't want any more regrets.

116

Yes, she's a prostitute. I wish she wasn't, but she is. Don't worry; I'm not deluded. I'm not so smitten that I've lost my sanity. And I'm not marrying, not to her, not to anybody, not now, not ever. And I don't want more children. I'm not in love. I'm living day to day."

Abe returned to Maia.

"What did he say?" she asked.

"It's too late. He's gobsmacked," a term he learned in London. "It means . . . . ."

"I know what it means," she snapped." Maia frowned and said, "Here's another British word. She's a slag, a slut."

"Oooh, ouch," Abe replied.

"He's in lust. We'll see how long it lasts."

Abe added that Elder had compromised. Stephanie's stay would be brief. He took unwarranted credit, and Maia was mollified. However, Stephanie did not leave that night or the next. For nine days, the household was disrupted. Maia stayed away. Abe didn't know what to do, so he took a brief unnecessary business trip to Sacramento. When he returned, he was extra careful not to antagonize his wife.

While still on her rant, Maia informed Jessica and Sam that Stephanie was a whore. They were appalled. They could talk to him but probably wouldn't. He would listen but rarely changed his mind. "Whoa," Jessica said. Her initial evaluation of Stephanie was that she was lovely and decent. But now, she hoped that her father would not be harmed in any way, morally, emotionally, financially, or physically. "You know," she said, "Sam, I still like her."

Sam frowned. He didn't like it. Not one bit, and extremely relieved that he had not frequented Ramona's. He had heard of the strikingly, beautiful new woman at Ramona's and had thought of visiting. "Good Lord!" he

117

thought, "a bullet missed." The thought made him shake his head and groan, "Oh my gosh!"

Chapter Eighteen: Lugo, Discontent

The day previous, Lugo, was standing across the street from Ramona's. What he saw, surprised him to no end. This he had not expected. "What," he thought, "She's leaving Ramona's--with him!?"

Matteo lifted a suitcase into the boot of the car and confronted Lugo's stare. Also helping was Caesar. Caesar started toward Lugo to confront him but was stopped by Matteo. This was the second time this little man had sent chills down his spine. In Lugo's memory was the night he had followed Stephanie and Elder to the popular Blackhawk Jazz Club in North Beach, owned by Robert, Abe's younger brother. Robert was the only one of nine siblings who had left Savannah.

Lugo recalled: It was 11 p.m. The tables and dance floor were packed. A faceted glass ball rotated from the ceiling, radiating spears of light. Revelers, blacks, and whites, dressed to the "nines" in style, danced. The sounds of rhythm carried outside, and Lugo's attention went to the piano, bass, and riffs of drums playing the "Boogie Woogie Stomp." He could play it. Attuned to the beat, he lost his concentration. The next piece was a rendition of "Down the Road a Piece." Lugo stayed where he was, listening, rocking his head, and tapping his foot.

After "Down the Road a Piece," he still temporized. Cars deposited passengers one after the other. He dithered as to whether he would go in to provoke a fight. He'd win. Elder would be embarrassed, and Stephanie would see that he was the superior man. Or, maybe, he'd stab Elder on the crowded dance floor and slip away. Or, if he waited, he'd shoot him from the alley. Somehow, he'd do it.

Backing deeper into the shadows, he bumped into someone. Not one to be intimidated, he whirled around and immediately stepped back. It was the damn little jockey man with his knife, itching to be set loose. Next to him was the tall Negro---Abe. Earlier, Lugo had seen Matteo pull up to the curb in the Caddie to drop off Elder and Stephanie. But evidently, he had parked and worked his way back. He didn't know how a man so small could instill fear, but he did. He thought, "He'd go for the testicles."

Lugo estimated Abe's physical strength. Lugo was larger, but the man was tall and impressive and gave the impression of someone who could not be intimidated—nor was he impressed by Lugo's uniform. Over the years, Abe had gained weight, but hadn't diminished his stature—still fit, imposing, and distinguished. Distinguished, elegant people made Lugo uncomfortable. They possessed intelligence, something he respected, and power, money, and connections.

After a few seconds of tense, quiet confrontation, Abe said, "Lugo, unless you want something bad to happen—to you—stay away!" While keeping his eyes on Abe and Matteo, Lugo walked backward seven feet. Then he turned and left, shaken. But it didn't stop the stalking.

Lugo's stalking included trespassing on Elder's property. In the darkest hours, he skulked around, peered in windows, and climbed trees for better viewing. With his back to a tree, Matteo watched from a comfortable distance. Elder had instructed him not to intervene, "Leave him alone. Eventually, he'll get tired and quit." Curious, Jessica sat in the darkness with Matteo and giggled at Lugo's antics. Climbing a tree, he snagged his pants leg. Attempting to yank it free, he almost fell. Giggling silently, she placed her hand over old Lubo's snout and whispered to be quiet. Lobo didn't care. He was content with these humans and their silly games.

Lugo's efforts were all for naught. Stephanie had already moved to a neat Craftsman-style home with a white gated picket fence, a front sitting

119

porch, fruit trees, grass, and roses, all attractively groomed, and a one-car garage. No car. She walked and rode the trolleys.

They were partial on rainy days to sit on the porch, drink hot tea and coffee, converse, and watch the passing scene.

Lugo knew that he was losing control but couldn't help it. Even fellow cops talked behind his back, saying that he was acting stranger than usual. He was not deterred, even knowing that his carefully concocted facade of a calm, even-tempered individual was eroding. He brooded. Obsession over Stephanie and how outclassed he was by Elder was all-consuming. All that mattered was getting through his workday so he could stalk, watch her from a distance, and plan to win her back.

Lugo's friend, Mack, and a prostitute provided Lugo with Stephanie's new address.

Chapter Nineteen: Home

Sam and Elder sat under the veranda drinking iced sun tea. The Spanish terra-cotta-colored Saltillo tiles had been resealed with a muted sheen. Two of the dogs, Bradley and the dachshund that Abe had named "Dog" after Jack's dog in Texas, romped across the green lawn. Lobo dozed serenely at Elder's feet. Matteo had finished his work in the greenhouse and tossed a ball for Bradley. Dog was content to romp around behind Bradley. It was dusk and time for sweaters. A light breeze rustled lightly through slender white bark birch trees. Chirping birds sounded in the background. Maia asked if there was anything she could bring them. Elder asked if Abe was going to join them. She replied that he would have to ask himself--if he could find him. He had been gone for hours.

Sam noted that age had not diminished his father's persona or strength: his arms were muscular, as well as his shoulders and chest. Perhaps there was a little extra weight in his stomach. Adding to his persona were two scars, one barely perceptible on his upper lip and the other on his left cheekbone. If his calm physical presence did not impress, then his personality did. But he could have an explosive temper. Sam had seen it when dealing with bad characters and when he came to the defense of his family. Yes, he mused. Dad has an aura of power, of authority, just like Abe. However, Abe preferred to be in the background, and not desirous of bringing attention to himself. Sam asked, "Dad, how did you get that scar on your cheekbone?"

"That and this little one on my lip. It happened in a fight in the oil fields. I was sucker-punched by Rory, another foreman. It didn't take much to set him off. I thought I'd walk away. Yeah, that's what I thought—walk away from trouble. He hit me in the kidneys so hard that even my hair hurt. Then, he hit me a couple more times. He used brass knuckles. Abe was a few feet away. He saved me. He knocked the shit out of him—yeah, kicked him down the road." Smiling crookedly, he added, "Never mess with Abe. Rory disappeared after killing a friend of ours. Rory's brother, Otis, was in on it. The story is that Otis was killed and dropped down a ravine."

While speaking, Sam noticed that his father had his right hand over his left—alternately squeezing and relaxing. Elder added, "He deserved to die. Too bad Rory got away." No more needed to be said.

"You know, son," Elder said, "life is hard but full of adventures. Even if something bad happens, if you survive it makes a great story. Money helps. Abe and I got rich young. Others thought we were the ones to follow. And I'm not going to feel bad for getting rich for working hard. But I'm going to tell you something. Whenever something big happened, it was like it was time. Like the future was waiting for me to come along. Like there was a reason, like meeting Abe. We were both far from where we were born, the card game, hitting oil, PeeWee dying, and being forced

121

to move to San Francisco. Even the earthquake. It led me to your mother. Now, I have you and Jessica. But I feel in my bones something else is coming. Is it good, bad? I don't know. I hope I'm ready." Then looking at his son with a crooked smile, and chuckling, "But maybe life is just a series of accidents."

When David Elder spoke about the past, he usually omitted information. He did speak about being raised in a small farming community. He spoke of his mother, Ella Grace, who passed away young. And he had a sister, Kathy, somewhere. He would speak of her briefly, reluctantly as if it pained him. Never did he speak about his father.

Sam had learned not to ask. His face would darken, and say, "Sorry, Sam, I can't talk about it." It was as if his life had started in Texas, where he met Abe. Sam had heard the stories before, including their struggle to strike oil, and some from Abe, including the violence at Ramona's. The thought of his father working in a dirt hick town with nothing to do except work from morning to night was fascinating. They were young. They had money. There was no place to spend it—no drug stores, restaurants, no movie theaters, nothing to do except play cards, drink, and, if one was so inclined, go to Ramona's house of prostitution.

Sam asked, "Dad, did you ever go to a cat house?"

"Me? With a sporting woman at a brothel? Of course not!" But his reply was with a grin and a twinkle.

While waiting to see if Abe would come, Sam and Elder discussed the projected end of Prohibition, that is the manufacture, sale, and distribution of alcoholic beverages. "Dad," Sam said, "Prohibition is going to be repealed (repealed December 1933). We'll change the Palace Speakeasy to the Palace Station Café. Someone else can be the manager. I'll be a bartender and get in touch with the working man. Later, I'll write. Maybe about you and Abe. You're colorful. You've lived full lives—from the hardscrabble oil fields of Texas to business tycoons tainted by association with the Mafia. Yes, I know about that." Surprised, Elder sputtered, trying to verbalize justification for his activities, but Sam stopped him.

"Dad, this is not a perfect world, especially with this infernal depression. I've watched everything you do since I can remember. And you're full of stories like Big Hat Sam. Remember?"

"Of course," Elder replied. "Sam, when you were born, you came out with a smile, probably gas. For some reason, Big Hat Sam came to mind.

"Big Hat Sam, Samuel Torres Mendoza, was the foreman of one of the largest cattle ranches in Santa Fe, New Mexico. When I got there, I was broke, hungry, and looking for work. I was told to ask for Samuel Mendoza at Diego's Cantina. I found him and introduced myself. He told me to wait. I waited over an hour, just standing there. There weren't any stools. He didn't say a word to me, just kept drinking and talking to his buddy. Once in awhile he'd look over at me. Maybe sizing me up. Well, eventually, he finished his drinks and walked to the door. My heart dropped; I thought that was it; I wasn't hired. But he turned and said, 'Come on, amigo, let's go.' I was hired.

"Big Hat wore a big sombrero. He was a hell of a man with piercing green eyes. He liked tequila, loved women, and dancing. We hung around him so much, pestering him for stories, that sometimes he'd chase us away. He was full of life. His laugh was loud and lusty; that alone made us feel good." Elder hesitated. "Like Jessica." A shadow crossed his face. "And like my dad."

Sam looked at him questionably. Elder shook his head and gave him a look that said, "Don't ask."

"Big Hat returned to Mexico and never returned. The last I heard, he was fighting alongside Pancho Villa in the Mexican Revolutionary War. Big Hat was probably in the thick of it. For all I know, he's dead."

123

The conversation touched on other topics. Elder asked if he had ever been mean and harsh to Sam. He hadn't. Sam said, "If anything, you were overly protective. But," as his lips crinkled mischievously, "you're not above lies."

"How so?"

"When we were kids, you read us fairy tales and butchered the stories."

"Yes, I did, for fun."

"You sure did. You said Little Red Riding Hood had a machine gun and that Jack and the Bean Stalk liked Mexican food. You also said that Jack was our great-grandfather, and that's how the family got rich with the goose that laid the golden eggs."

Elder laughed and said, "Sorry."

Sam continued. "Because of you and Mom, I was born one of the lucky ones. But I don't want to get complacent or disconnected from the regular working Joes."

Elder replied that he had been fortunate. "Too bad, it sometimes is to the misfortune of others. The depression offers great opportunities to those who have money. They have power and authority more than the poor. They're put to the front of the line. It's unfair, but life's not fair."

"Dad, I'll work under a different name. Begging your pardon, I don't want it known that I'm your son. You'll just have to tell the manager he can't fire me."

Elder took a sip of tea, and said, "Sure, why not?" I don't think our name is known among dock workers. But just in case, let's keep our name confidential."

"Done," Sam said and extended his hand for a handshake.

"Here's Jessica."

They watched her gliding gracefully toward them on her long, exquisite legs. At 5 feet 8 inches, Jessica was stately, with tempting, healthy lips,

124

dark brown eyes like her father, and long auburn hair. She was stately, beautiful and knew it. She was a lively extrovert and wouldn't hesitate to speak her mind.

"Your sister," Elder commented wistfully, "is beautiful, just like her mother. And look at her. She radiates energy."

"Yeah," Sam replied. "She has a zest for life, but she is louder." Indeed, she was lovely and slender, an elegant beauty with a robust, lovely laugh. At first meetings, boys and men were enthralled.

Jessica leaned in to kiss her father and sat next to him. Crossing her long, athletic legs, flouncing her white pleated skirt, she asked, "What's done? What are you two up to?"

"We're turning the speakeasy into a cafe and bar, and catering to the dock workers," Sam replied.

"What fun. Me too. I want to work in a bar."

Elder replied. "Hold on, Jess, you're still at Berkeley and have a job."

"My classes are easy," she replied. "I can do it part-time easily, and you know I'm not needed in the office. It would be great. I can do my master's thesis on the recreational activities of the unemployed versus the rich. At the café, I think I can convince someone who loves me to give me good hours."

"Who might that be?" Elder asked.

"Why," teasingly, "who do you think?" Winking, "You, Dad. You love me, don't you?"

Chuckling, "Why, yes, more than you can imagine."

Elder looked at his daughter, at her joyful personality. For the second time in an hour, he was reminded of his father before the change. Shuddering, he silently mumbled, "The asshole."

"Jess, we'll see," said Sam, "It's not even open yet."

"I don't know," said Elder.

Jessica wasn't having it. "Dad, after mom died, you moped around. You wandered around at night, and we followed behind you to make sure you were all right. I dropped out of college to get you back to life. I think you owe me. And you do remember that I convinced you to take a trip with me to Europe?"

"Yes, how can I forget?"

Their trip began in the hillside town of Nice, France. The first night was in a converted farmhouse in the foothills with scenic views of vineyards, the town, and the ocean below. In the evening, in the gardens, the proprietor, a friendly fellow carrying a bottle of wine and three glasses, asked if he could sit and visit. The next morning, they walked uphill to the historic medieval castle city of Saint Raul De Vance, a historic citadel town on a high hill overlooking the city below. It was a small thriving community with narrow alleys for streets. It had shops, a dentist, homes, restaurants, storage for food, a church, a cemetery, an outer defensive wall, and an inner defensive wall in case the outer was breached.

From Nice, they traveled by train to Naples, Italy, and from there to Firenze, Rome, Barcelona, and Paris. In ancient Roman times, Firenze was called Florentia; more recently, Florence by the British and the United States; and Firenze by Italy, Germany, France, and Spain. From Rome, they flew in a one-prop airplane to Barcelona, Spain, and from there by train to Paris.

People were polite and went out of their way to offer hospitality, often walking them to the door of a particular café or historic site. But unfamiliar with the currency, they were cheated twice, once short-changed buying tickets at the Louvre Museum in Paris built in 1190, initially as a fortress, and once in Rome by a taxi driver. The driver, paid in cash, turned away and back. By sleight of hand, he had concealed part of the payment and demanded more. Inside, the desk clerk informed them that it was a common trick. Jessica made the arrangements, the reservations, and the decisions. But after the incident with the taxi driver, Elder became involved.

At a café near the Cathedral of Florence in Rome, the waiter was greatly amused at their attempts at speaking Italian. In good humor, he served them wine, gratis, glass after glass, and taught them the word for butter, "burro," like the Spanish donkey. After a delightful evening and too much wine, they walked back to their lodging at Luciana's, drunk and giggling. It was the first real sign of his recovery. It was confirmed in a park the next day. While he went off to find a bathroom, four cute young Italian men cozied up to Jessica, flirting. Surrounding her on the grass, they said she looked like a modern Mona Lisa. Unfortunately, his return ended that entertaining moment but gave them pleasure and a little story to tell.

"Yes, great trip. Fine," Elder replied, smiling. "Since you're using that against me, I'll agree. But on one condition. One of our staff will drive you to and from work. He'll have the same working hours. It's near the waterfront. There's trouble brewing, about to explode. The crowd will be rough. There will be heavy drinking. Some will get out of hand."

She protested. "Protection? I don't want a bodyguard."

"How about the new fellow?"

"Who?"

"Caesar."

"Caesar? Oh!" A slow flirtatious smile crossed her lips. Caesar would suit her just fine. "Well, if I must."

"Sam," she said, "I heard you talking about working under a different name. How about Cock-er? From what I hear from my girlfriends, a name like that would suit you."

"That's enough, young lady," Elder said.

Sam grinned.

"Tah tah tah." "Well," she laughed, "Don't get into a tizzy; I'm just saying—and you know, I'll have to use the same name. How about Elger? Close, but different."

Elder said, "I wonder where Abe is, maybe making one of his deals?"

Twilight was coming, and a gust of wind scattered Scrub-Jays from the trees. They resettled. The dogs joined the group and lounged at their feet. "Ah, here he comes," Elder said. Seeing how serious Abe looked, they waited while he placed logs in the fire pit, moved them around thoughtfully, and set them on fire. Looking at Abe, Elder said, "Abe, you look worried."

"Maybe it's nothing. I was downtown with Matteo, and we hopped on the trolley. A man at the rear covered his face and jumped off as we got on. He looked like Rory with his red hair and pocked face. Yeah, I know, it's been years, but it was a shock. This is the second time that I thought it was him. The first time, I had a feeling of being followed. I turned around, and a man whipped around and ran. And Maia says she dreams of someone hunting me, and he's getting closer."

Chapter Twenty: Charitable Food Line. Rachael and Morgan

When the stock market crashed five years prior in 1929, Rachael, the young woman Sam had treated to a meal in Palo Alto, was in her first semester at the University of California School of Nursing. The Great

128

Depression began. Everything changed. There was uncertainty, insecurity, and constant worry about money and necessities such as food and shelter. It seemed unfair for her to get an education when money was a worry. Purchases were weighed carefully. She had to decide whether money would be spent on books and an uncertain future or for food and shelter. Money had to be saved for the unknown. Her dream to become a nurse was put on hold. Joe, her father, had been swept up in the exhilaration of the roaring twenties and fast profits. The booming stock market was making instant millionaires.

Ordinary folks, chauffeurs, cooks, and brokers had sold their Liberty Bonds and mortgaged their homes to invest, to make fast profits.

Between September 1 and November 30, the stock market value dropped from $64 billion to approximately $30 billion. Black Tuesday alone on October 29 wiped out around 14 billion. For Rachael's parents, all vanished in two days. Illusionary paper profits went to zero value. On the heels of that disaster, banks had a run on their deposits. His bank, and about 11,000 nationwide, went bankrupt. The shocks to his emotional health were horrific. Emotional weight loss and depression followed. Fortunately, he had a government job as a mailman. Every day, he went to work. In off-hours, he sat silently staring off into space. Slowly, determined, he recovered his humor.

Joe's usual demeanor was to have a positive attitude, but with the depression, he was wary and watchful of every cent spent—the same for Rachael's mother, Helen, a housewife, and stay-at-home mother. Emotionally devastated, she lost her effervescent personality and became solemn. Pinching pennies to keep the family fed, she worried about the $17 monthly mortgage payment on the two-bedroom, one-bath house purchased for $1700 in 1928 at a bank auction. They stopped buying clothes; instead, she made blouses, dresses, and underwear with her Singer

129

sewing machine. Socks with holes were repaired with needle and thread until they were so worn-out they were thrown away.

There were no more outings to restaurants. A rare movie was allowed. Vegetables were grown in the backyard, and apples and apricots from their trees were traded with neighbors. The children noticed the changes and adopted the spirit of economizing. Plans to upgrade to a nicer, larger house were set aside. With the personal loss of their stock investment of $1,500 and savings of $1,000, they were lucky to hold on to the one they had. It was small but had a garage. They sold the car. Rachael shared one bedroom with her teenage sister.

One day Rachael stepped off the trolley, and saw her old childhood friend and college classmate, Morgan, waiting in the food line at the Salvation Army with her father.

Morgan, seeing Rachael, ran her fingers through her thick hair and waved. She was prideful and pained her to be seen standing in a food line getting charity.

Morgan was slim, pretty, and known for her frankness and vivid imagination. Cute dimples set off her clear light peach complexion. Although slimmer than Rachael recalled, she looked healthy. Her dress was loose, and her white knit sweater was repaired with the same color thread, clean but tired looking. Gorgeous wheat-colored hair flowed below her shoulders.

Larry, Morgan's father, an out-of-work longshoreman, was eager to strike for better wages, treatment, and regular working hours. Also prepared to strike were warehouse workers, bargemen, Teamsters, seamen, wipers, boilermakers, marine firemen, and others. The ferry boats did not join.

The Industrial Union, an association of shipping, industrial, banking, railroad, and utility firms, was also ready. Scabs, a derogatory term for

130

those who took the jobs of regular employees, were hired. Hundreds were students at U.C. Berkeley. For their protection, they were housed and fed on a ship. Their pay was $1.00 an hour, the same amount demanded by the labor union.

Not wanting to lose her place in line, Morgan waved for Rachael to come over. Unabashedly, Morgan told Rachael of her travails. With the advent of the Great Depression, Morgan's mother had abandoned the family. Her whereabouts were unknown, and Morgan's younger brother, Richard, was sent to live with his paternal grandparents. Larry wanted her to go with Richard, but she refused; she wasn't leaving him alone. They had managed to hold onto their little house until seven months prior. Since then, depending on whether Larry was picked out of the jostling crowd to work, they would rent beds for the night, 35 cents to 65 cents, in Pioneer Square or Folsom Street. Or, if the weather was good, they might sleep in a park under the stars.

Rachael was distressed that her friend had fallen on such dire straits, but during the Great Depression, it was commonplace. California was doing better than most of the nation. The country's unemployment rate in 1934 was between 25% and 28%. In San Francisco it was 22%.

It pained Morgan to see her father struggle, but he had no choice. He was at the damp docks every morning, almost begging, hoping to be chosen by the various independent contractors. If picked, he would give the expected kickback to the "walking man," the agent who decided who would work and who wouldn't.

Before parting, Rachael paused and looked thoughtfully at her friend.

Morgan said, "If there is something you want to say, say it but please don't offer money."

"Morgan, would you be interested in waitressing? I'm getting 25 cents an hour."

131

"Oh yes, but where?"

"I'm working at the Palace Station Cafe. It's new and close to the waterfront, near the Ferry Building and Rincon Hill. It's a poor area but nice enough, and business is increasing. I've only been there for about three months. I met the assistant manager in Palo Alto. He's nice. He told me to come by. I did, and I've been working ever since. I can't promise anything, but I'll see what I can do."

Morgan replied, "So far, this is my lucky day. A few minutes ago, a cute priest came by. I've prayed daily for the Lord's help. Today, he heard me."

A few minutes earlier, a Catholic priest had come by, Father Raffael Bouvier, soliciting people to come to service at St. Mark's Cathedral. Morgan watched as he made his way along the line. She took in his starched white priestly collar and plain black shoes. She had not had a new pair in almost five years and stared. The leather soles on her pair were worn through and had a cardboard insert—otherwise, the sole of her foot would rub the pavement. It was commonplace to repair shoes with glue and cardboard; if shoestrings broke, the ends were knotted together.

Father Raffael almost passed Morgan, purposely. She was too pretty. He felt a tug of his heart, an attraction he thought it best to avoid. Her hair backlit by the sun turned to shimmering gold. And when he turned to her dark coffee-colored eyes, he saw that she was frankly appraising him. Intrigued, he stopped. She was perhaps of Irish descent. But no, she was of Italian heritage, Morgan D'Alessandro. To entice them to come to Saint Mark's for worship, he advised that coffee and donuts were served following each service, and food donations were available for the taking.

Morgan tucked loose strands of hair behind her ears and took in his appearance: dark eyes, black hair, and an accent. "Hmmm," she wondered, "A French accent?" She asked for the hours he officiated.

After Father Raffael went on his way, he carried a slight smile. She was pretty. Her hair was striking, and something was enticing about her lips and voice. "Sorry, Lord," he whispered, "but she is your creation." Raffael's God was personal, friendly, and had a sense of humor; He would be amused. "Don't worry," he added, "I'll be good."

Chapter Twenty-One: The Palace Station Café

The Palace Speakeasy was open almost two years before Prohibition ended December 5, 1933. In that month, during the Christmas season, it transitioned into the Palace Station Café.

The cafe had a relaxed rustic ambiance and mainly served workers from the docks and carryover clientele from the speakeasy. Many were well-off but liked the working man's company. Console tables bearing Chinese porcelain vases of fresh-cut flowers were at the entrance beyond the saloon's swinging doors. On the ceiling, between thick oak beams, ten ceiling fans slowly hypnotically stirred the air dissipating smoke drifting up from pipes, cigarettes, and thick cigars.

Longshoremen, warehouse workers, and sailors spoke incessantly of their sorrows and worries of the times and the unfairness of their bosses. They drank, planned, and shared gossip. The majority wanted confrontation and violence for newspaper coverage. Dissenters argued for peaceful talks and orderly demonstrations, with strikes as a last resort. The newspapers disparaged them and labeled them as commies, socialists, enemies of business, un-American insurrectionists, and dangerous.

Rachael approached the Palace Station and thought of words to use to convince Gus to hire Morgan. She was excited and in high spirits, but the closer she got to The Palace Station, the more she fretted.

Both Gus and Caesar were busy behind the long highly polished oak bar. Caesar nodded. Gus gave her a welcoming grin and wave, as did a couple of the regulars, and a dismissive look from a rude regular, a policeman, and his partner, Mack.

"Gus," she asked, "by any chance can you use another waitress?"

"I don't think so," he replied. "You're a bit late. I just hired two, but why don't you ask Sam?" Although Gus managed the day-to-day activities, she noticed that Gus often asked Sam for advice and respectfully listened, kinda like a subordinate. It made her wonder if Sam had hidden authority. But she didn't want to offend anyone and never asked.

"Sam? Really?"

"Yes."

"Well, that was strange." She wondered who had final authority. It was supposed to be Gus, but he told her to ask Sam. If there was a problem, the staff went to Gus. If he was away, they went to Sam, but never for something like this. Gus was an astute manager, and his cheerful, friendly personality and recall of names kept customers coming back. Sam was his assistant and bartender. But here, in hiring a new employee, one who wasn't needed, Gus sent her to Sam. "Fine, I'll ask him," she thought. "But where was he?"

"Gus, where is he?" She asked.

"He's coming in at 7:00," he replied. Annoyed, she repeated to herself, "Yes, about! That's Sam. He comes and goes as he pleases, sets his own hours, takes money from the cash register right in front of Gus, and puts it in his pocket."

In vexation, she asked, "How come he comes and goes as he pleases?"

134

Gus smiling mischievously, said, "Yeh, it is a mystery. Why don't you ask him?"

Seven was when her shift ended. Throughout the day, she fretted. Although Sam was pleasant enough, she barely knew him. She knew he looked at her when he thought she wouldn't notice, and she didn't know what it meant. "Maybe," she thought, "he's checking to see if I'm a good waitress. That has to be it."

Sam walked in nine hours later at precisely 8:30 p.m., late again, 90 minutes, casually strolling in, looking good, and wearing expensive clothing as if he had been to an important meeting. As usual, Gus didn't say a word. "What nerve," she muttered.

Crossing the floor, Sam's eyes took her in——legs crossed, wearing a mid-calf length light blue dress, white socks, brown shoes, and watching. She put down her Coca-Cola and smiled. He thought, "Nice!"

Following his eyes, although there wasn't much showing, Rachael discretely adjusted the hem of her dress and placed a hand on her knee. Usually, she didn't care if men looked at her legs, but if Sam did it, it made her uncomfortable. And considering that he was not much older, it felt awkward calling him Mr. Cocker. Giggling at the close play of words, she thought, "Sam Cocker sure is cocky."

Rachael told herself that Sam was a working stiff like her, an ordinary guy working in a cafe. Yet he didn't seem like one. He had manners, spoke well, had an excellent vocabulary, and carried himself in a way that spoke of a different life. His clothing was usually ordinary inexpensive cotton shirts and pants. But on rare occasions, like today, he came in looking fashionably sharp—high-quality wool pleated slacks and polished, hand-tooled shoes, maybe Italian, even his socks—out of place in the Palace Station Café.

To Rachael's way of thinking, fine shoes, or an expensive wristwatch instead of a pocket watch, "My gosh, a Patek Philippe," which Sam wore, indicated a man's social standing better than his clothing. Sam had everything. And why and how? To her annoyance, she liked him a lot, but he was her boss. As a result, she did not tease, joke, or treat him as anyone special. She spoke to him when necessary, indifferently but politely.

Sam sat on the adjacent stool and swiveled toward her. Surprising herself, she looked at his lips and, subconsciously, licked her own. Languidly she raised her eyes to his, only to see him watching. "Dang," she mused, "he saw me looking."

"Yes, Rachael?" he asked. "What is it?"

Unnerved, she said, "Uh, well, Mr. Sam, I mean Cocker," and thought, "What kind of stupid name is Cocker? "I would like to ask something, kind of a favor." She stopped, afraid to ask.

"Call me Sam, just Sam."

"All right."

Playfully, he prodded her. "Well, come on. You have something to say, or you wouldn't have waited two hours after quitting time. Say it!"

"Well," she began but again hesitated. She looked at his lips and eyes and saw that he was looking at her fingers. She was fidgeting with the middle button of her white blouse at the area of her bosom. Again, she licked her lips. He did the same to his. Blushing, she switched to a strand of hair.

"The, oh, ah, what?" she asked.

"Come on, Rachael. Tell me." She had forgotten her presentation. Sam patiently looked directly at her eyes and then her lips. He licked them. Not hers, his. "Wow," she thought, "he did that on purpose." Her cheeks were hot. Her lips parted, and she began breathing through her mouth. Her pulse quickened. Unintentionally, she licked her lips again. "Dang." Her cheeks were hot. "Darn it," she mused, "this is not going well." Before her nerve completely evaporated, the words spilled out in a rush. "I have a friend. We were in college together. She needs a job. She's destitute, homeless, and living with her father. He's a longshoreman, but with the trouble at the docks, he isn't working.

"She could die of malnutrition and ill health, and if things don't improve, her heart will break. Could you, by any chance, consider her for employment?"

Teasing, Sam asked, "Now, is it your heart or her heart that will break?"

"Mine."

For a moment, he didn't respond. "Did you ask Gus?"

"Yes, He says he just hired two, but that I could ask you."

"Oh, he did? Well, Rachael, we don't need another waitress. Maybe later."

Rachael never could hide her emotions. She was embarrassed for having asked. Her cheeks were hot. Her heart was pounding, and her face betrayed her. The bread and soup lines were an everyday sight, and it saddened her to think Morgan suffered while she never went hungry and had a clean bed to sleep in every night. The more she saw of life and its unfairness, the more it perplexed her, including the unfairness of God, who seemed to have his favorites, including her.

"Ooooh, oh, okay, Mr. Cocker."

"Sam, just Sam."

"I thought it wouldn't hurt to ask." Disappointed, avoiding his eyes, she swiveled her barstool to the counter, sipped the last of her Coca-Cola, put a nickel on the bar, and hopped off the stool.

Recalling the incident near Stanford, Sam had lost hope of seeing Rachael again and wished he had asked for her number. Almost two

137

months later, she walked in asking for a job. Sam had introduced her to Gus and left the two to talk. With her back to him, he had silently mouthed, "Hire her!" Gus looked puzzled and put his hand to his ear. Sam silently repeated himself, exaggerating the words, only to smile when he saw Gus's wink. Now, she asked for a favor, and he turned her down. Seeing her dispirited reaction, he didn't feel good.

Hopping off the stool, Rachael's dress hiked up, giving him a side peek at her young, toned thighs. A slow, guttural humming began, "Hmmmm." Reaching out for her hand, he said words he hadn't expected. "Rachael, wait! Don't give up so easily. Tell me about her. Sit! Dog-gone it," he thought, "now I've done it."

Solely based on Rachael's recommendation, Morgan was to show up ready for work on Friday, and today was Wednesday. To her surprise, Sam opened the cash register and gave her $10.00. It was, he said, for Morgan to buy a dress for work. But it was enough for a dress, a pair of silk stockings, and shoes, with money left over. And Morgan would earn 25 cents an hour, about $40 per month. Rachael thought, "What a lovely man, and Gus's permission wasn't needed. But ooooh, yikes, what's happening? He's looking at my lips and tapping my knee. He's touching my hand. Gosh, he's flirting!"

"Thank you, Mr. Cocker."

"Sam!"

"Yes, Sam, thank you."

As she headed for the door, Gus sidled up and said, "I saw that little by-play between you two. You had her so flustered she didn't know what to do with her hands."

"So," Gus said, grinning, "we have another waitress. Do you think we'll stay in business with all the people working here?"

138

"Gus," Sam said wistfully, watching Rachael walk to and out the saloon doors, "we'll manage."

"Nice back," Gus offered.

"Yes, nice."

"Nice legs too, and smart."

"Yeah."

"Pretty too, and just in case you haven't noticed. . ."

Gus, I've noticed." Smiling, Sam swiveled the stool back to the counter, "Yeah, I've noticed."

Going out the door, Rachael passed Jessica and Caesar coming in. Jessica was the only part-time waitress. Rachael liked her, but there had been some initial annoyance. Jessica got the best hours, actually any hours she wanted. Resentment faded once she got to know her. In addition to having questions about Jessica, she also wondered about Caesar. Caesar was hired at the same time and had the same working hours. Initially, she had paid it no mind but noticed that he brought her to work and left at the same time to drive her home, wherever that was. Sometimes, he returned to put in more hours. Like Sam, he had incredibly flexible hours. Sam put in 30 to 60 hours a week but came and went as he pleased. It sure was curious. "Oh well," she thought, "it's none of my business."

Caesar was nice looking, with brown eyes, funny, cute, intelligent, mannerly, solidly built, and exceedingly well proportioned. His hair was thick and black. His job was as a bartender and bouncer, but he kept his attention on Jessica, and everyone knew it. Maybe not the kind of attention that said he was interested, but like a protective brother or bodyguard. "Yes, like a bodyguard," she thought. There was also an air of calm about him and assurance among men. He easily escorted drunks out the door, courteously, without anyone being injured or offended—-often while they bantered back and forth and exchanged mock-play insults.

139

Chapter Twenty-Two: <u>Saturday.</u> The Palace Station Cafe

Beer distributors competed for sales, and temporarily a customer could get a beer and a sandwich for 15 cents. Pickles, pickled eggs, and pickled pig's feet were on the counter in large glass jars and could be had for a few cents more. The crowded cafe buzzed with talk about the unfairness of the employer's Industrial Union, the lowdown dirt pay of 60 and 80 cents an hour, and the horrific working conditions. Dockworkers wanted $1.00 an hour, maybe $1.30. Lowering their voices to a whisper, lest some spy listened, they drank beer at 05 cents a glass and got tipsy. Loose talk prevailed. Anger and urgency crackled.

Crowded and noisy, all tables, chairs, and stools were occupied. Many stood, beer in hand. There was major talk of a strike—others wanted peaceful negotiations. Sprinkled among the men were office workers, primarily women. Thick smoke drifted. Fans rotated. Rachael swept up cigarette butts. Behind the counter, Sam and Gus served drinks and wiped glasses. Two fry cooks were hard at work. A busboy cleaned tables. He and the dishwasher rushed back and forth from the dining room to the kitchen, clearing tables of dishes and empty glasses.

Sam watched Rachael and her quiet efficiency. To him, she glided gracefully on the roughly sanded plank floor. The floor was yet to be varnished, but nobody cared except him. He took his eyes off Rachael to remove money from the over-stuffed cash register. With his hand on the paper money, about to pull it out, he stopped and searched for her reflection in the mirror. He found her. She was staring back. He looked away. "Dog-gone it." Since he had done it before, he didn't think she'd notice. He looked again. She waved. He couldn't resist. He smiled.

"Gosh, he wondered, "who knows what she's thinking?"

Sam's athleticism, good looks, and outgoing personality had always won him accolades and female admirers. But none had won his heart. His interest leaned toward Rachael from their first meeting. Now, he looked forward to seeing her every day, even if only a word or two were spoken.

Chuckling to himself, Sam thought, "I either have to ask her out or fire her."

He liked seeing her. He liked the sound of her voice and laughter--even the sounds of her walk. Never had he felt this way before. And even though she treated him with polite indifference, she affected him in ways he could not define. He noticed that his habit of speaking softly made her lean in to catch his words—and she would look back and forth from his lips to his eyes.

On payday, while Sam was sitting with her at the bar reconciling her hours, she wore "the blouse," the one with the loose buttonholes. As usual, the top button had come undone. Visible were the delectable details of her neck and collarbone, and below, delightful freckles and the hint of cleavage. Feeling frisky, he spoke softer than usual, mumbling nonsense. She leaned in closer, and he got a quick peek of the swell of her upper breasts.

"Yikes," she wondered, "what did he do?" And their lips were so close they could have kissed. Sam's intention was not to look again, but he didn't catch himself in time and did. In glancing away from Sam's face toward the mirror, she saw his behavior. An unexpected rush of pleasure seized her, surprising herself—while Sam was chagrined--caught looking down her blouse.

Chapter Twenty-Three: Morgan and Father Raffael Bouvier

Morgan did go to services at St. Mark's Cathedral and occasionally sat through two. She participated in one communion. If she had taken two, he wouldn't mind. When handing her the wafer, her fingers brushed the top of his hand. Anticipating the touch and her upward glance, he looked for her.

After three Sundays, Morgan visited the rectory offices. She had decided that to increase their contacts, a request for counseling would work. Hearing her voice, he came out to greet her. She explained that she was physically and emotionally stressed because of the Great Depression. Sometimes, she thought of suicide but could not bear to leave her father alone, even though he was abusive. Also, she wanted to talk about her mother.

During the Depression, many men abandoned their families, but it was her mother who left them. Almost three years prior, she prepared breakfast, as usual, rubbed her husband's back, kissed and hugged him. Then she took the car, supposedly to visit a friend. Pulling out of the driveway, she stopped, hugged Morgan, and cryptically told her to take care of her sister. She pulled into the street and waved. That was the last time Morgan saw her mother and the car.

Three days after Christmas, the sessions began. It was raining. She had no umbrella. Still, she came, wet, out of breath, and on time. Feeling sorry for her, he gave her an umbrella and two dollars. To see how happy it made her made him sad, sad at her condition.

Father Raffael and Morgan met every other week and then, at her request, once a week. Counseling primarily concerned her faith. God, she said, wasn't helping her relationship with her father, and she was stressed about her father's daily disappointments at the docks. Work was scant before. Maybe he wasn't chosen because he looked elderly. Now it was virtually non-existent. There was talk of a major strike along the entire west coast of California, and the worry that scabs would take his job. His situation had worsened, and he was cranky, terribly upset, and was taking his frustrations out on her--yelling and shaking her. Would Father Raffael be so kind, she asked, as to allow her to come for counseling? Father Raffael felt that this was why God had chosen him to serve, to minister to people like Morgan. When she left, he was content. So was she.

Their meetings graduated to an occasional lunch and dinner. He was aware that she kept her eyes on him. He was flattered. He didn't know when it happened, but he eagerly looked forward to each meeting. Later, mulling it over, he thought it began when they first met. He thought of her incessantly during the day. Dreams of her invaded his sleep, and he began wondering about life outside the Church—outside the vows of chastity. What, he mused, would it be like to be married, have children, and love? He questioned his attraction to Morgan and the need for counseling. Were her complaints actual or a ruse to visit? After the first session, he believed her to be emotionally well and that her father was probably a kind man going through a highly stressful time. Even though she came with stories whose veracity he doubted, he listened, commiserated, and counseled. During one session, he swiveled his chair away so she wouldn't see that he was suppressing laughter.

Enthusiastically, Morgan was in the midst of her story of shoplifting: "I took the smallest chicken from the ice chest and put it high under my dress between my thighs. But I couldn't walk. I waddled and shuffled. And it was freezing. Just as I was leaning over the ice chest, putting it back, Mr. Simmons came up behind me and scared the cush out of me. I jumped, and a can of beans fell out of my bloomers. Oh, I'm sorry, I shouldn't have said that."

143

With an image of thighs and a can of beans hitting the floor, Father Rafael asked, "Then, what happened?"

"I guess the look on my face was so funny, Mr. Simmons laughed. Well, I had the two silver dollars you gave me. I told him I was sorry and would pay. He wanted to know where I got it. I told him the truth that a Priest gave it to me. Then, he gave me everything, including the chicken, for 75 cents. He tossed in another can for free and warned me that some people are in such dire straits that they steal and go to jail. Then he told me to go home. 'Go, Go,' he said and was still laughing when I left. I guess I'm lucky that he's known me since I was a kid."

"So, you had the two dollars I gave you last month?"

"Yes, I kept it because you were so nice. Silly maybe, but I did."

Raffael wondered if her story was true. Many were destitute and did steal.

Sitting across from her in his office, Father Raffael looked at her appraisingly. She was wearing red lipstick and a bit of blush; her smooth, unblemished skin glowed, and she radiated a feeling as if inwardly smiling. Her wheat-colored hair was freshly washed—lush and thick with a natural curl. Lately, he had desires to play with her warm honey toned hair, and to caress her. And her lips—he wanted to kiss her.

Now that he suspected that some of Morgan's stories, if not all, were concocted, he had to be alert. Maybe she was a habitual liar. As these thoughts went through his mind, he realized he didn't care. Each visit was a joy. After each, he looked at her exquisite ankles, all he could see under her long dress, and wondered. Then, he would pray.

Wanting her to continue a story, he said, "Tell me, my child," then stopped. "I apologize. You are not a child. I'm being pompous."

"It's fine, Father; you are a priest and older."

144

He winced, offended that she considered him old. "Is 31 old?" His heart sank while Morgan's rose as she saw that she got a rise out of him. She didn't care how old he was.

Morgan was seriously after this man and had the Church as her opponent. To her delight, she had found that he could flirt. It was only a matter of time. God, she believed, would forgive her. He would understand. He would have so much love in his heart, more than she could ever imagine; if he had a heart in the conventional sense, he would allow them to marry. Despite what the Bible said, she didn't believe there was a hell in the middle of the earth; it was just too silly. She read the Bible and the Catechism--the handbook of Catholic religious doctrine but considered herself to be a free thinker.

Unlike her father and most Catholics, Morgan believed in evolution, and wondered how it and religions conjoined. She decided it was beyond her ken and wouldn't worry about it. She was a regular at mass and prayed daily, asking for the Lord's intervention to make things better, primarily for her father and her mother, wherever she might be. Although she prayed, she wondered if prayer was worthwhile. God didn't seem to pay much attention to hers. Also, she did want to marry in the Church and wanted her children baptized as Catholics. "Hmmm," she thought. "If Father Raffael marries, he'll be excommunicated. Well, I'll have to think about that."

Before being hired at The Palace Station Cafe, Morgan applied at the J.C. Penny department store but was rejected, perhaps because of her tired-looking clothes. If she was going to get a job servicing customers, she had to be presentable. She needed money to buy a good dress. As a result, she went to Saint Joseph's to ask for alms for the poor. This is where she worshiped. A young priest told her that she would be given money, but first, she had to confess her sins.

She had told nobody, not even Rachael. He had tried for a sexual act, for gosh sakes. Instead of taking her to the confessional, he stood and walked around his desk towards her. His pants were unbuttoned and hanging loosely from his hips. And there "It" was staring her in the face. When he reached for her, she hit his chest so hard that his skull cap fell off, and he made a noise like an oomph. She ran out of there so fast that she almost lost a shoe—but still, while flashing past the font of holy water, she dipped her finger and performed the sign of the cross. Outside, safe, and nervously giggling, she thought, "What nerve. And he yelled after me to wait, that he would give me $1.00. Forget it. Maybe I'd take $1,000 for the indignation—the creep, and he had the nerve to say he would pray for my sins—cute, but a creep, a real jerk. If he wants sex, he should go into another line of work."

After having met Father Raffael, Morgan went to Saint Mark's Cathedral. She admired his intelligence, his cultured voice, almost like a smoker's voice with a French accent, and he stood tall and regal. She liked his black hair and blue eyes, and warm smiles. He was interested in what she had to say, and "he touches me when he thinks I don't notice." Thoughts passed through her mind that they would have cute children. She mused, "Mr. and Mrs. Father Raffael Bouvier. Oops, we'll drop the Father!" She wondered about his parents in Spain on the border of France. Tailors, he said.

Although Morgan looked forward to the counseling sessions, she was getting hard-pressed to develop concocted stories of strife, emotional depression, and problems with her father. He loved her dearly and was not the ogre she described. They had difficulties, but she was positive, even happy, despite it all. They were getting by, and she believed things would improve in time. Franklin D. Roosevelt, the president, promised a "New Deal." But she had to keep her stories straight. Father Raffael occasionally

146

returned to her earlier travails. Some she couldn't recall, much to his amusement. She asked if he was trying to trick her. He replied, "No, not at all."

Thanks to Rachael, she worked at the Palace Station Cafe, and her savings were enough to rent a small room at a house. Actually, it was a one-car garage converted into a living space. Its furniture consisted of two chairs and twin beds. But no kitchen or bathroom. In the house lived a young couple and one child. It was a tight fit, but the rent was right. Use of the kitchen was shared and limited to twice a day, in the morning from 5:30 to 7:30 a.m. and in the evening from 7:00 to 8:30 p.m. The bathroom was available all day, but she had to knock at the side door before entering.

When Father Raffael heard of these limitations, he was appalled, but Morgan was cheerful, even optimistic. Life was pretty good as far as she was concerned and getting better. He offered to loan her money for an actual apartment. She declined. He offered money as a gift. Again, she refused, saying the offer was kind but that she and her dad would manage. She asked, "Do you have so much money that you can give it to someone you barely know?"

Chapter Twenty-Four: Sweet Agony

While shaving and feeling good, Father Raffael thought of a recurring dream. He and Morgan stood on a balcony in their home in Spain. They had views of rolling meadows, vineyards, and children playing—theirs. His Labrador, German Shepherds, and his old Spanish mastiff were with them.

Shaving completed, he dressed in civilian clothes, black shoes, black slacks, a black shirt, and a priestly white collar.

147

First, he would pray before meeting Morgan. It was a beautiful day. A soft breeze caressed his skin, birds were chirping, hummingbirds were flitting at the trumpet vines, walks were swept clean, the sun was shining, and the air was clean and pure. The cathedral was magnificent, or was he cheerful because he was to meet Morgan for lunch? Light beams illuminating the cathedral streamed through the stained-glass windows. Prayers completed, he opened his eyes. Standing waiting was Father Raul Morrel, his friend, and confidant.

"Father Raffael," he said, "a word, please. Let's talk." Sitting together, Father Raul informed Raffael that others in the church were talking about his relationship with Morgan, saying cruel things. "They're saying she's a loose and sinful woman intent on stealing you away. I've had some terrible arguments in your defense, but it does no good. Rightly or wrongly, your reputation is sullied."

Raffael replied, "I've been counseling the young lady, that is all. If anyone thinks differently, they should come to me."

"I apologize, but we're friends. I thought you should know. Umm, one more thing. The gossip is that the monsignor has put a bug into the bishop's ear. He says you should be sequestered in the prayer cell to save your soul until you come to your senses. He should talk. Everyone knows he's been having an affair for years, and that little boy he takes for walks looks like him."

Raffael reflected on Father Raul's words. They irritated, but he was confident that neither he nor Morgan had done anything so improper as to be censored. Nonetheless, his cheerful mood had evaporated.

Walking to Washington Square, Father Raffael reflected on his relationship with Morgan. He questioned himself and Morgan. "No, she's just a friend," he mused. But Father Raul was correct. He did spend a good deal of time with her. Daily he thought of her, and it was disturbing to think of life outside the Church—to dream of love.

Twice they had taken the Eureka ferry across the bay with Sam and Rachael to Sausalito, a small town once populated by artist settlers. They had cheerful talks and laughter and walked so closely together he might as well have had his arm around her shoulders or held hands. If they received questioning stares, he quipped, "We're cousins."

She looked into his eyes, smiled happily, and joked, "Are we kissing cousins?" Amused, he grinned and didn't reply.

Father Raffael and Morgan were so compatible and in synchronicity that they knew what the other was thinking and about to do. He looked forward to their talks, walks, her quick wit, and lively dalliances over coffee, sometimes lunch or dinner, and a bottle of wine. Being with her gave him pleasure and a secure feeling of genuine friendship. He liked looking at her and hearing her voice and light laughter. Often, he listened more to the sounds of her voice than to what was said, with words, firm and soft, and with others like a caress. When together, time stood still and was always over too soon. Thoughts of life with Morgan filled his mind. Not all were chaste and distracted from priestly duties. When close, he wanted to touch her in ways forbidden. Sometimes when together, he would turn her to see something and drape his arm over her shoulders or waist and pull her close—feeling tender, innocent pleasure, or so he thought. When dining, he stroked the top of her hand, in a chaste manner, of course. She didn't seem to mind. Sitting next to her at the park with his arm draped on the backrest, he fingered her hair, thinking she wouldn't notice. Of course, she did. "Am I so sinful?" he wondered.

Seeing his approach, Morgan stood from the bench and waited. Before he could react, she hugged him and brushed his cheek with hers. He stiffened and wondered if she indeed had a crush on him. Smiling weakly, he pushed her away. Other women made advances, and he handled the situations gently and firmly. Never had he responded in a way that would lead anyone on. Yet here he was with Morgan.

On the table were two glasses of wine and one cup of coffee. He had gulped his wine and ordered the coffee. Distracted by Father Raul's comments, he added more sugar to his coffee. He had said hardly a word. Gazing at her golden hair, dark brown eyes, throat, lips, hands, and fighting desires to take her in his arms, he thought, "Father Raul warned me. Maybe he's right."

Following his eyes, Morgan realized, "Why, he's studying me!" Deliberately, she moved a hand to her hair. His eyes followed. She touched her lips. His eyes followed. She put her hand to her heart. His eyes followed. A sweet, sad mellow feeling of love filled her, almost making her cry. She thought, "He's beautiful. But something is wrong."

Breaking his concentration, she asked, "Father, you're staring. Is something wrong with my face or my hair?"

"Sorry, yes, I mean no, you're fine." To himself, he thought, "Too fine."

"Am I boring?"

Too quickly and distracted by his thoughts, he said, "Oh no, my child." In his vexation, he had reverted to calling her a child. Mentally, he chastised himself. "Am I ever going to get over being pompous?" He took another sip of coffee, made a face of distaste, and stood.

"What's wrong?" She asked.

Looking at her sweet face, he thought, "What's wrong? I'm in love with you." Instead, he said, "I have to get back."

The visit was short, 37 minutes, and he was abrupt, on edge, and eager to flee. There was no lunch. Following him outside, she reached for an

150

embrace. Recoiling, he excused himself and hurriedly walked away. In confusion, she watched until he turned the corner.

Returning to the Cathedral, striding fast as if to distance himself from trouble, Raffael worried. And his heart hurt, aching like his life force was sweetly bleeding out. He wondered, "Is this a broken heart?"

Chapter Twenty-Five: Morgan And Sarah

"Honey?"

Morgan's eyes, riveted on Raffael, was startled. It was the homeless woman, Sarah.

"Oh, Sarah, don't sneak up on me."

"Honey, you're concentrating so hard on that man; if the Union Pacific came through, you wouldn't notice. Be careful."

"What do you mean?"

"Your feelings are on your face. You love him, and he doesn't have a clue. He doesn't know, but he's in love with you."

As a homeless person, Sarah was well known. Often messy, but clean. Today she was neat and clean. Her hair was brushed. Her eyes were bright, and her speech was clear. Known on the street as a former prostitute, one much sought after who had abruptly quit, she briefly sought employment in fashionable shops and was surprised to find that she had a sizable reputation. The respectable crowd didn't give her a chance at the preferable jobs. So, temporarily, she lived on handouts, on charity. She felt free and resolved to re-enter conventional life after a time of penance for her "sinful" life as a prostitute.

"No, Sarah, I don't think so."

Sarah replied, "He's rigid. He's stuck in the tenets of the Church and can't break free. He might never know. He can't admit to loving, not our kind. The Church is his life. It has him by the short hairs--but look at how he looks at you."

"Don't talk like that. But am I so obvious?"

"I'm only a bag lady, but I think so. If you ever want to talk, I'm here."

"You're more than that. I've heard about you. How about now?"

Chapter Twenty-Six: Failed Appointment

Five days later, Morgan was scheduled to keep a counseling appointment with Father Raffael. She arrived with a sense of foreboding. She had not heard from him indicating anything different, but he had missed two coffee dates—dates that needed no reminding.

On arrival, it was Father Raul Morrel who was waiting. Raffael had asked him to substitute. Her heart sank. She understood. Raffael didn't want to see her. "No, I'll go," she said. Father Raul lightly touched her hand and asked if he could be of any help. "No, tell him I won't be coming again. Tell him it has nothing to do with him. Tell him I've met someone—someone crazy about me. Tell him goodbye and thank him for spending time with me. Tell him I don't need him anymore."

"Is there anything else?"

"Yes. Tell him he's a coward. Tell him anything you want.
No, don't tell him anything." Turning away, she exited through the side door, and walked briskly through the courtyard.

Father Raffael, standing at an upstairs window of the dormitory, watched her pass. Walking with her head lowered, she ran her fingers through her hair. His heart ached at his loss and her imagined pain, but he was optimistic that he had done the right thing. "Then why," he mused, "do I feel so wretched, and so….so sad?"

Father Raul told Raffael everything, including that he was a coward and had found a man who loved her. Raffael's heart was heavy, but he had been warned. "Am I a coward?" he wondered. What tormented him, possessed him, was that she had a new love. "Was he kissing her? Did they laugh together, maybe at him? Is he tall, short, thin, athletic, intelligent, with a sense of humor? Was he holding her hand? Did she kiss him? Would he take care of her?" And . . . "When she hugs him, does she think of me?"

Days passed, and his peers continued their criticism. He was, they said, walking around in a daze like he was in love. They whispered loud enough for him to hear. Feeling emotionally heavy, he confronted those he could identify, but it did no good.

The voice droned on about prayer, the rosary, and something else Raffael missed. Sitting in counseling with his Excellency Bishop Daniel O'Malley, Raffael tried to listen, but his mind couldn't concentrate. The bishop, commiserating with Raffael's dilemma and the loss of a parishioner, was saying that it was not unusual for women to get attached to a priest and to believe they were in love.

Asked if he was in love, Raffael lied and said, "No, not at all, only sincere friendship."

"Did you ever kiss or do anything else?" The bishop asked.

"No," Raffael replied and thought, "I wanted to."

The bishop, looking solemn, revealed something about himself, something he had never shared before with anyone, not even in confession. "Love," he said, "sometimes happens when you least expect it. It happened to me once—a real affair of the heart. We became undeniably attached. I stopped it."

Raffael asked if he had regrets. The bishop paused and replied. "It was the proper outcome. She went to another parish. Seven years later, I accidentally ran into Rose. That was her name. She was pushing a baby carriage with a baby dressed in pink. A little boy was by her side holding her hand."

Raffael asked for his reaction. The bishop heavily cleared his throat, adjusted his posture, and moved some papers aside. As if someone else was in the room, he stared past Raffael's shoulder and sat very still, pensive, wondering how candid he should be and the words to use.

"Frankly, it was a shock to see her. She was polite but uneasy and didn't want to talk. Feelings arose that I thought I had overcome. Yes, I felt pangs of sadness. But I knew I had done the right thing, serving the Church and its flock instead of her. But there she was. She didn't even say my name. It was uncomfortable. After a few words, I watched her walk away like she had years before. The image doesn't fade. She was wearing blue. Funny, she was some yards away when she turned. She ruffled her son's hair and had him look at me. She said something to him. He waved. Can you imagine? That cute little boy waved—to me." The bishop shook his head in wonder. "Until then, I hadn't paid much attention to him. He was about seven. His hair, his eyes—he looked like, like. . . ." With a deep sigh and an "Oh, well," he continued. "Rose gave me a little wave. I never saw her again. It is puzzling that I still think of her after so many years."

The bishop's face looked forlorn, sad, and lost. The corners of his mouth turned down. Rubbing his heart, he swiveled his chair toward the window behind him. Raffael wondered if he was being dismissed and if he should leave. Unsure, he waited. Finally, as he was about to leave, the bishop turned back. With his mouth turned down, almost scowling, he swept his hand over his desk as if removing dust, back and forth, back and forth, in little sweeping motions. Then, lifting his eyes to Raffael's, and, with a mirthless smile, said, "Evidently, she married. And I became a bishop. I have this beautiful cathedral, this office, and the gift of a jeweled cross from the pope. I made the correct choice. And now, my son, so should you. Observe the Lord's direction and choose correctly, as I did, to serve."

The talk with the bishop did not help. Raffael wondered if the bishop meant to give two meanings, one to stay with the Church and the other to follow his heart. It had been about 30 years since the bishop had last seen Rose, and he had never forgotten. And the little boy might have been his son.

For Raffael, thoughts of years of service to the Church, growing old, walking the same halls day after day, with the same dull routines, and being transferred from parish to parish seemed bleak. There was no consolation. Oh, sweet misery. And every time he talked to God, he spoke of Morgan. The more he tried to put her out of his mind, the more his longing grew. He missed her every moment, every day, and he was jealous of her new love. Her comment about his cowardice bothered him, and he wondered, "Does she think of me?"

Raffael went to the chapel to pray. He couldn't concentrate and instead reflected on Morgan. Prayer did not help. He wondered if he was being tested. He tried to believe, but emotional pain permeated his entire being. He could not understand. Still hoping for strength and peace, he prayed for answers. After prayer, he sat at the pew and bent forward. With his eyes on his shoes, he rehashed how he had come to this situation.

On their third meeting, Morgan walked into his office and hugged him. Astonished, he had blushed to his ears.

She asked if it was permissible. Unnerved, he had said, "Umm, oooh, probably, I guess so." After that, they hugged in arriving and departing, and he was disappointed if one was missed.

And there was that day in the rectory office. It had unnerved him. It should have warned him off. She had stepped to his chest and embraced him affectionally. It sent his mind and body reeling, and if she had not broken their embrace, he would have stood there forever. Afterward, he wondered about the extent of the hug. "Did she ever so slightly rub my back? Was it brief or semi-brief? Had she meant to do it affectionally, or was it an accident? Did I caress her hair? Did I kiss her cheek? Was it my imagination?" Both acted as if nothing had happened, and the moment passed. But after that, they brushed hands and bodies, and she never seemed to mind. Walking together, they would smile, pull apart, and do it again.

Oh, but there was that other time. It was the worst, the one he rejected, did not want to admit, couldn't resolve, and couldn't forget. He had lost his mind. After the last service, Morgan lingered until he finished his greetings with departing parishioners. She asked if she could have a counseling session—right then if he had the time. He did. They walked from the Cathedral to the rectory, to his shared office. Stepping in behind her, he closed the door. When he turned, he was caught totally off guard. Stepping to his chest, she nestled her head while emitting a sound like purring. It was a warm hug with both arms wrapped around his mid-back.

He questioned, "It was chaste, wasn't it?" But what he had not expected was that he was aroused. She felt it through his robes, and a powerful primal urge possessed him---and her. While his mind went elsewhere, she reached down to determine if what she felt was real. It was, and with her touch, his body and emotions froze like a tuning fork waiting. He didn't know what to do, so he stood still, frozen in place. She looked into his eyes, lifted his robes, and fumbled. Her lips parted with uplifted eyes towards his, and her breathing quickened. So did his. She never looked down. She locked her eyes on his and began a slow, delicate examining motion with her fingers.

He put his hands on her arms to push her away but did not. The feelings were exquisite. Standing so still and quiet, she looked into his eyes and

156

said, "Father, breathe." He couldn't take it any longer. His hand moved to her breasts.

"Oh God," he thought, "I'm sinning, and just after my sermon." Her gentle fingers moved until he stumbled forward, shuddering.

Morgan steadied his movement, dropped the robe, and shyly smiled, thinking she had done the unforgivable. She looked like she was about to speak. She also appeared stricken with mortification and about to run. She turned to leave.

"Morgan," he said, "don't go. Do not fault yourself. If there is blame, it is mine. I'm the one in authority and couldn't control myself. I gave myself willingly to bodily pleasure. Perhaps, we, I, have sinned, but not gravely. We're young, and even children of God, starting with Adam and Eve, are tempted. God knows and understands. Let's forget this ever happened. Now, let's talk about your problems."

Morgan noticed and appreciated that Raffael had said nothing about her lack of control.

Stiff and awkward, they talked, acted as if nothing had happened, and agreed to meet again. Later, neither could recall the words spoken during counseling.

Walking home, there was one thing Morgan wondered about. Aside from the incredible excitement of feeling the beating of his heart and the silky smoothness of his skin, it was that they had not kissed. Funny, as if kissing was more intimate than what had transpired. Something exciting and exquisite had happened and left a warm feeling. There was also a sad feeling. She didn't blame him, not at all. If anyone was to blame in the heat of the moment, she was. She softly touched her fingers to her lips and sighed, "Babies."

Following Morgan's departure, Raffael was distressed and reprimanded himself for his lack of control. Was he remorseful? He should be, but wasn't, which bothered him. He was a priest and had succumbed to the acts of the flesh. Falling to his knees, he prayed. In subsequent meetings with Morgan, this incident had seemingly never happened. Of course, they both played it over in their minds repeatedly. There had been other times when she had hugged him, and he felt aroused, but he didn't think she had noticed. "Or had she?" He considered breaking off but quickly put those thoughts aside.

Raffael rationalized that God was testing him to make him grow in the world's knowledge and the temptations of the flesh. He would rise in awareness and become stronger. The lessons, he reasoned, would serve him well when counseling.

"The Lord," he mused, "is using Morgan to make me a better man." In prayer, he asked God to take away his longing for her or make it less. Then came the day Father Raul Morrel warned him, and he had to admit he had been deluding himself.

Raffael's time with Morgan had ended, but emotional agony drove him to see her one more time. Perhaps, he wondered, if he confessed his muddled thoughts; if she told him of her love for this other man, he could forget her and live in peace as before. He reflected on his feelings, trying to sort them out to a positive conclusion. Prayer had done no good. "What," he wondered, "is God's plan?"

Father Raul asked, "Do you believe God has his hand in everything? If so, you have to trust, and it will be revealed." Raffael wasn't convinced, and wondered how long he had to wait, how long he would be racked with regret and sorrow over love?

There had been no contact with Morgan for 21 days. He wanted to see her once more but questioned his motives. Father Raul agreed. A final meeting might serve them well but advised that Raffael should speak the absolute truth, even if painful. Father Raul asked, "Do you her," and if so

158

would he tell her? Raffael said he didn't know. In any case, all efforts to contact her had failed. He had left messages with her father. She did not respond. After 27 days, unable to stand it any longer, he returned to Washington Square, hoping to run into her.

Father Raffael tried to appear nonchalant, but a downcast look had taken over his mind and body. Morgan had disappeared from the park, but on the 37th day, he saw her across the park walking toward the Italian district. She saw him. He waved. She saw, picked up her pace, and walked on. His hand was still up in mid-wave. Slowly, he lowered his hand, crushed. It flattened his day more than before. With mild weather, falling leaves, and a sweet soft breeze touching and caressing his skin, the day was amazingly beautiful, but not for him. He passed a young couple lying on the grass, running their hands over a carpet of tiny yellow dandelions. He and Morgan had done this when they were happy. Across the street, fronting the stores, multi-colored flowers were on display. He was unaffected. His mind was on Morgan. Feeling drained, his heart aching with longing, he crossed the street to Dominick's, thinking a glass of wine would calm him.

After downing two glasses, he stood and returned to the park to a bench where they often sat. Dogs played, reminding him of the joyful day when he and Morgan watched two dogs frolicking. They had sat close, legs touching, watching the dogs rolling over each other, nuzzling and licking muzzles like lovers. And Morgan was crossing and re-crossing her legs. He was fascinated. Her full-length forest green cotton dress revealed her delicate ankles and smooth, beautiful skin. He wanted to put his hand on her thigh. She was talking about something he couldn't recall. To his ears, her voice was music. As if reading his mind, she clasped his hand and brought it to her heart. For a second, he thought she might kiss him. Oh, sweet delirium. She must have purposely tempted him, but he didn't care.

159

Torn, and wanting to hold her and shout his love, he questioned if he would ever feel free again.

Now, on this beautiful day, alone, reflecting, he lifted his eyes and looked in the direction Morgan had walked. Then, as if his feet had their own will, instead of returning to the Cathedral, he walked through Little Italy, through Chinatown, and along the Embarcadero, toward the Palace Station Cafe. Unaware of his turmoil, soldiers guarding the waterfront from longshoremen waved cheery greetings and cried out, asking for blessings.

Upon entering the Palace Station, all eyes---Sam behind the bar, and Rachael, Jessica, Caesar, and Gus---looked to Raffael and Morgan and away, embarrassed for him.

With a dismissive look at Raffael, Morgan said, "Gus, tell him to go away." Then, she turned and went into the back room.

Raffael thought, "She must hate me."

Gus walked him out, put his hand on his shoulder, and apologized.

"Gus," Raffael said, "It's not your fault. Tell Morgan I'm sorry. Tell her I miss her."

As Raffael walked away, Gus gazed at his departing back. Barely perceptible and then more noticeable, Raffael's shoulders shook, and he wiped his eyes. Looking thoughtful, Gus went back inside.

"What did he say?" Morgan asked.

"He said to tell you he was sorry."

"Well, I guess that's it."

"Yes, but, well, uh . ."

"What? Tell me!"

Gus, feeling emotion, cleared his throat. "He was crying. He said he misses you."

"Ooooh, no!"

160

Chapter Twenty-Seven: Late Breakfast

Sipping coffee, Morgan and Sarah glanced out the window. With a clear view from Dominick's Café, they could see the comings and goings of Washington Square. Thoroughly enjoying their newfound friendship, they met a minimum of twice a week. Morgan commented that Sarah was looking better every time she saw her.

"Yes, I have a benefactor—Captain Blodger. One evening, he was injured, and I helped him to his ship. A few days later, he sent someone to give me four silver dollars. Now we get together fairly often. With the strike going on, he can't work. No ships are going out or coming in, so he spends his days waiting for the end of the strike. Although he's quite shy and awkward, he looks for me and pretends he's not. He brings me flowers. He says he finds them, but I think he's lying. Now, I've made it easy. Instead of having to look for me, I wait on the bench under the olive trees every day at three. Usually, he comes.

He isn't pretty and looks rough, but I think he's cute and a softy. His name is Edger, Ed, about 40, maybe younger, maybe older."

"Isn't he too old for you? What does he want?" Morgan asked.

"Nothing, I guess, except friendship and my company. I don't think he's old. I like his hands. I like his craggy face, and I like the way he looks at me, and who knows when our maker is coming? He's decent. He's taken me shopping for clothes and food. We talk a lot. And he's strong. One night in the park, I saw this shadowy figure going from one sleeping person to another. It was Ed, looking for me. I was half asleep when he picked me up. Afterward, I thought about it. He cares about me. Well, anyway, I thought it was romantic. He carried me back to his ship and put me to bed, and tucked me in. I don't know where he slept. He doesn't ask for anything. He looks for me at night to see that I'm safe. I am. Families sleep in the park. Most I know. We look after each other. Well, anyway, Ed has come looking for me so often that he got me a job at Lee's Chinese restaurant. I'm the only white woman there, but we get along fine. I have a small room in the back, next to the kitchen. That's where I sleep."

She did not say Blodger was paying her wages and room and board because she did not know. Her duties consisted of menial cleanup work and cook's helper. It was a start. She took the job but intended to stay only until Stephanie's boyfriend, David Elder, got her a job at City of Paris, the prestigious department store at Union Square. Blodger was displeased. He didn't like Elder.

"Look," Sarah said, "Here he comes, right on time." Father Raffael Bouvier entered the park and looked around without enthusiasm, looking lost.

"Yes," I see him. Do you think he looks all right?"

"No, the man is pitiful. You know, he's looking for you. You should talk to him. Tell him to get serious or to get on with his life in the Church."

"I don't think he cares, not enough. He'll forget me."

"He might give you up, but he'll never forget you."

"Let's forget him. Tell me about your life at Ramona's."

Sarah told her story: When the depression hit, Sarah's parents had financial problems. Her father owned a hardware store. Business had drastically fallen off. In trouble, he sold it while it still had equity. Now, he worked part-time at the store he had previously owned. They had been solidly middle class, but the depression reduced them to bare subsistence living, careful with their money. And they didn't waste a bit of food. Yet,

162

her parents continued to maintain appearances they couldn't afford. Sarah was told to help out. She quit college. She wanted to become a teacher. Quitting didn't help. She couldn't find employment, not in South Carolina. She heard there were more jobs in the West than in the East, so she came to San Francisco.

She and Sue Ellen, a teenager she met on their journey, ate in soup kitchens, and earned money any way they could, including picking fruit and eventually small sex acts, like showing their breasts. Sometimes, they allowed fondling. What they did was to survive, for spending money, food, and a clean bed. In an apple orchard, both tried sexual intercourse for the first time. It was with rosy-cheeked teenage boys working as hard as any man. It was also their first time.

They looked outside. Father Raffael was making a second desultory circuit around the park. A woman stopped him and gestured at her little girl. Raffael placed his hand on the child's head, perhaps giving a blessing, and said a few words. Morgan and Sarah turned back to each other.

Sarah resumed her story: Her southern accent, youth, and beauty attracted the well-to-do. Like her friend, Stephanie, she was a favorite at Ramona's and limited herself to the most mannerly men. She was earning an obscene amount of money and living well. However, her moral and religious upbringing never gave her peace. She felt guilty, soiled, and repulsed by her weakness for security. She did not like the secretions of the men on her body, worried about disease, and always washed as quickly as possible. It was not what she had expected in life. She wanted a husband and children and a family of relatives and friends.

Sarah knew that many prostitutes were intelligent. Many married. Some became successful in business, entered sophisticated society, and engaged in philanthropic causes, like Ramona. This is what she should have worked for, but Sarah first thought of her parents, and they cut her off when they

163

found out how she earned her money. Nonetheless, they continued taking it.

Unable to tolerate men paying for sex, panting over her, she couldn't take it anymore. After an offhand comment at Ramona's about growing old in the profession, with her breasts hanging down, and ending up in one of the cheap alley cribs, she ran into the unknown without a place to go and little money. "I thought, if not now, when?"

"Was it awful? I mean, your first night alone?" Morgan asked.

"That first night here in the park, in expensive clothing, it was horrid. I was propositioned so many times, I can't say. Finally, to get some sleep, I gave in to a one-eyed, bald, toothless old geezer for 15 cents. He was so ugly, hair was growing out of a mole on the tip of his nose, and snot was running down."

Making a face, Morgan exclaimed, "Oh no, how terrible. You didn't really, did you?"

"Well, what could I do? That's all he had." Barely surpassing a smile, Sarah tapped Morgan's hand and added, "You're right; I didn't. I'm joking. It was peaceful. I never intended to be a street person. I think I'm doing it to atone for my sins. But lately, I'm thinking perhaps I've punished myself enough."

Taking bites and sips of their food and drinks, they looked at each other and outside at Father Raffael.

"Morgan, I think you should talk to him. Or maybe, we should shoot him to put him out of his misery."

"Yes, I think I better. He came to the Palace Station, but I wouldn't talk to him. He looks so sad. Sarah, will you deliver a message for me?"

After visiting with Sarah, Morgan went to the Palace Station Cafe. There, she confided in Rachael.

"Well, I'm not Catholic," Rachael said, "and I've always thought it was unreasonable for them to have that rule about not marrying. But they do take it seriously. What are you going to do?"

"I'll meet him one last time. We'll be civil and say our goodbyes. I'll do it, but I know it will be hard. I've been mean and miss him. One day, we were sitting on the grass, and he knelt to tie my shoelace. I touched his hair. He looked up at me with the sweetest smile. Right then, I loved him so much that my heart ached. But it's probably all my imagination."

So it was that Sarah stood one day in the path of Father Raffael as he circumvented the park. He started to walk around her, but she moved to block his way. Sighing, he said, "Yes, Sarah?"

"Morgan will meet you Thursday at 10:00 a.m. at the cathedral."

"No, not then. I have other commitments."

"Listen, Father, that's it, that's the time. You're not getting another chance. If you let her go, you're an idiot."

With a thin smile, he agreed. "All right, Thursday, at 10:00."

Chapter Twenty-Eight: Chinese Elders

David Elder walked the long stone floor hallway listening to his footfalls and thinking of the two prominent Chinese elders, Shen Lee and Zhang Yi, wondering if they were there to ask for business advice or help in some other way.

The Chinese community, in self-preservation, resorted to activities that skirted the law. Knowing that Elder disliked discrimination against minorities and was inclined to help the oppressed, they had a situation that called for his help. They knew he was respected in many circles, even by the infamous, and had authority in circles they did not.

In keeping with tradition, the Chinese addressed each other by speaking the family name first, followed by the given name. There were exceptions.

As a sign of respect for Elder and Abe, they asked to be called by their given names, Lee and Yi.

It had been well over a year since they last met, and it was because of young competing Tong members terrorizing shop owners. Lee and Yi could not go to the San Francisco City leaders or police. These entities did not concern themselves with the Chinese unless they became a nuisance to the white community.

Lee and Yi could have confined the matter to Chinatown, but to avoid an internecine war, they sought Elder's help. There were two chief competing miscreants. They hoped they would disappear or be convinced not to be greedy. Abe took care of the matter. He had lunch with a member of the San Francisco Lanza Mafia family. Two nights later, the targeted individuals were grabbed off the street and taken to a remote part of the bay. Under a clear night sky, they were pushed to the edge of lapping water and told to wade in. Terrified and shaking, they waited to be executed. Standing in the undulating water to their waists, fighting to keep their balance, they expected to be shot. "All right, turn around," they were instructed. Two burly men, with another standing off some distance by the car, pointed revolvers at their faces. In no uncertain terms, the Tong boys were given the choice of being reasonable in their extortion of merchants or dying. They chose the former. Without another word, the men drove off. Frightened, the boys looked at each other, made peace, and together found their way home. The matter was resolved.

Almost two years later, as Elder entered the study, Shen Lee and Zhang Yi rose from padded chairs and proffered an exquisite black lacquered engraved box. The Chinese were great gift-givers. Lowering the box to his desk, he thought, "Always polite, even though they'll try to outsmart me." And chuckling, "Maybe they will." Maia entered and served tea and sweetbreads. She looked questionably at the lamps. Elder, watching her,

166

understood, and nodded for her to adjust the lamps to subdued light. Lee and Yi courteously remained standing until she left.

"Gentlemen," Elder said, "let us relax while we wait. Abe will be along shortly. Meanwhile, tell me about your families. It's been a long time since we shared tea."

Abe arrived ten minutes later. Lee and Yi stood. Abe nodded and moved to sit on the dark leather couch. Seeing this, Elder left his chair and sat with Abe.

Abe was dressed in black woolen slacks, matching socks, cordovan leather slip-on loafers, and a white button-down shirt open at the neck. Elder looked at him and envied him for his sharp looks. Abe was meticulous in his clothes. And his body and facial features were so handsomely defined that he could wear rags and look regal. His chiseled face and strong, even teeth reminded Elder of a tintype photograph of an Egyptian king he had once seen. Abe, handsome and slender yet broad-shouldered, was imposing, and his regal bearing matched his intelligence. In conversation, words eloquently flowed. If there were strangers in their midst, they quickly realized that he was a formidable man, and above their pecking order. If stubbornly not convinced, they were when it became known that he welded considerable economic power and that he and Elder were partners and closer than family. He might be resented as a Negro, but when he spoke, men listened lest they lose out, especially concerning the economy and investments.

Seeing the contemplative way Elder looked at him, Abe asked, "What?"

"Nothing, my friend."

Lee and Yi told their story: A freighter was bound for San Francisco from Shanghai with a cargo of merchandise. The issue was that it also bore a load of humanity for the businesses and homes of San Francisco—

167

coolies, men and women, and one baby born en route. Some had paid a specified amount. But most were to be sold. Merchants, Caucasians, and Chinese were eager to buy them for cheap indentured labor.

"Are any for prostitution?" Abe asked. He was assured they were not, but he didn't believe it.

Chinatown centered on Grant Avenue and Stockton Street where the coolies would be dispersed or sold at auction, an auction that the city knew about but ignored.

The Chinese were under the heel of the white men and needed Elder, a man they trusted, to intercede on their behalf. Edgar Blodger, the captain of the Morning Glory, a tough cunning man, had double-crossed them and demanded more, even from the ones who had paid.

If Blodger's demands were not met, he would keep monies already paid and sell the coolies to the highest bidders. Because of the prevalent anti-Chinese discrimination and the illegality of their contract with Captain Blodger, they feared going to the police. Police could be bought off and weren't trusted. Two, they especially despised. One lived amongst them, Lugo Spaak. The other was Lugo's friend, Mack.

Abe asked if the matter couldn't be handled by the Chinese Consolidated Benevolent Association, which provided social and legal services. The association, they explained, was aware of the issue but chose not to be involved. It could explode and bring unwanted attention to their district. Elder and Abe understood. Everyone in San Francisco knew that slavery in Chinatown was tolerated and ignored, but not by Elder or Abe.

It was decided. Elder would negotiate with Captain Blodger. If additional payments were required, he would pay. Repayment to Elder would be money or services, as he chose. Elder demanded two conditions: Photos were to be taken and a record kept of each coolie, and their progress. He said, "I'll keep track of each, and I better not find one of

168

these women or men at the slave auction on St. Louis Alley or in one of the whore houses in Bartlett Alley or Cora's." Do you agree, Shen Lee? Do you agree, Zhang Yi?" He uttered their family names first to emphasize his meaning.

"Yes." They fully realized the meanings of Elder's words. The coolies would be under Elder's protection and watched over and aided in every way possible.

Elder walked them to the doors of the study, where Maia waited to escort them out. To Shen Lee, he said, "Something has gone unsaid. What is it?"

"Ah, yes. You are a wise man," Lee replied. "Some months ago, a young boy disappeared from a short walk from his house. He was nine. A Chinese boy. We fear he is dead. The parents grieve. Madame Zhao, of Cora Street, was his grandmother."

"I know her," Elder said.

"She offers a reward. We have witnesses who saw the boy with two police officers in a family market. One was Lugo Spaak. We know he gives you trouble. He's disrespectful and extorts money from merchants. He uses our women."

"What can I do?" Elder asked.

"You have the ear of the police. If you come into additional knowledge of this boy's disappearance, please tell us. If the men we suspect disappear, do nothing."

Chapter Twenty-Nine: Visitor From the Past

Shen and Zhang had departed. Abe and Elder had a late-night snack and said goodnight. Elder returned to the study, snapped on the desk lamp, set a fire in the fireplace, and opened his wall safe. He counted stacks of money on his desk, more than enough to meet Captain Blodger's demands.

The fireplace burned low and cast dappled shadows against the walls. The spacious, generous room was semi-dark but sufficiently at his end illuminated enough for the task.

The grand hallway was dark. Elder, hearing footsteps, called out, "Abe, is that you?" To his amazement, standing in the doorway, glaring in triumph, was Rory, Rory from the dirt, no-name town near Conroy, Texas, who, with his brother, Otis, had killed PeeWee, Elder's friend. Elder and Abe had exacted revenge against Otis, but never found Rory. And now, here he was, as mean looking, only older with straggly thinning hair, jowly--and curiously with a crust of blood in place of an eyebrow. His sneering smile revealed worn and yellowed teeth. "He still has his pink face, bloodshot eyes, and just as stupid," Elder mused.

Elder took in the thick leathery welts on the left side of Rory's pocked face, ear, and hands, like worms, and surmised that they were from burns from the fire at Ramona's years ago. It had been about 26 years, and he was intent on revenge. His dim brain had never forgotten, and he always believed that he should be the rich one living in a mansion, not David Elder. Rory had almost burnt up himself before jumping out of a flaming window. Thoughts of revenge had festered. Now he would kill.

"Yeah, it's me," Rory spat. "You look like you've seen a ghost. I'm real."

"Yeah," Elder replied, "and fatter than ever."

Waggling his revolver at the money, nervously cocking and un-cocking the hammer, "click, click," Rory motioned to the stacks of cash and said, "Put it in a bag, all of it and everything you have in the safe."

Elder's mind was racing. Maybe he could rush Rory between clicks, but his damaged ribs would slow him. Suddenly everything changed. In a blur, in rapid exchanges, Abe walked in and was knocked to the floor with a sharp blow to the head.

170

"What luck," Rory said. "I'll kill both of you." Pointing the revolver at Elder's chest, his eyes flicked to Abe, now kneeling, and back to Elder. Saying, "I'll make it quick," he lowered the barrel to the back of Abe's head.

"Hold it. Don't you want to know how Otis died?" Elder asked, stalling for time. "Also, there's something I've always wanted to say."

Rory raised the revolver.

"We dropped him down a ravine."

Full of hate and loathing, Rory's face contorted. "What's the other thing?"

"You're really stupid."

Rory cocked the hammer and fired a deafening shot at the desk, causing a long ugly scar. Savoring the moment, Rory smiled hatefully. "The next one is for you." He cocked the pistol, but in the next instant, he suffered a searing, agonizing pain in his buttocks, followed by two more in his lower back. "Aaaaahh." Screaming and leaning backward, a wild shot went into the ceiling, raining down plaster and dust. Elder and Abe rushed him. A furious tussle ensued. As fast as it started, it was over. Matteo, breathing hard, was sitting on Rory's chest, his knife sticking crookedly out of Rory's heart. Rory was still, slack-jawed—eyes open.

Elder, Abe, and Matteo looked down at the body, then at Maia watching from the door. With a fist tightly held to the nape of her robe, she nodded at her men, turned, and returned home.

Elder instructed Matteo to return to his quarters. The police would be told that Elder had killed the intruder.

"Abe, Matteo, how did you know?" Elder asked.

"Maia suddenly sat up in bed, nervous. She said that the man haunting her dreams was here—that you were in trouble. She insisted I call Matteo and to have Xavier check the grounds. She was so adamant that I came right over. In her life, she has visions, usually about danger or death. Her mother and grandmother are the same."

Chapter Thirty: Illicit Cargo

In the thick fog of night, Pier 30, 3:00 a.m., Captain Edgar Blodger led a group of coolies—25 fearful individuals, five couples, five single men, 10 single women, and a baby toward a warehouse. Thick unseen clouds drifted overhead. Moist air and drizzle covered their faces.

On each side of the coolies were Blodger's merchant seamen. Once inside, the human cargo, unable to speak English, were lined up against the wall. Two Caucasian individuals, a pretty, young woman in a dark gray overcoat, and an imposing man wearing a black wool pea coat, waited behind a metal table. The woman gave them a smile, giving them hope. On the table was an open briefcase of money. The high-ceiling cavernous warehouse was empty except for the individuals, the table, and two trucks at the far end. Canvas tarps covered the beds of the trucks. Men stood by the doors. Jessica had prevailed in her argument that she should be with her father to learn all aspects of the family business, even the unusual. Abe, Sam, and Caesar were at the trucks—also a young Chinese student from the University of San Francisco.

All those with Elder appeared calm, except a photographer. Blodger had been on edge until he saw their demeanor. Realizing they would cooperate, he was relieved. He said, "So, you're David Elder. I've heard about you. I'm Captain Edgar Blodger."

"Yes, and I know you," replied Elder.

Blodger, taken aback, didn't know what to think of this, but said, "Good. Now, to business. I'm not here to negotiate. You'll pay $100 for each!"

"Captain, you've already been paid and reneged on the deal. This is not good for your reputation."

"I don't give a damn. And anyway, this is the last time." Blodger's nervousness returned, but he forged ahead. After dickering on the price, Elder agreed to pay $100 each, with the baby thrown in for free.

The exchange began but was too slow and careful for Blodger. Two coolies at a time were moved to the table. The captain was paid. Their names were recorded in a book. The interpreter, the Chinese student politely introduced himself, handed each a sack meal, and led them to the trucks.

Agitated and with anxiety rising, Captain Blodger snapped, "It's taking too long. For the rest, I want $125 for each. Take it or leave it. If you don't like it, we'll back out of here, and I'll sell them on the street." Elder nodded. The Captain said, "Ah, too easy. Add on $25. No, add $50. That will be $175 for each."

"No," Jessica shouted, "that's not right." Knowing that her father could explode at someone trying to cheat him or not keep his word, she grabbed his arm. Elder's physicality had changed to one of menace. With eyes flashing, glowering, he appeared larger, hostile, and dangerous.

Blodger, thinking Elder was going to attack him, stepped back and looked to his men for backup.

Jessica restrained her father. Grasping his arm, she whispered in his ear, ran her hand soothingly over his back, and signaled to those behind her. Infuriated but restrained, Elder kept his glaring eyes on Blodger.

Seeing an angry dispute, five coolies came off the wall and started forward, and were pushed back. The baby cried. The mother cooed and

173

rocked the child. Contemptuously, Elder pushed the briefcase toward Blodger, saying, "Take it all!" Surprising Blodger.

"We're done," Elder said, "Are you satisfied?"

Blodger sarcastically replied, "Yeh, thank you kindly."

With a wicked smile, Elder chuckled and said, "Enjoy it while you can."

Although wondering what Elder meant, Blodger was pleased. He snapped the case closed and joined his men.

Jessica approached the woman with the baby. The mother, uncertain, shyly smiled. Jessica extended her hands palms up, hoping she was understood and motioned for the woman to follow. The young Chinese student moved to help. Excited chatter erupted amongst the coolies. Negotiations were completed, but the majority wondered if they were gaining freedom or sold into slavery. In truth, these fortunate souls didn't know that Elder's involvement forever enhanced their futures. They were under his umbrella of protection, and it would be honored.

Blodger said, "Damn, what a sight." Feeling good and thinking Elder was a fool, he snapped a departing wave and said, "Well, good luck to them and to you. Come-on boys. Let's go."

Although Blodger had said there would be no negotiation, he would have taken half of what he got. Gloating and chortling, pleased with himself over the obscene amount paid and, to boot, a bonus of an expensive leather briefcase, he followed his men out of the warehouse. "Move it; let's go." In good humor over their success, they pulled their jackets tighter, tucked in their chins, and stepped out into hail and rain bouncing off the quay.

When Blodger had entered the warehouse, two men were posted outside; three entered with him. To his surprise, the posted men were prone on the ground spread eagled. Standing over them were seven armed

174

men dressed in black. The leader, a short, diminutive man, reminded Blodger of a jockey. He giggled when he realized that this little guy, the only one wearing a hood, was the leader. It was Matteo. The other six were his son, Xavier, and five on loan from the Mafia. The sailors had immediately surrendered, not caring to shed blood, much less their own.

"Get going," Matteo snapped. They started to walk off, including Blodger, but Matteo stopped him, "Not you Captain."

"Wait, little man," Blodger blurted. "Don't be hasty. Let's negotiate."

For his comment, Matteo rammed the stock of a confiscated shotgun into his stomach. It went off, making everyone jump.

Matteo whispered, "Ay caramba!" Luckily no one was hit. Blodger bent double, gasping for breath.

Matteo handed the briefcase and sack to Xavier, and said, "Don't call me little."

Blodger was having difficulty accepting the turn of events. A few moments before, in the warehouse, he was in command.

The hail stopped, replaced by pattering rain. While gasping for breath, Blodger was taken to the ground. Blodger heard Matteo ask for a knife. Over the sounds of thunder and lightning, the snick of a switchblade knife was heard.

"Captain," Matteo said, "hold still, or it'll be worse. I'm going to cut your tendon."

"No!" Blodger screamed and struggled to be free, to fight, but it was no use. With three men holding his upper body, and two his lower, he felt a cold blade on the back of his ankle, then pressure and searing pain.

"The cut's not all the way through," Matteo said, "so get it fixed as soon as possible. Try not to put weight on it, or it'll tear. Too bad you got greedy. Mr. Elder was going to let you keep it."

"You have just enough connection to get back to your ship."

Glaring with hatred and screaming obscenities, Blodger would have snapped Matteo's neck had he been within reach. Walking away, Matteo stopped and looked back.

"One more thing, don't come looking for Mr. Elder or me. If you do, I'll cut the other tendon, or maybe I'll take a leg or fingers from that hand that's already missing one." Matteo faded into the raining darkness and left the captain grimacing in pain and frustration.

Blodger examined his leg; blood colored the cuffs of his pants. Carefully standing, he began his trek toward his ship at Pier 32. Fearful of snapping his tendon, he hopped on the good leg and slowly hobbled. The pain was subsiding. Adrenaline, he guessed. Pausing to rest, he saw a woman ahead, heavily clothed against the weather, watching. Seeing him, she closed an umbrella, rose from a squat concrete bench, and approached. No words were spoken. After looking him up and down appraisingly, she put his left arm around her shoulders, and, with her right arm around his waist, pulled him close for a secure fit. She was taller and strong. Noticeable was an odor, a combination of onions, garlic, and sweat. After helping him to the concrete bench, she lowered him carefully to a sitting position. In a soft southern accent, she introduced herself, "I'm Sarah."

Blodger didn't care who she was but nodded. She knelt and raised his pant leg.

"Hmmm, it looks raw."

"Is it ugly? How bad is it?"

"Your skin is abraded like a tool or fish knife was used. It's seeping but doesn't look serious."

He couldn't believe it. "What?" he cried, pulling his foot up to the edge of the bench and staring. "Why, that God damn son of a bitch played me for a fool," he shouted. Sarah curiously watched him erupt with a loud, exultant laugh. Relieved, his manners returned.

He looked at Sarah. It was the homeless woman to whom he had given money a few days prior. He said, "I'm Edgar Blodger, captain of the Glory Queen." Taking a better look, he saw that she was wearing an oversize seaman's cap and what appeared to be layers of bulky clothing. Seeing that she was nice enough to help him, and feeling good, he suggested she was welcome to clean up on his ship, but "Don't stand so close. Sorry honey, you smell."

As they ascended the ramp to the hulking gray ship, Sarah took it in, from bow to stern, the smokestacks, the control tower—everything. In his quarters, Blodger showed her the small efficiency bathroom with a shower. While she showered, he reached for a coffee can from a cupboard and made coffee. After about 20 minutes, and hearing contented humming and singing, he wondered if she would use up all the hot water, and if he had done the right thing inviting a bum onto his ship. The shower stopped. She asked for towels. Two large white towels were handed through the door. After a few seconds, she came out with a towel wrapped around her body. Her dark hair was wet; her skin glowed, and she was lovely.

He had never seen such a beautiful woman, a woman with blue eyes and delicate honey-colored skin. Catching his breath, he almost looked in the shower to see if a trick had been played. Unable to speak, he jumped to his feet and mumbled that he would wait outside while she dressed. She told him to sit. He did. And with his hands on his knees pressed together, he nervously looked left and right and back to her.

It didn't seem right, now that she was clean, that she should put on dirty clothes. A seaman was summoned to wash her clothes. The sailor gaped when he saw her. Blodger handed him the clothes and, to the sailor's departing back, shouted, "Get her a new cap!"

While waiting, they sat at a metal table, sipped their coffee, and chatted. She was truthful: She had been a prostitute at Ramona's but had

177

quit; her parents had disowned her but had continued taking her money. Now that she was out on the streets doing penance. She would accept money if offered but not from prostitutes. She had her pride. After a period of penance, she would return to her prior respectable self, a person she liked and decent. She would get through this. The way she dressed was to discourage men Although, she said, "Despite my appearance, somehow too many men still think I'm attractive."

He was surprised when she told him that she knew Elder's mistress and that Elder was quite nice. Also, a surprise was that Elder's mistress, Stephanie, was going to talk to Elder about helping her to get a job at City of Paris, the premier department store and tourist attraction.

Sarah readjusted the towel. He averted his eyes only to look back at her transformation. As she adjusted the towel, he caught innocent glimpses of her collar bones, lower legs to the knees, and delicate, downy hair. Embarrassed, aroused, and rattled, he looked away. Curious, she thought, "He's shy for such a rough man." He offered his quarters for the night. She declined, wondering if he was propositioning her. He walked her to the gangway, shook her offered hand, and watched until she faded into the night.

His skin quickly healed. All that was left was a superficial scar. For that, the loss of the money and being played for a fool, he bore a heavy grudge toward Elder.

Chapter Thirty-One: Ending A Forbidden Relationship

On the appointed day, although it was overcast with dark clouds, and cold, Morgan wore a light summery cotton, blue floral dress. To accentuate her slim waist, she wrapped a thin twisted scarf around her slim waist. She stepped into low heel shoes, examined herself in a mirror, applied red lipstick, pinched her cheeks, and she was ready. She thought, "Wrong dress for cold weather, and too dressy for work, but oh well, it'll only take a minute. We'll say a few trite words, be polite, and say goodbye. I'll leave, wave once, and go to work. Easy."

Meanwhile, Father Raffael at his dormitory showered, shaved, and brushed his hair. Having decided to make him feel strong in the faith, he wore the distinctive clothing of a priest: black slacks, black Cossack robe with a gold thread cross sewn into the lower left, a black sash, and black shoes. He placed the black skull cap, the zucchetto, on his head, made tiny adjustments, and was ready.

Apprehensive and engrossed in thought, Raffael walked the short distance from the dormitory to the Cathedral. Then, he sat in the first pew in front of the sacramental wall and waited. Other priests wondered why, on a weekday, he was dressed so formally.

His eyes roamed over the great room and the numerous rows of pews. He studied the white speck on his shoes; he looked at the marble floor, at the travertine walls, and at the vast, thick, granite columns supporting the immense ceiling. Full of anticipation, he turned to the confessional stations and the small chapel to his left. Sighing and leaning back, he turned to the entrance doors and the 10-foot-wide scarlet wool carpet running the length of the center aisle. He thought, "Scarlet, like my sins." He imagined the statues of Mary, Joseph, and Jesus looking down at him, judging. He glanced at the raised rectangular slab of marble, the altar where he said the sacraments—and glanced at the front doors, nervous, waiting.

Morgan appeared suddenly, magically, at the open doors. Even from a distance their eyes locked. Transfixed, he watched her approach and thought, "Why, she's beautiful—and glowing." Rays of colored beams from 120 stained glass windows danced around shimmering, from her feet to her wheat-colored hair until, with a bright flash, it was extinguished, except for the face and hair. Goosebumps erupted on his skin. He remembered to breathe. Rising from the pew, his hunger for her strong, he wanted to meet her halfway but resisting, he whispered an agonizing, "Oh, God, you sent me an angel to tempt my soul. I love her. If I let her go, I'll never be whole. Lord, I pray, make me strong." Years later, he would recount the experience of the glowing. Most doubted, saying it was a trick of the eyes, but he knew. He hadn't meant to fall in love and thought, "I'm going to hell for eternal damnation." Fighting for emotional control and a rational brain, which he doubted was rational, he waited.

Catching his eye, Father Raul Morrel entered from a side door and hurriedly approached.

Turning his attention back to Morgan, Raffael, relishing her touch, took her hand. But Father Raul was there, nervous.

"Please excuse me," he said, "His Excellency, the bishop wants to see you."

"All right, in a few minutes."

Father Raul fidgeted. He had more to say but was constrained by Morgan's presence.

"Father Raul, is there something unusual in your message? When does he want to see me?"

"Immediately!" he stammered, clearly embarrassed.

Morgan asked, "Is something wrong?"

Heavily sighing, Raffael slowly sat down, rigidly straight, then folded forward, with his hands on each side of his face and swayed ever so slightly.

Morgan and Father Raul looked on in concern. Was he praying?

With a grim expression, Raffael stood. Taking her by the elbow he said, "Come, Morgan, I'll walk you out."

Another priest urgently called out, "Father Raffael, his Excellency is waiting."

Sounding angry, Raffael snapped a reply, "I'm walking this young lady to the door."

The acoustics of the cavernous cathedral crisply carried his words.

"What is it? What's wrong?" Morgan asked.

"It's nothing; the bishop says I spend too much time with some parishioners." Taking in her sweet face, he sighed and said, "and that I've lost my way."

"You mean me. You spend too much time with me."

He made no reply. Just a look.

As they started up the aisle, Father Raul's admonition followed, "Be truthful!"

A group of visiting nuns in their black habits, near the votive candles, realized something unusual was occurring.

Raffael and Morgan innocently moved close. "God knows," he thought. "If we've sinned, we're washed clean by his grace."

"Dear Lord," muttered a nun, "they're in love." Passing pew after pew, rays of light from the artful stained-glass windows softly shone down on them like the love of God. Morgan felt like she was floating in a dream, on stage with an audience.

Raffael stopped at the threshold of the ornately carved oak doors. Looking somber, he took Morgan's hand and pulled her to his chest. Gasps of indignation were heard.

The bishop had joined the spectators and, like everyone else, was transfixed.

"Scandalous," muttered the monsignor. "Should we get him?"

"What, by force? No!"

At the entrance, Raffael ignored the frigid wind, the cold, and the curious. Taking a deep breath, he said, "Morgan, somehow, I've ruined our friendship. I've been fumbling, stumbling through my days since I met you. It's so embarrassing, for you, for me. Maybe, I've misled you." And glancing at the onlookers, the priests, nuns, and tourists, "These curious, pious people think that I, uh, have strong feelings for you."

"Do you?"

Instead of answering, he explained, "I'm married to the Church. Waving toward the onlookers, he said, "In their eyes we are sinners, but we are innocent. As for me, I'm at a loss to understand myself. I meant to be professional, but all I know is confusion. I think of you every day."

Astonished, she asked, "Oh, really? Really? You do think of me? Often?"

Staying with Father Raul's admonition to be truthful, he replied, "Yes, but my life is here. I took vows."

"Are you sure?"

"Yes, positive."

"Then, yes," she replied, "I'm sorry I've caused so much trouble. I understand. I'll go. You won't see me again. You're a good, sweet man. The Church is fortunate to have you." Leaning toward him, she gave him an awkward one-arm-sideways half-hug and said, "Goodbye, Dear Father," and stepped away.

Sadly, he nodded.

Stepping outside to drizzling rain, she stopped. She couldn't go any farther, not with him holding her hand. There they stood, two people in love, separated by extended arms. She tried to shake loose, but he held tightly.

Puzzled, she met his eyes. "Father, let go." But he held. Carefully, she stepped away. He followed. With claps of thunder and crackling lightning, the clouds let loose their burden. Drizzling rain turned into a torrent. She took steps, paused, and continued. After each pause, he followed.

He was standing tall, but when he raised his full sleeve to his eyes, she realized he was in torment. Shivering from the cold, she said, "Father, it's all right. I'll be fine. Let me go!" She continued down the next tier of steps. Still, he held tightly. Nervously, with her free hand, she played with the red ribbon tying her wheat-colored hair. It fell loose, making him sigh.

Almost inaudibly, softly, he said, "Morgan, I. . . . . We were more than friends. We did have good times together. It's over. We will never see each other again—never laugh, never talk again, hear your voice, see your sweet face, your hair. . . . . . Dear sweet Jesus!" Attempting to compose himself, his chest heaved as if short of breath. "Dear Lord," he whispered, "it's not fair."

"Father Raffael, will you miss me?" Rachael asked so softly, he almost didn't hear.

"Yes."

"Will you miss my face and my voice?"

"Yes."

When he said no more but just stood looking at her, she asked:
"And?"

"And what?"

"What about my lips?" She asked mischievously.

183

"What about them?"

"Will you miss them?"

Weakly, he smiled. "Yes."

"Touch them! Go ahead."

Astonished, he grinned. "Yes, I'll miss your lips, but I won't touch them."

"You almost kissed them once."

"When?"

"We were walking across Washington Square to Dominick's. We got caught in a downpour, like today. We ran. I slipped. You tried to catch me, and we both landed on our backsides. We were in stitches, laughing hard. You picked me up. You looked down at me. I looked up at you, and you almost did it. I wanted you to."

"I didn't know."

"Raffael, you do think of me?"

"Every day, with every breath."

The onlookers had followed them outside, absorbed in the drama, oblivious to the pelting rain. A priest asked no one in particular,

"What are they doing?"

Father Raul whispered, "Love talk."

Standing close, still lingering, Raffael said, "It's time. Morgan, someday come back to visit, to say hello. Make this your place of worship. Bring your children."

Bristling at his words, her temper flared. Hell, if she was going to demean herself. Heatedly, she shouted, "You dumbbell, you ninny, are you blind? Can't you see that I love you? There is no one but you. Do you love me or not? If you don't, give me back my hand. But if you do, I mean my hand, and I walk away, you'll regret it for the rest of your sorry life. I'll get on with mine. I'll get married and have children. I'll be happy, and you'll

184

stay here and get old and wrinkled with your ugly black shoes and stupid memories."

Raffael was dumbfounded at the force of her words. Then, smiling wryly, gazing at the face he loved, he said, "Morgan, you forgot numbskull, nincompoop, knucklehead, and ignoramus. And you're right about my shoes."

Humor softened the tension, and she felt a glimmer of hope. The wind and rain whipped her body. She gripped his hand, and ever so softly and imploringly she said, "Raffael, Dear Father Raffael, look at me! See me!"

"Yes."

Wet, cold, and shivering, her dress clinging to her body, she closed her eyes for a moment. Then her words came out, quaking, "Dear Reverend Raffael Bouvier, you don't have to miss me. Dear sweet man, I love you so much. Can you do it? Why don't you come with me? Come with me. Please. Now."

Raffael was immobile. Gripping his hand, she questioned, "Raffael?" She knew that this was a pivotal moment. If she let go, he would disappear into the Church; he would be reassigned, and she would never see him again.

His mind swirled with conflicting thoughts until, with clarity, it was just two people standing together with longing. He took a step closer, staring into her dark brown eyes. Whereas he had not relinquished her hand, she now firmly grasped his with both of hers and started backing away with him in tow, down the last tier of steps. With her eyes on his, she said, "Come with me. Spend your life with me."

He felt fear, but it was diminishing, vanquished by a warm, rich feeling flooding his heart, giving him courage. He looked at those at the cathedral doors and back to Morgan. He took in the lovely features of her face, her

185

eyes, lips, and wet hair framing her face. His eyes went to her slim fingers, fingers that were delicately removing strands of wet hair from her face. And he was lost in dizzying, swirling love.

Gazing into the eyes he loved, he cupped her cheek. And knowing he would always long for her, he said. "May God forgive me. I choose you."

Moving away from the imposing cathedral, they stopped and looked back at the fascinated spectators. Father Raul waved. One nun trying to suppress a smile failed and clasped her hands to her heart. Another, tight-lipped, scowled. The bishop's expression was benign. Making the sign of the cross, very silently he said, "May the Lord be with you. Be happy and multiply."

Raffael's robes flapped wetly at his heels. Holding hands, they were almost jogging. Looking toward the sky, he said, "Dear heavenly Father, if I am not doing your will, please forgive me, but if I am, thank you." Inclining his face toward Morgan, he said, "We'll have a wonderful story to tell our children."

Morgan was beside herself, floating—elated—giddy with happiness.

Chapter Thirty-Two: Treat a Woman Like a Dog

Blodger and his first mate, Bob, were having breakfast of eggs and toast at Dominick's. Blodger barely spoke. A favorite pastime of recent days was daydreaming of revenge. Being imaginative and angry with Elder, he conjured various revenge scenarios of throttling Elder in his home, on the waterfront, or in an alley, wherever he could catch him. The possibilities took him to a reverie of improbable options.

Elder would apologize when he held him by the throat. And if his body turned up in the bay, with the troubles at the docks, the matter would be on the back burner of the police and the back pages of the news. He sipped his coffee. The problem was how? It could be done, even if it took years. One

186

imagined scenario was that he and his most trusted seamen would go to Elder's house to Nob Hill, where he thought he lived, in the dead of night. He thought, "I'll riddle it with high-caliber bullets. Gatling guns would do the trick until it looks like Swiss cheese. "Or I'll plant dynamite around the entire house and blow it to high heaven." The mindful vision of masonry flying to the sky, flashing brightly with red, white, and blue colors like rockets, made him chuckle aloud, drawing the attention of other diners. "Yeah, that's what I'll do," and chiding himself, he thought, "and I might as well write fairy tales." Interrupting his thoughts, he saw Sarah crossing the street to Washington Square.

Sarah dressed in warm clothing for the crisp, cold weather, sat at one of the benches under a strand of pines. Watching from his window seat and seeing Sarah adjusting her clothes against the frigid weather, Blodger forgot about Elder.

"Bob," he said. "Do me a favor. See that woman out there, the one on the bench? The cute bum. The one with the long dark hair. She has blue eyes. Give her this." It was four silver dollars. From his window seat, Blodger watched her talking to Bob and her reaction to the gift. Bob pointed toward the café. She waved. Blodger leaned back on his chair as if struck. Even though he and Sarah had been visiting casually, occasionally, he had attached no importance to them; they were simply to pass the time.

Bob returned and said, "She said thank you."

"Yeah, well, good," and he looked again. Seeing him looking, she waved again. Caught, he looked away.

"Are you interested?" Bob asked.

"My gosh, no. Look at her. She's a bum."

"She looks a bit more. If you look closely, there is something about her. She's pretty. She seems intelligent. She speaks well, with a southern accent. It's odd; she's a bum with an expensive leather satchel and seems

187

classy. Cap, it's not my business, but if you're interested, be careful. Women can be a whole lot of trouble, and they're more sensitive than men."

"You're right; it is none of your business, but what do you mean?"

"All right. For instance, they take it hard if you don't keep your word. They'll remember and bring it up later in an argument. That's trouble. You have to kiss them, caress them, and not only when you want sex. If you don't, that's trouble. You have to tell them you love them—often. Women are complex. When they hear music, they close their eyes, like it touches their heart and maybe rock and sway. My opinion is to treat a woman like a dog, but a special dog. Pet them, brush them, comb them, kiss them, take them on walks, and give them baths and treats. Treat them great, and for gosh sake, listen and pay attention, or they'll catch you unaware. Maybe you'll be lucky, and she'll treat you like a dog." Nodding toward the woman outside, "If you like her, assuming she has all her marbles, give her flowers."

"The dog thing is interesting," Blodger replied, "but flowers, that's not me. Anyway, how do you know so much?"

"Sorry, Cap." looking down into his cup. "Don't mind me. I learned the hard way when it was too late. I'm just talking."

After minutes of silence and seeing that Blodger was looking out the window, distracted, Bob stood. He wasn't going to wait any longer. He surmised that the captain would stare out the window until the woman left.

Blodger did. When Sarah left, she picked up her bag, lifted her eyes, and looked directly at him. A breeze tousled her hair. She waved. His heart jumped. He had to admit, he liked her. He raised his hand to acknowledge the wave and called the waitress for more coffee. Then, he sat thinking for a long time.

Four days later, he saw Sarah again. Probably due to the improved weather, she wore a pale-yellow dress and navy-blue sweater—very attractive. He had been sitting on the bench for nearly an hour, waiting. He handed her a bouquet of daffodils. She was pleasantly surprised. "It's nothing," he said, "Someone gave them to me. I'm giving them to you." Why he lied, he didn't quite know—embarrassed maybe at his new interest.

She asked if he was busy. He wasn't. She invited him to go with her to the Palace Station Cafe to see Morgan, a woman she had met at the park.

Morgan was pleased to see Sarah but chagrined at being introduced to such a rough-looking character, and wondered if Sarah was going back into the business. She decided she was unfair. After all, Mr. Blodger was polite and treated Sarah kindly. He and Sarah acted like friends, ate a meal of meatloaf and mashed potatoes, drank beer, and animatedly conversed.

Chapter Thirty-Three: June 30. In A Den OF Thieves

The Palace Station was crowded, standing room only, and full of talk. Men big and small, tempered by the strenuous work on the docks, moved from table to table, bolstering each other for the impending strike. Over 40 men stood, unable to find a seat, holding drinks, smoking, making comments, and arguing. A showdown was coming between them and the Industrial Union, their bosses. The customers, longshoremen, sailors, warehouse workers, teamsters, and others crowded through the doors, eager for the latest news and gossip. One table remained conspicuously empty. It was reserved, Sam said, for friends who would come in later. "Curious," Rachael thought. "We never reserve tables."

189

The front doors were wide open for fresh air in the smoke-filled room. The fans were overpowered. Five waitresses glided from the kitchen and bar to tables, delivering food and drinks.

Rachael had a nagging feeling that the day would be unusual. In the morning, she passed from a table toward the bar and looked into the mirror to see if Sam was looking. He was. And his behavior was different. Throughout the day, he moved closer and away, like he would say something, then change his mind. Morgan also noticed and said, "Rachael, Sam has been watching you."

"In the mirror?"

"Don't look; he's doing it again. You know what, I think he has a crush on you."

"Really? I don't know if he's staring because he likes me or is doing it to creep me out."

"Well, I think he does. Especially when you wear this oversize white blouse. The buttons come loose, and you pop out, and he sneaks looks."

"No, he doesn't, does he?"

"Yes, in fact, his eyes follow you whenever you leave. Then he sits still, like a statue, like he's thinking. He doesn't move until you're out of sight."

"How long?"

"Long enough. I'll tell you what, next time I'll use my stopwatch."

"Do you have one?"

"No."

"Well, let's see." Rachael undid the top button and the second, toyed with the third, and left it buttoned. Then, she went to the bar near Sam, made a humming sound, and leaned over the counter to get a rag. She straightened and cheerfully said, "Hi, Sam."

190

When Rachael returned to the floor, Morgan said, "Holy moly, you're wicked; I saw the whole thing. He's still looking. If he were a dog, his tongue would be on the floor, and he would be ready to, well, you know."

Rachael was pleased, but she had to be careful. She liked Sam but he was her boss. She didn't know if he was really interested or just randy. She said, "Morgan, I can't jeopardize my job over a fling. I do like him, but I don't know. I want someone with better prospects. He might remain a bartender. I hate being poor and want someone at least on the same educational level. It might take 10 years, but I'm going to graduate. But what do I know? Nice young handsome millionaires with eyes like his don't just grow on trees. Although have you noticed there is something not quite right about Sam, something mysterious? Sometimes, he seems like he might be someone else, like someone important. Look at his shoes and his wristwatch. For gosh sake, it's a Patek Philippe. I looked it up. Expensive. He has money, more than he earns here, and his speech is refined. I'm smart, but sometimes he'll use a word I pretend to understand. Later, if I remember, I'll look it up."

"Yeah," Morgan said, "maybe he's a crook selling drugs, making crime pay."

"Do you think so?"

"No, Rachael, I don't. I do think you have quite an imagination. And if you want a man with an education and rich, you're not going to find one here, not in this place. As for me, I'm happy with Raffael, although he doesn't seem to care about employment. I've encouraged him to apply for a bank job or cable car driver, but he says we can go to his hometown in Spain. He says his parents will give him a job. They're tailors. Oh well, we'll do okay between the two of us."

Rachael felt Sam had never been more than civil, except that one time when she thought he was flirting, when she asked if he would hire

Morgan. "He was just playing with me." Never was there a hint of personal interest", at least not until recently, not seriously, not that she could tell. Seeing Jessica passing, she stopped her for a second opinion, and asked, "Jessica, let me ask you a question. Do you think Sam's acting weird, or do you think he might be interested in me?"

"Oh," Jessica replied, "he is weird in a cute way and sometimes annoying, but he's interested."

"How can you tell?"

"He told me."

"What?"

"I'm his sister."

"No!"

"Yes!"

"Oh, no! Gosh. I'm so sorry, I have the habit of putting my foot in my mouth. You never use your last name, and I don't want to be nosy. Well, I guess that explains why you get the best hours, and never gets on you for being late or talking back. Gee, wiz, I did it again."

"Don't worry about it. I do get special treatment."

"Jessica, I apologize. I don't know very much about Sam. He never talks about his family. I didn't know he had a sister. Who are his parents? I mean, who are your parents, or should I ask?"

Jessica replied, "My father is a good old guy who spends most of his time at home. He rarely works since our mom passed away. For now, that's all I can say. He doesn't like us to talk about him."

"Oh, I understand. Don't feel bad. My father works but hasn't had a raise for the longest time, and Morgan's father barely gets by at the docks."

Jessica looked at Rachael with a crooked smile. Rachael thought she was going to say something but didn't.

192

Rachael had nagging thoughts that Sam might be a gangster lying low and hiding out, maybe from the law. Or perhaps the Palace Station Café was part of a criminal enterprise laundering money? "How else, she wondered, could Sam come and go as he pleased, take money from the cash register, and hand out cash like it didn't matter? And lately, he's been giving away free meals, and Gus doesn't say anything.

"Jessica," Rachael asked, "when I met Sam, he was working at a speakeasy, and criminals go to speakeasies, don't they?"

Giving her an amused look, Jessica diverted the question and asked, "Who's the new dishwasher? He doesn't look like a dishwasher—so handsome and with a French accent." It was the former Father Raffael.

When the kitchen closed at 11:30 p.m., Raffael upended the chairs, put them on the tables, and swept and mopped. Patrons could continue drinking at the bar until 1 a.m. Morgan usually stayed to help.

Observing them, Gus said, "Sam, I had that once. My wife passed away four years ago. I miss her." Motioning toward Raffael and Morgan, he added, "Look at them. He's a dishwasher; she's a waitress. Maybe between the two they can afford an apartment? But they don't care. They're in love."

Jessica placed an order at the bar. Steins and two pitchers of dark beer were placed on the platter. "Sam," she asked, "are you worried about something, or are you thinking about Rachael? You look like you're somewhere else."

"Am I so transparent? Should I ask Rachael out for dinner? Will she accept?"

"Eat here. Tell her that you're eating here before going home. Ask her to join you. Act casual. That way, it's not a date, just a casual, impromptu sit-down. Or don't you think this place is good enough?"

193

By the time Sam worked up the courage to ask Rachael to stay, her shift was over. He hopped off his stool but was too late. In a rush, she passed him without saying goodnight, without a nod, without a glance, nothing, making him wonder if she was angry.

Rachael was on her way to California Street to catch the cable car to Hyde Street. From there, she would walk five blocks to her house. Her mind was on Sam and gangsters. She had to think.

Rachael's thoughts went to the strange and colorful people who had come in that day. Also pressing on her mind was the true purpose of the Palace Station Café. She guessed that it was some sort of nexus for illegal activities, maybe for the Mafia. She should have seen it before. Sure, it sold food and alcohol. They were busy, but she questioned whether it was sufficiently profitable. Recently, one or two nights a week, they gave away free beer and sandwiches. It was for two hours, and customers never knew the day except that it would be after 9:00 p.m. They came in hoping to be lucky.

"Sam," she was thinking, "has money, and it sure isn't by working as a bartender. For gosh sake, he gave Morgan $10 like it was nothing. He has money from somewhere, and he comes and goes whenever he wants, not like anyone I know." Her thoughts returned to the customers who had come in that day. The first group of note was a young bunch at mid-afternoon: four pretty, well-dressed young ladies, accompanied by three young men, all looking like money. They had caused a bit of commotion with Caesar because of Jessica. The second group came in a little too early for dinner but stayed late, and visitors came and went as if doing business or paying homage.

The young group had spilled through the doors, laughing, and jostling one another with an air of privilege. Overheard was a comment, "How quaint." The men wore quality wool slacks, white shirts, argyle socks, and

194

fashionable shoes. Yes, they were expensively dressed, young, and rambunctious, like they owned the place, or knew the owner. "Upper class," she thought, "slumming near the docks to see how poor people lived."

The prettiest, a very perky, shapely blond wearing a white blouse and ankle-length blue skirt, got Caesar's attention and told him, not asked, to call Sam. Caesar looked annoyed, but Sam was soon with the group, joking and chatting, and gave them the reserved table. The perky one draped her arm around Sam's shoulders. Much to Rachael's annoyance, she kissed him twice, once on the lips. She thought, "She's a floozy," and immediately reprimanded herself. "Now, Rachael, be nice." Ruefully she admitted they were a little noisy but behaved sufficiently well. "Sam isn't in their social class, is he?" she wondered. "Except for his shoes and wristwatch, and all that money in his wallet."

"Jessica," Rachael asked, "How does he know them?" Jessica looked at her and was about to answer. Before she could, surprising Rachael, Sam called Jessica to join them. "Oh, she knows them."

Morgan noticed and said, "I think you better stop staring. I know it looks funny. Maybe, he used to be somebody. Maybe his family lost it all in the stock market crash."

The young people shared pitchers of beer and were having a good time, but one fellow had made a mistake. He flirted with Jessica and playfully pulled her onto his lap. To Caesar's annoyance, she was responding. In an instant, he was there, astonishing all, especially Jessica. Extending his hand, he helped her up from the young man's lap, and with words and body language, aggressively told the guy to back off. The largest of the four took offense and started to rise. "No, Stacy, not a good idea," said his friend, pulling him down, "He's Caesar O'Sullivan."

"So?"

195

"He's a professional boxer. He fought Jake, The Bull Tanner, and flattened him. I was there. I saw the fight. Tanner is trying for a fight with Joe Louis the Brown Bomber. You know Louis might be the next champ. This guy is better. But if you insist, go ahead. After he knocks your block off, I'll carry you home." Stacy stayed seated. "Nah, I didn't think so."

The peacemaker looked up at Caesar and said, "Sorry, we meant no offense."

Caesar, shaking from adrenalin, retreated to the end of the bar with Jessica. She rubbed her hand over his back to calm him, squeezed his hand, and told him to relax. Seeing his sad look of unfulfilled love, she impulsively put her hand behind his neck, canted her head, and pulled him to her lips—to kiss soulfully, something she always had urges to do. "The guy's a friend," she said. "He was playing." But she was pleased. After all, her father had allowed her to work at the Palace Station for "protection." Initially, she balked at the idea, thinking it was silly, but she wanted Caesar from the start, from the first day she laid eyes on him. She had resisted temptation, except once when she had impulsively grabbed him in the hall, kissed him, and nonchalantly walked away. After that, she refrained, not sure what the family would think.

Two minutes later, Morgan couldn't contain her curiosity and asked, "Jessica, is Caesar your boyfriend?"

"No," I want a college man. Caesar's my friend. He gives me rides."

"Did your father go to college?"

Casting a glance at Caesar, Jessica answered, "No, but that was in the old days. Why do you ask?"

"Oh, umm, I saw you kissing. And you're always looking at each other. But it's none of my business."

"Oh, shit. Excuse me." Jessica blushed and looked flabbergasted. "Does everyone know?"

"I think so, including your brother."

The young people stayed out of pride to save face but were uneasy. Caesar looked their way. It did not go unnoticed. He knew he had overreacted but couldn't help bristling when he saw Jessica on the fellow's lap.

The peacemaker laughed, patted his friend on the knee, and said, "Stacy, I think you pissed him off."

Sam had seen the whole thing and was amused.

Three hours later, two men entered and took the reserved table. Although wearing common casual clothing, they wore quality shoes and expensive wristwatches, not pocket watches like most, and gave off an aura of confidence and money. One of the men was Caucasian, and the other was an olive-skinned Negro with green eyes. The Caucasian looked somewhat familiar but couldn't place him. They were unhurried and in good spirits. Shortly, a well-known politician, Jacob Woodson, joined them. His pleasant manner had everyone laughing.

The table was in Rachael's section, but Sam with a wave of his hand had sent Caesar. The men stood and shook his hand. Rachael realized, "He knows them too."

He had just served them beer when a striking woman with shoulder length strawberry blond hair and emerald, green eyes entered. Pausing at the second pair of saloon doors, she surveyed the room. The noise in the jam-packed room went down to a low hum. She had captured the room.

Some blatantly gawked. A woman reached across the table to her companion and cupped his chin, turning it back to her. Stephanie sat and crossed her legs. The modest slits to above the knees revealed skin. "Wow," and "Oh, mama," were uttered from somewhere.

Stephanie's clothing was ahead of her time and considered risqué. Her dress was an emerald, green sheath, Asian style, with a modest high

197

scooped neckline and a relaxed corded belt draping her hips. The dress flowed over the curves of her bodice and hips to the ankles—quality low-heel shoes to match. Delicate pear-cut emerald, green earrings set in gold complemented her creamy complexion. Her fingernails were polished red.

Seeing her friends, Stephanie smiled warmly from her mouth to her eyes. After she sat, the spell cast on the room was broken and returned to its prior din. Stephanie looked up directly at Rachael and smiled.

Sam joined the table, hugging everyone, and so did Jessica. Sam motioned for Rachael to come over. She did, briefly. The men were introduced as David and Abe, and the woman as Stephanie Ruth Rosen, her actual name. In acknowledging Rachael, Stephanie's voice was soft, dusty, and German-accented, and the impression was that she took care to speak correctly. The surnames of the men were not given. Rachael said, "I'm pleased to meet you, Mr. uh, David," and wasn't corrected. With a friendly wave, Gus was also acknowledged. After a few minutes of polite words, David, Abe, and Stephanie were left alone. Privacy was short-lived.

Another young, attractive woman entered accompanied by a balding muscular man. Leaving the woman at the table, the man went directly to the bar. In passing, David and the man exchanged glares. Stephanie and the woman hugged.

Adding more to Rachael's curiosity, two stylishly dressed Italian men in suits and Homburg hats entered shortly thereafter, contrasting significantly with the clientele. One stopped at the table and sat. The other, a tall, somewhat effeminate thin man, paused, shook hands, and went to the bar. Despite their suits, they looked dangerous and disreputable. The larger of the two wore oversize pants, evidently to fit large legs. Distinguishing features, besides his size, were his slicked-back white hair, a small brown mole on his chin, and an aquiline nose. Leaning slightly to shake hands,

198

his jacket flapped open revealing a shoulder holster and black gun. Mr. David reached up and closed it.

The thin companion sat at the bar next to the balding, muscular man. The thin man removed his gray felt bowler, placed it on the counter, and asked for a beer. Seeing Rachael glancing at the table, he proudly said, "Doll, the big guy--that's my goombah, Luigi Bonnaducci."

"Goombah?" she asked.

"Yeh, you know, my godfather, my buddy, my uh, like special family."

"And you are . . ?"

"I'm Sonny Fruttuchi from Joisy."

"Joisy?"

"Yeh, Joisy, you know, New Joisy."

"Oh."

"(H)ave you hoid [sic] of us?"

"No!"

Disappointed that his boasting was failing to impress, he tried again. Preening, he slicked back his black hair and opened his jacket to show he had a gun, just like Accordion Luigi. Smiling broadly, he said, "I (h)ave another moniker. Can you guess?"

Rachael's eyes went over his tall skinny frame, thin dainty hands, and narrow, bullet-shaped head. "Could it be slim or bullet?"

"No," he laughed, "My real name is Paolo 'cause I'm Italian."

"No!"

"Yeh, usually I'm called Sonny, but sometimes I'm called Munchi because I eat so much. But mostly, I'm called Fruiti."

"I don't get it."

Somewhat dispiritedly, he replied, "Yeah, me neither."

Taking a chance, she asked, "Do you know Sam?"

"Oh, sure."

"Do you know his father?"

"Sure do." Now that he had her attention, he puffed up and said, "If he needs a little muscle, we're there. Bat-ta bing, ba-ta boom, and it's done--if you get my drift?"

"I'm afraid I do." She tried again, "Do you work for Sam?"

"Umm, more like for his father. He's right there at the table. He and our boss, Francesco Lanza, are friends. So, if he wants us, we're there."

"The Mafia boss?"

"Huh? Hey, hey, take it easy. Wadeaminute, waaadeaminute! WaaddidIsay? I ain't talkin'. Don't put woids in ma mouth. Did I say anythin' about da Mafia? Mr. Lanza's a respected businessman."

"Just great," thought Rachael, "Lanza, the boss of the San Francisco Mafia. I'm surrounded by a bunch of crooks.

"Let me understand, you work for the Mafia, and Mr. David Cocker can tell Mr. Lanza to do something, and he will."

"I tol [sic] you he ain't Mafia, and that ain't his name."

"It ain't? I mean, it isn't? It's Sam's name. Then, what is it?"

Fruttuchi had enough. He was thinking, "What's a matta wit this ditzy dame?" Furrowing his brow, he picked up his beer and moved to the other side of the muscular balding man, muttering, "I ain't talkin.' Fogitaboutit."

Rachael walked away with a little smile, thinking, "Wow, phew, I got his socks in a knot."

"What's so funny?" Morgan asked.

"I got that skinny, bullet-headed man's tidy whities so tied in a knot that he farted--twice, pop, pop. The second was a doozy, phew. The man beside him got up and moved."

No one paid. Not the first group, not the second, nor anyone who had stopped by their table. Rachael had looked at Gus for instruction, and he mouthed the words, "It's okay." The only one who paid was the balding,

200

broad man at the bar. At his insistence. Not even Fruiti Fruttuchi paid, nor did two men seated at a nearby table; one was a short, trim guy like a jockey. She had not made the connection until, with a nod, Mr. David, Mr. Cocker, or whoever he was, pushed back his chair and stood. So did everyone else in his party. Everyone stood as one and followed. More mysteries. "Bodyguards? Mafia?"

Unable to reconcile the events and Sam's connection to the Mafia to a favorable conclusion, Rachael fidgeted. The streetcar was not due for another ten minutes. One passed, going in the other direction, loaded with cheerful Chinese returning home from their day's labor. Thoughts strayed while she watched them pass, then returned to the day's events: "I have to stay away from Sam. There is something secretive about him. Maybe he's dangerous." Upon more reflection, "Sam's father held court, receiving visitors while bodyguards watched. And Gus must be Sam's henchman. Oh my! And Caesar doesn't bother to have his work schedule posted. Neither does Jessica. Just like Sam. They work whenever they feel like it. Caesar must be Jessica's bodyguard and lover. Gosh, it's a crime family!

"Why," she wondered, "does Sam want me when he can get one of those gangster molls, a floozie with high heels, platinum hair, and lots of makeup, one with her breasts showing? He can't be serious. On the other hand, gee whiz, why does he have to be so cute?"

Chapter Thirty-Four: Morose Thoughts

Lugo, knowing that Stephanie was inside, was standing at the entrance to the Palace Station Cafe, dithering about going in to have a beer. He thought he might sit at the bar just like any other customer and stare at them to make them uncomfortable. But Accordion Luigi, Elder's Mafia friend, passed going in and gave him a scorching look. He decided against it. Elder had too many friends.

Sullen and jealous, Lugo walked past the Ferry Building, not caring that he was talking aloud to himself. At Louisa's, at Fisherman's Wharf, he drank a pitcher of beer and daydreamed about violence: He imagined passing the small gate at Stephanie's and quietly ascending the steps. He'd break down the door, run to the bed and kill Elder. Unsteadily, he paid his bill at Louisa's and continued home.

Stewing in anger, Lugo continued walking along the Embarcadero toward his small second-floor walk-up. He considered whether he should have gone into the Palace Station Cafe and what might have happened. Also on his mind was another incident where he had the opportunity to talk to Stephanie, to convince her to take him back. But he couldn't control his temper: It had occurred a few days prior. Stephanie and a female friend were having lunch in Little Italy. He strolled by pretending to pass by accidentally, hoping she would invite him to join them. She did not.

Cautiously, she introduced him and turned back to her friend. He felt disdainfully dismissed. Nonetheless, he persisted. To the back of her head, he asked if he could join them. Giving him an askance look, she curtly replied, "No." He tried one more time, suggesting they meet later, and added, "I don't mind sharing you with Elder." With a withering look, she looked away. His mind exploded with anger. Turning vile, he gripped her arm and yanked her to her feet. When her friend protested, he sarcastically spat, "Do you know she fucks for money?" The manager and other customers intervened. One was a tall priest who arose from a nearby table. Seeing him coming, Lugo wheeled away and stalked off, admonishing himself, "Why, couldn't I have controlled my temper?" The confrontation went around and around in his head. He truly believed that had he used the proper words Stephanie would have recognized his genuine affection for her. Instead, he had exploded with anger. "Ah, nuts."

Watching Lugo walk away, Stephanie apologized for Lugo's remark, and said, "If you want to leave, I understand." Her friend responded, "For such a good-looking man, he sure is awful. Don't worry, I don't care in the least."

To the priest, Stephanie mouthed the words, "Thank you."

Lugo was consumed with thoughts of Stephanie, and of late, his failures, and boring life. He knew eyes were on him as he walked away and felt like a dog with its tail between its legs. Another failure and another headache suffered when angry and under stress. He guessed he had gone too far in saying he didn't mind sharing.

Lugo's life was usually a succession of dull days broken by his work routine, making arrests, hassling drunks, and prostitutes, and using them when he felt the urge. Stalking Stephanie had become his interest, something to do. She was a goal to attain. "God damn that fucking Elder," he mumbled. "He stole her with his money. I'll kill him and her too. Well, not her, not right away. I'll take her and win her over with affection and sex. I'll be sensitive. If that doesn't work, then I'll, aaaaha, kill her."

Passing the prostitution house on Cora Street, he impulsively entered and stormed past an astonished madame Zhao, a tall narrow-faced bony woman with stringy black hair, wearing shapeless all-black down to her black slippered feet. Two sinister Buddha-like bouncers looked to her for instruction. With a long bony finger, she waved them off. On edge, Lugo grabbed the youngest by the wrist, a nubile girl with budding breasts and a hint of pubic hair and pulled her after him.

"Yesssss," hissed Madam Zhao.

Under his bulk, unable to move, hoping it would end quickly, the delicate girl kept her eyes closed and held her fists tightly to her side. Lugo groaned and rolled off, sexually sated but not satisfied. The girl curled into a ball, eyes filled with tears, and looked at the wall.

"Ah hell," he experienced something new, remorse, even guilt. Not one to have such feelings, he muttered, "What is wrong with me?" and tossed a $5.00 bill on her legs. Storming out past Madam Zhao's poisonous glare, he growled, "I'll be back tomorrow for my money!"

Madam Zhao flicked a bony finger toward the "Buddha" bodyguard to check on the girl. As an afterthought, she instructed, "Take her to my quarters." Then, gliding on slippered feet, she followed Lugo. Outside, throwing mental daggers at Lugo's departing back, she turned her attention to two men across the street. Nodding and, with a "Yessssss," she pointed her delicate finger at Lugo. "Yessssss." Hissing, with lips moving, voicing words no one could hear, she returned inside, leaned heavily with both hands on a desk, mumbled something, and went to check on the girl. Things were going as planned. Everyone in Chinatown knew that Lugo and Sgt. Frank had murdered her grandchild. An ominous shadow had been cast, and an inevitable outcome.

Still, on edge, Lugo considered going to the opium den but dismissed the thought as too expensive. His use had increased from an occasional once a month to three and four times a week.

Lugo continued to his building in a foul mood, cursing loudly, mumbling like an idiot, appearing mentally impaired. Passerby's enjoying the crimson sunset and crisp air gave him a wide berth. Burning with adrenaline, furious at being undermined by Elder, he ignored the polite greetings of merchants. Somehow, he had to vent his anger, or he would explode. In his high emotional state, he felt like running amok, yelling, to shove men, women, and children aside. He wanted to hurt someone to show that he was fearsome, important--- someone to be reckoned with.

Ahead of him, an elderly couple strolled taking in the evening air, impeding his progress. Walking between them, he shoved them apart. Snarling, he, spat, "What are you looking at?" The man struck him with his cane. Lugo moved to retaliate, but the couple was quickly encircled protectively by other pedestrians. As he turned away, angry insults followed. Lugo shouted, "Go fuck yourselves."

Ignoring the yammering insults hurled at his back, he considered going to the Barbary Coast—-ominous, dangerous, sexual, cheap whores, down-and-out bums, alcoholics, and drug addicts. Under his breath, he said, "I'll pick out one or two, maybe one squatting against a building or maybe a whore, someone with red hair like Stephanie. I'll beat them to a pulp, yeah, behind the Horseshoe Bar." Then, thinking of Elder, he mused, "I'll kick out his teeth. The mother fucker. Then we'll see what she thinks. Yeah, he won't be so pretty, will he?" Looking around, he saw people staring and wondered if he was talking out loud. he shouted, "Shit, can you hear me?" Inexplicably he yelled at the closest man, "Shut up." With head throbbing, he continued walking, whispering to himself, "Am I losing my mind?" He muttered, "Fuck no!"

His thoughts returned to Stephanie. To get her, he reasoned, he needed money. "I'll get more from the Chinese shopkeepers." Opium use was draining his pockets. "I'll get it. She'll want a nice apartment." He thought of his apartment and neighborhood. He wasn't liked. He didn't care.

Although Lugo portrayed himself to his fellow cops as calm and even-tempered, he was capable of the unthinkable. And now, with his damn fixation on Stephanie, his mind was jumping all over the place. In frustration, he mumbled, "Ha, shit, I'll get her back." But nothing would quell his growing feelings of being a loser and inferior to Elder.

In his youth, Lugo's sister, Josie, had been his conscience, mentor, and guide. Without her, he was left to his own devices, morally and socially rudderless. It was usual to feel he was acting, which he was, and he took pride in doing it so well. With fellow cops, he could laugh at a joke along with everyone else, even though he thought it to be obtuse or stupid. He

205

expressed opinions on matters that he did not personally believe but believed to be the ones they wanted to hear. It was best to say little—or to tell a well-practiced joke. Sage nods and grins did the trick and buying drinks to be one of the guys. But living a lie and suppressing an explosive temper took its toll. With true feelings squelched, severe headaches followed.

Still tense, he passed Chow Fat's neat two-story department store and Shao Long's dreary tattoo parlor. Next to the tattoo parlor was the more attractive Green Lantern lounge. He went in to have another beer. Across the street, the Chinamen smoked and followed.

A pastime for Lugo was frequenting the late-night lounges in Chinatown, drinking, and listening to music and singers, singing songs to words he did not understand. It was to kill time until the next day to repeat the same routine. That he was the only Caucasian bothered him not at all. The locals stared to make him feel unwelcome, but time passed. He was neither friendly nor unfriendly; he was a fixture, like a piece of furniture, a miserable solitary creature without friends. After three beers, he left, feeling the beer, and still agitated. The men waiting outside followed to his building. Then, lighting up another smoke, they waited until a black car, driven by a sinister-looking Buddha-like man, slid to the curb.

Entering his dingy apartment, Lugo's frustration exploded. His fist went into the bathroom door, cracking it. Flopping on the bed, he thought of Stephanie and fought the urge to go to the opium den below to curb his anxiety. But he had to pay. The building and den were owned by a Caucasian and could not be pressured. Instead of opium, he drank two more beers.

During his first week as a policeman, Lugo was introduced to the use of opium by Mack, close to retirement. Although it was available when Lugo lived on the Barbary Coast, he had steered clear of its use. Bums used it,

206

and he saw how it affected them. However, at the police department, he was surprised some cops used it. As a devotee of history, he knew that Thomas Jefferson, the third president of the United States, had used opium for coughs, aches, and headaches. Also, George Washington used laudanum, a liquid of opium and alcohol, for pain from ill-fitting false teeth. Therefore, he reformed his opinion of the drug. He surmised that only weak-minded, lazy individuals become addicted, certainly not people of quality like himself. Lugo decided that if such intelligent men used it, it had to be good if used wisely. Mumbling "To hell with it," he headed for the door.

Lugo stepped into the candle lit, dank basement opium den and looked around. The pitted concrete floor was liberally covered with oriental rugs to disguise the dinginess. Mixed fragrances from the thick melting candles, incense, and opium vapors competed with the musty smell. At the entrance, out of place, was a thick black electrical cord bearing the weight of an exquisite multicolored glass globe with hues of greens, reds, yellows, and blues. Jackets, coats, and purses hung on thick nails hammered into the concrete walls. Seven others were in the room, all Caucasians, smoking or already in a stupor. Three women with their dresses in disarray, riding high on their thighs, were watched over by attendants.

Lugo ran his fingertips four inches above his head along the low, uneven ceiling. The mat, a hard wooden pillow, mahogany pipe, and spirit lamp were ready. The attendant warmed the sticky paste at the end of a long steel needle similar to a knitting needle. Turning it constantly until it swelled and turned golden, he inserted it into the hole at the top of the enclosed bowl of the pipe (made of a peculiar mixture of sand and clay). The process took about three minutes, and about one minute and 10 to 12 whiffs to smoke it out. Lugo took it, lay on his side, and turned the bowl toward the flame to keep it warm. He took a whiff and thought of

Stephanie. He smoked 12 more. An hour later, looking disheveled, he was assisted by two teenage boys up the stairs to his apartment and flopped on the bed. The after-effects of alcohol and opium were so intense that he almost soiled his pants, but he made it to the toilet. Drunkenly, he mulled over the possibility of crippling or killing Elder.

Until Stephanie, Lugo had never loved any female in his life except for his sister, Josie. Women were playthings with whom he had sex. If they wanted a relationship, he was annoyed and dropped them. Whores aptly served his needs and were not demanding. And being a policeman, he usually got it free. A quick poke and he was done. Then, he met her. Everything changed. Told that he had to pay, he didn't care a whit. Dazzled and consumed, he wanted her, if not as his wife, then as his live-in woman. He was enchanted with her lips, slim fingers, laugh, accented voice, sophistication, and the pink areoles of her breasts. He liked her green eyes, strawberry blond hair, and the darker, thick hair of her pubic mound. She was a piece of art. He liked her walk, her delicate scent---everything. In her presence, he felt fantastic, and unlike his so-called friends and co-workers, she listened. Whenever he was in her company, he felt an intense high, a high he wanted to replicate again and again. She was something to live for, like opium. But, he mused, "Now, she treats me like a nobody."

During his third and last visit with Stephanie, he asked why she had been so passionate only once, the first time. Impressing him was that she ejaculated, squirted, much like a man—something he had never experienced in a woman. Her reply was simple. She had been without sex for months and was corny. She meant horny, but he knew what she meant. The remark left him deflated in an unexpected way. Unable to perform, he left with a dull headache. Then, she refused to see him and moved in with David Elder. "Yeah, for his money." Thoughts continued to run through his mind of destroying Elder. If he were dead, Stephanie would return to Ramona's. Then, he would be the one to rescue her. Gulping down a beer, he opened another and thought of her body. "Shit." He wanted her.

Sitting on the edge of the bed, blinking forcefully to clear his vision, he looked around the apartment. It was small—a 15 by 17 feet combination living room bedroom with a fold-down Murphy bed. Near the bed was the blunt, short kitchen counter, one stool, and next to it was the bathroom with a shower, and a toilet squeezed in so tightly that it barely allowed clearance for his knees. To allow more leg room, the bathroom door had been removed and left leaning against the wall. Thinking of Stephanie, he said loudly, "She'll want something better." Lurching out of bed, he almost fell. Fumbling with the telephone, he called Mack at his regular drinking spot. Mack didn't like it. It was 11:00 p.m. He wanted to catch the last ferry to Sausalito, but Lugo swore and insisted that he come to pick him up. His intent, he said, was to rough up Stephanie, nothing more, and he would be in disguise. Mack reluctantly agreed.

Lugo changed to a black shirt, black leather bomber jacket, black pants, and black shoes. Drunkenly, he combed his hair. At the door, he snatched a stiff, starched red Chinese mask and a black wool cap from a hook and put them on. Drunkenly swaying, he looked at his reflection in the bathroom mirror. Muttering, "You handsome devil," he pulled the cap down over the upper part of the mask to just above the eyelids. Satisfied, he went to the street wearing his disguise. Mack arrived. Seeing Lugo in his mask and cap, he was greatly amused and jokingly commented that he looked silly and should wait until he was sober. Lugo shouted a muffled command, "You'll do as I say. I know what I'm doing. It'll be easy. In and out."

At Stephanie's house, Mack again admonished, "Lugo, I've never seen you this drunk. You should wait."

"Shut up," Lugo responded.

"Do you have your gun?"

"Nah, don't need it. I (h)ave my club. I'm only going to scare her."

As expected, Elder's car was parked in the driveway, and as expected, Mack didn't notice. No streetlights were on this street. Evergreen trees added to the darkness. They waited an impatient five minutes and craned their necks, looking for possible witnesses. None. Mack knew Lugo's intention: His part was to wait down the street around the corner.

Swaying with vertigo at the short gate, Lugo surveyed the lawn, porch, and door. Blinking to clear his vision, he held the gatepost to steady himself. Then he headed for the porch. He wobbled off the flagstone walk. Drugged and drunk, he had trouble getting his lower body to cooperate. Adjusting the mask, wasted, he glared at the porch steps and tried to focus. Taking the first step, he lost his balance, stumbled back, sat on his butt, waited for the dizziness to pass, pulled himself up, and started over.

He had visited the house while Stephanie was at a yoga class in Chinatown. Each room and piece of furniture was memorized. After three practice swings with his oak club, he barreled forward, and crashed through the pine door. He spun once around, regained his bearing, nine paces to the left as he had practiced, and was at the bed.

Chapter Thirty-Five: Fight To Live

Two hours earlier, Elder sat on the edge of the bed, looking at Stephanie. He said to himself, "What a gift," and wondered how long it would last. He had grieved for the passing of his wife, Georgia, not only when she died but for days, months, and years after, even after wonderful times with Stephanie. Georgia's memory would come to mind for the rest of his life at the most unexpected times, and his heart would ache.

210

He wondered whether he should tell Stephanie that Maia had invited them to church. He was prejudiced toward religion, a mythical God, and an afterlife. Abe and Maia believed, but not him. Abe was an elder in the Negro Baptist Church and sang in the choir. As far as Elder was concerned, God had let him down too often and did a piss poor job. What he had accomplished, he had accomplished on his own and with Abe, not by God's intervention. "Yes, Abe does a better job, and so do I." He didn't like churches and religion, especially after his mother, Ella Grace died and his father went to hell.

The only time Elder felt there might be a God was when he was stirred by black choirs singing gospel music. He chuckled at the thought of a Negro friend who sang in the choir at Abe's church. The man didn't believe but loved to sing; if he had to fib about being a Christian, so be it. He was part of the church family. Elder and Abe disagreed about religion, and the subject was avoided.

"What are you thinking?" Stephanie asked.

"Nothing important. Maia invited us to church. You know how I feel, but would you like to go?" She opened her arms and told him to come to bed.

"Yes, we'll go," she said. "Maybe, Maia is softening toward me and wants to save my soul."

The bed and headboard were in a corner under a window. When the door shattered, Elder was on the inside against the wall, snuggling flush against Stephanie's backside. One hand fondled a breast. He nuzzled her neck. Her hand covered his.

Lugo's footfalls pounded loudly on the hardwood floor. Stephanie leapt out of bed screaming. Lugo threw a straight blow to her chin, but she was a moving target. Connecting with her forehead, he sent her bouncing off a wall, to the edge of the bed, and to the floor. In haste, Elder attempted to throw off the blankets but became entangled. Lugo struck him in rapid-fire with the truncheon. The first was a glancing blow to arm and chest, followed by solid blows to his side and mid-back, cracking ribs. Grabbing a fistful of Elder's hair, he hauled him over Stephanie's inert body onto the floor and caught the piquant aroma of sex. Thirty-seven minutes earlier, he would have found Elder between her legs, leisurely kissing the smooth curves of her inner thighs and moving to her moistened pubic mound. He tasted her delights, pleasing her, until she pulled him up to reward him with kisses.

Elder weighed 227 pounds, yet Lugo easily pulled him, the sheet, and the blanket off the bed, over Stephanie, and to the floor. Lugo punished him rapidly with repeated blows to his upper and lower torso, careful to avoid the head. Before caving in his skull, he wanted Elder to suffer—to know his end was near. Elder, attempted to crawl away and was trying to clear his mind. Lugo held him in place. Never had Elder feared anyone, no matter the adversary. Nor was he ever intimidated. He had been in a fair share of fights, but this time he was caught unaware. His fear was for Stephanie. He was failing to protect her, just as he had failed his sister, Kathy, and Georgia, his beloved wife.

Lugo stood over Elder, eyes wild, excited, gleefully rocking back and forth, savoring the moment before delivering the death blow to the skull, smashing it open like a ripe tomato.

Elder desperately struggled to remain conscious. With his head bowed between Lugo's knees, holding his calves, gathering strength, and gulping air, he sprang upright smashing his forehead into Lugo's face. A cracking sound was audible. Lugo's head snapped back. Stunned, he reeled. He swayed. The room tilted. The cap fell to the floor. The mask was knocked askew but held. The smashed mask, opium and alcohol had dulled the blow. Nonetheless, it gave Lugo a terrific shock, so much that for a few

212

seconds, he swayed in place, disoriented, not knowing where he was or what he was doing.

Elder feebly clung to Lugo's torso. Coming somewhat to his senses, Lugo pushed him to the floor. Defenseless, moaning, and on his knees, Elder gamely tried to rise but couldn't.

Swearing, dazed, and swaying, Lugo placed a finger on Elder's head on the spot where he would strike. To test himself, he lowered the club to Elder's head to touch. But woozy, he tilted and missed. Drooling, intoxicated, and seeing double, he thought he might rest for a moment, maybe sleep. There was no rush. Stephanie was unconscious, and Elder was entirely at his mercy.

For a second, he didn't feel the bite. Old arthritic Lobo had stiffly roused from a deep slumber and sank what he had left of his teeth into Lugo's ankle. Lugo's reaction was to throw the poor fellow against the wall, almost killing him.

"Crap," Lugo exclaimed. He liked dogs and considered them nicer than most people. He hadn't thought of the possibility of a dog. Returning his attention to Elder, he heard whispered cursing. Before he could react, an excruciating blow to his rib cage sent him flying to his hands and knees. Another sent him crashing onto a side table, breaking the lamp, and shattering the bulb. It was Stephanie, grimacing—full naked breasts heaving, wielding a bat, and attacking relentlessly and mercilessly, striking anything and everything on his body. Blows struck his feet, lower legs, knees, and back. Missing his head three times, she twice clipped the same ear, hurting like hell. Raising his arms in defense resulted in a strike to his elbow, disabling it. Strikes, fast and furious, gave him no time to stand. An attempt to grab the bat resulted in a fractured thumb. On hands and knees, he scampered to the front door to escape. Stephanie followed, grunting when landing a blow. His knee was struck. She connected again. Most were solid, some glancing.

Before tumbling out the door, to the porch, and down the steps, a blow connected solidly on his buttocks. He righted himself, hobbled toward the little gate, lost his balance, and fell on the gate, knocking it askew.

Stephanie stood on the porch, glaring, naked, chest heaving, and holding the bat. In her accented voice, she screamed, "God damn you, Lugo, I'm going to dich umbringen, uh, uh, kill you."

On his backside, holding the broken gate with his right hand, looking at Stephanie, he marveled; "Damn, she's beautiful." In his intoxicated condition, mind swirling, he fleetingly wondered if he was in a bad dream. He thought she would come after him, naked though she was, and scrambled into the street. Stephanie gave him one last scorching look and went inside.

If there had been an observer, he would have said that he witnessed a bloody drunken man with a gimp, staggering, weaving, and putting out his hand to buildings and fences to steady himself—and cursing with the most colorful language one could imagine, interspersed with exclamations of, "I don't believe it." Almost to the car, he gagged, stopped, and vomited.

When Lugo came around the corner Mack was casually leaning against the car, feet crossed, leisurely smoking. Seeing Lugo beaten, limping, soiled, and crookedly lurching toward him, Mack's quizzical expression would have been comical had it not been for the situation. Squelching laughter, he thought, "What? She beat him!?"

Ripping off the mask, Lugo threw himself into the car. Incredulous that it had gone so badly, but couldn't deny it, Mack asked, "Can I guess? It didn't go well? What happened? Your face is bloody. Here's a rag. You're dripping. Your nose looks broken. I told you to wait. Look at you, beat up by a woman."

214

"Shut up. Get going."

It was a fiasco. Despite the darkness and mask, he lost his club and cap, and Stephanie knew it was him. Realizing that the police would be called, Mack repeatedly told him to forget that he was ever there. Lugo replied, "Forget it. You're in it now."

Stephanie knelt over Elder to see if he was alive. He was but in a bad way. With his head spinning, barely conscious and grimacing, she helped him onto the bed, and threw on a dress. The ambulance and police arrived simultaneously. An officer questioned her and took her report. Reluctantly, she sat at the kitchen table to give a hurried description of the attack and assailant. Firmly, she said, "It was Lugo Spaak, a policeman. I know him." Impatiently, she answered questions. Elder was being carried out, and she wanted to accompany him to the hospital.

"No, I didn't see his face. No, I didn't hear his voice," she said, "but it was him."

Neither Lugo's name, nor the accusation that it was a police officer were included in the report. Another officer found Lugo's black lacquered truncheon poking out from under the dresser. His cap was on the floor. He walked the items outside to the police car and tossed them to the floorboard.

At the hospital, Elder was treated for bruises to his chest, two fractured ribs, and three fractured fingers on his left hand, defensive injuries.

Abe was in anguish, lamenting that he had not, somehow, been there to help. In frustration, he asked, "Is there something about us that attracts evil men, or does God send them to us to rid the earth of them? I had hoped that part of our lives had ended."

Elder, in pain, coughed out a reply. "If we don't take care of him, he'll come again. Maybe he'll come for you. Maybe for Sam and Jessica, and Maia and the girls. First, let's see if he goes to work and his condition."

215

The next day, the San Francisco Examiner ran stories of disorderly dock workers, inflammatory talk of communist organizers, and ten lines of an attack on a prominent citizen. The assailant was described as a large, stocky Negro wearing a mask.

A middle-aged woman with a child reached into the gutter, picked up a trashed news copy, and read with interest.

Chapter Thirty-Six: Aftermath

Lugo took off from work, sick. Cho at the opium den set his broken nose. Painfully, he iced and used makeup from a beauty shop to cover the discolored skin. His ribs were severely bruised. Every move made him wince; his elbow and thumb ached like hell; his heel and ankle were tender. Teeth and gums ached. Hell, his whole body ached. There was no worry about anyone seeing the injuries, except for his face and ear. The thumb he set on his own with two popsicle sticks cut to size and wrapped with tape. The makeup did a poor job of concealing the damage.

When he called in, asking for more time off, Sgt. Frank refused and ordered him to report to the station immediately. When Lugo walked into the sergeant's office, he concealed his injuries as best he could but didn't fool anyone. He limped, his busted nose was swollen, and despite the makeup, his two black eyes were evident. His club and cap were on the desk.

"You look like hell."

"I got in a fight at the docks."

"Yeah, sure! Here's your club and cap. You dropped them."

"Where?"

"Oh, God, don't play dumb. I'm covering for you for now. We'll see where this goes. It isn't good. She didn't see your face but swears it was you."

"Yeh, she's going to insist and try to pin it on me."

Sarcastically, Frank said, "Well, it was you, wasn't it? But maybe you want to say your club was stolen? Then you can get a few witnesses to perjure themselves, to say they were with you somewhere else?"

"Hey, that's not bad."

"You knucklehead, your initials are carved on the handle. You're damn lucky I was the one who got the call and that Eugene found it before anyone else. He's a good man. He won't say anything."

"Yeh, okay, it was me. Now, we have to get rid of her. I can't take a chance. With Elder behind her putting pressure on the chief, they'll come after me. We have to get rid of her, fast. Anyway, it will be just one more dead whore. No one will care."

"Except Mr. Elder. And don't say 'we.' You're on your own. If you're so hell-bent on murder, you do it. Not me."

"Listen, you owe me big time. Before your promotion, remember? We both know about your little pastime and that little Chinese kid, maybe 10 or 11, you killed. Yeah, he shoplifted a couple of pieces of candy. You scared him. You told him he was under arrest and his parents would see him in jail. Yeh, we were both drinking but you were drunk. But if he did a little favor, you'd let him go. So, instead of letting him go with a warning, you took him to the alley. The poor kid was crying for his mom, begging, but you didn't care. You forced his head down; he gagged and threw up on

217

your pants. You lost it. There he was, just a poor dumb kid, and you hit him with the butt of your gun and split his skull. He fell on your shoes and died. You panicked, blubbering that your life was over. We dumped the body together. His parents are probably still looking for him. It was awful, even for me, but I covered for you. Now you help me one time, and we're square."

Sergeant Frank scowled; he didn't like it, not one bit. It was all true. There was no way Lugo would implicate himself in a cover-up without destroying himself, but he couldn't take the chance that Lugo would blab that his partner was homosexual, a queer, a fairy, preying on young boys, and in this case, a pedophile. It would destroy his carefully groomed reputation and career. He'd go to prison. Weakly, he said, "All right, when?"

"Tomorrow, there's going to be a big demonstration at the docks. We're going to be there in force. Yeah, lots of noise and commotion. Lots of confusion. We'll do it late. It'll be easy. Everyone will stay off the streets because of the riots and curfew."

On the way out, Lugo passed other officers. Three patted him on the back like he was some kind of hero, but another almost toppled backward on his chair laughing hilariously. Barely able to contain himself, he quipped, "Hey Lugo, I hear you got in a fight with a girl and lost."

"So much for Eugene keeping his mouth shut," Frank thought. "Stupid, stupid."

Elder was in the hospital Saturday, Sunday, and Monday. Tuesday, Sam, Jessica, and Stephanie took him home. An argument was made for Stephanie to move into the big house immediately. But she declined, saying she would do it the next day, in time for lunch on Wednesday, the 4th of July. Tonight, she wanted to bathe, clean up, and pack some clothing.

218

Unknown to Lugo, the day following the attack, Abe paid a visit to the opium den. First, he relaxed and savored a glass of excellent wine at Dominick's. Forty-five minutes later, a young Chinese boy approached to say that Lugo was doped up. Abe gave him a coin, and the two walked together to the den.

Abe knelt beside a stupefied, uncaring Lugo in the throes of addiction. Carefully, he loosened the scarf around his neck to see the damage; then he lifted the shirt. Bruises. He pulled up the hem of the pants to see more. While examining the torso, Lugo moved and threw his arm over Abe's wrist. But Lugo's eyes were closed. Abe carefully removed his hand, stood, and pulled out his pearl-handled pocketknife. Cho shook his head. Abe mused, "All right, can't kill a sleeping man."

Abe returned to the streets. Strolling back to Little Italy, tall, lanky, and impressive, he drew attention. Ahead of him, Chinese men and women excitedly, hurriedly, crossed the street and made an orderly line. Abe was cautious, but they were smiling and not threatening. He was waved forward. He passed from one to the other, politely acknowledging each. At the end were four he recognized from that foul day when he and Elder saved them from Captain Blodger. Nodding, smiling with little bows, and beaming, they excitedly shook his hand and thanked him for his service.

Pleased, Abe looked around. "Ha, there they are." As expected, Matteo and Xavier were following discretely, or so they thought. Matteo looked embarrassed at having been detected so easily. Abe waved for them to join him. The Chinese had started to disperse but, upon seeing Matteo and Xavier, reformed the line, just as excited as before, and waited for them to pass. Abe, thoroughly amused and enormously pleased, thought, "Life is good. After they pass the gauntlet, we'll have a leisurely Italian dinner, and I'll see if I can get Matteo to have a glass of wine."

Chapter Thirty-Seven: Tuesday, Daytime, July 03rd, Riots at The Docks

Nerves were at the breaking point. Ninety-four ships lay idle in the ports of San Francisco and hundreds more up and down the West Coast from San Diego, California, to Seattle, Washington, almost 2000 miles.

Tuesday, July 03: The day Elder was released from the hospital, all appeared peaceful, with no incident, not until 11:00 a.m. Trucks with merchandise, driven by scabs, and protected by the police, moved freight from the waterfront to inland warehouses.

Seven hundred policemen were at the waterfront armed with clubs, tear gas, rifles, shotguns, and pistols. Not only did Sergeant Frank have to deal with the fiasco caused by Lugo, and causing more trouble, the newspapers had been whipping up a frenzy with talk of anarchists, communists, and socialists taking over the country. Hundreds of pickets, tired of ill-treatment, were in the streets. Scattered riots began. Adding to the confusion, ordinary folks, to show support joined the strikers.

Thousands of onlookers mingled in streets overlooking the Embarcadero, caught in the unfolding drama, hoping to see the action. It started at the McCormick Steamship Company's Pier 38. Loaded trucks exited the warehouses and were met with charging, yelling men. Waves of violence ensued with the police charging, and the strikers retaliating. Innocent spectators crowded together at windows of nearby buildings were hit by wafting tear gas. With tears streaming, they fell back. Pitched battles went on throughout the day; clothes were torn, faces were bloodied, many were seriously injured.

William J. Quinn, the police chief, led his men. Sgt. Frank was in the thick of it, and so were Lugo and Mack. Bricks, stones, boards, and fists were used against the police. Police fired errant bullets. One crashed through a window of the Bank of America, grazing a teller over the left eye. Police shot into the strikers. One emptied a riot gun and his pistol. Two strikers were wounded, one in the ankle.

Sgt. Frank, distracted by thoughts of the crime they were to commit that night against Stephanie, was almost run over by one of his own, a police car.

Scabs, those taking the jobs of the strikers, were pulled from trucks, and beaten. Sacks of rice, corn, and beans were slit open and scattered in the streets. Standing amidst spilled corn, Lugo was rhythmically beating the bejesus out of a striker with his fist. Sgt. Frank pulled his revolver and fingered the trigger. "Should I shoot him?" With Lugo's death, the events he had set in motion would stop. As if reading his mind, Lugo turned and glared at Sgt. Frank. Their gaze was broken by a tear gas canister. Both ran with burning eyes and distressed lungs. Screams and shouts filled the air. It was chaos. Four mounted police officers galloped past, choking, coughing, with tears running from their eyes. Held in reserve by the police was another type of tear gas, a nauseating vomiting gas.

Chapter Thirty-Eight: July 03rd, Tuesday Night. Kill Her!

Lugo, Sgt. Frank, and Mack had to move fast before Stephanie moved to Elder's house. Arriving at her house at 9:45 p.m., they sat patiently in an unmarked police car, and watched her house, and its lights. So intent were they watching that they were startled by a cute elderly lady in her late 70's. Peering over her horn rim glasses, she tapped on a side window, and asked, "What are you men doing here?" They identified themselves and explained they were on a stakeout for a home burglar. "God bless you, boys," she responded, and brought them coffee and banana bread. "After

221

you're finished, leave the cups on the stoop, by the geranium pots. Her son, she said, gave her the Italian ceramic pots, and had painted the one-step stoop red.

At 10:25 p.m., the lights of Stephanie's home were extinguished. The house was dark. The porch light remained on. "Okay, let's go. Nobody's out," said Sgt. Frank. In quick step, they briskly walked to Stephanie's porch. Sgt. Frank rapped on the newly installed oak door. A light went on. Lugo and Mack stood to the side, out of sight.

He knocked again. Stephanie opened the small speakeasy door. "Sgt. Frank," she exclaimed, "What are you doing here? Has something happened to Elder?"

"I apologize for coming so late, but we have talk. It's about your assailant. I think it was Lugo Spaak, just as you said. We have to act fast before he flees the city. Can you give me five minutes?"

Stephanie unlocked the double deadbolt lock and the chain. "All right, five minutes. But sergeant, please, let's make it fast. It's late, and I'm tired."

In the process of opening her door, Sgt. Frank, heart pounding, shoved it wide and stepped in. Stephanie's eyes widened in puzzlement, then realization. To their astonishment, she let out a shrill blood-curdling scream, freezing them momentarily in place, and barreled forward at Sgt. Frank. Jumping on his body, she wrapped her legs around his torso, grabbed his hair, and bit down hard on his right ear. Thrown backward, he would have fallen had not been for a wall. While chewing his ear, drawing blood, she went for his eyes, missed, and raked her fingernails deeply, digging down his cheek. He threw her off, but she wasn't through. She was nimble, fought, dodged, and screamed, hoping the neighbors would hear. If she was going to die, she would leave her mark. She swung to Sgt. Frank's right, almost behind him. This put him between her and Lugo. But

Frank grabbed her hair and whipped her back into the middle of the three. Managing to grab his wrist, she kicked out blindly and connected with something solid.

Lugo grabbed her robe. In full light to the kitchen for a weapon, she let it slip off. But Lugo grabbed a handful of hair and punched her in the kidneys. In terrible pain, gasping, she fell. He wasn't through. Pulling her back up by the hair, he struck her stomach and let go.

Mack stupidly hopped from spot to spot from one foot to another. But it wasn't in him to manhandle women, and he ended up simply observing.

Stephanie, on the floor in a fetal position, rolled over on her back, naked, her eyes glazed, barely conscious, and groaning.

In haste Lugo undid his belt and dropped his pants. Frank and Mack stared, transfixed, looking down at Lugo's hairy butt. His pants were at his ankles, and he had the biggest penis they had ever seen. Their sensibilities, and morals were in confusion. Lugo was raping an unconscious woman.

Sgt. Frank knew they were to kill Stephanie. Mack, being the dummy he was, somehow was under the misconception that they would only rough her up. Neither imagined it would be so difficult, terrible, and messy.

Sgt. Frank's mouth dropped open, gaping, staring. Fingering his revolver, he thought, "This is horrible," and slid it half out of its holster. A thought flashed through his mind of shooting Lugo and maybe Mack and getting out of there.

"Good God," Mack exclaimed, "This is awful."

Stephanie, regaining consciousness, moaned. Slowly, she lifted her arms, caressed Lugo's back, and moaned in ecstasy, or so he thought.

"Lugo, oh, Lugo," she sighed.

Lugo, full of himself and believing Stephanie's moans were of pleasure, couldn't imagine otherwise. Too bad, he thought, but she has to die. "Yeh, you love it, you bitch, always did," he said, thrusting his hips.

Stephanie's head was pounding, but lifting her hands to his thick, touseled hair, she nuzzled his neck. Lugo, making ugly guttural sounds, reached his most vulnerable moment.

"Yes, Lugo, yes," she whispered. In the next moment, he was screaming, "Get her off, get off, help me." With both hands holding fistfuls of hair, she had locked his head in place. Her teeth bit deep into his neck. Clamped forcefully, she jerked her young jaw side to side, yanking, attempting to rip it open, and drawing blood. If not for his thick bull-neck, she might have bitten his jugular vein.

Screaming, he grabbed her hair to pull her away. He changed his mind, afraid he'd lose a chunk of flesh.

Sgt. Frank stepped in and delivered a short kick to the ribs but hit her elbow. Trying again, he kicked the side of her face, splitting the skin. But her bite held. Again, he kicked, short kicks, again and again. Between a whimper and a groan, Stephanie's eyes rolled up; she went limp, and the rise and fall of her chest stopped. Her face and teeth were a bloody mess—blood mingled with Lugo's and Frank's. Sgt. Frank, feeling revulsion and breathing hard, stared at her lifeless body.

Lugo rose with his hand on his neck to staunch the bleeding. Blood seeped through his fingers, down to his chest, spotting his shirt. Grabbing a couple of white crocheted doilies off the arms of a chair, he pressed them to the wound. "Is she dead?" he asked.

Nudging Stephanie's face with his shoe, Sgt. Frank replied, "Yeh, sure, looks like it." Adrenaline pumped so hard that it wasn't until then that he touched his fingers to his cheek and ear and came away with blood.

Mack exclaimed, "Damn that was exciting. Is this the woman you said you were going to marry?"

"Shut the fuck up," Lugo screamed.

"Damn, she's gorgeous,"

"Go ahead, take a turn, she's still warm."

"Hell no, I'm not a pervert. I won't fuck a dead woman."

Breathing deeply, in pain, Lugo pulled up his pants, buckled his belt, and glared at the inert body. Snatching a small pillow from a chair, he knelt, hit her a fierce blow, and pressed it to her face.

Sgt. Frank, panicked, lifted his foot to Lugo's side and shoved him off. "Lugo, give it up. She's dead. Lugo rose, looked down, and muttered, "Rotten bitch. You could have had me."

Mack standing stupidly, said, "Geez, you messed her up."

"Mack, understand this," Frank replied, "We messed her up. You included. You're here, and let it happen. If one goes down, we go down together."

Next door, a couple sat up in bed, listening. "Did you hear that?" They listened. Nothing. "I thought I heard screaming." Hearing nothing more, they returned to sleep.

Sgt. Frank was shaken. "We have to get out of here."

"Hold on," Lugo said. Holding his hand to his wound, and leaving a trail of blood, he moved to the kitchen sink. Snatching an unopened Jim Beam fine whiskey bottle from the counter, he cracked the neck on the counter's edge. Sgt. Frank and Mack watched astounded as Lugo splashed the alcohol over his wound. Lugo emitted ugly excruciating sounds. Suddenly, twisting side to side, groaning horribly, and rocking back and forth, and up and down, he finally flopped down on the floor, looking disoriented. Sgt. Frank pulled him up and toward the door.

"Let's get out of here," Frank said.

Frank and Lugo headed for the door. Mack delayed. He bent and ran his hand over a breast, fondled one, then the other, squeezing like they were balloons. He thought of putting his mouth to a pink nipple but thought he better not, not after saying he wasn't a pervert. Muttering, "What a waste,"

225

he positioned her head to get a better look at a once beautiful woman. Then, picking up her flannel robe, he wiped blood from his fingers, and casually tossed it over her body. With a second look, he bent and adjusted it neatly to cover the face and body. "Sorry, honey," he said.

Outside, the cups and saucers they had placed on the old lady's porch were gone. "Hold on," Lugo said. With a shove and sounds of cracking wood, he broke in. What followed was a woman's panicked voice. Sgt. Frank, in remorse, lowered his head, ashamed. Moments later, Lugo returned with banana bread and one geranium pot and said, "Let's go."

"My gosh," Mack said, "she was a nice old lady. I can't believe it. You even took her pot. This isn't good. It's not what I thought."

Lugo asked, "Not good?" No, Mack, murder means someone dies. It's messy. Did you think we were going to talk?" Handing him a slice of banana bread, he snapped, "Stick this in your yap."

Silently, Sgt. Frank was seriously questioning his sanity. "Why," he asked, "did I allow myself to get into this mess?" It was a fiasco and much dirtier than he had expected. And Stephanie's fierce fight to live was not anticipated. It made it worse. Distastefully looking at Lugo sitting next to him, he thought, "I should have killed him."

Mack was not the brightest candle on the police force, and he knew it. He was like a complacent old cow, easily led but competent enough to be a patrolman. He had no ambitions, was never promoted, and didn't care. He reflected little on life and left worries to others. After the attack on Stephanie, he dimly reasoned that he went along with the night's events only because Sgt. Frank was in on it. "Yeah," he thought, "I never touched her. So, I'm innocent."

226

Chapter Thirty-Nine: Fourth Of July

On Wednesday, July 04, Independence Day, the strikers took a holiday.
At breakfast, Elder received a call from the police.

Stephanie's neighbors had heard screaming. They sat up in bed to listen
but heard nothing more and thought it might have been their imagination.
But at sunrise, they walked their dog and passed by the house of an
acquaintance, that of the elderly lady. The door was askew, smashed in.
Entering cautiously, they found her body half-in and half-out of the
bedroom.

After calling the police, they passed Stephanie's house. Her door was
wide open. They looked at each other. Something was wrong. They went
to the porch and called her name. No response. They were afraid of what
they would find but peeked in. And there was the body, mostly covered by
a bloody white flannel robe. In horror, they backed away. This was two
murders near their home on the same night—a veritable crime wave.
Moments later, Matteo arrived, and called Elder.

Elder was bereft. Striding up and down the hall, he shouted, "No, it
can't be," and, with his fractured ribs, went into a fit of coughing. Abe had
attempted to stop Elder from going to Stephanie's, arguing that he was still
recovering, and the police undoubtedly would not let them see her. "I'm
calling Fred Kinder. I want him there," Elder said.

When Elder, Abe and Maia arrived at Stephanie's, five police cars were
there, two parked in front, one across the street, and two investigating the
murder of an elderly lady. While Elder waited in the car with Maia, Abe
talked to the officer posted at the front door. No matter what argument he
used, he was flatly denied entry. His temper was flaring, but he held it in.
While stepping back, the medical examiner, Fred Kinder, M.D., arrived.

"Abe, I got your call." Kinder was kindly disposed toward Abe. Abe was in his social circle and a font of information, including profitable tips. Taking Abe's arm, he blithely waved the officer aside and walked in.

Abe surveyed the room. Sgt. Frank, tall, balding, and reedy thin, with broad but scrawny shoulders, was kneeling over a partially covered body. Two other officers were at his side, staring uncomfortably at Stephanie's bloody matted face.

The doctor took charge and asked for an estimate of when she was killed. They didn't know. He asked if the body had been touched in any way. Sgt. Frank assured him that it had not. They had examined every room and surrounding area but not the body.

Abe was chilled. She was so still. He liked her. She had a wonderful open personality, full of jests and laughter, marvelously intelligent, and world traveled. Bile rose in his throat. He waited.

"Alright," Kinder said, "let's do this." Kneeling to her body, he examined her forehead, semi-dried bloody nose, and the entire bruised left side of her face. There was a rupture in her cheek where she had been kicked. Her jaw, teeth, and lips were particularly bloody, and semi-dried matted blood extended from her throat to her hair. Kinder gently moved the hair from her face. Patting it to the temples it stuck. The young, clean-cut officer standing next to Abe gagged and looked away.

The doctor checked for a pulse and her heart. "Well, well," he said and continued to repeat himself, "Well, well."

Sgt. Frank put the back of his hand to his mouth, aghast at the damage they had inflicted. "Well, well, what?" He wondered.

Kinder paused. Pensively, he looked at Stephanie's face. Carefully opening her jaw, his fingers moved inside, checking for damage.

228

Sgt. Frank stared, fixated at the condition of the corpse but also startled. "Her eyes? Weren't they open when we left?" Now, they were closed. His anxiety was rising. "Shouldn't rigor mortis have set in?"

The doctor leaned back with a questioning look, leaned forward, and, for a second time, checked for pulses in her throat and wrist. "Hand me that pillow," he instructed.

"Jesus Christ," Frank thought, "She better be dead. What does he want with a pillow?"

"Somebody call an ambulance," Kinder said. And, as if the living deserved more modesty than the dead, he said, "Move back, give the lady some privacy."

"Don't you mean the meat wagon, the hearse?" asked Sgt. Frank.

Kinder didn't answer immediately. He lifted Stephanie's head and positioned it gently on the pillow. Then, he replied, "No, it's interesting. I'm guessing some of the blood is not hers. She had a nosebleed, but it's not broken. Her cheek is cut, but there is no wound inside her mouth. She has blood all over her teeth and gums, but the teeth are not loose; they're firm. She's a mess but alive. She's been brutally beaten and raped. She probably has fractured ribs. Her brain is undoubtedly concussed. Her breathing is shallow, but her heart is strong and steady. Yes, she's a mess but she sure put up a fight. Look at her fingernails, defensive injuries." Eyes went to her fingers, nicely manicured with red polish—two bloody fingernails, one held by a thin tendril of tissue.

Abe, who had not said a word, started to ask a question. "Doc?" Stephanie's green eyes flicked open. Her eyes met Abe's. With a sigh, she noticeably inhaled, exhaled, closed her eyes, and went to sleep. She had groggily become aware and heard Sgt. Frank's voice. But until she heard Abe's voice, she hadn't moved a muscle. Hearing him speak, she knew she was safe.

One of the officers, alarmed, jumped back and frightfully spat, "Good God, she's alive!"

Sgt. Frank blanched; his coffee and breakfast was coming up. He rushed to the kitchen sink and vomited until he was dry heaving. Wiping his mouth with a towel, he turned back. Everyone was staring, especially Abe, focused on the strip bandage from the corner of Frank's eye to below the cheekbone, and his ear. Under the bandage were four stitches and a drying crust of blood.

Sgt. Frank said, "I'm sorry, the brutality to this woman got to me." He touched his cheek and said, "Cut myself shaving. Doctor, could there be brain damage?"

"Unfortunately, yes, but let's hope for the best. I'm guessing when someone inflicted these injuries maybe she was faking and holding her breath. Maybe she managed to relax enough to absorb each blow. Look at this knot on her temple. It could have killed her. She must have a strong will to live. These Irish women are tough." Someone corrected him, saying she was German. Fred quipped, "Okay, whatever."

Abe asked, "She opened her eyes. Is she awake? Can she hear us?"

"She was," responded the doctor, "Now she's asleep, as opposed to unconscious."

Forcing himself to appear calm, Sgt. Frank withstood the rest of the examination, dreadfully afraid she would open her eyes and look at him.

Fred gently palpated bruising around the thighs. Then he covered her to her chin. Standing straight up, abruptly, he said, "Monsters, we have monsters on the loose. All right, where's that ambulance?"

After the ambulance personnel placed Stephanie in the ambulance, Frank climbed in. "Hold on," said Abe. "Get out!" Disdainfully, he grabbed Sgt. Frank by the arm and forcefully pulled him out.

Sgt. Frank protested. "If she wakes up, she might be able to identify her assailant. It might be our only chance. She could die on the way."

"Sergeant, you're not going anywhere with her. Do your interview at the hospital!"

Elder watched from the car. When Abe told him the news, his eyes grew moist. Wanly smiling at his friend, he thanked him for watching out for him and Stephanie. "Abe, now what?" he asked.

"I'm riding with Stephanie," Abe replied. "Maia will drive you to the hospital."

In the ambulance, Stephanie awoke. Abe wiped oozing blood from her nose. Agitated and desperate, she reached for his hand. Weakly, struggling to speak, she said, "Abe, komm naher." He lowered his ear to her lips. By the time they arrived at the hospital, he knew everything.

At the hospital Elder turned to Maia. "Maia, I love her. I wish you would try."

She nodded and said, "Yes, I will." Abe had also implored her to be friendly, saying Stephanie was exceptional, and she was, but not in the way he thought. Maia mused, "As a successful manipulator of men, yes, as a temptress and femme fatale, yes."

Maia had tried to ostracize Stephanie, to make her feel so unwelcome that she would forget Elder and move on. Georgia had been greatly loved, and accepting anyone in her place was difficult. But Stephanie had saved Elder's life. Her characterization of her as a tramp had to be reconsidered. It would not be easy. Begrudgingly, she would be civil and polite. "I don't have to like her. Abe says I'm being unreasonable. Maybe, I am."

Upon receiving the news from Sgt. Frank that Stephanie was alive, Lugo and Mack were filled with disbelief, then dread. The consensus was that they had to get to her immediately to finish her off before she woke. It had to be at St. Francis, and Sgt. Frank was the one to do it. He certainly

231

couldn't trust the other two dummies to do it right. If challenged, he would say he was investigating a crime.

Within the hour, Sgt. Frank was at the hospital. Weaving in and out among patients injured in the previous day's rioting--family members, friends, and medical staff, he checked the nursing stations, and the location of Stephanie's room and its proximity to the stairs.

Standing at Stephanie's room entrance, Abe brusquely stopped Sgt. Frank from entering. Inside, four individuals stared back at him: Maia, Elder, and a doctor and nurse.

Hearing Sgt. Frank's voice, Stephanie's fingers tightened on Elder's. "Sgt. Frank," Elder calmly said, "she's in a coma. There's no telling if she'll wake up." But Elder knew everything, including the rape. Stephanie had agreed to pretend she had amnesia in exchange for revenge.

Sergeant Frank made his way out of the hospital, astounded she was alive. Worried thoughts filled his head: If she awoke hopefully her brain and memory would be gravely impaired. If she accused him, he would say she was crazy and needed a psychiatric evaluation. He would assert innocence and say she was incompetent but knew he was wishful thinking. Fatigued and ashamed that he had ever aligned himself with Lugo in this despicable farce. he wondered what his loving father would think of him now. As for his mother, she was a Bible thumper and hated that he was gay, a homosexual. She called him a lousy pansy going to hell and urged him to kill himself. On the day he moved out, his father was supportive and sad. She rejoiced.

At 10:00 p.m., Sgt. Frank tried again. Attempting to exude authority, he entered the hospital in full police uniform, including his holstered revolver. Nobody challenged him, and there was so much activity in recent days from the riots that it was commonplace for police to come and go. Again, he was thwarted. The halls were full of activity. Once again, he had to retreat, and he was tired. There was the constant trouble from the strikers at the docks, the long workdays, and now he had to deal with this fiasco caused by Lugo. Exhausted and hungry, he fell asleep in his patrol car.

Chapter Forty: July 05, 1:00 a.m. Eve of Bloody Thursday

Playful young men pounded on the car's hood, waking Frank from a stuporous sleep, and laughed at his startled face. Lethargically, he forced himself to move. Fortified with black coffee from a nearby bar, he tried again. He entered a side entrance, and took the stairs thinking, "This has to end tonight."

Perspiring a clammy sweat and not because of the weather, Frank worried about this damned woman. "Why is she alive?" On the 3rd floor, he peeked out from the stairwell door. Compared to the earlier activity, it was eerily quiet. Lights were dimmed. Stephanie's room was two doors away; the nurse's station was beyond it. Her door was slightly ajar. Two nurses were halfway into a room, pushing a cart. Dashing to Stephanie's dimly lit room he moved to the bed. Breathing heavily with urgency, he carefully opened the adjustable curtain. Pausing, feeling pangs of conscience, he looked down at the sleeping form. But out of self-preservation, she had to die. He was so concentrated on staring at her bandaged head that he did not see the short, diminutive man, Matteo, with his long hair tied in a ponytail. The rustle of the curtain had awakened him from his dozing sleep. Startled by the sound of movement, Frank snapped his head to the left to see Matteo's eyes roaming over his uniform, weapon, and face. In Matteo's right hand was a knife. It snicked open. The sound almost made Frank bolt for the door. But holding his ground he faked an appearance of calm.

Sgt. Frank had expected to kill Stephanie easily, quickly, either with a well-placed pillow over her face or, since she already had so much discolored skin, he would throttle her. There would be a delay, then an investigation, but it would be too late. But now, here was a reversal. Haltingly, he said, "I'm Sgt. Frank. I'm investigating the attempted murder of this young lady. I hoped she would be awake—to get information."

This little man with his short black hair, dark eyes, and olive skin, made no reply.

Sgt. Frank asked, "Do you speak English?" Still no reply.

Of course, Matteo understood. He was Matteo Canales, holder of a Ph.D. In botany from Williams University of the Andes, Venezuela. Elder had helped him immigrate to the United States. Matteo had been prosecuted and detained more than once for political activism. After completing his studies, he gave up his sideline as a stable boy and jockey. But after years of disturbing political activism and having been alerted to another pending arrest, he fled the country.

Sgt. Frank took his eyes off Matteo and glanced at Stephanie. Only then did he realize that someone else was in the room, someone at the foot of the bed, someone holding a shotgun. Frank reeled back and retreated toward the door. The little man stood and followed. Frank waited at the Otis elevator. The little man watched from the entrance of Stephanie's room. Two nurses at the nurse's station also watched. One said, "Sir?" Whatever had possessed him. He knew he looked guilty but couldn't help it, and the staring by the little man was unnerving. It took forever for the elevator to arrive. It was seconds.

Sgt. Frank walked out of the front door into the parking lot and looked up at Stephanie's room. The lights were on. He broke his gaze and turned to his car parked close by. Emblazoned on the side door was the word "Police." It made no difference.

234

"Gawwwd." The little man was standing by the car's door. Sgt. Frank reached for his service revolver. But the little man, with a slight motion of his right hand pointed to a nearby group of slender decorative trees. Standing there, a husky young man casually held a half-raised shotgun. It was the man he had seen at the foot of the bed. The barrel was lowered but could, in a heartbeat, be raised to blow Sgt. Frank away.

Sgt. Frank veered away and walked rapidly up Hyde Street. Looking behind him, he began running. With heart pounding, he ran down a wet alley, feet splashing, to the next street, through another alley, down another street, another alley, and stopped to get his breath. He stepped into a doorway. Craning his ears for sounds, he heard pursuit and men talking in Spanish. Desperately, he continued his pursuit to safety, moving from one dark patch to another. Firecrackers exploded nearby, set off by celebrants of the 4th of July. It was close, making him jump. Two hours passed. Tightly gripping his official short barrel .38 special revolver, he cautiously moved from one recessed doorway to another. He was tired, and his lower back ached. He knocked on a few doors. No one answered. He heard muted voices or thought he did. He shouted, "Help, help me, please, someone." Lights went on only to be extinguished. One man looked down from his window. Looking directly at Sgt. Frank, he closed the shutters and extinguished the light.

Exhausted, Frank entered a dark recessed doorway, and slumped down. He almost nodded off, but his head snapped up with every sound. He was not a coward. He would fight if he could see his enemy. To be hunted down and killed in an ignoble way was not how he expected to die.

The icy air and nighttime breeze kissed his face and chilled his hands. He lost track of time and was incredibly cold. Cursing at his futile attempts at the hospital, he pulled his coat tighter and closed his eyes.

A newspaper smacked him in the face, startling him awake. It was the paperboy with bags of newspapers balanced on each side of the handlebars. The boy called out, "Sorry, sir." Sgt. Frank ruefully grinned and muttered, "At least I'm alive." At the door behind Sgt. Frank, a man in a washed-out pink robe cautiously peeked out. Peering around his shoulder was his wife. "Young man," he asked, "can I help you?" Frank identified himself and asked for the use of his telephone. With the couple looking on, Frank explained his situation to an incredulous desk sergeant. It was an incoherent story of marauding strikers chasing him. Thirty minutes later, a car arrived. The young officer, clearly puzzled, asked no questions, and dropped him off at the hospital. Frank's car was undisturbed, just as he had left it. Now, if lucky, he would get an hour of sleep. Then he had to get to the waterfront to supervise his men at another demonstration by the strikers. It would be Bloody Thursday, a day of infamy, taxing his already exhausted body to its limits.

In his car, Sgt. Frank fitfully slept, constantly worried about how they had botched Stephanie's killing. Very possibly, his distinguished career was coming to an end. The whole thing had been futile. He would be arrested and go to prison for attempted murder and accessory to murder, that of the elderly woman.

As for Matteo and his son, Xavier, Matteo never pursued Sgt. Frank. He immediately returned to guard Stephanie. His son, Xavier, had pursued one block. It was the sergeant's imagination that had chased him through the night.

Back in Stephanie's room, Matteo thoughtfully flipped the knife up and down, catching it, and considered the night's events. He would inform Elder at breakfast.

Matteo's interests were horse races, investing in real estate, gambling, and making exquisite exotic knives, including the finely turned knife in his

236

hand. Some called him the jockey; in fact, he was in his earlier years in South America.

Chapter Forty-One: July 05, Bloody Thursday

Four days prior, two competing companies demonstrated tear gas products for the police, including vomiting gas. Police were ready with 1,700 to 2000 officers.

Starting at daybreak, more than 5000 strikers gathered at the docks. Family men, single men, white and black, fathers and sons, brothers, cousins, and friends agitatedly circulated, bolstering each other for the forthcoming battle. Swarming about in the vast areas fronting the Embarcadero piers, many were dressed in suits and ties for an important event.

It started at 8:00 a.m. and continued into late afternoon. It was strikers and sympathizers against the police, like two armies, but only one side had firearms, horses, and motorcycles. Although, once, a demonstrator fired a revolver at police but hit no one. Spectators stood across the Embarcadero, watching, many from hotel windows and lobbies. Hundreds gathered at a fenced rise on Rincon Hill to see the spectacle unfolding below. Gas grenades broke through the windows of the Seaboard Hotel, making guests flee. All day, up and down the Embarcadero, riots raged. Strikers and sympathizers charged the police, attempting to take over the docks. They were thrown back by police using tear gas, revolvers, and short-barreled riot shotguns fired directly into the strikers. Strikers retaliated with stones, bricks, fists, and boards. For the first time, vomiting gas was used.

Strikers rocked police cars, attempting to turn them over. Police fired into the crowd killing two. Thirty-one were wounded, 17 seriously. Hundreds were arrested. Tear gas wafted indiscriminately over police, strikers, sympathizers, and spectators. Sixty-eight police on horseback and more on motorcycles rode into the crowds with clubs and lead saps swinging. Frenzied skirmishes were ongoing. Sirens blared; fire trucks and ambulances swept in and out. Cops were pulled from their motorcycles and horses and beaten. One was hit in the face with a brick. Another raised his revolver to fire. His partner knocked it up and away. Spectators scattered from errant bullets. Smoke permeated buildings, causing those inside watching to fall back. Many ran out to the streets, adding to the pandemonium.

Among the uproar, ordinary folks went about their activities. Disembarking from cable cars, they walked through and near the commotion. They parked their Fords, Studebakers, Chryslers, and Packards, hardly casting a glance, seemingly not interested in the chaos. This did not stop the police from bludgeoning and arresting anyone who gave them a dirty look, looked like a commie, socialist, insurrectionist, or just looked funny. Most ladies were told to go home. Rioting continued throughout the day.

At the Palace Station Cafe, a few blocks away from the Embarcadero, Morgan fretted about her father. Despite her pleas, he went to the Union headquarters and intended to be in the thick of it. A man burst in, excited. The rioting was coming closer. Morgan was obviously agitated. She was sorry but had to see if her dad was all right. "Oh, hell," Sam said, "I'll closeup and go with you. Anyway, we only have one customer. There's too much happening."

Sam, Caesar, Father Raffael, Morgan, Rachael, and Gus rushed out. The last to leave was Jessica. "Charlie," she instructed the old white-haired codger, "help yourself to no more than three and lock up behind you when you leave."

"How about four?"

"Alright, don't cheat."

As it turned out, the police had already closed every saloon and restaurant near and around the Embarcadero.

Sam and the others saw the action moving their way. Within a block, the sounds of battle and the cacophony of voices, sirens, shouts, and smells of battle were louder. Unexpectedly, a large phalanx of police swarmed headlong towards the group, clubs swinging right into them. Sam and Gus were hit broadside. The rest were thrown down but rose back up to resist.

"Hey, we're not involved," Sam yelled. The others likewise protested. It didn't matter. Cops were all over. Sam was dragged toward a police van while another whacked his legs. Resisting resulted in more enthusiastic pummeling. Caesar took offense and, to the astonishment of the cops, knocked one out and sent another reeling. All hell broke loose. Other cops joined in and piled on Caesar. To their chagrin, he did not take kindly to unfair and violent treatment. A horse reared up. Sam slapped its flank. It took off wildly, flipping its rider backward and to the ground. Its momentum knocked Caesar, Gus, and three cops to the ground. Sam helped the officer up. The officer thanked him and ran after the horse.

Caesar, exhilarated, feeling almost out-of-body, performed flawlessly, thrumming like a well-oiled, perfectly coordinated machine, and didn't hold back. Grinning happily, his joyful face was unnerving. Every blow put an officer out of action, either as an outright knockout or left them down and holding their chests, gasping for breath. One fist hit a cop between the eyes, snapping his head back and reeling into another. Both toppled over a railing onto concrete below, to thuds and groans.

Gus moved in and out of the melee, picking targets, striking well-placed blows, putting cops down. He was thinking, "I still have it." It was a brawl.

Sergeant Frank and Lugo working nearby noticed. "Look," Lugo called. "What luck." Above the din, he shouted, "Let's go."

Sgt. Frank thought, "Do your own killing."

Lugo raised his club and moved to strike Sam from behind, thinking he would disable him out with one blow, but was intercepted by Caesar. He swung and missed. Caesar had deftly moved to the side, threw a left, and connected with Lugo's ribs. Lugo had never seen a doctor, and his fractured ribs were still inflamed. He recoiled. Seeing his reaction, Caesar struck the ribs again and again with all the force he could muster. Protectively, Lugo lowered his arms. With his legs firmly planted, Caesar unleashed a powerful left to Lugo's nose, a right to his ribs, and another left to Lugo's face. Lugo staggered back, grimacing, eyes watering. Rushing Caesar, he grabbed him in a bear hug, and attempted to squeeze the life out of him. Seeing that Caesar needed help, Jessica jumped on Lugo's back, Morgan grabbed a leg, Rachael grabbed the other. Breaking free, Caesar returned to the attack. Lugo, recoiled from another blow. He had to give up---and he had dropped his club. His nose, previously fractured by Elder, and somewhat healed, was fractured again. His eyes watered, his nose dripped blood, his ribs ached, and his thumb throbbed. Although enraged, he retreated outside the circle of fighters. Then he saw Gus fighting with another cop and attacked with his lead sap.

Raffael did not condone violence and tried to stop the melee but failed. His participation was limited to grabbing cops and throwing them to the ground, that is until one cop attacked Morgan. Fury boiled over. Grabbing the cop by the shirt, Raffael swung him around and punched him solidly, sending him tripping over a curb and down. Another came at him with raised club. Raffael held up his hands, chest high, palms out, and said, friendly enough, "Hey, Charles, hold on. I'm Father Raffael from Saint Mark's. You know me."

240

Charles stopped, and said, "Hi, Father."

Raffael hit him in the stomach. Charles bent double. His breath gone, Raffael pushed him down and away.

"Sorry, Charles."

Gus, for a man of 60, was inflicting bone-crunching blows. No one in their group was pulling punches. Nonetheless, the odds were against them. Inexorably, they were pushed toward a brick wall. The police had been fighting in confusion, even striking their own and running into each other. One pulled his revolver, but another stopped him from using it. Finally, screaming, and yelling overlapping orders, they formed some organization.

The sheer number of cops won out. Sam and the others were down and attempting to cover themselves as much as possible. The blows were relentless. Raffael covered Morgan with his body. Sam was doing the same with Rachael. Caesar was unconscious from a blow to the base of his skull. Jessica attempted to cover his body with hers while warding off Lugo's kicks.

Gus, well Gus, looked bad—bloody and still, knocked unconscious by an attack from behind. One ear was lacerated. Blood covered the side of his face.

Although already down, the police, in a frenzy, continued punching and kicking mercilessly. Defensively, their targets tried to ward off the blows, but the attacks continued. Absorbing another kick, Raffael grunted. Morgan whispered, "We're going to die."

"No, we're okay, but Gus does look bad," he replied.

The blast of a shotgun rang out. A young lieutenant arriving on the scene took charge, shouting, "Stop! That's enough!" To a sergeant, he said in a low voice, "Oh, no, that one there is David Elder's son, and that woman," pointing at Jessica, "is his daughter."

241

Breathing hard from combat, the sergeant said, "My gosh, do you mean David Elder, the businessman who supports the policeman's fund?"

"Yeh," was the soft reply, "and personal friend of the Chief, the mayor, governor, and anyone else who matters."

"Are we in trouble?"

"Not if they started it. They did! Right? Write it up that way. Make the reports short, simple, and the same. They started it! Understand? Let Elder's daughter go. Maybe that will appease him and make us look fair. There's going to be blowback. Now let's get a police van and ambulance. It looks like the old guy is dead."

The next day, Friday, July 6, 1934, the headline of the San Francisco Chronicle trumpeted, "TROOPS GUARD FRONT! 2 DEAD, 109 HURT IN RIOTING." Front-page articles blared: "S.F. Embarcadero Rocked By Death, Bloodshed, Riots,". . . "Military Rule Put Into Effect on Water Front;" "Governor Calls State Troopers for Protection;" and "Paris Denies Part in Hitler Revolt Plot."

That evening the California National Guard moved in. The next day 2,500 troops guarded the Embarcadero with sandbag machine-gun bunkers and tanks. The perimeter extended about 5.5 miles along Fisherman's Wharf to China Basin, near the construction of the San Francisco Oakland Bay Bridge. Thousands more were held in reserve nearby at the Military Presidio and more in Oakland.

Chapter Forty-Two: July 05, 1934. Politicians, and Mafia

At 11:00 p.m., Elder received two visitors, both political power brokers, Eric Von Steiner on the Board of Supervisors, and Jacob Woodson, chief deputy of the police commissioner. Clouds hid the moon.

It was late, it was dark, and streetlamps competed with fog. Large evergreen trees abundant with leafs added to the darkness. Maia escorted the dignitaries to the kitchen. Then she joined a large man cutting vegetables at a food preparation station opposite the stove.

"Gentlemen," Elder said, "I apologize for bringing you out so late, but I have a problem; something very personal. I'm asking for your assistance."

"Mr. Elder," Maia asked, what shall I serve?"

"A bottle of red wine for Abe and me and a bottle of cognac and whisky for our guests."

"Mr. Elder," Mr. Von Steiner said with annoyance, "it better be good. I didn't want to come, certainly not at this ungodly hour. I wouldn't be here at all except for Jacob's insistence."

Ignoring his insolence, Elder said, "Jacob, you know Abraham, but your friend doesn't. Abraham, meet Eric Von Steiner. Mr. Steiner is on the Board of Supervisors.

While Abe was extending his hand, Von Steiner snidely said, "Mr. Elder," It's Von Steiner, not Steiner," and ignored Abe's hand.

Elder looked at Abe. Abe shook his head to say, don't bother. Elder speared Von Steiner with a look of malice.

Von Steiner was corpulent for one so young. His flat, fleshly nose called for attention. He was expensively dressed, and his hair was parted in the middle, pasted flat with Brilliantine wax.

Elder was amused and thought, "Such a trivial man and doesn't know it."

Abe sat near Elder and pushed the wine aside. Maia replaced it with a cup of coffee. Von Steiner and Jacob sat nearby, across the table.

Sitting silently for a few moments sipping their drinks, they gauged each other's worth. "Now, to the point," said Elder, "My son and my employees were arrested. They're in the city jail. Here is a list. I want them

243

released immediately. One is in the hospital." He held up broken eyeglasses. "These are his. All arrest records, fingerprint cards, notes, journals, anything that has to do with them are to disappear."

Von Steiner smiled arrogantly, taking his sweet time in replying and relishing his authority. "You have a lot of nerve. Who are you to ask? Your son started the whole thing, him, and his gang. They attacked the police. Some are in the hospital. They're charged with misdemeanors and felonies: vagrancy, assault, battery on police officers, drunk in public, resisting arrest. They're in the system. Nothing will stop that."

Elder smiled wickedly. Abe inscrutably stared at Von Steiner, not in a friendly way, which Von Steiner thought rather uppity for a black man. And his unrelenting gaze in the face of insults made him increasingly uneasy. Abe looked fearsome. It suddenly dawned on him that he was very alone in his insolent behavior.

"What do you say, Jacob?" Elder asked. "Before you reply, I remind you of our prior dealings. As for you, Steiner, I will destroy you. Presently, you are leading a commission to uproot corruption, but you are the rotten core. You're leading the commission astray." Pausing to assess his reaction, he added, "I have proof, documents, and witnesses."

"This is blackmail bullshit. Jacob, let's go," Von Steiner said. Pushing back his chair, he stood and walked to the double doors. However, Jacob remained seated.

Breathing heavily and with a flushed face, Von Steiner tried one knob and then the other. Locked. His forehead grew clammy. Sweat trickled down his armpits. He dumbly looked to Jacob for assistance, but Jacob remained seated, and seemingly amused.

Von Steiner dumbly looked at Elder.

"Sit down! Steiner," Elder said softly but firmly.

Jacob said, "Mr. Elder, I understand."

244

Von Steiner was perplexed. His eyes flicked back and forth from Jacob to Elder.

Von Steiner relented. "All right, tell your cooks and colored boy to leave."

"Oh no," thought Maia, "he did it again." She looked at her husband. He seemed calm.

Von Steiner continued, "I don't want them listening."

Abe was stoic. Elder flushed, frowned, bared his teeth in an angry grimace, and dealt with conflicting emotions of whether to kill him now or later. Afraid that Elder would erupt, Abe stretched his hand across the table, gripped Elder's forearm, and said, "Patience, partner." He had not seen Elder this angry since they burned down Ramona's house of prostitution years ago.

"You know, Steiner," Elder said, "I don't like you. You don't know Abe or me. Jacob will educate you."

Jacob nodded and turned toward the broad man standing with Maia at the four-by-six kitchen cutting board. "I see you have Accordion Luigi here."

"None other," responded Elder. I call him Accordion Louie."

Von Steiner was fuming and didn't care who Luigi was. Almost shouting, he said, "Let me understand; you are threatening us. And my name is Von Steiner, not Steiner. I'm going to have you arrested. Tonight."

"Oh, pardon me, Steiner," Elder said. "Would it help if I put my demands in writing?"

"Yes!"

"Abe silently chuckled, and thought, "What a moron."

Maia's thought was quite colorful, and she tried to squelch it as unchristian. It had something to do with a pig's asshole.

Jacob thought, "What an idiot!"

Elder waved his hand toward the door and said, "Maia, tell Aida and Matteo to come in, Xavier too. They're listening outside the door" When they entered, he motioned them to the table. They stood respectfully, with their hands clasped at the waist.

"These men here," pointing at Eric Von Steiner and Jacob, "say I'm threatening them. They think I'm going to slit their throats. The way I feel right now, maybe I will. Now listen carefully, Aida, Matteo, Xavier, Abe, Maia, am I threatening these men?"

Maia had moved so that she was standing behind Von Steiner and Jacob. She shook her head and mouthed the word, "No."

"No," Matteo said, "It looks like you are having drinks with friends." The others nodded.

"That's the way I see it," Abe said.

Seeing the dark look on Elder's face, Maia was uneasy. His fingers drummed on the table, and his expression was malevolent. Suddenly, he brought his fist down hard on the table, rocking it, and thundered, "Well, by God, if they can't see that I am most definitely threatening them, then they're fucking idiots."

"Sorry, Aida, Maia, I can't stand stupidity."

Maia gripped her fists in exasperation.

With anger and frustration, Elder said, "In the last six days, I was attacked by someone in the police department, my girlfriend was almost murdered, and police attacked my children and employees. I am in no mood to play around. I'll be specific. I am threatening you. If I don't get what I want, I'll slit your throats and dump you in the ocean." Again, he turned to his employees. "Does that sound like a threat?" They shook their heads, making him grin.

To Von Steiner's surprise, Jacob also shook his head.

246

With palms flat on the table, Elder closed his eyes, inhaled deeply, and exhaled. Then he sat very still, unmoving. The impression was that he wasn't breathing. Afraid Von Steiner would speak, Jacob patted his forearm, indicating patience.

Elder opened his eyes with a flat, dead look fixed on Von Steiner, alarming Abe. The last time he had seen the look was when PeeWee was murdered, and bloody violence followed. Shaking Elder's arm, he said, "David, David Elder!"

Coming out of his trance, Elder very slowly and deliberately looked around at each sitting at the table, including Abe. His expression was hard, ominous. Darkly gesturing, barely able to contain himself, with tension in his voice, he said, "Steiner, you asked me to have my cooks leave and my boy. If you insult my so-called 'boy' again, I'll slice your throat ear to ear. I'll take that bobbing Adam's Apple of yours and stuff it up to your ass."

Abe, seeing a chance to lighten the mood and with a sense of the absurd, took out his switchblade knife and said, "Right! And when he's done with you, I'll cut out your heart and stuff it up your ass. Then, I'll kill you."

Everyone except Von Steiner thought the gross overkill was amusing. A smile played around Elder's lips.

After Abe's fun, Elder continued, "Abe is my brother, and business partner. Maia, there with Luigi, is Abe's wife. Yes, he is Accordion Luigi Bonnaducci. He is Mafia." Canting his head toward Luigi, he said, "What do you say, Luigi? Would you like to leave?"

Luigi put down the long sharp knife and cracked his knuckles. With a raspy voice, low and slow, he replied, "Only when you say so, sir."

Von Steiner started to speak, but Jacob whispered, "Shhh, be quiet."

Von Steiner didn't like being corrected and said, "What!?"

"Shut up!"

247

Eyes returned to Luigi---hulking, slicked back snowy white hair, Roman nose, and unblemished skin, save for a small scar and a brown mole on his chin—attractive in a rugged way. In his thick, meaty hand was a butcher knife. On his thumb was a crude, faded tattoo of a heart. His dark eyes went from Elder to Von Steiner. Looking at Von Steiner, it turned into a glower.

"Okay, Luigi, you can go," Elder said. "Thanks for coming."

Taking his time, Luigi drizzled olive oil onto a skillet, heated it on the burner, scooped in the vegetables, and wiped his hands. He walked around the cutting table, his lower body as large as his upper, and removed his apron. All eyes were on him. Luigi's clothing was high sartorial quality: a white dress shirt, gold cuff links, red suspenders, maroon tie, black socks and shoes, and slacks especially fitted for his bulky legs. Casually, he moved to a clothing tree standing in the corner and removed a suit jacket and gray vest. Revealed was a shoulder rig with a holster and revolver. Extravagantly adjusting the rig to his chest, he shook his shoulders and played with the straps. Lastly, he put on his black wool overcoat, a cashmere white silk scarf, and a black cap. "Goodnight, sir; I'm here for you anytime."

"Tutti bene, grazi," replied Elder.

Making a show, Luigi paused at the doors and turned to face the table. He opened his overcoat, removed the revolver, and fixed his eyes on Von Steiner. With a withering look to kill, he spun the cylinder. Not unnoticed was that it was fitted with a suppressor. Then, to Steiner's surprise, he winked, easily opened the door, and was gone.

"What do you think, Abe?" Elder asked, "Do you think they understand?"

Abe often expressed a silly bent to his humor, and said, "Well, Massah," but seeing the distaste on Elder's face, he got serious. "No, I

248

don't think they do. So, I'll put it another way. I've put this blade to good use before." With the push of a button, the switchblade sprang open. And with a swift downward motion, he buried its tip in the tabletop and left it vibrating. Looking at Von Steiner, he said, "Hai capito? Do you understand?"

Elder intervened. "Abe, put that away. It makes me nervous."

"Well then," Abe said, removing a cocked Colt .38 silver revolver from his leather vest, "I better get rid of this. Maia put it away."

Maia carefully took the gun with both hands. In the process it was pointed at Von Steiner. She fumbled and dropped it. It hit the table. The firing pin struck home with a loud crack, and Von Steiner fell out of his chair.

"Golly, silly me," Maia said, "I'm so clumsy. I guess we're lucky no bullet was in the chamber." Steiner righted himself with fear on his face. Maia winked at Jacob and gave him a cute smile.

Elder said, "Answer. Now! Give me a yes, or you're not leaving unless it's in a body bag." Seeing hesitation, he shouted to the door, "Matteo, get the bags!"

"Okay, okay, fine," Von Steiner said. "We'll do it for your son and daughter."

Jacob sighed in exasperation and said, "Oh, for Christ's sake, of course, we'll do it—for everyone. Consider it done. Give me the list."

Von Steiner was scared shitless. His mouth flapped open, but no words came out. "How," he wondered, "can Jacob be so calm?" Steiner's underarms were dripping sweat; his legs felt weak, and he had to pee but was afraid to ask to use the bathroom.

"Now go," Elder said, waving his hand dismissively. Jacob leaned across the table and offered his hand. Elder accepted it warmly, as did

Abe. Words were exchanged, words Von Steiner could not hear. He stared, confused.

Eric Von Steiner and Jacob hurried down the front steps to their chauffeured car. Jacob leaned back into the plush leather upholstery and sighed. Chuckling, he said, "Well, that was absolutely great. What a performance—much better than I expected. Maia was exceptional, and so was Abe with his knife, although a bit overdone."

Von Steiner, regaining his sense of importance and feeling safe, was fuming. "What the hell are you talking about? I'm going to have them arrested, them and their fat thug—tonight. What a laugh! They don't know who they're dealing with."

Jacob was amused. Von Steiner calling Luigi fat was odd, especially coming from a man so chubby he waddled when he walked.
"Eric, you're dumber than a stone," Jacob said. "It's the other way around. It's you who doesn't know whom you're dealing with. Call the cops if you like, but I'll testify that everything you say is a lie. Star witness, that's me."

"What? But he threatened to kill us. Even the maid had a gun."
"Where?"
"In her apron pocket. She was armed, and so was that little jockey guy. And who in the hell is Accordion Luigi or Louie, or whatever his name is?"

"Eric, you're not very observant. Only your life was threatened. I have an excellent relationship with Elder. I knew his children were arrested. I expected a call. Now about Luigi—also known as Accordion Louie. He plays the accordion and piano at Italian weddings, parties, and funerals. He plays beautifully, amazingly with those thick butcher's fingers. And he's colorful. He can play and sing to make you laugh or cry. He's also a thug, but an intelligent thug, extremely dangerous, and the little brother of Nick the Nose Bonnaducci, a 'made man' in the Mafia."

"Accordion Luigi is a living legend. Do you know the word consummate? Of course, you do. He's a consummate killer. There are stories about that man that you wouldn't believe. One is that he cut out an arrogant guy's tongue and took a bite. Then he stuffed it into the guy's mouth. There was a time when there was bad blood between the Bonnaducci and Frascati families. Two brothers, Fino and Vincenzo of the Frascati family knew Luigi frequented the library. He's a big reader— spends hours reading newspapers, books, whatever. Fino and Vincenzo followed him to the main library where they expected to get him in one of the book stacks. But being readers themselves, taken there when they were kids by their dear mothers, they couldn't bring themselves to do it. Not there. They put it off, and by the time of the Italian Club Christmas party, Luigi knew. So did Francesco Lanza, San Francisco's Mafia boss. He ordered them to make peace. Now they're thick. Eric, Luigi was there for a reason, and you, my friend, are the reason. If you don't do it, he'll slice your dick into nickel-and-dime pieces while you're alive, just for the fun of it.

"You'll be screaming in the trunk of your car as it's run into the bay. Understand, Elder doesn't like to repeat himself and wasn't mincing words. If you don't take care of it, Luigi will take care of you, and if he doesn't, then that ebony bastard, Abe, will.

"The Nose, the mafia? What about you?"

"Is that all you heard? Yeah, the Nose is another story I'll tell you another time. Now, listen. I'll tell you why I said you, not me."

"You're trying to scare me."

"I am because I'm not getting through your thick skull."

"Is Elder Mafia?"

"No, he and Lanza are friends and have a personal arrangement. They exchange information that can benefit one or the other. Elder steers clear of anything that smacks even a little bit about anything illegal, even if it's just information—maybe it's just how the wind is blowing on some deal. Did you know Lanza owns Fisherman's Wharf? He's not a man to cross or to cross his friends. Elder asked us if we understood. I do. Do you? Do you really?"

"What happened to the guy whose tongue was cut out?"

"Oh, he choked to death on his own blood. Too bad. He made the mistake of beating up a homosexual kid whose mama is a friend of Lanza."

"So, you're going to do it?"

"No, Eric. You are. Alone. You have enough clout. That's why I brought you along. I told Elder I'd do it, but he says it has to be you. He told me to bring you along. He could have gone directly to the Chief of Police but didn't. I think it has something to do with wanting you in his pocket. You must do it. If you don't, I'll let him know. Then I'll work it out myself. And you'll be dead in this town. Maybe just dead. Damn straight, I'll do it."

"You set me up. I don't like it."

"Yeah, I did, and you'll do it. You gotta. Too bad for you, but it's the way for him to forgive you for being such a jerk. If you don't, you might as well burn your house down yourself, and move your wife, your kids, your mother, and dog and cat to Alaska. Your connections here will dry up. Contractors won't deal with you. You'll be dropped from the social register. If you have a favorite plumber, they'll get to him. Eric, it's not a big deal unless you refuse. He doesn't hold a grudge unless you cross him. But get this, Elder has a quirky code of conduct and he's decent in his own way. His word is gold, and someday there will be some payback. Probably not money, but some favor that's just as good, probably better. But not for you. I'll get it. You, he doesn't like. He was royally pissed when you

252

insulted Abe. If you cross one, you cross the other. 'Tell your colored boy to leave.' Oh my gosh, Now, that was scary. I just about had a heart attack. I thought he would jump across the table to tear you apart. If he had, I would have helped clean up the mess. Meanwhile, Abraham was sizing you up, deciding your worth. He wasn't impressed. Elder said Abe is his brother. He meant it. They are that tight. That so-called 'boy' keeps a low profile, but he's a power broker in his own right and smart. If you ever got into a discussion with him, you would quickly realize you are outclassed. If you hadn't been shooting off your mouth, you would have noticed I hardly said a word. All the refusals and insults came from you. Eric, Abe is exceptional. Important people know him. He acts humble, but he's more than he seems. He's a major landlord and investor. Tell me, who holds the mortgage on your house?"

"Republic Pacific."

"He owns that."

Von Steiner groaned.

"Eric, you'll be finished wherever you go. They have connections with the Italians, the Chinese, the Japanese, the governor, with people you can't imagine."

"Hold on. Why didn't you let me know?"

"Curiosity runs deep in my character. The behaviors and interactions of men are illuminating. And frankly, it wouldn't have been entertaining. You were perfect. And that thing with Maia and the gun, 'Golly and silly me, I'm so clumsy'---That was priceless. And I have to keep it to myself. Believe me; she is not clumsy. I thought you were going to shit your pants."

"Do you know her?"

"She didn't recognize me, but I recognized her as soon as I walked in. Years ago, in the 1906 earthquake, she was an emergency nurse. The hospitals were flooded—pure bedlam. The nurses were doing the work of doctors. My hand was cut; I wrapped it in a rag and went to the hospital. And there she was at the head of a line suturing up hands. I enjoyed every minute of the wait. What a beauty. I love her tawny skin and eyes, a cross between gray and green. She sutured my hand nice and clean. I tried to date her, but she wanted Abraham. Maybe that's why I've followed his career for so many years. It's just as well. With her skin, she passes for white. But she's mulatto. As you know, the laws don't allow marriage between the races. We would have had a tough go. Damn the miscegenation laws. I still wonder, but it would never have worked. Too much prejudice. It's a wonder they've made it."

"Is there anything else?"

"Well, Elder was a gunfighter, and a friend of Wyatt Earp, you know, the infamous sheriff and gunfighter. But that's not the story. And if this doesn't convince you, nothing will: They came here from Texas and got here in time for the earthquake. They left in a hurry after burning down a whore house to get revenge for the killing of their partner, a guy by the name of PeeWee. Get this, PeeWee had a buddy, a giant, seven feet tall, a Hercules, by the name of GeeGee Poopindinski, a hell of a name, hard to forget. Quite a pair, PeeWee and GeeGee Poopindinski. Anyway, Elder and his buddies won 20,000 acres of land in a poker game. It was supposedly worthless, but they hit it big time and became filthy rich. The guy who lost it was pissed, and one evening, he and a bunch of his friends took it out on PeeWee. They stomped him to death. That same night, Elder, Abe, and GeeGee found them in a cat house owned by Ramona. Yes, the same Ramona who has the place here on Broadway. They shot the killers in the legs, torched the building, and burnt them alive. There was no mercy. If anyone tried to escape, they were pushed back with two-by-fours or given the coup-de-grace on the spot. You can imagine the horrible

254

screaming. So, you see, unless you want to get burnt to a crisp in a fire, maybe in your house, it would be much easier to cooperate. Now, do you understand?"

In the telling, Jacob got it slightly wrong. The story had been told and re-told so many times that it had become corrupted, and the facts and numbers were exaggerated. It was 1700 acres won, not 20,000, GeeGee was not seven feet tall, and his name was Popindinski, not Poopindinski.

Von Steiner's face took on a queer shallow color. He said, "I understand." He looked sick but nodded. He repeated, "Yes, I understand."

The car slowed and pulled to the curb. Von Steiner asked, "Why are you stopping?"

The driver turned to face him. It was Accordion Luigi. Spittle shot from Von Steiner's mouth. Shrieking, "Oh no, no, no, no, no," he pressed his back into the back of the seat and pumped his legs up and down, profoundly shaken. The urine he had been holding ran down his leg, down onto the upholstery and floorboard. His late dinner rose in his gullet. Placing his hands over his mouth did not prevent some from squeezing out. Forcing it back, he swallowed, coughed, and vomited.

Although startled, knowing the unexpected could be expected from Elder, Jacob retained his composure. Luigi, laughing heartily, tipped his cap, and exited, replaced by Jim, the chauffeur who had followed in Luigi's.

Jacob found it hilariously funny and rocked in laughter. Jim didn't care for his boss and grinned widely. Careful not to soil his hand, Jacob gingerly patted Von Steiner's head and said, "I'm glad this is your car. Your mess. Hey, don't look so glum. He's just breaking you in." Whacking his leg, he added, "Hey, you did it, didn't you? You shit your pants. Jim, pull over; I'm getting in front. What a fantastic night. What a story. You even asked him to write it down. But Eric, look at the positive; you're not dead, well, not yet. Eric, I'm sorry, but this is too good to keep to myself." After barely getting out the word 'sorry,' Jacob laughed himself silly. A squeaky giggle escaped Von Steiner's mouth.

Chapter Forty-Three: Back at the House

The lights were set low. Maia had retired. Elder and Abraham sat at the table smoking cigars and sipping cognac. After a few minutes, they discussed the events of the evening. The long-necked bottle of Dago Red had been pushed aside.

Abe said, "You know everyone thinks we only drink this Dago Red. Maybe we should give it up."

"I like it."

"Will they do it?" asked Abe.

"I think so, and if they don't, we'll kill them.

"Really?"

"No, Abe, of course not. I'm pulling your chain. Jacob will do his best. I don't know about that pissant, Van. But if they don't, we'll go to the Chief or lawyer up. Abe, I want to tell you something, kind of a confession."

"You're not going to get maudlin on me, are you?"

"Maybe. Abe, the first time I set eyes on you, I was on the oil platform pounding in a flat-head nail. I looked up, and there you were, coming toward me, walking on the driest land one could imagine. You were still a ways off. It was hot. Heat waves radiated up from the ground, making your body look distorted. Anyway, I had a feeling. I said to myself, 'Well, here he comes.' Don't get me wrong. I don't believe in divine intervention or predestination, but I do believe we were meant to meet. You're my partner, my friend, sometimes my protector, and my confidant; Together, we've come a long way.

"You gambled on that faro game with me, and now we're rich, can't deny it. We're free not to be pushed around anymore like those poor saps, the dockworkers barely getting by. We've been on a great roll. It couldn't be better. If it ended, I think you would be there to pick me up. Whatever worries bother me, I find you. I said you're like my brother. I meant it. Sometimes when I look in the mirror, I see you. Well, that's it."

"Only, I'm colored."

"Oh. Yeah."

Looking at each other, they fell into paroxysms of laughter. Gasping for breath and holding their sides, Elder managed to say, "It's the color of your soul that matters. By the way, that thing Maia did, dropping the gun. Was it loaded?"

"Nope."

"Did she do it on purpose?"

"Yep."

They grinned. Again, they couldn't restrain laughter.
Getting solemn, Elder said, "This thing about Stephanie, we can't let it go. We have to do something. Lugo's obsessed with her."

"And with you," Abe replied. "I'll take care of it with Matteo. You know, Stephanie really messed him up. It was Lugo, Sgt. Frank and someone else. Let's find out who.

"What do you suggest?" Elder asked. "I already have Matteo and most of Chinatown watching Lugo."

"Brother, whatever we do, whatever happens, we'll be together, like always."

After a thoughtful pause, Abe said, "Elder, the word in Chinatown is that Captain Blodger is carrying a heavy grudge against us. He says he was cheated. He's angry at being made a fool. He's shooting off his mouth, talking revenge. Two of his men were caught trespassing on the property here. Maia and Xavier told them to scat. So far, he hasn't been able to figure out how to get to us, but from what I hear, he's persistent. We have to deal with him. I should ah, talk to him."

Elder replied, "The captain is taking care of that homeless woman, Sarah. She's Stephanie's friend. She says I can't hurt him, so I can't. I won't."

"Well," Abe said, "I'm glad I brought it up. I told Luigi to drop him off a bridge."

"You didn't?"

"Ha, I got you," Abe laughed. "No, I didn't." Abe continued, "So, you're bringing Stephanie here. I don't think she'll stay unless you marry her."

"That, my friend, is exactly what I'm going to do."

"Does she know?"

"Not yet. As for Lugo, that snake has bitten me twice. Shame on me. I've arranged to have him patrol the Ferry Building at night. Don't hurt him, Abe, not yet. I never thought I would marry again, and certainly not to a prostitute. I was lost. She came just in time."

"Well, it's a good thing we've never sinned," Abe replied, "like taking justice into our own hands, like dropping a body down a ravine or taking advantage of down-and-out businessmen. By the way, remember Petey in Conrad? He met Two-Bit Sally at Ramona's, fell head over heels, and married her. You wouldn't be the first or the last."

"I get your drift," Elder replied, "Everyone in town turned out for the wedding. We partied all night. PeeWee was his best man. He kicked up his heels, got tipsy, and as usual, butchered his jokes. I sure miss him."

"Abe at our wedding, there may be some men who had Stephanie. What do you think about having them bumped off? Maybe, four or five."

258

Abe looked soberly at his partner and replied, "That many? Are you serious?"

"Abe, I got you. I'm joking. No, I don't know who they are, and I'm not going to ask. The gossips will have some juicy stories. I'll live with it."

"My friend, in some circles, you'll be roundly criticized. In others, you'll be envied."

Chapter Forty-Four: July 06, 12:10 a.m., Friday, Early Morning, July 06, City Jail

The telephone ran startling awake Captain Gary Luther of the San Francisco Police Department. Annoyed, he picked it up on the second ring. After hearing a few words, he roused his boyfriend and told him to go into the other room. Then he slowly and carefully wrote the names of five individuals, four in the city jail and one in the hospital. Captain Luther was instructed to release them immediately. All records concerning them were to be gathered personally by him and placed in a bag. If he failed, there would be repercussions. "What," he wondered, "are we doing messing with the Elders?"

At the station, Captain Luther checked and re-checked to see if all was complete. The phone rang. A voice he recognized inquired as to his progress. Yes, he had followed instructions. Now, he was to issue verbal orders for their release. There was to be no written record, not even of their release. The bag with all records was to be personally handed to Sam Elder.

At 3:30 a.m., with sounds of grating metal on metal, the cell door opened. They were free to go. Rachael wondered why, and the jailers were overly courteous. "Strange," she thought. "Morgan," Rachael asked, "Do you think Sam's in the Mafia, and that's why they're letting us go? You know, he has connections."

Morgan had no idea and didn't care. She said, "Sam's not Italian."

Rachael replied, "His name is not Cocker."

"What is it then?"

"I don't know."

"Rachael don't get yourself into a tizzy about something you don't know. I don't care as long as he treats us nicely. Ask Jessica. Boy was she mad when they didn't arrest her. I wonder why they let her go."

It was early morning when Rachael and Morgan stepped from the stairs to the sidewalk. Sam and Caesar were waiting by a taxi. Despite their protests, Raffael had already left. He wanted to walk, to think.

Rachael and Morgan were delivered to their homes. At Elder's big house, although it was still dark outside, everyone was up. An early breakfast was almost ready. Coffee was the item everyone wanted. There was much to be said. Matteo and Xavier had also come in, wanting to hear. Lilith and Julie, setting the table, touched Maia's shoulder affectionally in passing, and waited for her to be seated. Elder, observing, was glad. After her son, Mikey, passed away, Maia carried a sadness.

The radio played "Minnie the Moocher," a recent big band song:

"Whoa-a-a-ah, hee-dee-hee-dee dee ho...

She was a moocher hoocher coocher

and messed around with a bloke named Smokey. . .She

loved him though he was cokey...Hi- de- hee-dee ho

Whoa-a-a-a-ah...

She had a dream about the king of Sweden...

He gave her things that she was a-needin'. . . .

Skip-de- diddly-skip-de-diddly-oh. . ."

Maia turned it off.

Sam recounted the incidents of their fight with police. Lugo's crude attempts to batter Sam had failed, owning mainly to Caesar's presence. Everyone was impressed with the fight in the women. They were right in there, getting in the way of the cops, grabbing their batons, arms, and legs, hampering them as much as possible. Rachael was thrown down five times and got up to fight some more. Sam said, "If they had not been there, the cops might have shot us. It's too bad about Gus. He was laying them out until Lugo got to him."

"How is Gus?" Elder asked.

"He'll be in the hospital for two more days, maybe more. Lugo cracked his arm at the elbow when he was down with kicks, that asshole." Raising his eyes to the women, he said, "I apologize for the profanity. We thought he was dead. When he's released, I'll bring him here. But he probably won't stay. He's too proud. He wants to be independent, on his own."

All were amused when they heard that Father Raffael tried to be a peacemaker but fought when the police wouldn't listen. Elder suggested that Sam invite Raffael, Morgan, and Rachael to dinner. Sam replied, "I'll invite Raffael but not Morgan or Rachael. They don't know about our family, and I'm not even sure Rachael likes me."

Meanwhile, the whereabouts of Raffael was unknown, and Morgan was worried. In the morning, she went to his apartment. The door was unlocked, as was his habit, and his priestly garments were gone. Had Raffael suffered remorse and returned to the Church?

261

Chapter Forty-Five: Sadness and Resolution

Raffael fingered a carefully folded letter. It was from the bishop, personally hand-delivered by Father Raul. It was a generous invitation: Since it was only a few weeks since he had run from the cathedral, should he decide to return, he would be forgiven without penalty. In addition, he would receive favorable evaluations, and after perhaps 15 or 20 years, he would be elevated to a bishop.

After release from jail, Raffael had returned to his apartment in the dead of night to retrieve his priestly garments. Their return, he thought, was long overdue. By the time he arrived at the cathedral two miles away, it was 5:00 a.m., too early for most. At the Cathedral, he took in the beauty of the magnificent edifice. He climbed the tiers of steps, unlocked the grand front doors, and walked to the communion rail. Morning sun penetrated the stained-glass windows, casting myriad soft colors. Feeling the spirit of The Lord, he knelt in prayer and talked about his love for the Church and Morgan. For an hour, he contemplated and prayed, silently moving his lips, asking for understanding, begging for forgiveness, and God's blessing. The prayer finished; he kissed the robe and respectfully laid it full length on the far side of the rail. The key to the front doors was laid on the robe—also the black zucchetto cap. He placed his sterling silver rosary ring on the robe but changed his mind. He returned it to his finger. It was a gift from his parents. He also kept his colorful Italian corded olive-wood rosary beads. He removed the thin gold neckless from his neck bearing a gold and silver cross. It was a favorite but decided that a new initiate might use it. It would be replaced with something less ostentatious. He placed the letter from the bishop at the head of the robe, and on it, he laid the neckless and cross.

Touching the robe with affection, he reflected that life in the Church had been good. Now, he was entering a new chapter of life with some sadness. Exiting through a side door, he disturbed a flock of colorful hummingbirds feeding on red and yellow tubular flowers of tangled Trumpet Vines. While they flitted around him, he glanced up at the second floor of the dormitory windows. Looking down at him, Father Raul raised his cup of coffee in greeting.

A cold breeze cut through Raffael's clothing. Shivering, he buttoned his jacket to the neck and continued walking. Friendly early risers, and delivery men waved and nodded greetings. At the Palace Station Cafe, he slipped a note under the door asking Morgan to meet him at Washington Square. At Washington Square, he waited and considered the course of his life. He thought of Morgan and his family on the border between Spain and France, Figueres, Catalonia, Spain. At 7:30 a.m., single individuals and couples arrived for their dog's constitutional. He was reminded of his Spanish Mastiff, an affectionate dog, despite his huge size.

At 8:00 a.m., the park was alive. Fifteen elderly Chinese ladies performed their ritualistic tai chi exercises like a stylized dance. One man joined in but dropped out, unable to keep up. A milkman in white uniform and white cap, and produce men made deliveries. Cooks carried garbage outside in pails to be tossed in larger cans. Sanitation workers came by to pick it up. At 9:00, Raffael took a window seat at Dominick's, ate a breakfast of two eggs, toast, and coffee, and returned to the park. At 11:00 a.m., he saw Morgan walking rapidly toward him, looking worried.

Morgan had been unable to sleep, apprehensively believing Raffael had returned to the Church. She had always worried he would regret choosing her over the Church. He had never really asked her to marry him, but she blithely assumed all was settled. "Foolish, foolish girl," she thought. Steeling herself, she knew she would have to do it, to let him go. There could be no rancor. She'd hide her disappointment. After all, this mess was her fault. She had been after him from the start. She would not wilt and allow tears to flood her eyes, nor would she beg him to change his mind. Seeing him seated, waiting at the bench, her heart ached. She had wanted them to grow old together, to share happiness and sorrow. To have children. To live fully until their end days, old, wrinkled, and content. Determined to be strong, she drew closer.

She could see that Raffael had his eyes on her, but he sat like a statue and made no move. There was no smile, no wave—only a look she interpreted as grim. Talking to herself, she said, "I can be strong. I can do this. I will not cry. I will be kind." Fighting an urge to flee, to not hear the words that they were through, she hiccupped. He started to stand but exhausted, fell back and started over. As lovers often do, they had misunderstood what each was thinking, and contrary to her decision to be strong and hiccuping, she quietly burst into tears and covered her eyes.

Raffael realized what she had been thinking. He stepped close and cupped her face with his hands. Lovingly, gently enfolding her to his chest, he kissed her hair and trembling hands, and said, "Morgan, you have my heart. Will you marry me?"

Chapter Forty-Six: Figueres, Catalonia, Spain, Bordering France

Philippe, Raffael's father, wearing a coffee-colored canvas apron, was cutting red and yellow roses. Raffael's mother, Anna, leaned from the edge of their overhead balcony. With a strained voice, she called for him to come quickly. A yellow Western Union telegraph had arrived from San Francisco, California, U.S.A., delivered by a town clerk. He handed it to a maid, who gave it to another, who walked it to Anna. Each had read it, including the clerk, who shook his head in pity.

Seeing faces of concern, Anna was struck with dread. She would not read it, not without Philippe. Seeing his wife's worry, Philippe fingered the telegraph. His hands shook, and his heart raced, fearful that something fatal had happened to Raffael.

It was brief: "Have quit the priesthood—getting married to Morgan D'Alessandro. Come Soon. More to follow."

Philippe slowly raised his hands and, in a quaking voice, exclaimed, "Oh my God, my dear son has left the priesthood. He's getting married!"

To the surprise of their staff, and the clerk who had followed them in, Philippe and Anna looked at each other, hugged, kissed, smiled, clasped hands, and proceeded to dance in the grand entrance, shouting, "He's getting married, praise God!"

Confused, the maids stopped sniffling. Raffael had left the priesthood? Was it not a disgrace to the family and the town? A travesty! Not to Philippe and Anna. They never wanted their only son to go into the priesthood. Their name would come to an end. They had a daughter. She had children, but they wanted more from Raffael—grandchildren, little boys, and girls playing and running through their house. They called for the majordomo. An announcement would be made. In their spacious gardens, a grand feast would be held for all, for family and the whole town. The tables with white tablecloths would be laden with food and wine from their vineyards. There would be toasts and music and dancing.

Morgan D'Alessandro had to be quite a woman to pull their son out of the priesthood. It did not matter that she was an American. She was Italian—close enough.

They would petition for an interview with the Cardinal and, hopefully, with the Pope. Surely, they could get special dispensation for the marriage with generous emoluments gifted to the Church.

Perhaps their neighbor, Salvador Dali, the distinguished world-famous surrealist painter, would put in a good word. At that time, Dali was not popular with the Church, but he was famous, and even Priests liked to be associated with celebrities, even the disgraced. But no matter, even if Raffael was to be excommunicated, nothing could dampen their happiness.

Via Western Union, the Bouvier's received additional information regarding the marriage. Mr. David Elder and Abe Jackson would host them. Planned was a trip to the wine counties of Mendocino and Sonoma. Elder, desirous of growing his family of friends, hoped to interest the Bouviers in bringing their business interests to the area.

Chapter Forty-Seven: Prelude to a Wedding

When Rafael and Morgan kissed, it was almost more than she could handle; she could hardly wait for the honeymoon. That's what she told Rachael. They would drive up the coast and stay in a small cottage in Mendocino. Rachael was curious and asked if all they had done was kiss. Morgan grinned and winked. She would get a simple dress for an at-home wedding. The bridesmaids would wear dresses from their own wardrobes. It would be with family and friends, about 25, at Rachael's house. As for rings, they couldn't afford anything but plain silver, but Raffael offered an alternative. His parents would bring ancestral family rings from Spain. The house was too small for more than one table and food. Guests would mingle inside and outside, and the Palace Station Cafe would provide the drinks. The thought that they could have the wedding at the Palace Station Café had crossed Morgan's mind but was dismissed, and Sam hadn't offered.

"How about a rehearsal?" Rachael asked.

No rehearsal," Morgan replied. "For such a small wedding, it's not necessary. I'll come out of the bedroom into the living room, and the judge will say the words. A big wedding would be nice, but I'm happy. No frills. It will be wonderful."

As requested by Morgan's father, who by tradition purchased the bridal gown, Morgan and Rachael went to the most expensive department store in the city, City of Paris, at the corner of Market and Geary Streets. Jessica was otherwise occupied and would do it later. The purchase of new shoes was considered unnecessary and frivolous. They would use what they had.

Standing at the entrance of City of Paris, intimidated by their low social standing and its grandeur, they wondered if they should go in and if they would stand out as poor. Inside, awed by the beauty of the rotunda's tremendous circular interior, ornate flower stands and artwork they hesitated. Above them was lacy grill works on the upper floors, and departments. Circular walks allowed panoramic views of floors above and below. The ceiling was a towering historic ornate stained-glass dome depicting a sailing ship. Rays of sunlight penetrated the interior, providing warmth and illumination. Suitably impressed, they found the woman's dress department. Going through the racks, the cheapest dresses were priced at $25.00. "Oh, my," Morgan exclaimed, expensive. To their dismay, the saleslady, upon hearing they were there to purchase a dress for a wedding, escorted them to the bridal section. Morgan protested, "We only want simple white or cream-colored dresses." To her surprise, her name was found in a registry book, and the saleslady snapped to attention. Perplexed, Morgan asked, "Is it all right that my name is in the book?"

"Yes, of course." Leaving them confused, the woman replied, "Wait here. I'll be right back." She went to a back room and returned with two seamstresses.

Morgan took Rachael's hand and started to back away. With a sweeping motion towards the dresses, she said, "No, I think there's been a mistake. We can't afford anything in this department. "Rachael, let's go."

"Wait, please," the woman said, "Are you not Morgan D'Alessandro marrying six weeks from now? If you leave, we'll be reprimanded, maybe fired."

"Yes, that's my name, but how do you know? And I don't like to say it, but we're simple girls on a limited budget."

"Miss D'Alessandro, someone confidentially placed your name in our registry, and our instructions are that you be given every courtesy. It's underlined. I can't reveal the name because I don't know. The directive came from the office."

Morgan tried again. "Look, I don't understand, and I don't have the money. My friend doesn't have the money. We don't have it. And the wedding is small, tiny actually." She looked to Rachael for support.

Rachael jumped in, "Yes, teeny tiny. So tiny the vows will be said inside, in the kitchen, and guests will be looking in the windows."

The saleslady looked shocked, and Morgan couldn't help laughing. Rachael did have a vivid imagination. Morgan continued, "Well, not that small. I don't know who you talked to. It's a bad joke. We'll go to J.C. Penny."

To her chagrin, she was told that she could do as she wished, but money was not a problem. They treated each customer as someone special, whether rich or poor. And business was slow. "Please, it will be our pleasure. We have dresses to meet every budget. Why not have a little fun?" Morgan looked at Rachael and shrugged as if to say, what can I do?

Although perplexed, thinking the women had nothing better to do, Morgan picked out a plain cream-colored dress costing $25, still more than she had expected. Following directions, she stood on a box while the seamstresses took detailed measurements and inserted straight pins at the sleeves, shoulders, torso, waist, and hem. With measurements completed,

268

Morgan was encouraged to pick out another dress, a gown, one that would be her dream gown if she could afford it. Rachael too.

"Why not? For fun," they were told. In her mode of frugality, even though she longed to do so, Morgan declined. "Then I'll pick one for you," said the saleslady. It was a gown Morgan had fingered longingly. Not wanting to be rude for their friendliness, she consented.

It was a Bianca, a beautiful ultra-white Bianca, and a tulle veil, a brand she had read about in magazines, much too expensive. Morgan looked at her hands to make sure they were clean. An assistant salesperson opened a box containing elbow-length gloves and another with matching three-inch high-heeled shoes. The symbolism of the gloves was not lost. Upper-class women wore gloves. Morgan stood before the three-sided mirror. Looking back at her was someone happy and wealthy, a princess. Her eyes grew moist. The gown was too big for her. She didn't care. For once in her lifetime, she would have the experience of wearing an exquisite designer gown, even if briefly.

Gazing at her, Rachael said, "My gosh, you're beautiful." Both women were so giddily enthralled that no notice was given to the continued actions of the seamstresses tucking and pinning.

A supervisor, a male, came by to observe. Morgan and Rachael fell silent, worried that they were in trouble. It was not the case. What courtesy! The saleslady and the supervisor stepped aside and exchanged quiet words. The spirit of the moment was contagious. The supervisor ordered champagne. Morgan remained standing on the box and was told not to move. More measurements. Chilled champagne in an ice bucket was offered. Rachael mentally counted the change in her purse and asked, "Umm, how much?"

"Nothing dear" was the reply. More fussing by the seamstresses, more pins.

Morgan thought, "It's too bad Raffael can't see me in this gown."

A matching bridesmaid grown was presented to Rachael. "Try it on dear," she was told.

That evening, Morgan related the events at the store and the excellent service.

"Even though the dress I bought fit quite well, they insisted on taking measurements, for what reason I don't know. Then they did it for Rachael. Mine was a little loose but good enough. They wouldn't let me take it because of alterations. It's to be delivered three days before the wedding. I refused, but they bragged about their impeccable service and promised the dresses would be free if they were even a minute late."

Her father asked, "Was there anything else? What else did you see?"

"Well dad, there was one gorgeous gown. The saleslady insisted that I try it on. It was fun."

"I'll get it for you," Raffael offered.

"Oh gosh, no. Raffael, the price is $600, and a Bianca. Can you imagine? Ridiculous. And the bridesmaid dresses are $95. Sweetheart, I'm happy with the one I got. Anyway, it would look silly at our wedding."

A larger venue for the ceremony had not been found. They would go ahead and have it at Rachael's house as planned. Morgan was content. The invitations had been mailed. Rachael's parents had, at their insistence, completed the task. Everything was falling into place as planned. They talked of the number invited and the expected overflow into the front and back yards.

"Raffael, do you think your parents will come?" Morgan asked.

"Oh, yes, I sent a cable. They're on the way on the Italian steamship, the SS Giulio Cesare. They're bringing the rings, the rings my great-grandparents wore. You don't mind, I hope."

"Of course not. But can your parents afford the voyage?"

270

Raffael leaned back and smiled widely. "Oh, I think so."

"Didn't you say they're tailors?"

"They started as a tailor and seamstress. With the depression, they hung on. When all the others went out of business or moved, customers came in from surrounding areas. My mother encouraged my father to add textiles from Egypt and Portugal. They did better. Now, they also sell wine. Business is good."

Morgan peppered him with questions about family. But he told her that she would have to wait until the wedding and to trust him.

"Well then just tell me about Figueres."

"Ah, I love figures It's a small rural town of about 7000 in Catalonia, Spain. It has rolling green countryside, sloping hills, dirt roads, vineyards as far as the eye can see, and wildflowers carpeting the hillsides in the spring. On the highest hill, we have a historic stone and brick military castle, constructed in 1753, the Castell de Sant Ferran. My parents live outside of town but near enough to walk to anything important."

Raffael described the language as closely related to Castilian Spanish and similar to French. "It's also spoken in southern France right across the border."

Chapter Forty-Eight: Rachael

After release from jail, even though they were both to be in Morgan's wedding, Rachael attempted to have as little contact with Sam as possible. She couldn't break the suspicion that he was involved with criminals. Nonetheless, when Sam invited her to go with him on the paddlewheel ferry, the Ukiah, to Sausalito, she meant to say no but said yes. "Dang," she thought, "he got me."

271

There were no bridges to Sausalito, not yet. The Golden Gate Bridge was under construction. They made a day of it, starting with an early breakfast at Louisa's at Fisherman's Wharf.

In Sausalito, Spanish meaning Small Willow Grove, they took in the small boat harbor, antique shops, craftsman shops, and art studios.

Lugo and Mack, having breakfast at a nearby café, noticed Sam and Rachel leaving Louisa's Cafe. Immediately, impulsively, Lugo stood, threw money on the table for his meal, and followed. Mack let him go alone, but not without saying, "You're acting crazy. You're out of control. Your obsession is going to bite you in the ass."

Rachael had softened. Holding hands, she and Sam went in and out of trade shops. Glancing into a clothing window display, she saw a reflected furtive movement. "Sam, that cop, the one who was beating us at the riots, is following us." Even though Lugo was across the street, she could see his face and the bruises. "Gosh, his face is messed up. He looks awful."

"Where is he?"

"Across the street. Near the bougainvillea, behind the tree. What are we going to do? Wait! Don't look."

Alarmed, Sam peered into the glass covering the display window. There he was, Lugo.

Lugo had followed discretely, or so he thought, mainly at a respectable distance, except for a few moments when he got impatient.

Sam didn't want a confrontation or fight. They could go to the local police station, but they would laugh when he told them a cop was following them. He and Rachael were to board the ferry at 7:30 p.m. for the return trip. Lugo would undoubtedly follow. Would he attempt something on the ferry in a crowd of people?

Mulling over their situation, Sam held Rachael's hand and led her to the curb-side patio of a small cafe. While looking at the menu, two men entered. One was the small jockey-man, as she was calling him, and the other, Rachael guessed to be his son. In passing, the jockey sharply finger-double-tapped the table. Rachael looked up, startled. Sam said, "I'll be right back." Entering the café, he went to Matteo and Xavier. "Matteo," Sam asked, "Did my father tell you to follow us? If he did, I'm glad."

"Not exactly; we're following Lugo falling you. Your father has us and most of Chinatown keeping an eye on him. Today, we hit it."

"Can you be on the 7:30 ferry ahead of us?"

"De Seguro, of course, all the way. We will be with him, and he won't know."

Sam rejoined Rachael and explained that the two worked for his father and would keep them safe. "Do they also work for you?" She asked. Not realizing that her imagination was in overdrive, he nodded. She assumed they were hoodlums in his gang. Nonetheless, she was relieved. She asked, "Do they have guns? Do you?"

Amused, he nodded and said, "They might. I don't."

His answer only made her think, "He doesn't have to, his henchmen do." She didn't like guns but found it comforting that they had the means to protect them.

On its return to San Francisco, the ferry was caught in a cold, dark mist, that turned to fog. The droning, heavy vibrational thumping of the steam engines below was hypnotic. Sam said, "Let's go outside."

Rachael didn't feel comfortable about the idea because Lugo lurked, but thoughts of Sam possibly making a move to get affectionate did. She moved closer and playfully hooked a thumb in his belt. The other, she placed on his waist. "Gosh," she thought, "I'm daring" and wondered if a bit of danger had brought it on. When she looked at Sam, her eyes betrayed her. It was with desire. Sam, she noticed, was doing his humming thing.

273

Outside, the ocean water simmered from the churning wake of the boat, and in the far distance the colorful tableau of hazy colors from the city lights beckoned—-and somehow, she was in the mood. After climbing to the topmost deck, they stood in the darkness and leaned against each other, Sam told her stories of ferries racing to be the first to dock. However, if they raced and were caught, they would be fined, and the loser fined double.

Despite Sam's involvement with the criminal element, Rachael's emotions were stirred. It was lovely to be with him. As for Lugo, she surmised that he was keeping his distance.

Hips touching, they leaned over the railing. Looking at the swells cut by the ferry, they pulled nearer for warmth and blew little puffs of air, turning them into tiny white clouds. The sensuous deep sonorous pulsating of the 1500 horsepower engine affected their emotions. Hearts and breathing were attuned to its rhythm. Sam's arm encircled her waist. "Oh my," she thought, "he's doing it," and responded by turning and wrapping her arms around his back.

Sam opened a borrowed umbrella and held it low over their heads. Not unexpectedly, he tilted his head and his lips met hers. She took a breath and didn't resist. The kisses went on. He grew bolder. She sighed and returned his passion. Feeling his hand at the top buttons of her coat, she pushed it away. It was too cold for such nonsense. "Maybe, later," she thought. Reasoning her resistance was weak, he grew bolder. Kisses were increasingly passionate. Pausing, they looked at each other and did it again. Wondering how much she would allow, Sam's fingers returned to the buttons. While kissing her about the face and neck he made some progress, but the sharp snicking sound of a switchblade knife interrupted. Placing her hand over his, she asked, "What was that?"

Lugo had followed them outside. He planned to rush them, to throw them overboard, still kissing, he thought, as they hit the water. Snickering, and climbing up the last rung of the access ladder, he wasn't quick to notice two men on the far side of the lovebirds. The hazy night air didn't help. One was the little man with his damn knife. Lugo froze. Matteo made a low-slicing motion toward the testicles. Lugo backed down and went inside.

Chapter Forty-Nine: Stalking The Palace Station Cafe. A Premonition

Lugo resumed stalking. Thinking Stephanie might visit the café, he went there, but unknown to him Stephanie was recuperating at the big house.

Lugo now had a hatred not only for Elder but also for Caesar, the only man who had ever beaten him in a fight--and knew he was inside. Caesar had refractured Lugo' nose, and thumb. "Hell, my whole-body aches." Whether his nose would ever return to its original shape was worrisome. Everything was wrong. The dark shadows around his eyes were more pronounced than ever. He needed a win.

Lugo waited until the evening hour when Caesar would retrieve the parked Chrysler to drive Jessica home. He always hoped to catch Elder or Sam, but his timing was always wrong. And they were always with someone else, usually with that infernal little man, Matteo.

Jessica positioned herself in the hall of the cafe knowing Caesar would pass her on his way out to get the car. Impishly, she tugged his arm and said, "Hey cutie, kiss me." She kissed him twice, and said, "Hurry." Employees saw, amused. Against the wall, they kissed passionately,

275

deeply, like a needed drug, dizzying, intoxicating, floating, and blended. "Say you love me."

Grinning happily, he replied, "Sweetheart, you know I do. Meet me in front."

Caesar's heart was filled with fulsome joy. The relationship with Jessica had flowered a few weeks prior when her friends came to the cafe, and he got jealous. Driving her home, he was remorseful, and still tense. Adrenaline coursed through his body. The fellow who was flirting with Jessica was big, as big or bigger than Ricardo Santana, a foreman he fought in Santa Fe. In thought, Caesar recalled the fight: He had underestimated his opponent, thinking him old, and too big to be fast.

Deep in his thoughts about the past, and also mentally beating himself up for his jealousy, Jessica told him to pull over. Unexpectedly, without warning, not caring if her bare legs showed, she climbed over the back seat, leaned in, placed her hand on the back of his neck, pulled him in, and kissed him. He blurted, "I love you."

Smiling playfully, Jessica replied, "You're impetuous, but I don't mind. I love you too. Kiss me."

That was then, now Caesar was going for the car, and Lugo was waiting for him.

Jessica cheerfully waved goodbye to her brother and was mid-way to the to the cafe's front door when the phone incessantly rang, stopped, and rang again. She almost turned to answer but thought someone else could get it. She didn't want to keep Caesar waiting. It was Maia with a terrible premonition.

Entering the car parked a block away, Caesar, was in a loving mood and thinking, "Everyone knows about Jessica and me but pretend they don't. Tomorrow at breakfast, we'll make an announcement. Then everyone can relax." Smiling, imagining expressions of feigned surprise, his peripheral vision caught sight of a metallic shape coming through the open window. Lugo's gun was pointed at Caesar's temple. He wanted Caesar to see him, to know that he, Lugo, had beaten him. But Lugo had again misjudged. Caesar deflected the barrel, grabbed the gun and hand, and bashed them against the metal steering wheel. Thrown off-balance, Lugo's nose bumped the window frame, making him yowl. And his thumb, which hadn't healed, felt like it was squeezed by a pair of pliers.

"No," Lugo howled. A wild shot shattered the front windshield. A second shot went into the dashboard. Caesar was gaining control. Quickly, forcefully, and repeatedly, Caesar bashed Lugo's gun hand and wrist into the metal steering wheel. Before Lugo could recover, Caesar delivered two snapping left backhand blows to Lugo's nose.

With labored breathing, and struggling, Lugo thought of giving up and running. But if he did, if he failed, he would be arrested. His grip slipped. Caesar was gaining possession of the gun. But although fighting for his life, Caesar was a kind person and hesitated. Quickly, Lugo lifted his boot for the snout nose .38 revolver. There was a flash of surprise from Caesar. Lugo fired. The bullet went into Caesar's shoulder. The second skimmed ribs, a lung, and out. "Damnit, die," Lugo shouted. It was supposed to be simple murder, but "The damn idiot wouldn't cooperate." He turned to see people running toward him, shouting. He reached in with his left hand and retrieved the first revolver from Caesar's fingers. Holding his wrist and running, he turned the corner and entered the waiting car. Putting a rag on his bleeding nose, he said, "Drive, quick."

After a block of silence, Mack said, "God damn son of a bitch, stupid. Damn me for being slow. I'm done. You're bat-shit crazy. Your nose is a mess. Again. Criminy, I had no idea you would go this far with this stupid crap. And in plain daylight. They're going to get you and me. We're through. Don't call me anymore."

At the sharp reports of a gun, patrons, and employees rushed outside. Jessica saw a big man running from the Chrysler. She thought she knew who he might be but wasn't positive. She raced to the car. Sam sprinted past her.

The only car on the street, a Model-T Ford, turned right on Folsom toward the piers. Sam knew a Model-T had a top speed of 40 to 45 m.p.h. He could catch it if he cut through alleys. Previously, as a track star at the university, he was known to explosively pass other runners like they were standing still. Behind him, he heard Jessica's anguished screams over and over. Willing his pounding legs to run faster, the gap closed. He could see the driver wearing a police uniform, and a passenger with a cloth held to his face. Seeing Sam running alongside, the driver screamed in horror. Staring into his terrified face, Sam reached for the door handle, stumbled on the uneven road, and fell. The car picked up speed—and out of reach.

Chapter Fifty: Lugo, Depression

At his apartment, Lugo anxiously hurried up the stairs to look into the mirror, to see the destruction of his once handsome face—battered horribly. What was left of his once nicely shaped nose was ruined, splayed flat, bleeding, and discolored. Icing somewhat mitigated the pain. Thoughts raced through his mind—another humiliating failure. Every attempt to cause harm to the Elders had been thwarted. Wincing, he checked the wrist that Caesar had pounded into the steering wheel. He prodded the flesh of his neck where Stephanie had bitten. Mushy. He had failed again. "Failed, failed, miserably repeatedly failed." He was re-injured, and possibly recognized. Feeling a great lassitude, he washed his face and examined his reflection. Not usually one for self-evaluation, he contemplated the days since he had started on this path. He was no longer handsome, invincible, indestructible, and winning. He had underestimated his enemy, notably Stephanie, who had caused the most damage. "God, she tried to kill me." His error was believing that mannerly, civilized individuals couldn't be violent like him.

People were shying away from him, even dogs. Aside from his face, there were other lingering injuries: elbow, ribs, discolored thumb, ankle, and heel. Even his teeth ached. He thought of his sister Josie, what she would think of him, and what he had become—an out-of-control, unthinking brute. Force and murder weren't working. He washed his hands and face, dried them, and did it again. A sob escaped his lips. Carefully reexamining his tender nose, he stared in the mirror. There were tears on his cheeks. Depressed, he got into bed fully clothed, covered himself to the chin, and stared at the dull room: peeling ceiling, shabby, tiny, dingy. He didn't give a rats ass about the apartment. It was a place to sleep, that's all. Except for his vivid, colorful paintings of the streets of San Francisco, all unfinished but one, the room was colorless.

Lugo's mind went into flights of fancy. He imagined a promotion to captain and living the good life with Stephanie. He would become a famous painter. They would have an attractive apartment with quality furniture, flowers in vases, and a little boy for him and a girl for her. The visions faded, replaced with despair. It wasn't going to happen. His body shook. Tears welled. He mused, "Why wasn't I born rich like David Elder? I'm never going to get her. Who am I kidding? She'll never forgive me--- the whore!"

In comparison to Elder, he mused, he was small and insignificant. There would be no promotion. He wasn't liked, considered strange, peculiar, and even stupid. He was tolerated, never welcome, shunned, never invited to parties. Others would advance, and he would be pitied. He was so tired of being the oddball outsider, and he had lost his reputation as a tough, durable cop. Anyway, he hated the police department. "They," he mused, "don't know they're the stupid ones." But there was one thing for which he received some credit. If anyone had a question about history, the American Civil War, Finland, Russia's Vladimir Lenin, or the population of Greenland, he knew. He was the go-to person. But the ignoramuses were so dumb that he was never asked.

Not even Mack was a true friend. He only stuck by him because of shared protection money.

Lying in bed, sniffling, he asked himself, "How many days and nights will I be alone?" He touched the latest injury, a cut to his lower lip puffy and aching. He re-examined his left eye and the skin around it. The eyeball was red and sunken, and he wondered if the socket was broken. "At least," he mused, "my teeth are okay."

"What would Josie say? She would tell me to go to church, to follow their guidelines, and to practice manners and kindness." To Lugo, kindness and manners were abstract concepts, but intellectually, she made him understand the benefits and the rewards that would rebound from others. He had strayed from her teaching. "Maybe, I can change. Yes, Josie, that's what I'll do. I'll let her go." He continued musing: "If I don't change, I'll die of loneliness. Or I'll kill myself. But first, I'll go to the opium den, just one more time. Then I'll quit."

Lugo was positive Elder knew about his stalking and that Stephanie had identified him as their assailant. "God, she's a tough bitch. And today, they saw me running away." He mused, "What a mess." But the police had done nothing. They were protecting one of their own, even if they didn't like him. But Elder was the type to take his own revenge. He groused, "Let him come. I'll be waiting. After I kill him, I'll change." An amused smile creased his lips. He thought of Stephanie and Elder. "If Elder dies, she'll

280

return to Ramona's, and I'll rescue her. With him out of the way, I'll get my hands on her, and maybe . . . ." Suddenly, raising his eyes to the ceiling, he shouted to his long-deceased sister, "I love you, Josie."

Chapter Fifty-One: Lamentation

No one had considered that an assassin would strike so blatantly, so recklessly in a business area with the possibility of witnesses. Unexpectedly, abruptly, Caesar's life had ended.

Elder took it hard. It was a mistake to tell Matteo to follow Lugo only during daylight hours out of consideration for him and his family.

Accordion Luigi, Nick the Nose Bonnaducci, and Fruiti Fruttuchi came to the house and asked Elder if he wanted them to "whack him," meaning Lugo. Elder was reluctant, saying he had to look Lugo in the eyes to let him know he would die. But perhaps they could be of some help.

Jessica was devastated, inconsolable, and sequestered herself in her room. On the third day, she emerged to seek out her father. First, she went to the kitchen, where she encountered Abe and Maia.

Elder was in the study at his desk. Seeing her enter, he moved to the couch and beckoned for her to sit. Leaning quietly against his shoulder, she looked up to meet his eyes.

Elder stroked her hair. His heart went out to her. Thoughts arose of the women in his life whom he had lost, his mother, Ella Grace, his sister Kathy, and his wife, Georgia. He thought of love, death, and

281

consequences. When his mother Ella Grace died, his father changed. He didn't love Elder and Kathy anymore. Then, when Georgia died, Elder feared he would be like his father. Thankfully, he wasn't, but he was vigilant of his behavior. He had remained present. He loved Jessica so much, and here she was grieving. He would do anything for her, anything within his power.

Jessica needed him. He recalled the night that he and Abe had been sitting in the dark late at night under the veranda of Abe's house. Abe opened a box of Arturo Fuente cigars. Good friends, they sat in silence, taking puffs, blowing out smoke, and sipping wine. Bradley and Lobo were comfortable at their feet. The small dog, Dog, was inside with the girls. Señor, the wandering cat, appeared, climbed on Lobo's back, contentedly massaged his paws into the fur, and settled snugly between the two. In greeting, Lobo licked its face. Bradley raised his head and whined, calling attention to the second floor of Elder's house.

The lights in Caesar's room had come on, then extinguished. As if coordinated, the lights of Jessica's room came on. A few seconds later, Jessica closed the curtains. But before she did, back-lit behind her was Caesar. The lights went out. Abe looked at Elder for his reaction.

Elder wistfully grinned. He could banish Caesar from the house, but what good would that do? He recalled Georgia's father, Mr. Sandbourne ranting at her for loving him. Everyone knew Caesar and Jessica were in love, and people in love had powerful urges. "Yes," he mused, "love is precious." Looking back, Elder was glad Jessica and Caesar had time together and experienced sweet, young, innocent love. But life had taken its course. A new chapter was open, one not foreseen. Perhaps fate brought the two together, just as fate had brought him to Georgia and Stephanie. But what about fate and death? He didn't know and didn't want to think about it, not now. Caesar had died, and Jessica needed him.

282

Almost inaudibly, Jessica said, "Abe is singing in the kitchen. He's drunk. Maia is watching him."

"What is he singing?"

Softly she sang,

> "In the Sweet by and by, we shall meet on that beautiful shore
>> We shall sing on that beautiful shore. We shall sing on that
>>> beautiful shore, and our spirits shall sorrow no more in that
>>>> sweet by and by."

"Sorry, Dad, that's all I know."

"You have a beautiful voice, and it's a beautiful song," Elder said. "He's grieving. He loved Caesar. It's like losing a son for the second time. He'll sing at the service at Abe's Baptist church since the high and mighty white Presbyterians don't care for colored folk."

"I think Caesar would like an outdoor service. Dad, I have to say something."

Inwardly Elder cringed, thinking she would admonish him for not being vigilant, for letting Caesar die, but he was wrong.

"I think I'm pregnant. We were going to tell you, but now he's gone. If you want, I'll leave. Mom left me enough, so I won't have to work."

"Honey, when you were born and put into my arms, I said, 'So this is love.' You grabbed my finger, and I was hooked. Don't ever let go. You stay, you hear? Please."

With a teasing tone, she asked, "Do you love me more than Sam?"

"Unfair but let me say it this way. I love Stephanie dearly, but I would choose you if she came between us."

She tried again. "How about Sam? Would you choose him?" She asked.

"Now, you're pushing me, young lady. But you are my favorite."

"Dad, Sam says you say the same about him."

"Have you told Stephanie how you feel about her, that you're in love with her?"

"I think she knows."

"Not good enough. You better tell her before it's too late. Has she said anything about loving you?"

"Yes. She whispers, 'I love you,' when she thinks I'm asleep."

"Dad, there is something else. Will you do something for me?"

Adjusting his arm to better stroke her hair, he said, "Yes, sweetheart, what is it?"

"I want to go with you when you find Caesar's killer. I know you will."

"No, you can't. But yes, I will. Soon."

"You will take Abe with you, won't you?"

"Yes."

"And Matteo and Xavier?"

"Yes, and Accordion Luigi. Now, will you return the Winchester to the case?"

"I know how to use it. I think I know who did it, but I'm not positive."

"Sweetheart, I'll do it."

She stood. "I hope I am pregnant. If it's a boy, I'll name him Caesar David Elder O'Sullivan after you and his father. I wish Mom could see her grandchild. You know how she was. She would dance in the hall, in the kitchen, all over holding my baby."

Elder reached out for his daughter's hand. "I don't mind if you are, and I want you to stay. Stay until you tire of me until I'm a tottering, doddering old fool who needs help getting up from a chair."

"Dad, I love you. We'll take care of each other."

Caesar had no known enemies except for Lugo. Gus, as well as everyone else, was in mourning. Gus had also come to view Caesar as a son and Caesar's two sisters as family. Alone in his boxing studio, he was

284

bereft. When he hinted that he was lonely, his meaning was not lost. After a few weak protests, he agreed to move in to take Caesar's room. Additionally, a decision had to be made regarding Caesar's sisters.)

As Jessica took her leave, Elder returned to his desk, and sat still considering events. The phone rang making him jump. It was the doctor. He had a shocking message. Caesar was alive, barely. An orderly wheeling the body to the morgue downstairs, noticed a flicker of fingers. This wasn't unusual. Involuntary bodily movements occurred after death. But to be sure, he notified the doctor. Caesar had already been given blood transfusions when he arrived at the hospital, but despite their efforts, they believed he had passed. Now that there was a flicker of life, they placed him in a hyperbaric chamber.

"I don't understand," Elder said.

"Treatment with oxygen under pressure has been around since about 1877. Frankly, it's rarely used, and I believe we have the only chamber on the West Coast. The patient is placed in a chamber for periods of time. Oxygen is infused into the chamber under pressure. It increases the oxygen saturation in the body. It helps healing by bringing oxygen rich plasma to tissue, such as for burns and other wounds.

The downside is damage to lungs, or eye damage, if there is too much pressure. With Caesar, we're playing God. He's badly wounded, and although every cell of his body is infused with rich oxygen, he might not respond."

"Do it."

"Alright, but I caution you to keep this to yourself, for now. It might be fruitless."

Chapter Fifty-Two: Funeral

Julie and Lilith grieved. Caesar was their brother, their support, strength, and more of a father than their actual father had ever been. There would be no morning kisses and hugs, no shared laughter—no more of his strong loving presence they had taken for granted.

Initially, sympathy went to Jessica and then to Julie and Lilith. That's what the girls felt, but it wasn't that they were intentionally ignored. The girls were not consulted about funeral arrangements but were appreciative that the matter was in Elder's capable hands. It was quickly arranged.

Caesar's service was open-air near a tall maple tree with branches shielding mourners from the hot sun. The casket was closed. Mourners stood in a semi-circle, held hands, and said a prayer for his soul. Abe sang his solo, followed by words spoken by Abe's pastor. Then an old Negro gospel song, "Just A Closer Walk With Thee," sung by a Negro quartet,

"I am weak, but Thou art strong, Jesus, keep from all wrong,

Just a closer walk with Thee, Grant it, Jesus, is

my plea."

The quartet finished the song and began another, "The Old Rugged Cross."

"On a hill far away stood an old rugged cross

The emblem of suffering and shame

So, I'll cherish the old cross

Till my trophies at last I lay down. . . . ."

The mourners joined in the singing. For Elder, it brought back dark memories of his mother's funeral, his sister Kathy, and the awful days that followed. He glanced at the mourners. He held a secret, he felt he could not divulge, not yet. "God damn it," he cursed.

Maia glanced at Elder and her husband. Singing together, Abe's arm was draped over Elder's shoulders. It was the first time she had heard Elder sing. He sang beautifully like his father, but she didn't know this.

Julie and Lilith stood next to Maia and Abe, their shoulders shaking with heart-rendering sobs as the highly polished rosemary casket was lowered into the ground. It was time to leave. Abe nodded to the quartet. As everyone turned away, departing, they began singing "Danny Boy" normally reserved for Catholic services, but Elder, half-Irish, half-English, and one used to breaking convention wanted it.

The lyrics swelled:

"Oh, Danny boy, the pipes, the pipes are calling

From glen to glen and down the mountainside.

The summer's gone and all the roses falling.

It's you, it's you must go and I must bide . . . . ."

Chapter Fifty-Three: New Beginning

Julie and Lilith were told that the family would talk to them at breakfast. Worried, the girls stayed up talking all night, wondering what would become of them. They thought they would be told they were to leave the family they loved. The household rhythm was returning to normal, but not for them. It had been a month since Caesar's funeral. They anticipated this time would come. Steeling themselves for bad news, they had worn their favorite dresses.

Their parents had not responded to their letters, and their grandparents had long passed away. Maybe the Elders would take them to an orphanage. They could only hope that they would remain together.

Descending the stairs, Julie and Lilith held hands. Stepping into the kitchen, the warm aroma of freshly brewed coffee hit their senses. The room hushed. They received nods and words of greeting, but it didn't seem the same as before. All were there except Stephanie. The room looked solemn, on edge, evidently waiting to tell them the bad news. Greetings seemed stilted. The only hug was from Jessica.

The cooks removed the yellow daffodils and replaced them with platters of crispy bacon, sausage, eggs, succulent ham, country fried potatoes, gravy, cut pears, pitchers of fresh orange juice, and two carafes of steaming coffee. For once, Maia let the cooks do their chores without her. At mid-breakfast, with everyone quietly eating, Jessica couldn't wait any longer and caught her father's eye.

Elder was thoroughly enjoying the meal and in an excellent mood. The cooks had outdone themselves. However, getting the hint and seeing that the girls were somber, he put down his cup and cleared his throat. With everyone sitting straight at attention, he dropped a thick bacon strip into Bradley's mouth and stroked his muzzle. Lobo was snoozing under the table at Abe's feet.

Looking up, Elder said, "Julie, Lilith, with the passing of your brother, we've re-evaluated your stay here."

"Dad!" Jessica said and gave him a disapproving look.

Julie's heart tightened. Her left foot nervously bounced. Lilith reached for her elder sister's hand. "Here it comes."

Jessica shook her head disapprovingly.

"Okay," Elder thought, "wrong words." He started again. "Julie, Lilith, I love you and would miss you if you left. But I don't know about the others here."

Of course, he knew but was going for the dramatic.

"We must vote, and it must be unanimous. The decision comes with a major condition, a caveat. You'll hear it after the vote. Do you agree?" For a moment Elder thought of Kathy, his sister, who of late was heavy on his mind. He mused, "Kathy, I'll vote for you." He continued, "If the vote is for you to stay, you must consider the condition. It's a big one."

Impatient, Jessica said, "Come on, Dad."

To Jessica, Elder said, "To my darling daughter, I say, patience. To the girls, I ask, do you agree?"

Julie nodded.

"Well then, let's vote."

Maia, Abe, Jessica, Sam, Gus, consider whether we should keep these delightful girls. But don't let my opinion sway you. We'll go around the table, and each can say aye or nay.

"Sam?"

"Aye!"

"Jessica?"

"Aye!"

"Fact?"

Elder had used Abe's old nickname. Abe grinned.

"Aye!"

"Maia?"

"Aye!"

Pausing for effect, he took a bite of bread and a sip of coffee and leaned back. "Gus?"

"Aye."

Quickly, he held up his hand. "Wait, it's not over. All right, Stephanie is in bed, still recovering. Her vote is yes. Now, the deciding votes are from Lobo, Bradley, and myself. Lobo is sleeping, so we'll skip him, but he told me earlier that he agrees. Now we have the pesky condition." With a grin, he added, "First, I have to have another cup of coffee."

"Dad!" Jessica exclaimed.

Smiling broadly and seeing the crestfallen look of the girls, he said, "Of course, I say aye, but what about Bradley?"

All eyes went to Bradley, thumping his tail, his tongue lolling out, soulfully glancing hopefully from Elder to Abe. Elder dropped another strip of bacon into his mouth and said, "Bradley, by the thumping of his tail, says aye."

The table erupted in smiles, moist eyes, and hugs. The dogs caught the mood and emitted excited, short barks. Lobo, being old but no fool, was now wide awake. Seeing everyone clustered around the girls, he put his paws on the table, scanned it from left to right, from the ham and sausage to the bacon, and chose the entire ham. Bradley saw and tried to imitate his father but was caught.

Thinking he couldn't drag it out any longer, Elder called for quiet. "Now for the caveat." But looking around as if he had lost his train of thought, he leaned and scratched Bradley's head.

"Oh, yes, the girls." Thoroughly enjoying his little drama, he returned to his cup, took a sip, and with everyone in high anticipation, raised his eyes over the rim to see his family staring back. He set it down.

"Alright, here it is." He paused for effect. "If they agree, they'll move in with Abe and Maia to be raised as their daughters."

Abe and Maia held hands, hoping, and looked at the girls, barely suppressing their emotions.

For Lilith and Julie, it was fulfilled hope, something secretly longed for. With their eyes on Abe and Maia, they brightly smiled and emotionally said, "Yes."

"Then," Elder continued, "beginning today, you can call them mom and dad, mother and father, or Abe and Maia, whatever pleases you. I now decree you are family, living with us, being one of us, caring for and loving until, well, you know."

It was too much emotion. After that day, forever until their last days, the story would be told of how the family became stronger, how Elder made everyone wait and suffer, and how beloved Lobo gorged himself sick on the ham.

Chapter Fifty-Four: End of Strike

Monday, July 16, 1934, a four-day city general strike of the city began. Participating were approximately 12,000 longshoremen, non-union sympathizers, stores, movie theaters, non-union truck drivers, nightclubs, and 130,000 to 150,000 workers from other unions, 63 in all, including Teamsters. In and around the bay, San Francisco was closed for business.

Thousands left the city, afraid of carnage. The Industrial Union, comprised of ship owners, dock owners, banks, and other vested interests, had reached the limits of their patience. The next day, July 17th, the National Guard cordoned off both ends of a block with truck-mounted machine guns to allow scabs and paid vigilantes to attack and decimate Union headquarters. Police were present but did nothing to prevent crimes against the union. Hired goons wearing leather jackets laid waste to furniture, equipment, pianos, windows—anything they could destroy with their axes. After they were done, the police went in and arrested any hapless union member still present. Throughout the day, anything and anyone associated with unions was attacked, including a union school, kitchen, library, the Communist party headquarters, the ex-service men's headquarters, and even private homes.

Along the Embarcadero, police arrested union members and others considered suspicious and charged them with vagrancy.

The strike was broken. The Teamsters voted to return to work, and so did the longshoremen. On the 20th of July, the first ship in 70 days was unloaded. Arbitration followed. The Industrial Union had not expected the strike to last more than a couple of weeks, but after 70 days, it was almost over. The strike limped along for a few more days until the unions formally capitulated.

The military was pulling out. Left temporarily was a token presence at the southern end of the Embarcadero. The regular patrolling police were withdrawn, and Lugo was assigned in their stead. This assignment was made after David Elder had spoken to the police chief.

Chapter Fifty-Five: Celebration

On Saturday, September 01, 1934, Elder had an elaborate party to celebrate the end of the strike. Chief of Police William Quinn was the honorary guest. Captain Luther ordered Sgt. Frank to attend. After all, Sgt. Frank was intimately involved as the investigator in the crimes against the Elders. Also, Mr. Elder was adamant he be there. In attendance was a large contingent of off-duty police officers of all ranks, celebrities, politicians, would-be politicians, business associates—the cream of society. Music, dancing, lively chatter, and laughter filled the air. Waiters and waitresses circulated with platers of hors d'oeuvres and champagne. Two hundred seven guests sidled up to tables laden with catered food: sliced meats, fish, lobster, German potato salad, tossed green salads, wafers, caviar, dips, olives, pickles, desserts, and three crowded open bars.

Sgt. Frank turned into the round-about driveway and turned his car over to a valet. The revelers were everywhere except in the rooms upstairs. They were blocked off. Warily, Sgt. Frank's eyes cast about for Stephanie. Attempting to be inconspicuous, he mingled with the largest concentrations of revelers. He reasoned that if Stephanie saw him, it might shock her into recognition; she would scream bloody murder. Her doctors said she had traumatic amnesia. Would it last, he wondered?

Sgt. Frank moved to a buffet table and exchanged small talk. All the while, his eyes cast about for the presence of Stephanie. At one point, she looked his way. Cringing, he turned away. At 10:30 p.m. sharp, he felt he had been there long enough to satisfy the captain and would leave. Hurriedly walking toward the front door, he brushed a woman. To his horror, it was Stephanie. Mumbling an apology, he took in her face and was fascinated by the crescent shaped scar on her cheek—caused by his kick, the kick delivered while she was down and fighting to live. She looked into his eyes. There was no overt sign of recognition. He thought, "She doesn't remember," and, "Not quite so perfect anymore."

Noticing, his stare, Stephanie deliberately turned her face to give a profile view. Not one for self-pity, she embraced the scar as a badge of survival. Tonight, when he arrived, she was notified and steeled herself for this confrontation. She remembered everything but pretended otherwise. She wanted to scream and to go for his eyes, this time to succeed in tearing them out. Instead, after delivering a crimped smile, without a word, she walked rapidly to the closest room, to the bathroom. She vomited. Maia, hovering protectively, was with her. Elder had argued against it, but she wanted Sgt. Frank to know that she was alive and thriving.

Frank was immensely relieved. Stephanie had shown no reaction to his presence. Not at all. "She doesn't remember a thing." Suddenly, his appetite returned. Unusual for his personality, he did a happy little skip-hop and took two champagne drinks from a passing waiter. Moving to the buffet, he heaped his plate with lobster bisque, potato salad, and olives. Very low, he sang, "Yes, siree, I'm in the clear," and looked around for Elder.

Elder, in a small group, and in high spirits, holding a bottle of Dago Red wine, was weaving drunkenly. A few minutes later, at 11:00 p.m., Sam and Jessica, trailed by Matteo, were seen helping him into the house. Abe stayed, circulating. Frank kept an eye on him but eventually lost interest. When he looked again, he was gone. Frank thought, "Can't hold his liquor." Sgt. Frank was so relieved and happy that he helped himself to another drink. A great weight of worry had evaporated.

While Sgt. Frank contentedly popped black olives into his mouth, Elder, Abe, and Matteo were driving to the Ferry Building.

Chapter Fifty-Six: Midnight, Behind the Ferry Building

Matteo cut the ignition, pushed the clutch to the floor, and smoothly coasted the Chrysler under the cast-iron pedestrian bridge to the curb of the Ferry Building directly in front of the imposing double doors and stopped. Elder leaned forward and instructed Matteo to look for them after 12:15 a.m. They would be walking north on the Embarcadero toward Chinatown.

Abe looked up at the 75-foot-tall four-sided clock tower—11:45 p.m. Casually held was the 12-round Winchester Model 1892 lever-action rifle.

Seeing the glum look on Elder's face, Abe asked, "Are you okay?"

"Yes," but I'm not happy about this. It makes me sick."

"I understand, but remember he tried to kill you and Stephanie, He left her for dead. He killed Caesar."

"Yeah."

Expecting to intersect Lugo walking his rounds, they pushed through a gap in the temporary barbed wire fencing at the North end and looked towards the rear of the building. It was eerily quiet, except for lapping water and the foghorn's mournful sounds from Alcatraz Island. Abe pointed out Sarah hiding in a recessed doorway. He went to a place of concealment, and Elder went to confront Lugo.

For Lugo, time dragged. The opium was urgently calling. The day had started balmy, and the weather was still crummy. Now, he had to wait out

294

the night. Miserably ill at ease, he walked the rough-hewn piers on the Embarcadero. He hated the weather: damp, foggy, and drizzling rain. And he was lonely. He was appropriately dressed in his wool uniform, cap, and overcoat, but still shivered. This assignment was to keep him out of sight until time diminished the suspicion that he was the perpetrator of the brutal attacks on Elder and his mistress. He understood but didn't like it. "It's crap," he thought. "Her brains are scrambled. We're in the clear." He wanted his regular daytime routine. His mind returned to Mack's worrisome comment that he was crazy. "Maybe," he thought, "maybe he's right; maybe I am crazy." To a pelican sitting on a piling, he shouted, "MAYBE I AM," making it fly off and making him lean back and manically howl like a wolf. "Hmmm, not bad," he said to himself.

Bored, he listened and heard nothing, not even the sounds of birds and seals, only the foghorn, the lapping of the water, and an occasional wheezing breeze. The tanks and military trucks were gone. A nine-man squad of National Guardsmen remained at the Southeastern area of the Embarcadero, too distant to be seen or heard. He scrutinized the darkened length behind the Ferry Building, and the approximately 20 to 25 feet between the back of the building and the 10 to 12 feet drop off into the ocean. Harbor lights fought to penetrate the gray undulating fog and failed. Visibility was poor. He removed a glove. Shrugging his shoulders, shivering, he lit a cigarette, and peered into the darkness, and pondered whether he should walk the length. Flipping the flaming match aside, he stepped forward. Midway, he stopped and listened. An obscure figure paced back and forth. Approaching cautiously, he discerned a man of medium height, not tall but stocky, and not a bum by the look of him. "What are you doing here?" Lugo asked. "This is a restricted area."

"I'm James Blodger, captain of the ship Glory Queen. I was ordered to be here."

Lugo didn't care who he was and ordered him to leave the area, but curious asked, "Who told you to be here?"

Blodger explained that he had been at Lee's restaurant in Chinatown with a couple of mates: "When we walked out, a large gangster-type character was waiting. He told me he was Mafia, and that someone I had dealings with, Mr. David Elder, wanted to see me. He told my mates to get lost. I laughed. 'Tell him to go to hell,' I said. But he said he was Accordion Luigi, and to check him out. If I didn't come tonight at 11:00 my ship would be sunk. So here I am, with you, a man I don't know, a policeman to boot."

At the mention of Elder's name, Lugo physically reacted. His facial expression changed to one of alarm, and his hand went to the inside of his coat.

"So, you know him," Blodger exclaimed.

"Yeh."

"Did you do something to him?"

"No, nothing," he lied.

"What did you do to Elder?" Lugo asked.

"I reneged on a deal," Blodger replied.

Blodger examined Lugo's face, and said, "I'm thinking you're lying about Elder. He wants to see us both. So far, I've been lucky, but maybe luck's run out, yours too."

"Nah," Lugo replied. He checked the gun in his coat and bent to check another in his boot.

Blodger said, "I think the man who wants us is coming through the fog."

Lugo turned, looked, and listened. Indeed, someone was approaching.

"Son," said Blogger, "maybe you know what's coming. I'm guessing you have a broken nose. Your eyes look bad. You walk like you're in pain,

296

and you have a wound on your neck. You look like dogs got to you, or. . .
.?" His eyes widened. He didn't finish the thought. "Ah, I see. The man is
coming to finish the job. But you're armed. Maybe you have a chance. Me,
I'm beaten and tired. It won't do any good to run. But I'm hoping. I love
this wicked town and don't want to leave."

If not for the thick fog, they would have seen the sky heavy with
moisture.

Blodger muttered, "I don't like this. Something bad is coming."

As he finished his words, the sky erupted with rolling claps of thunder
and torrential rain. Thunderous lightning briefly illuminated everything
and drowned out the ominous sounds of frigid ocean water lapping the
piers. Shadows played off buildings and crates.

Blodger buttoned his black wool pea coat and turned up the collar.
Sitting on the barrel with a bowed head and water dripping off his cap, he
was in a reflective mood and began talking. "There was a time when I was
a good man. I got greedy. I wanted money, even illegal money. I didn't
care. My conscience went away until all I cared about was the all-mighty
dollar. Was it worth it? I thought so. When I'd long given up on meeting a
good woman, I did, someone I care about, a decent woman. Now, I
wonder."

"Well, old man, nice confession. Maybe you're ready, but I'm not. Your
so-called wicked ways are pathetic." Lugo reached into his coat for his
revolver and twirled the cylinder.

"Your doomsday man is here," Blodger said.

Lugo squinted into the gloom. The wet footfalls had stopped. The
foghorn sounded low and mournful. Lugo pointed his gun from the waist.
He was a good shot but couldn't be premature in firing too soon. Panic
could get him killed.

Elder, wearing a black overcoat and black cap, stopped a good 45 feet away. He was alone. His hands were in his pockets. Blodger, sensing the tension, distanced himself away from Lugo. Lugo smiled at his good luck and looked at the man he was about to kill. Midnight and the clock of the Ferry building began to sound the hour. As if in reverence, both men waited until the last gong.

"Well, well, Mr. Big Shot," Lugo shouted. "You're here to get revenge for your bitch." Despite the obscure weather, Lugo saw Elder flinch. "I couldn't have set this up better. The jealous boyfriend comes alone to get revenge for his lady, right where I work and is killed himself. I even have a witness who you conveniently sent."

At the sound of levering of a rifle setting a cartridge, Lugo snapped his head to the left. Lugo threw himself sideways and prone. In quick succession, he fired in the direction of the sound and two shots at Elder. But Elder had moved. He also had closed the distance. He fired twice at Lugo's lower body. One connected and tore Lugo's calf near the bone, making him fall. His hands flew out to cushion his fall. One open hand landed on top of the revolver. Excruciating pain shot through his leg. Maintaining his sense of survival, Lugo's fingers tightened around the guns grip. Blodger stepped up and put his boot on his hand stopping him. Reaching down, he removed the gun from Lugo's fingers. While pointing it at Lugo's face, he pulled up Lugo's pants, reached into his boot, and removed the .38 snout-nosed Colt revolver.

Seeing Blodger with two revolvers gave Elder pause. "Toss them," he ordered. Blodger tossed them into pool of rainwater. Lugo awkwardly got to his feet and cantered backward toward the pier's edge. Limping badly, attempting to distance himself from Elder, he fell again.

Standing ominously above Lugo, both soaked with rain, Elder asked, "Who was with you?"

"What are you talking about?"

"When you tried to kill Stephanie. Who was with you?"

Elder put his foot on Lugo's ankle and pressed down hard. Lugo tried to pull away, but Elder bore down.

Grimacing, Lugo held his leg, "It wasn't me."

"Yeah. Sure," Elder said and shot him in the upper thigh. Writhing and howling with pain, subsiding to mewling like a starving kitten, Lugo rocked back and forth. The pungent smell of cordite was strong. He was afraid but thinking. Blood soaked his pants and boot and mingled with the water. He looked around. One other man was out there, but whoever it was had not shown himself.

"Who was with you? Say it, and I won't kill you. It's not worth killing you over a prostitute. I want to know. We were both fools." Elder was lying, but deception with his enemies was permitted. They lied to him; he lied to them. "If you won't say, I'll shoot you in the other leg and then your hands. You will tell me!"

Steeling himself, Lugo shouted, "No one."

Elder shot him again in the same thick thigh, eliciting yowls, and whimpers.

Lugo yelled, "It was Sgt. Frank and Mack Donovan."

Elder knew Sergeant Frank's involvement, but Mack? Mack was an old police veteran nearing retirement, not very bright, but nice enough—and not known to get involved in criminal behavior. He was a follower. He had been at Elder's house at various functions. They were on speaking terms.

"Say again," Elder said and kicked Lugo's leg.

"It was Frank and Mack, I swear. Damn it, ask Mack, the dumb schmuck."

299

"One more question. Why did you kill my employee at the Palace Station? His name was Caesar. Why? He had nothing to do with Stephanie."

Lugo didn't answer.

"Blodger, take off his boots. Help him up," Elder instructed.

Lugo stood shakily, barely, glaring at Elder.

"Lugo, back up."

"Hold on. You said you were going to let me go."

"Did I? No, I said I wasn't going to kill you. Tell me. Why did you kill him?"

Lugo shrugged. "I wanted it to be you."

"Lugo, so much hate. It didn't have to be this way, over a woman."

For a frozen moment, they stood eye to eye. Then, as if speaking conversationally, Lugo said, "You know, she isn't just any woman. She's different."

"No." Elder agreed, "Not just any woman."

Alarming Lugo, two more men came into his line of vision, Accordion Luigi and Fruiti Fruttuchi, in black. He was so concentrated on Elder that he had not previously noticed. Hopping backward, searching for an escape, Lugo hatefully glared.

"Lugo," Elder said, "I'm not going to kill you. They will."

He continued, "Lugo, you are amazing, still standing, still defiant. Why didn't you just leave us alone?"

As offensively as he could, Lugo sneered, "She was mine. I fucked her first. She sucked me off and swallowed. Dimwit. She fucked them all. Fuck you and your bitch."

Elder flinched. He felt like his heart had been ripped from his chest. Wincing, he stopped breathing. Revulsion, hate, despair, and anger welled up. Feeling sick, he put his fist to his mouth and said, "Goodbye, Lugo."

300

But Lugo wasn't through. Eyes brightly burning, as if he could see into Elder's inner soul, he said, "You lying dumb son-of-a bitch. You're a murderer, just like me. You think it's over; it's not." Intently watching Elder, he saw his chance. When Elder greeted Luigi with an extended hand, Lugo, in that split second of distraction, lunged for the drop-off. Gimping with a frenetic skip, hop, crippled dash, he tumbled headfirst into the turgid freezing water. A barrage of shots followed.

Abe joined the others and added the firepower of his lever-action rifle. Looking down, it was dark. They saw nothing. Nonetheless, shooting randomly, they hoped to score a hit.

Elder, Abe, Luigi, and Fruiti went up and down the water's edge shooting at imagined movement.

"We botched it," Elder said.

"Maybe, maybe not," Abe sighed.

Blodger hadn't moved. He could have run but caught in the drama, he stayed. Elder turned and saw Blogger's shocked expression.

Turning to Abe, Elder said, "Abe, we're done here. Give me a moment. I'm going to talk to Blodger." To Blodger, he said, "Come on, walk with me."

As they walked, Elder informed Blodger that his sailors were caught surveilling his home. Also, he heard that Blodger wanted to blow up Elder's home with dynamite and riddle it with heavy caliber bullets from a Gatling Gun. He wanted Blodger there to show him what would happen if he tried to exact some type of revenge from the coolie exchange. "I don't want to kill you," Elder said.

Blodger was unaware his sailors had been to Elder's house and told Elder the same. As Elder talked, Blodger was amazed that Elder apologized for the injury to his Achilles tendon. That was not his intention,

Elder said, and the man who had done it had been "taken care of." Blodger stopped walking.

"Do you mean he's dead?" Elder nodded. A lie. Blodger snapped, "Jesus, you shouldn't have done it," surprising Elder. Blodger, for all his bluster, noise, and imagination, had never killed anyone. He liked his tough guy reputation, a reputation nourished and helped along by tall tales. Sure, he had been in some rugged, challenging ports. He had been in shoving matches and had broken up fights, but that was it. His appearance alone and lashing tongue usually dissuaded the unruly. Gruff and formidable, but he wasn't a killer. "You didn't have to do it," he said, shaking his head. "Not for me. God, no," he blurted, "I'm a blowhard; that's all I am."

"Damn," Elder thought. He hated making misjudgments.

The clock sounded 1:00 a.m., It had taken longer than expected, and Matteo was probably looking for them.

Across the square, buildings were closed. Except for three cable cars parked in the turn-around, all was empty in the vast area, and damp. In the quiet of the night, they stood facing each other—no sounds except the pitter-patter of rain and their breathing.

The desired object of the night was inconclusive. It was time to leave. But before Elder let Blodger go, he asked, "What did Lugo say at the end? A word. Did you catch it?"

Sounding dispirited, Blogger replied, "Yes, he said Josie."

"All right," Elder said, walking away, "that's it; we're done. Now, call your gal, Sarah. She's out there watching to see if you're okay."

Feeling glum, Blodger called out, "Sarah, if you're out there, you can come out." Sarah walked out of hiding. Despite layered clothing, she appeared small. "Sarah," he said, "are you looking out for me?" She nodded, and it touched him. It made him sad and happy at the same time. "Thank you, Sarah. Sarah, I'm a fraud."

Sarah and Blodger made an interesting couple. Sarah was 5 feet 8 inches tall, long-legged and slender, fine-featured, and pretty. He was stocky at 5 feet 5, broad and barrel-chested, with good cheekbones and a slightly flat nose from a childhood wrestling accident. He was "different looking" with his physical appearance and receding hairline. No one except a loved one would say he was handsome-maybe cute. Ed did look fearsome, and frankly, Sarah was initially wary of him, but in his treatment of her, he was gentle and mannerly. It was weeks before he placed his hand on hers and asked if it was all right if he did.

Sarah liked him and looked forward to their visits. When she heard at work, at Lee's restaurant, that Mr. Elder had ordered him to meet him behind the Ferry Building, she was surprised at her degree of concern. Frantically, she looked for and found her derringer. Not knowing the time of the meeting, except that it was near midnight, she hid in a recessed doorway and waited.

Abe joined Elder at the North-end corner of the Ferry Building. "David, I heard him say those things about Stephanie. Are you all right?"

"Abe, he ripped out my heart. Yes, it hurt."

The big Chrysler coasted up beside them. On the return trip to the house, Elder was depressed and quiet. Lugo's last comments rankled about being a murderer and seeing him in hell. He already carried around a demon. He thought of Lugo's words, 'Just like me.' "Yes," he thought, "I'm flawed. I'm a murderer, a dimwit. I have guilt I'll carry for the rest of my life."

Abe gently prodded but gauged Elder's mood and fell silent. The car pulled to the rear of the house, behind the kitchen. Elder, distracted, in thought, stepped out and stumbled forward. If not for Abe, he would have sprawled on the ground.

Maia was waiting. She helped them off with their coats and examined both. A bullet had pierced Elder's coat and grazed his side leaving a red welt. She palpitated the wound, "No problem. I'll clean it and cover it with a bandage." She took his revolver to be melted down and disposed of. When she reached for the rifle, Abe shook his head, "Uh, uh." Talk ceased while she cleaned and applied a salve to Elder's wound.

Elder was dispirited, worried about Lugo and the possibility of unwanted repercussions. Abe also had concerns but would not voice them. Not yet.

"Now what?" Abe asked.

"Abe, this is my problem. Why don't you and Maia take the girls and go to Europe? Matteo and I will take care of the other two. It's too bad about Mack. Until today, I liked him."

"Brother, you offend me. We're in this together. I'm staying."

Moving into the study, Maia placed Cognac on the desk and filled three glasses. They clinked them together and downed the liquid in one swallow. After pouring a refill, she massaged her husband's shoulders.

"Stephanie is coming down," Maia said. "She's been waiting. She didn't know you were going to do it tonight. She came down looking for you when you didn't go to bed. She was frantic. I had to convince her that it would be impossible to find you. She's been in a dither, rocking back and forth on that chair you gave her.

If she wasn't rocking, she was pacing, afraid that something would happen to you. Elder, did you know that she was once in love with a childhood friend? His name was Ezra. He was a private in the War to End all Wars. It was his bad luck to be caught in a cloud of poisonous mustard gas just a few months before the wars end in 1918. He was a tall, thin young man, only 18. Although he returned home, he never recovered. The irony is that he was Jewish and dedicated to Germany. If he had lived, the Nazis, now in power would reject him. Now, she's afraid of losing you."

"She's a good woman," Abe said.

Elder looked down at the floor and shook his head. "I'm not leaving."

Seeing that Elder's glass was empty, Maia refilled it.

"I'll be glad when it's over," he said and shuddered. "It had to be done, but it wasn't noble."

Abe replied, "Yes. I'm glad he didn't beg."

Stephanie entered the room wearing a fluffy, soft white bathrobe over a chiffon nightshirt and barefoot. Without a word, she went to Elder. Gently, she kissed and hugged him, touched his face, and caressed the back of his neck. Unable to discern his mood, she decided to say nothing, and led him to the dark leather sofa. There, lifting her eyes to his, she leaned against his body and held his hand. Looking sorrowful, he offered a wan smile.

"Well," Abe said, "It's been a long night. We'll leave you two alone." But Elder was tense and in conflict. "Abe, stay," he said.

"Elder," Abe asked, "Did we do the right thing with Blodger? He planned to get revenge, maybe kill you, me, and the kids. The man has a reputation for being volatile, sneaky, crafty, and other things. We could have rid ourselves tonight of any worry."

Stephanie, snuggling close to Elder, feeling safe and loved, raised her lips for another kiss. A good half of her body covered his chest. His arm draped her shoulder and bosom, resting it heavily—a picture of warm intimacy.

It looked like Elder was not going to reply to Abe's question but did. First a swallow of Cognac. "Abe, Blodger shoots off his mouth. He was angry but had no intention of murder." Elder took a deep breath and continued. "He reminds me of my father, a confusing man, but not as bad.

305

"Blodger talks like him, looks like him, walks like him, but nothing compared to him—not a saint, but he's okay. He's getting another chance.

My father, my dad, was a great dad. He loved us. I'll clarify. He loved us until Mom died."

A long pause made it seem he was through, but then, "Abe, you've wondered about my father. Well, I'll tell you. We had a good life, but it fell apart. We lived on a farm in York, Pennsylvania, with beautiful fields of corn, cows, and pigs. We had friends and belonged to a little country church. You would think we were Baptist holy rollers by the way we sang, so strong the walls vibrated. Mom and Dad told us stories, and when they went to bed, they held hands and giggled like kids. She died trying to give birth. The midwife didn't know what to do."

Maia sat to listen. Elder had spoken fondly of his sister and mother but never of his father.

"Memories haunt me. I want to tear them out but can't. When Mom was alive, Dad played a game with us. Steamroller. He would roll over Kathy and me, saying, 'Here comes the steamroller,' back and forth, careful not to hurt us. We laughed so hard. My heart breaks thinking of the love we had, of the way he once was. We shut our eyelids tight, pretending he couldn't see us. Gently, he opened our eyelids to see if we were inside and say, 'Ah, there you are,' and smothered us with kisses. He was fun— funny. We were happy.

"But Mom died, and he changed. When we lowered her into the ground, singing, 'Lord, I'm Coming Home,' he changed before our eyes. He glared at us as if we had caused her death. Kathy saw it too. I tried to hug him, but he pushed me away."

With a tremulous voice, almost a whisper, Elder continued.

"Dad was an elder in the church and filled in when the minister was away. When he prayed, it was with faith. He moved the congregation to

306

cry out, 'Yes, Lord, hallelujah. Praise the Lord.' Oh, he had a beautiful voice. When he sang, the words rumbled out with passion like God listened. I wanted to pray like him, be like him, walk like him. But it didn't work. After Mom died, he was a total, crazy bastard like his father, a slobbering falling-down drunk. He hardly spoke to us. Inside, he was dead."

Elder's words slurred. His mind had slipped from tipsy to drunk. His mind filtered to his sister and father.

"I prayed like he used to, every day. I made deals with the Almighty, crazy with faith that the father I knew would come back and love us again. But I guess the Lord heard but didn't care or was too busy somewhere else. Maybe he was in France enjoying a glass of wine at a sidewalk cafe and looking at the pretty girls, or maybe in Italy, helping someone more worthy. Where was he when I needed him? The father I loved died at Mom's funeral and was replaced by an ugly bastard. Kathy looked like her mom. She got the brunt of it. She started hiding. He wouldn't leave her alone."

Alarmed, Abe said, "Elder, stop. That's enough. Don't say anymore."

"No, old friend, I have to get it out before I die."

"You're not dying."

"Feels like it."

"While he raged around the house, stone drunk, staggering, breaking things. We hid in a little storage room. He called, 'Kathleen, Kathy, where are you? Come here.' We didn't answer. He found us. He ripped the door off its hinges and threw me across the room. He got Kathy and called her Ella Grace, Mom's name. She was screaming. I tried to protect her. God only knows where she is now. Maybe dead. You wouldn't think things could get any worse, would you? I couldn't wait to leave. Prayer was a God damn waste of time."

307

Maia looked at Abe, unsure if they should stay or go. The combination of Elder's sadness and rancor was alarming.

Elder continued, "We fought. I woke up the next morning on the floor. Dad mumbled, "Sorry." Then he paced up and down impatiently while Kathy made him meatloaf sandwiches for lunch . He was going to church to write a sermon. She walked him outside. I couldn't believe it. He hugged her as if nothing had happened. And do you know what she said? 'I forgive you, Dad.' His reply, 'What for?' If I had my knife, I would have plunged it into his throat, right there. At the gate, he stopped and looked at us. For a moment, just for a moment, it was my old dad. I saw regret, remorse, and love. But it passed. Kathy gave him a little wave and said, 'Daddy, I love you.' Maybe he didn't hear. He walked away. I'll never forget it. I failed her."

Elder's memories and feelings of inadequacy for failing his sister were forever with him. "I tried to find her. God only knows where she is now. Maybe dead."

Maia said, "This is the first time you've talked about your father. Do you know where he is?"

Elder shook his head. The corners of his mouth curled down, and the skin of his face contorted until he looked ugly. He was in agony and angry. His father and God were on his mind.

"God damn, where was goodness, grace, and mercy? 'Hallelujah, and praise God.' What bullshit. He didn't help Kathy, Georgia or Mikey, my mother or father—or Lugo, but I guess Lugo doesn't count. And he sure as hell didn't help PeeWee. We make our own rewards or damage." Slurring his words, "Vengeance is mine, I will repay saith the Lord, Romans 12:17-19? No! If I left it to him, I'd be dead. Abe does a better job. I can depend on Abe. He gives it when I ask for his help, not like an imaginary deity.

308

"You ask where my father is. He always said that those who go to hell deserve it. Well, I gave him a one-way ticket."

Coming to his senses, he said, "I apologize, Maia. I'm sorry. I know you believe."

"How old would Kathy be?" She asked.

"Twins, we're twins. That day, Kathy helped me to bed. In the morning, she was gone. She left sweet peas and a note saying she couldn't take it anymore and hoped we would see each other again, someday."

Maia started to ask something else but caught Abe's eye. He urgently shook his head and said, "No! Enough."

Maia said, "Abe, I didn't know. But your life wasn't good either."

"No, in comparison, mine was fine. I had a good simple roof over my head, good parents, friends, and plenty to eat. The countryside was open with fields of cotton and tobacco. There were ponds where we fished, and places I wandered and still miss. We had our church. I was just upset that it took me so long to leave. I'm sorry to say my parents acted like slaves until the day they died. I tried to get them to move here, but they were used to the Jim Crow laws: separate drinking fountains, separate seating in restaurants and buses, separate bathrooms for whites and colored. They stayed where they were, with their church and friends. Only my little brother, Robert, came."

Abe looked at Elder. "Elder," he said, "we're leaving, we're going home."

Elder replied, "Stay awhile, my friend." Mumbling, he closed his eyes. A whisper, "Vengeance is mine." Then, a tortured groan and "Awwwww, dad, forgive me," stunning Maia.

Baffled, Maia turned to Abe.

Abe shook his head and said, "Don't look at me. I don't know." But he had a dark idea of what might have happened between Elder and his father.

309

Maia went to the RCA record player and selected "Stormy Weather."

"Don't know why

There's no sunup in the sky

Stormy weather

Since my man and I ain't together

Keeps raining all of the time. . . ."

"Abe, dance with me."

"You could have picked a happier song."

"I like it."

Sliding into each other's arms they slowly danced, cheek to cheek.

Swaying, Abe said, "Maia, there is a question I've been meaning to ask." She nodded.

"When those two fellows were at the house after the kids were arrested, you smiled and winked at Jacob."

"Yes, what about it?"

"Do you know Jacob?"

"I was wondering if you would ever ask. Yes, I know him, but not in the Biblical sense, just in case you're wondering. During the 1906 earthquake, the hospitals were overwhelmed. The doctors couldn't see them all, so the nurses stepped in.

"With all the chaos, men didn't wait to find gloves, they went right at it, digging and lifting debris off the dead and injured. They injured themselves. There was a man ahead of you. I sutured up his hand. That was Jacob. He was young then, like you, and he had a crush on me. He came around to ask me out. He sent me flowers. But I held out. You see, there was a young fellow in line. When I saw him, I tingled. I was struck. Abe, it was you. Yes you, and you were so dirty. Even your hair. I told you to take off your shirt and to wash off at the basin. Then, when I disinfected your hand, I tried to get you to talk, but you wouldn't look at me. You

310

barely told me where you worked. You were supposed to return to have your stitches removed. I told you to ask for me, but you didn't. I had no choice. I had to go looking for you. Were you interested at the hospital when I stitched your wound?"

"Oh, yes, I was. While I waited, I watched every move you made. I watched your fingers. I looked at your hair. I looked at your lips and eyes. I was smitten and trying to figure out how to ask you out, but you said something that dropped me like a stone. You said, 'You, wash up!' Whew, and bossy. I didn't know if you meant me. I looked around. You said again, 'Yes, you, Moreno, wash up there, at the basin.' Moreno around here is a slur, meaning a dark person or darkie. I thought you were talking down to me. You're white. You know the laws. But two weeks later, on Market Street, you were standing across the street looking at me. Remember? I was loading bricks onto a flatbed. Until then, I thought I had no chance."

"Oh, Abe, you didn't know I'm Puerto Rican. In Spanish, Moreno means dark-toned, brown, or dark olive-skinned. In Puerto Rico, it's often used as an endearing term. You didn't know that my father is black, and my mother is white. I didn't mean to hurt you. Lucky for me that you forgave me. We married within a month. Oh, one more thing. It wasn't necessary when I told you to take off your shirt. I wanted to see your chest and arms. Then, I forgot what I was doing. I wasn't sorry. The other nurses weren't either. My God, your body was sculpted, and handsome too. They teased me mercilessly. I got hot and thought I had died and gone to heaven.

"After that day, I was unhappy if I didn't see you. On our 21st day, yes, I was marking my calendar, I went home and my sister, Lourdes, asked me if I was all right. I couldn't talk. You see, you dressed like a common laborer, and you were always dirty. Remember? I used to wait for you to

311

get off work, and we took walks. One day we passed a nice building, totally untouched by the earthquake. I casually remarked that the quake had destroyed my sister's bakery, and she needed a new place to start over. That day upended my world. You see, you said you would buy it for me, for Lourdes. I laughed, but you reached into that raggedy leather jacket of yours and pulled out a wad of cash. I couldn't believe it. You bargained with that man, and the next thing I knew, it was yours. It was a side of you I hadn't seen before. I was impressed.

"Abe, you rascal, you looked and dressed like a charity case. You sure fooled me. I thought you were barely getting by. I bought your meals, even clothes, and you let me. I always wondered why you had that sly smile. I wasn't going to let you get away. Lourdes said I looked dazed. I told her what had happened. While she was ecstatically jumping up and down, I told her I was getting married. But you were so slow. I had to tell you we were getting married. You asked, 'When?' You're not sorry, are you?"

"Dear heart, if you were not my wife, companion, precious love, friend, my life, I would wish myself dead. So please don't die. When Mikey left us, our sweet dear little boy, I thought I'd lost you. I had to go to Puerto Rico to bring you back."

"I was waiting."

"So, you got hot when I took off my shirt?"

"Yes, very."

"How about now?"

"Uh-huh."

"Look at them," Abe said. "They're sound asleep." Elder's empty glass hung limply at the tip of his fingers. Abe looked at his friend of so many years and felt grateful that Elder was his friend to walk life's path.

Maia removed the glass and covered Elder and Stephanie with a white cotton herringbone blanket. She tucked it, touching their sides. They

312

turned off the lights and left them alone. Outside in the chill night air, midway to their house, Maia said, "So, his mother was Ella Grace, and his sister is Kathy. I'm going to talk to Jessica. Maybe we can find her. Now, tell me about PeeWee?"

"I'll tell you, and you'll learn something ugly about your easy-going husband. It's quite a story. You might not believe it."

Chapter Fifty-Seven: Aftermath. Ravens

Police found Lugo's size 14 boots behind the Ferry Building. Inside were his two revolvers and badge. In the creases of the thick planks of wood, a pink tinge of blood remained.

Sgt. Frank was greatly relieved. Lugo was missing, hopefully dead. One less witness, he mused. The only other witness was Mack. If Stephanie recovered, she might make accusations, but the degree of her recovery and memory would be suspect. And since Mack hadn't touched her, maybe she couldn't identify him. "Maybe," he thought, "he can be a witness for me. Shit, why do I even have to think about this?"

But Lugo was alive. In addition to the wounds inflicted by Elder, one shot from the Winchester had struck him in the fleshly left portion of his waist, just below the ribs. Determined to live, he worked his way east toward China Basin and the construction of the Oakland Bay Bridge. Grabbing pilings, sandy boulders, and debris he struggled, often going down, reaching the bottom, and thrusting himself back up, gasping for breath.

Unknown to Lugo, three shadowy figures had seen everything, from Elder's arrival at the Ferry Building to when Lugo had dropped into the black undulating water. Marking his progress, they followed. Not wanting him to drown, they tossed anything that would float in his path—something for him to hold onto. When he tumbled into the water, he shed his heavy overcoat. As he struggled, he lost the rest of his clothing except the undershirt. Spitting out water, dizzy, exhausted, shivering, bleeding at the thigh, and laboring for breath, he eventually reached an open rocky shore. There he rested for a few minutes in the darkness gathering strength. With determination he started forward, crawling toward a distant light, abrading his knees and hands on the rocky shore.

He took stock of his situation. Wounded but not severely enough to die, he would recover and kill Elder and that damn little jockey man. Abe too. Coughing violently, he thought of Elder's words. "Yes," he whispered, "I am amazing, still standing and defiant." His hand touched a soft stone. No! It was a shoe. And the shoe was connected to a leg and the leg to a man holding a machete. Next to him was another man and a tall thin woman with stringy hair and blazing eyes. "Yesssss," she hissed. The man whose shoe Lugo was touching looked down and said something in Chinese. He repeated in English, "For my son."

Lugo muttered, "Oh, crap."

Two days later, boys throwing stones into the sea turned their attention to loudly cawing ravens covering a mound. Having fun, they mimicked the cawing and threw rocks, scattering the birds. To their horror, the mound was a body. A machete was embedded in the skull.

314

Poor Lugo had died, sad, disordered, never understanding why he never fit in, never knowing that he was short-changed at birth with defective love genes, indeed not imbued with the full complement of emotional capabilities, including humor and other attributes others took for granted.

The means of Lugo's death confounded all, including Elder and Abe, the Mafia, the police, and his friend, Mack. Although never a favorite among his fellow officers, Lugo's death, and struggle to live rose to heroic proportions. As a member of the police brotherhood, there was talk of finding and killing the bastard who had done it. But there was also an unsettling belief that he deserved it and that the same could happen to them. Mack commented that it was amazing that Lugo made it to shore because he didn't know how to swim.

There was talk that David Elder and Abe Jackson had done it, but all was supposition. Elder and Abe had perfect alibis. They were seen by dozens drinking with Police Chief William J. Quinn to intoxication at the party.

Chapter Fifty-Eight: Unfinished Business

"What luck, Lugo's dead," thought Sgt. Frank. But his relief was short-lived. Within days, rumors circulated that David Elder had killed Lugo—also that he and Mack were next. Abe had planted the rumors, wanting them to worry, to look over their shoulders wondering when they would be next. Frantic, Mack urged Sgt. Frank to call Elder, to tell him they had nothing to do with the attack on Stephanie. After talking it over with Captain Luther Ewing, he did.

Elder took the call. Taking a deep breath, Sgt. Frank said that he had heard rumors that he and Mack were involved in the attack on Stephanie. Frank swore he was home having dinner with friends, including Mack and his wife. Lugo, he asserted, was unstable and had a fixation on Stephanie, but there was no proof that he had tried to kill her. Now, they would never know because he was dead.

Elder listened and commented that the call wasn't necessary. He had heard the rumors and had completed his own investigation. He said, "No problem. By the way, my fiancé bumped into you at the party. She says you stared at her scar." Elder dug in, "Now she can't stop talking about it; and yours, on your cheek-- and ear. Sergeant, do you know why?"

Frank slowly put the phone on its cradle.

Mack asked, "What did he say?"

Frank touched his ear. "We're dead. He didn't believe a word I said. And she knows!"

Mack panicked. Sgt. Frank, although rattled himself, calmed him. He didn't believe that a man even as powerful as David Elder would kill two respected police officers. Anyway, Elder had no proof, and Stephanie's memory could be challenged. Maybe Lugo did finger them, but he was known as a strange man, undependable, a known liar, and dead. He had to talk with Captain Ewing.

Captain Ewing agreed to temporary police surveillance on both Elder and Abe, and for a protective team for Sgt. Frank and Mack. It would be for a minimum of three weeks and then reconsidered. Time usually cooled tempers. Also, it would give both officers time to make plans, perhaps to join another department in a distant city.

Lying to Captain Ewing, Sgt. Frank said, "If Miss Rosen ever recovers her memory, she'll clear us."

The captain asked Frank if there was anything to the rumors.

"I swear to God and on my mother, no."

The captain had heard it all and did not challenge but inwardly cringed. He knew that Sgt. Frank's father had accepted his son as a homosexual and continued to love him, but as for his mother, when he confessed, she was

316

outraged. At the top of her lungs, she screamed, "Pervert! Get out of the house. I hope you die and go to hell."

The captain also knew Sgt. Frank's mother had passed away three years prior. There was little that he did not know about his men. The captain was also homosexual, unknown to Frank, a secret held close to a select few. As Frank took his leave, the captain said, "Frank, be careful. You've been a good officer. Everybody makes mistakes. Good luck." Frank felt uneasy at the words but shrugged them off.

As Sgt. Frank departed, Captain Ewing murmured, "Too bad. Goodbye, old friend.

With their lives possibly in danger, schedules were arranged for Frank and Mack to work the same shifts. Those assigned to guard them felt they had to protect their own. It was easy duty, and their attitude was, "Nobody kills a cop and gets away with it, even if the cop is corrupt." The story of Lugo's club being found at the scene of a crime was widely circulated. Also, there were strong rumors regarding the attack on Stephanie, and the involvement of other officers.

After the riots, this was boring duty. But on the second day of the second week of surveillance, two officers, Marcus and Dennis, following Frank's car, panicked. Traffic had come to a stop. At Folsom Street in Chinatown, a large party of colorfully dressed Chinese revelers was crossing, separating them from the sergeant's car. Dennis got out of his vehicle, and ignoring the dirty looks shoved his way to Frank's car.

Frank looked out his driver's side window, and said, "Dennis, I'm glad you're on the ball but we're fine."

Across the bay from San Francisco was Sausalito's sleepy, picturesque seaside town. In 1937, the Golden Gate Bridge would open, making it considerably easier for commuters, but for now, ferries were used. Hillside and lowland homes dotted the landscape, and it was fast becoming a tourist destination with charming shops and a harbor for fishing and recreational sailboats. Here, in modestly priced homes, lived a sprinkling of fellow police and corrections officers. Both Sgt. Frank and Mack were residents and shared rides.

Sgt. Frank drove his car past boat repair shops onto the rattling wooden ramp of the Eureka Ferry. He parked in a long row. The car, a new Ford Roadster Model 40, was purchased on impulse to boost his dark mood. The surveillance car followed. White seagulls with black and gray markings floated in the ship's wake. All was tranquil. The evening lights of the city blinked on. The ferry cut through the water. The engines throbbed. Double smokestacks emitted black smoke.

It was a multi-colored sunset when Sgt. Frank pulled into his driveway. The house was attractively painted beige with white trim. Its lawn was neatly cut, and carefully tended roses and wisteria indicated pride of ownership. They parked outside the garage, opened it, and searched for a possible assassin. They did the same in the backyard. They went through the kitchen and pantry and checked the small living room, the two bedrooms, the closets, and under the beds. Following the house search, they went to the porch, sat on wicker chairs, and shared a bottle of Zinfandel red wine.

While Marcus stayed with Sgt. Frank for the night, Dennis drove Mack to his house. In contrast to Frank's house, Mack's was a square white box and appeared vacant. No care was given to its appearance, not to its peeling paint, abundant weeds, and messy porch. There, he resided with his wife of 45 years. It was said she was unhappy and considering moving in with a daughter.

At Sgt. Frank's house, Marcus slept on the couch. At Mack's house, his wife went to bed and left him on an easy chair drinking Jim Beam whisky.

Dennis hadn't said it, but because the place was musty and depressing, he chose to sleep in the car.

The following morning, at 7:00 a.m., Marcus fried bacon, scrambled eggs, and brewed coffee. Coffee ready, he poured a cup and looked toward the bedroom door. With all the noise he was making, Frank should be awake. Marcus called for Frank to rise and shine. After turning the bacon and a sip of coffee, he rapped on Frank's door. After a decent interval and more raps, feeling uneasy, he hefted his revolver. With a slight push, the door slowly swung open.

Sgt. Frank was on his back with his head on a pillow. His arms were crossed on his chest. His fingers were interlaced.

"Frank?" He called.

The window shades were drawn. There was minor illumination. Marcus moved closer. Something indiscernible was sticking up between Frank's fingers, perhaps a pencil, and dark narrow strings of loose threads lined his bare chest. Carefully, Marcus pulled back the sheet. His eyes, having adjusted to the dim light, widened in shock. It was dried blood, not threads, and not a pencil. It was a thin blade similar to an ice pick pushed deep into the chest. He reeled back and rushed to the kitchen.

Marcus called Mack's house. No answer. The bacon was aflame and smoking heavily. He turned off the burner, placed a lid over the pan to smother the fire, and called again. Mack's wife answered. "Ruth," he said, "let me speak to Dennis."

"Hold on, Dennis is outside. I'll get Mack. He's sleeping in his chair." Marcus heard a scream and a dropped the telephone.

A long thin blade like the one used to kill Sgt. Frank protruded from Mack's heart. There was no sign of struggle. The empty bottle and shot glass were on the floor at his fingertips. Adding to the embarrassment, outside two red roses adorned the police car's hood, and it had four flat tires. Dennis had slept comfortably, wrapped in his blanket, a thick scarf around his neck, and a warm wool cap pulled low over his ears.

Later that day, police visited Elder's house. He was questioned about his whereabouts and that of Abe for the night prior. Elder referred the investigators to dignitaries and their wives with whom he and Abe had dined. Police did not think to ask him about his man, Matteo, or his son, Xavier. If they had, Elder was ready.

Chapter Fifty-Nine: Wedding Day

Rachael kissed her parents and went off to work as usual. She would see them later at home at the wedding. She was excited, and so were they, especially her mother, who she thought seemed unusually happy. She even seemed, well . . . .healthy. It would be a wonderful day--a simple wedding ceremony for Morgan with friends and family to be held at their house in the afternoon.

Bottles of wine and soft drinks were in ice buckets. Snacks were ready. But Rachael was worried. The dresses had not been delivered despite repeated calls. She called, complaining. City of Paris firmly asserted hers would be delivered to the Palace Station Cafe at precisely 1:00 p.m. This wasn't reassuring. They were closing early at 3:00, and the wedding was at 4:00. Filled with anxiety, she restrained herself from shouting protests.

At the Palace Station, Sam and Gus with a skeleton crew were busy serving customers. Raffael was in the kitchen but soon left, saying, "I can't be late for my own wedding."

At precisely 1:00 p.m., a delivery van arrived. Two women carrying a long rectangular box were led into the combination pantry room and office. Hurriedly, Rachael lifted the top. But inside was not the dress she expected. With rising concern, she tucked aside the crape paper to see if the correct one was underneath.

She fingered the fine material and dropped it. Stepping back, heart pounding, she accusingly looked at the two women. Shaking her head in disbelief, she exclaimed, "Oh, no, no, this is all wrong," and almost burst into tears. Unsteadily but forcefully, she said, "This is not what we ordered. This is horrible."

It was not a simple dress for a simple wedding, but a gown, a bridesmaid's match for the expensive Bianca Morgan had wished for, plus gloves and soft white suede shoes.

Almost in tears and desperate for them to understand, she loudly exclaimed, "I can't afford this dress, not in a million years. And I can't wear a dress more beautiful than the brides."

"No, it's fine." It was explained that changes were made, and everything was as it should be. "Dear, it's paid for. Now, please put it on, and we'll fix your hair and makeup."

Disbelieving, Rachael exclaimed, "What did you say? It's paid for? Are you beauticians? No, this is too much. What's going on? Go away. Take it back. No!" She shouted. But they prevailed. After she was dressed and coifed, she looked at her reflection in the mirror and marveled at the beautiful imposter staring back.

As in a dream, she heard, "Now, follow me. And don't cry. Your makeup will run."

Rachael walked through the hallway into the dining room. Everyone was standing, waiting. Sam was at the saloon swinging doors. She crossed the room to shouts and whistles and took his outstretched hand. She said, "Sam, I'm afraid. What is happening?"

Sam said, "Wow, you're gorgeous."

"Sam, tell me. I don't understand."

"I know, princess. More surprises await."

Outside, she was escorted to the little jockey man elegantly dressed in a tailored tuxedo, wearing eyeglasses, standing by a highly polished, decorated Bentley Roadster convertible. Introduced as Matteo, she recalled him as the one who had protected them in Sausalito, one of Sam's henchmen. Today, he looked like a professor. Matteo handed her an elegant bouquet of red roses and helped her into the car.

Four convertibles made up the procession—one four-door white Bentley convertible bearing Morgan, and another for Rachael. In the third car, a Packard, were Rachael's parents and her sister, wearing elegant clothes she had never seen before. Her mother, who had been so careworn, was beaming in a way that had been absent far too long. In the fourth car, also a Packard, were friends.

Seeing Morgan in the Bianca gown, and Sam talking to a policeman, Morgan shouted, "Morgan, what's happening? What on earth is going on?"

Morgan didn't know and didn't much care. She shouted, "Raffael told me to trust him. I am, but my heart is thumping. So far, it's good."

"Where is Jessica?"

"I don't know."

"Where's your father?"

322

"I don't know. I hope he'll be wherever we're going."

"Who's paying for all these snazzy cars?" asked Rachael.

"Maybe a secret admirer. Sorry, I don't know anything."

"Maybe you should marry him instead of Raffael?"

Giggling nervously, Morgan shouted back, "Yes, maybe. Rachael, I don't know what to think. I'm scared."

Rachael leaned forward, "Excuse me, Mr. Matteo, please tell me. What is happening?"

"Miss Rachael, It's a beautiful day, like a dream. A wonderful story, like a fairy tale. Sam wanted to tell you but doesn't want to ruin the surprise. Just wait; you'll see."

"That's it? That's your answer?" Grinning, he nodded. Her eyes went to Sam and four formidable motorcycle police officers—courtesy of the Chief of Police. Sam saw Rachael looking confused and in awe. Standing tall, moving from the cars to the officers and back, obviously in charge, he gave her a strong, confident smile.

To his watching customers, he announced, "I'm going to a wedding, but first, drinks on the house."

The procession pulled away, sirens blaring. Sam, with an amused smile tossed Rachael a kiss and waved.

"Oh, wow. Who is this man?"

"Sam," she shouted, "I don't want to go without you. Sam, I'm afraid."

His shout, "I'm the best man. I'll see you there," was drowned out by the sirens.

The procession took a circuitous route through North Beach, past Washington Square Park, and up tree-lined Columbus Boulevard. Shady poplars and cypresses lined the streets. The cars made a U turn and drove slowly through Little Italy and Chinatown. On-lookers gathered on the sidewalks in front of stores and cafes. Words of congratulations and good luck were shouted. Glasses of wine, beer, sodas and water were raised in a salute.

"Why I'm in a parade." Mystified, Rachael waved to onlookers. Thoughts swirled.

The streets became more elegant, the houses larger, the streets cleaner, and the cars more expensive. Passing through the high-class neighborhood of Nob Hill and lavish mansions, Morgan, mumbled, "This doesn't look like a simple wedding." In Cow Hollow, the procession entered the wrought iron gates onto the curving stone driveway, glided past white bark aspens, and stopped at the front steps. Numerous cars were parked in the driveway and lawn. More were arriving, and taxi cabs were disgorging passengers.

Matteo led Morgan and Rachael up the Spanish steps, through the double wide doors, and into the hallway. He paused to let them take in the beauty. The house was intimidating. Feeling awed and out of place, they looked down the long wide hallway and its high barrel ceiling to the glass doors at the far end. Arriving guests passed, smiled, and joined those outside. Some they knew. Many they didn't. Cut glass chandlers evenly spaced ran the length of the hallway. Flowers, yellow daffodils, red tulips, and red roses were everywhere. "Oh, gosh," Morgan exclaimed, "My heart is pounding. What are we supposed to do?" Matteo, thoroughly enjoying his role in the conspiracy, took Morgan's hand and led them through the hallway past evenly spaced console tables in the center. Each bore vases of flowers. On the walls were tapestries and large pastoral paintings. Around them maids, cooks, and others moved about, preparing for a feast.

Entranced, Rachael and Morgan followed Matteo. He stopped mid-way at a spacious alcove, very much like a spacious room. To their right were stairs.

324

Upstairs, in the bride's room, Morgan and Rachael were impressed—more plush carpet, settees, and makeup tables with mirrors and flowers—more daffodils. An RCA radio played soft ballads. Rushing to the windows, Morgan and Rachael looked down at the yard below. Guests milled about drinking champagne. Uniformed wait staff circulated with hors d'oeuvres. A band was tuning their musical instruments. Food and drink stations were strategically placed.

Morgan exclaimed, "Golly, look there. Is that Raffael?"

Engaged in conversation, Raffael was resplendent in a black tuxedo, white ruffled shirt, black bow tie, black waist sash, and shiny black shoes. Next to him was Morgan's father, similarly attired.

"Golly, he looks good and, ah, wealthy. Where did he get the money? And look at my dad. What is going on?"

Raffael and his conspirators had been to City of Paris department store and fitted for tuxedos. They also paid for the gowns for Morgan, Rachael, and Jessica. Female clerks, hearing of the two handsome men and the shorter and cute, interesting friends, casually passed by to ogle. One liked Xavier. His father stopped him from following her. "Later," he said. "Come back tomorrow."

Looking down at Raffael, Morgan exclaimed, "He's turning our way." Quickly backing up and in wonder, she quipped, "Rachael, if I see any more flowers without knowing what's going on, I'm going to scream. Someone will walk through that door and say it's a mistake, a big joke. We have the wrong dresses—the wrong house. All of this is for someone else. But that was Raffael out there, wasn't it?" Hearing a sound, they turned to the door. Breathing sighs of relief, it was Jessica. They immediately peppered her with questions.

"Whose home is this?" Morgan asked."

"It's my father's, David Elder."

325

"Wait!" Rachael asked, "Jessica, isn't Sam your brother?" Rachael asked.

"Yes."

"Do you mean David Elder is Sam's Father, and Cocker is not his real name?"

"Yes, it does, and no, it isn't."

"But" Morgan asked, "who is David Elder?"

"One second," Jessica replied. She went to the radio and listened.

"Cuddle up a little closer, lovely mine

cuddle up and be my little clinging vine

like to feel your cheeks so rosy. . .

Like to make you comfy cozy. . .cuz I love from

head to tosey, lovely mine. . ."

"Sorry, funny song. It was a favorite of Caesar's." She turned the dial to turn it off. "Now, I'll explain. Sam, you know is my brother, and David Elder is our father. You met him at the Palace Station."

"Does this mean Sam isn't a regular working man?" Rachael asked.

"I'm afraid not."

"I'm sorry, but I have to know. Is all this from the Mafia?"

"My goodness, Rachael, heavens no. We're into many things, but nothing illegal." Turning to Morgan, Jessica said, "Morgan, there are more surprises. I'm supposed to wait, but I can't let you suffer anymore. Today was Raffael's last day at the Palace Station."

Alarmed, Morgan asked, "Oh, no! Did you fire him, and just when we need the money?"

"No. He quit. He doesn't need the money and doesn't have to work."

"What?"

"I hope you don't mind, but Raffael is wealthy. He's an only son and heir to a large family enterprise. His parents manufacture textiles, and their vineyards produce wines. They sell throughout Europe. They're here for the wedding, sisters, husbands, relatives, grandparents, children, and a dog.

Morgan steadied herself on an armrest. She looked at Jessica and sat.

"Now you know," Jessica said. "Wait until you see your rings."

Raffael had talked about his family, and their occupations, but Morgan had imagined a small tailor shop crowded with sewing machines with a few shelves for textiles and wine. She had heard his words but fell far short of understanding. Accepting Jessica's words, Morgan, put her hands to her eyes. Full realization dawned: She was marrying a man she loved, a man who could support their children and, very importantly, take her father out of poverty and away from the backbreaking work at the docks.

Rachael didn't know whether she should console Morgan or congratulate her. She put her hand on Morgan's shoulder and asked, "Do you feel deceived?"

"I don't know. He told me about his family, but I didn't get it. I'm overwhelmed with my good luck. I hope his parents like me and my dad."

Jessica interjected, "Oh, from what I've heard, they're so thrilled they're about to burst. They never wanted their son to be a priest. They want him to marry and have children to carry the family name. They already love you. Now get this. Somehow, they even brought their priest. Don't ask me how. Maybe they did it with money and influence. You're having a Catholic wedding in English and Spanish. His English isn't good, so he's been practicing."

A maid entered. It was time. Downstairs, they were paired, Morgan with her beaming father, and Sam walking with Rachael. Caesar was meant to be Jessica's partner, but with his death, she chose to walk alone.

The music of the wedding march began.

327

Morgan sought out Raffael's family in the first rows. Nearing the front, she was astounded to see the bishop, the monsignor, and Father Raul in the fourth row. She would find that everyone she loved had conspired for this wedding. Rachael's mother and Maia had sent out the invitations. They were identical to the ones selected by Morgan, except for the wedding address. Morgan, swamped with emotions simultaneously sniffled and smiled.

Rachael couldn't decide whether she should be upset or happy. Had Sam been playing with her? She was puzzled, but at least now, maybe, she understood his strange behavior. With her hand in the crook of Sam's arm, she glanced up at him. He crookedly grinned. Grasping her hand, he whispered words too softly for her to understand. A little annoyed, she thought, "Sam is too good-looking for his own good." While wanting to pull his ears she also wanted to kiss him.

Sam removed something from his breast pocket. It was wrapped in vellum. He pressed it into her hand. It had the unmistakable feel of a ring. Her heart quickened. He nodded and whispered, "Wait, don't look until after the vows." She waited in anticipation and forced an appearance of calm. The priest completed the vows and instructed Raffael to kiss the bride. Everyone stood and clapped.

Rachael opened her fingers and unwrapped the vellum. It was a rectangular Marquise Emerald-cut-two-carat diamond ring interwoven with silver and gold. On the vellum was a note. It started, "Dearly beloved." Gasping, she put her hand over her mouth and looked quizzically at Sam. Everyone's attention was on Raffael and Morgan-- except eight: Elder, Stephanie, Jessica, Abe, Maia, Gus, Raffael and Morgan. They were watching Sam and Rachael. Sam and Rachael were in their own bubble despite the activity around them, oblivious to all. He held her hand and said, "I hope you like it. I . . ." His voice cracked, "I didn't

328

want to upstage Raffael and Morgan, so tomorrow, I'll ask you to marry me." Nodding, she replied, "Yes. I will. Tomorrow," and raised her lips to be kissed.

A few weeks prior to the wedding, a woman with her daughter had picked up a discarded newspaper. She read about the attack on a prominent businessman, David Elder, and his mistress. She reread the article, wondering if it was her brother. But could it be? Was he famous and wealthy? It had to be some other David Elder.

The thought that the man mentioned in the newspaper article could be her brother was constantly on her mind. With urging from her daughter, she decided to take a chance. They took the cable cars as close to Cow Hollow as possible. Then they walked and asked directions from gardeners and anyone else who appeared approachable. Coincidently, they arrived on the wedding day. The woman's cloth purse carried a few coins, just enough to return to their temporary lodging. Her daughter convinced her mother to make the effort, to go to the door to ask for David Elder. But they were closed, and she was too timid, tired, and undecided. And there was a party.

They loitered until a latecomer drove up in a sparkling two-door red Cadillac convertible and parked directly in front of the entrance. A huge man held open the car door to a petite woman. They started up the steps, but seeing the woman and child, he cheerfully said, "Come on. Let's go inside."

In the Book of Guests, a maid found the name of GeeGee Popindinski but not those of the woman and her daughter. She invited the woman and daughter to wait and led them into the hall to a marble replica of an ancient Roman bench. She then escorted GeeGee and his wife outside to the reception tables.

329

Waiting in the great hall, the woman and child felt awkward, decidedly uneasy. Sunbeams from the window over the front doors and the glass doors at the end of the hall washed warmly over the interior.

The child looked up and down the hall, taking it all in, awestruck. She looked at the polished floor, the marble benches, ornate vases of white, and red roses, red tulips, and white daffodils. The peace lily also had a prominent mid-way placement with brilliant white tapered blooms, golden spadix, and dark broad green leaves. Maids and waiters passed from the kitchen into the party area with platters of champagne and appetizers.

"Mom," the girl said, "it's beautiful, even the floor. And the ceiling is curved."

"Sweetheart, I think it's called a barrel ceiling."

"Could he really be your brother?" The child asked.

Her mother was embarrassed and intimidated. They were surrounded by opulence; they were in sad clothing and hadn't even washed. Everyone they had seen was expensively clothed and coiffed. She steeled herself. If she panicked, so might her daughter. "I don't know. Maybe," she replied and wondered if they should leave.

The maid found Maia and explained that the woman thought she might be Elder's sister and asked to see him. Maia was dubious. The detective agency had had no luck, not after only a month. But in their eagerness, they had come up with two imposters who were very willing to be the long-lost sister of Mr. David Elder. But very well, she would take a few moments to see her.

Maia approached the woman and her daughter, and two words came to mind, destitute and desperate. The woman had dark eyes and facial features, much like Elder. "There is a resemblance," Maia thought, "but it could be my imagination. Her face is gaunt. Maybe if she looked healthier, and cleaned up, I'd have a better impression." She led the woman and her

330

little girl into the study. The woman spoke of being born and raised on a farm in Pennsylvania with Elder, and their mother dying in childbirth. This information had been reported in the news. The woman could have read about it. Elder had a mean scar on his shoulder, but the woman did not mention it. Nor did she say she was his twin. Perhaps it was due to nervousness, but Maia wouldn't prompt her. The woman could not provide any defining identification. Fearful, and beset with emotions, she could only offer one letter addressed to a Kathleen Pritchard.

Dubious and cautious, Maia thought, "No, another imposter." She thought, "I'll give the woman some money and escort her to the door. But instead, she said, "Well, I don't know." As she sat undecisive, but ready to call the maid to escort them out, she turned to the young girl. "I'm sorry, child. What is your name?"

"Ella Grace."

"Ella Grace???"

"Yes, Ella Grace Elder, after my grandmother."

Maia's eyes widened. Surprised, she sharply inhaled. This name had been kept confidential. Her face flushed. Then, extending her hand to the child, she said, "Well then, you better come with me," and led her and her mother outside to the sounds of music.

When Kathy and Ella Grace were escorted to the table, Kathy saw her brother. Although it had been almost 30 years and remembered him as a teenager, she recognized him instantly. He had filled out and was a man, much older, and his hair had touches of gray but thick as ever. And he had a mustache. She took a step toward him, but his eyes met hers, paused, and passed. There was no recognition. None. She wanted to run to him, to embrace him, but he looked distinguished, important. And, no matter how her heart ached, she would not force herself on him. She wrung her hands, hoping. A second time he looked their way, paused, and moved on.

331

Before the wedding ceremony, classical violin music was played. Afterward, the music changed to cornets, saxophone, and drummer. Now, guests were dancing the Charleston.

Maia had taken a chance and placed Kathy and Ella Grace at a table by the grassy space used for dancing. On the opposite side was Elder's table. Perhaps after all these years, Elder would still recognize her. Maia returned to the main table, whispered in Stephanie's ear, and sat close by.

Julie, observing, asked, "Mom, what's going on?"

We'll see," Maia replied. "Maybe something wonderful."

Stephanie laid a hand on Elder's forearm and nodded toward Sam and Rachael. She said, "Well, sweetheart, it looks like we're going to have another wedding."

"Two," he replied. We're going to have two. Steph, I love you. I want to marry you."

"Ich liebe dich auch mein hertz, verzweifelt. I love you too, desperately, with all my heart. Could we have two children, maybe more— perhaps one like that little girl hanging on her mother's arm by the fountain?"

"If you mean the lady across the dance floor with the graying hair with the little girl, about 10 or 12, three tables from the fountain on the left, yes, I've noticed. She's been looking our way. She looks sad."

"I hoped you'd notice. Maia brought her in. She moved guests around so you might see them."

"I don't understand."

"She thinks you might be an old friend."

"There something about her. Maybe it will come to me."

"Elder," Maia said, "we might have a special guest here, someone you haven't seen for years. Look around and tell me who you see."

"Good idea," Stephanie said, and placed her arm on Elder's, hoping to draw his attention back to Kathy.

"Well, I see Harry Bridges, the leader of the International Longshoremen's Association. There's some Mafia: Francesco Lanza and his guys, Accordion Luigi, Nick La Duca, and Fruiti Fruttuchi. I've told Nick to cut his hair, but he won't. He likes it long. Some of my friends from the F.B.I. are at the next table. Lanza's amused. Captain Blodger and Sarah are sitting with Xavier, Aida, and Matteo. Blodger is looking at Matteo rather suspiciously. I told him he was dead." He chuckled, "Over there is Ramona with her husband, Travis, and a few of her girls; I'm sure the pious here will have a lot to talk about. There's the mayor and a representative from the governor. And over there is Nick Naso the nose and his wife, Nancy. There's Jacob, Mariano Bonaventura, the taxi driver, and his two sons, Joe, the judge from Las Vegas, and Paul, the jockey with his wife, Marlyn. Their sisters are at the next table. Is that enough?" She told him to look again, closer."

Abe interrupted and said, "Elder, look who's here. It's GeeGee."

Upon seeing Elder looking his way, GeeGee's face lit up in joy. Elder noticed he was bigger than ever and had given up on the beard and mustache. Immediately they stood and met halfway. GeeGee lifted Elder in a bear hug.

Walking back to the main table, clapping each other on the back and grinning like kids, GeeGee introduced his wife, Betsy, PeeWee's widow. After delivering the papers to PeeWee's petroleum partnership, he stuck around and never left. At the table, they continued gabbing about the past and bringing each other up to date. GeeGee, seeing Ramona, threw her a kiss.

Patiently, Maia waited. Catching Stephanie's eye, she motioned toward Kathy. Catching the hint, Stephanie tugged Elder's sleeve. "Dear heart, is there someone you might know, someone else from your earlier days, someone before GeeGee?"

Perplexed, and seeing that she was dabbing her teary eyes, he asked, "Sweetheart, are you alright?"

"I'm fine, please look around, for me."

Catching the urgency in her tone, Elder's eyes swept the tables, back and forth. "No. But there is something about that woman with the little girl. Is she all right? She's crying. Now, why would someone come to a party and spend most of their time crying? Maia, why don't you take her to the study to rest? People are staring. How did she get in? She looks homeless."

"She thinks you might know her. Why don't you talk to her?" Sighing in exasperation, he said, "All right, give her an appointment. I'll see her next week."

"I'll do it, but I don't think she has money. I'll give her some to come back, but I don't think she will. She's exhausted. She's frightened and held together by a thread." Looking steadily at Elder for his reaction, she said, "The little girl's name is Ella Grace, Ella Grace Elder. It's the name of her grandmother." Finished, she turned toward Kathy and Ella Grace.

Elder's hand flashed out. "Wait!" Turning his attention back to the woman, he saw her rising from the table and holding her daughter's hand. "It looks like they're leaving." Like Stephanie, the woman was wiping her eyes. Puzzled, he turned to Stephanie. Filled with emotion, unable to speak, she directed him with quick little nods back to the woman.

Timidly, barely holding herself together, Kathy lifted her eyes to Elder. Attempting to smile, she put her hand to her right cheek, palm out. Her thumb touched her nose. Then, she curled her fingers down and up once, twice, three times, jolting him to the core. It was goodbye, but with a hopeful palm-finger wave, roiling his memory. As if struck, realization dawned. Intently watching, he wondered if a tossed kiss would follow.

Struggling with emotions, Kathy brought her fingers to her lips.

"Yes," Elder thought, "barely, but there it is."

Shaken, breathing heavily and sighing, Elder's eyes burst forth with tears. Their mother had used this finger wave as a playful family thing, followed by a tossed finger kiss. The last time he saw it was when his sister stood on the wooden stoop of their boxy little farmhouse in the early morning, wiping tears from her eyes and waving goodbye to their dad. They were 15. He would never forget that day. It was overcast. The fields of corn lightly swayed with a cool breeze. A falcon flew in circles in a cloudless sky. The following day, he awoke to find multi-colored sweet peas on his bed and a note saying she loved him and hoped they would see each other again, someday. Kathy was gone.

Thirty years later, David Elder was looking back in time. The champagne glass he held tilted and spilled. He stood and sat down twice. He studied the woman's face, her eyes, how she moved her fingers through her hair, and the way she hugged her daughter. She was taller now. When last he saw her, neither had achieved their full height or maturity. He cleared his throat and swallowed. He did it again. He put his hand to his mouth, blinked, and wiped away tears. "Can it be?" he murmured. Old memories opened; her features fell into place. Feelings of warmth and weakness flooded his being. His right hand lifted. His face contorted. Tears streamed down his face. Reaching out, sobbing, he whispered, "Kathy, oh Kathy, I remember." He remembered everything, including the last hugs; when she helped his beaten body to bed; the tears, and the apologies of a teenage boy for not protecting her from their father. And her last kiss on his cheek.

Across the way, his sister, trembling, and sobbing covered her mouth. Seeing her mother so distraught, Ella Grace hugged her mother and said, "Mama, don't cry. We'll be okay. We can go back."

Kathy managed to say, "No, honey, we can't. Not ever."

The gaiety of those nearby became muted. Guests were staring, curious. It spread.

Elder, aside from looking at his sister and spreading his hands wide on the table, couldn't move. Wiping his eyes, his heart swelling, he said, "Am I dreaming? Can it be? Abe, help me up. My legs are weak." Abe and GeeGee stood him upright. With a hand on Abe's shoulder, Elder looked across the years of separation. Extending his arms out to his sister, he cried, "Kathy, oh Kathy, you're here. Come. Come here. I've missed you." Then, falling into each other's arms, mingling tears, they couldn't stop crying, laughing, hugging, kissing, and looking at each other.

Kathy nestled her face into the nook of her brother's shoulder, into the cloth of his jacket, rubbing away tears of gratitude.

Elder lifted her chin and said, "Kathy, I can protect you now. You're home." She reached for her daughter, Ella Grace, and pulled her into the embrace.

Looking on, the assembly was struck with awkward, stunned silence. Something momentous was happening—a special reunion. Guests stood. Scattered applause began and erupted into clapping, cheers, and whistles. A violinist caught the mood and played. The harpist joined in.

Elder raised his arm and, with a robust, exultant voice, shouted, "My sister, Kathy, has come home. Home at last."

Watching, Stephanie held her hands to her heart and struggled with emotions, longing desperately for a reunion with her parents, brother, and sisters. Hesitantly, she reached out and touched Maia's shoulder—Maia, who was always civil but had never shown warmth. Maia turned, smiled, and opened her arms for an embrace. Her heart had melted and filled with love. They turned to the sounds of weeping. It was Abe, seated and sobbing, and GeeGee trying to console him. Maia put her hand on his shoulder and asked, "Honey, what's wrong?"

"I'm so happy. I can't handle it," he replied.

The joy was contagious. All around the assemblage, guests, waiters, waitresses, musicians, bussers, prostitutes, criminals, and clergy, were touched at this delicate reunion, sobbed, hugged, laughed, and dabbed away tears. Although they did not know this woman, almost all had experienced loss, had been wounded by sickness and the loss of a beloved friend or family member or knew someone who had. Accordion Luigi and his brother, the Nose stood beaming and clapping.

Gus intently watched Kathy. When she had stood to leave, she was oblivious to his hand steadying her. She reminded him of his beloved departed wife, Nora.

Off to the side, Jessica and Sam were clapping. Filled with lightness and joy, Sam said, "Well, Jess, our family is growing. I'm getting married, and we have an aunt and cousin we can spoil." She nodded.

"I'm pregnant."

"Caesar?"

"Yes, silly boy. Of course. I loved him."

"Fantastic! I'm going to be an uncle."

Meanwhile, the bride and groom, holding hands, returned a salutatory wave from Father Raul. Raffael kissed Morgan and said, "Morgan, I'll live anywhere you desire, in Spain or here in San Francisco, but decide after seeing the house in Figueres, Spain."

"You have a house? Is it large enough for children?" she asked.

"It's different. It's a villa with a central courtyard. It has many rooms, large windows, a large kitchen with a fireplace and thick overhead beams.

Five bedrooms are upstairs with balconies. Our's has a fireplace. We'll be able to look down to see our children playing. And there are gentle fields of rolling vineyards as far as the eye can see."

"A villa? Can we live here and there? Can I have help to clean it? Are you rich?"

"Of course, and yes, we are."

"And a cook?"

"Yes."

"Shoes?" she whispered.

"What did you say?"

"Shoes. Can I have new shoes?"

"My darling Morgan, all you want."

"Then fine. You know, my father is coming with us. He's not to work anymore at that horrid waterfront."

"Yes. We'll keep him busy with our children, dogs, cats, sheep, horses, and anything else you desire."

"It couldn't be better, could it?"

"I don't see how." But at breakfast, an unpleasant topic was discussed. The fascist Italian dictator, Benito Mussolini, was aligning himself with Adolph Hitler. There was talk of war, perhaps involving all of Europe, and the worry that it would come to France and Spain.

Chapter Sixty: A Heavy Heart

With a heavy heart, Captain Edgar Blodger thoughtfully walked in the setting sun to Sarah's apartment. Their relationship was ending. For the

338

past week, cargoes were loaded on the Morning Glory. Truck after truck arrived with shipments. The last were perishables.

Sarah's one-bedroom bungalow, close to the Ferry Building, was one of eight English cottages. Birch trees and rose bushes attractively bordered the units. Every day from Market Street, Sarah took the cable car to deposit her directly at the front doors of City of Paris Department Store.

It was Sarah's third week as a sales trainee in the wedding gown department. She had invited Captain Blodger, Ed, to celebrate.

At her door, he re-tucked his shirt and ran a hand through non-existent hair. With trepidation, he knocked.

Although Sarah was always polite, fun, and pleasant, he considered her sophisticated and above his cultural level. The thought nagged him that she could do better and saw him only out of a sense of gratitude for the help he had rendered. Intimacy had been limited to hugs, and kisses on the cheek.

At his knock, she opened the door, and he handed her a bottle of dark Zinfandel wine, and white and red daffodils. Smiling, she pulled him inside and led him to a small plain wooden table. On it was a short, fat burning candle. She noticed his tobacco-colored leather jacket, polished cordovan shoes, white dress shirt, and black slacks. Not his usual dress. And he acted like a boy with a crush. She handed him a beer. They chatted about the wedding, the end of the strike, and the economy.

They had eaten. It was past midnight, and conversation dwindled. The candle flickered, about to burn out. He wondered if he should go. "I guess I should leave," he said. Without replying, she reached across the table and put her hand over his. After a moment, he turned his palm to hold hers. He asked, "Sarah, would it be all right if I see you sometime, maybe to go out together?"

Sarah squeezed his hand, and said, "Ed, I thought we were, but right now, why don't we sit on this blue velvet couch you got me? Then we'll see." So, seated, in her southern accent, she said, "Honey, come a little closer--closer."

Edgar's pulse quickened. His heart leaped, and he wondered if he had heard correctly. So innocent in the ways of tender love, his mind fumbled.

She leaned against him, placed her hand on his chest, and offered her lips. "Ummm, yes," she sighed. But despite offering herself, Ed was clueless, afraid he would do something wrong with this poised, refined woman. Just being with her was bliss. After another kiss and another, she unbuttoned his shirt and caressed his chest. Passively, he accepted the foreplay, waiting to see what would happen next, if anything. She pulled her dress up to mid-thigh revealing symmetrical thighs, delicate knees, and peaked calves. He held his breath. "My gosh." Heart pounding, he looked from her long, shapely legs to her eyes, to her lips, but still refrained.

"Dear Captain," she murmured, "this takes two." The candle flame flickered a wild dance and died. Their hearts beat staccato.

Chapter Sixty-One: Goodbye Love

Sarah stirred and playfully rolled over on Ed. Following her lead, he had moved in while his ship was being readied for a trip, but now it was ending.

The fully loaded Glory Queen was ready to depart. It would take routes to various ports: Hawaii, the Orient, Australia, and Europe, including the Baltic seaports of Germany, Denmark, Finland, Norway, Sweden, Estonia, and Russia. Manifests would be replaced, delivered at various ports along the way, and others returned to the United States.

At 7:00 a.m., Sarah and Ed walked to Louisa's Café at Fisherman's Wharf for an early breakfast and from there to Pier 32, to his ship. His legs felt heavy, unwilling to move forward. Edgar had secretly placed a considerable amount of money in her top bureau drawer, enough to pay the rent on the cottage and daily expenses for months. She would find it after he was gone, and with her employment she would be more than all right financially.

Although Stephanie had told Sarah that the captain was bonkers over her, he had never uttered words of love nor that he missed her when they were not together. He felt he couldn't; he always knew that he was leaving, and so did she. And he doubted that a woman of her quality could love him.

The strike's duration had allowed Ed a window to meet her, to spend time with her. True, they had lain in each other's arms and awoke to kisses, but she had not asked him to stay, and he fretted about her true feelings. He had never married, had no children, and never had he felt such fulsome satisfaction in the company of a woman—never in love until now.

Softly, she said, "Ed, I will miss you. Will you miss me? Will I see you when you return?"

Stabs of love filtered through his heart, but he could only muster nods. As they walked the quay the background noises of longshoremen at their tasks, clanking chains, machinery, shouts, and rumbling carts, assailed the ears of all but them. They were oblivious except to the presence of the other. Bob, at the railing, saw them coming and waved. Stopping at the foot of the gangplank, Sarah and Ed turned and faced each other. Feigning bravado he did not feel, Ed said, "Well, how about a hug?"

Sarah gave him a long enveloping hug and pulled him tight. She gazed at his rough face, memorizing, to keep it forever. She kissed his lips and screwed up her courage to say, "Ed, I'll think of you every day. I'll miss your looks of love. I know you love me. I haven't said it, but I love you. I don't want you to go. I want to see you every day. I want to talk to you. I want you. I want your children. I'm in love with you." Wiping a tear, she said, "My heart's breaking."

Blodger was dumbfounded. He gave her a quick hug and ran up the gangway. He began talking to Bob, his first mate, and seemed to forget her. The second mate joined them. An animated conversation ensued with hand gestures and waving arms. She sighed, looked up, and waved, but he didn't see. She lowered her head and pulled her coat tighter. She was 30 yards away before she heard running feet.

"Sorry, love," Ed said, "I'll lose my job, but I'm delaying our departure. Let's go to City Hall."

Sarah looked at him, wondering, "What is he talking about?"

"We can get a married—maybe? Please say yes. When I return, I'll quit the sea. I've wanted you from the first, maybe not when you came out of the rain, but now I'm glad Elder cut me. That night, instead of money, I met you." She was silent, and he couldn't read her expression. "Oh, Sarah, please, don't tell me I'm wrong." She made a happy humph and pulled him toward her.

Walking arm and arm toward Fisherman's Wharf, back to Louisa's café, to talk, Ed said he would quit immediately and stay, but he had made a promise. The promise was to David Elder.

He explained: In the port of Cuxhaven, Germany, five women would be brought on board to be smuggled to America: Stephanie's mother, maternal grandmother, and Stephanie's three sisters. They had ignored Nazi prohibitions limiting Jewish activities and movement and fled Hamburg. They were in hiding. The rest of the family was gone. A sympathetic former employee had provided the information. Given the world's political turmoil, they were to be rescued as quickly as possible.

"There will be another war," Ed explained. "Shipping from the U.S. to Germany will stop. Elder has plans of having them sit in the front row at their wedding, right behind them, while they say their vows. Maybe it can be managed. The trick is to seat them so that Stephanie doesn't see them. I don't think it'll work. Even with her back to them, she'll hear them speaking German and realize it's her mother, her family. They'll break down crying. There will be a big interruption in the wedding. Who knows? I think we should tell them, but he disagrees. It's his call. He wants her to see them after the vows when they turn to the audience.

"I'll be wiring Elder to keep him up to date, precisely the return date to San Francisco. Invitations will go out. Her mother, sisters, and grandmother won't know what's happening except that a Jewish benefactor has arranged for their rescue. Although he's not Jewish, that would be Elder. What a surprise for Stephanie. She doesn't even know they're alive."

"What if someone turns them in?" Sarah asked.

"That is a concern, but if that happens, some people won't get paid, and there will be hell to pay. Elder is dead serious about this, and they know it. He's a strange man. He's kind, he's mean, he's warm, he's cold, and he cries when he's happy. I've never known a man to cry so much when he's happy.

He's forgiving, he means what he says, and it's better not to get on his bad side.

"The plan is to put them in specially constructed wooden crates, truck them to the docks, and load them like any other cargo. They'll be uncomfortable, but it has to be that way. The Nazis patrol the docks. Some other families might be with them. And, if we can pull it off, we'll take them too. They'll stay with Maia and Abe when they get here. They won't know what's happening, except that they're safe. It's tight. The wedding will be the in the yard. Mayor Rossi will officiate.

"When Stephanie and Elder turn and are presented to the audience as husband and wife—all very secretive. You can imagine. She'll see them; they'll see her. Wow, what a scene! Elder is over the moon, excited, anticipating Stephanie's reactions. Heck, I'm excited. The trick is to keep them apart until the wedding. Yeh, that's how it will end.

"He's adding to the house. Stephanie was told it was for Elder's sister, daughter, and the babies. You know Stephanie's pregnant with twins, just like him and Kathy, but she can see that the addition is almost as big as a house. She's been asking why. He makes excuses."

Sarah pulled him closer. "Did you plan this with Elder?"

"Well, yes. Remember when Stephanie invited you to the house for breakfast? You said she insisted you bring me along. I didn't want to go, but you promised he wouldn't be there. He was, and you left us alone—on purpose. After staring at each other, he ignored me and turned his back. Frankly, I was boiling mad and felt like putting my foot up his, excuse me, his ass. I was talking to his back and cursing myself for trying. Well, I had been thinking about it and offered a plan to bring out Stephanie's family. But he just sat there with his back to me. I thought to hell with it. I wasn't going to repeat myself. But after a long minute, he went to a cabinet. At first, I thought the jerk was walking away from me. I was about to tell him

344

to go to hell. But he came back with a bottle of cognac and two crystal glasses. He gave me the strangest look like he was seeing me for the first time. He filled a glass and slid it toward me. To my surprise, he gave me a big grin and offered his hand. I was still mad, but he said, 'I've been pigheaded. I'm sorry.' Since then, I've had sit-downs with him and his family. Excited is putting it mildly."

"You didn't tell me."

"He swore me to secrecy, and you are Stephanie's best friend."

"Did he offer to pay you?"

"Yes. I turned it down."

"I'm glad."

"Stephanie is starting to wonder. She caught them jumping around the kitchen when we told them. But as Fruiti Fruttuchi says, they ain't talkin'. We have a bunch of co-conspirators."

"You're a good man, Ed. Does this mean you've forgiven Mr. Elder?"

"Yeh, but I'll still thinking about that little jockey guy with the knife."

Epilogue

At Cuxhaven, Germany, two tall, good-looking, masculine, strapping, Nazi officers came on board and watched the loading throughout the day. As the cargo was loaded, one grew suspicious of the extra careful diligence given to three large containers. Unfortunately, they wanted to inspect them and met a bad end.

The officers were stripped of their clothing. Then two crew members, both of German descent, put on their clothing and left the ship. They were also tall and spoke the language. They pulled their hats low and snug, pulled the collars of the great black leather overcoats to their ears against the chill air, and left the ship. Walking away, they waved a backhanded dismissive farewell to Captain Blodger. A German lieutenant, an officer of lower rank, approached but was contemptuously waved away. Twenty minutes later, the crew members returned in their own clothing. Also loaded that day, in addition to Stephanie's family, was a frail, elderly man of 80 and his eight-year-old grandson.

With the disappearance of two officers fervently devoted to Hitler, the Nazis suspected foul play. The Morning Glory was one of three stopped on the high seas by a battleship and searched. Armed Nazi sailors and one officer walked around the ship. Their attitudes were stiff and imperious. Descending to the cavernous hold, they ordered the largest containers to be opened. But they were sealed. Blodger called for tools and two cases of Lordanov Vodka to drink while they waited. Lordanov, made in one of the oldest distilleries in Germany in Koblenz, highly prized and costly, arrived promptly.

Tense, Blodger shouted, "Where are the tools?"

"Sorry, Cap.," a sailor responded, "Here they are," motioning to another sailor.

Crates were opened. Nothing found—only uninteresting merchandise. Welding the tools, the Nazis moved to the next. Meanwhile, the prized Koblenz vodka was offered to the officer. Seeing the reputable emblem stamped on the wooden boxes, he nodded in approval.

While another huge shipping container was opened. Blodger hurriedly filled two glasses, one for himself and one for the Nazi officer. He raised his glass, and made a toast, "To der Fuhrer." After the toast, Blodger invited his own merchant seamen to drink. Seeing this, the officer scowled, but Blodger refilled his glass and asked if he could also serve his men. Pleased, the officer nodded. The men with the tools stopped, curious. More vodka and the mood morphed into one of camaraderie. Feeling genuinely gregarious, Blodger clapped the Nazi officer on the back--a serious breach

346

of etiquette. After receiving a stern look, and an "Oh, oh" look from Blodger, both feeling the alcohol broke out in laughter. More was served. There were no more scowls and unfriendly orders. Blodger gave them the half-empty case and two more for their ship. The crates were forgotten.

On Saturday, December 22, 1934, at 5:00 a.m., the Morning Glory sailed into San Francisco Bay past the construction of the Golden Gate Bridge. With morning mist coating their faces, standing at the railing, Stephanie's mother, Gretchen, her maternal grandmother, Gert, and sisters, Elka, Birgitta (Gita), and Marta, were delighted. They were entering the land of liberty where they could walk about freely. They had heard about this land of opportunity, where one could speak his mind without fear, without regard to religion or race. Grateful and wondering about their benefactor, they witnessed the early morning lifting of the fog and the city's unveiling.

So much to see---beautiful skyscrapers with lights blinking on; high hills, pleasure and commercial boats sailing in the harbor, Alcatraz Island, hundreds of white flying seagulls, pelicans diving in the undulating water rising with fish, and basking sea lions.

At 11:00 a.m. Maia and Kathy arrived in the Duesenberg and the Chrysler. The elderly man, Simon, holding his grandson's hand, stood aside, lost in the vast docks. Not knowing this new land and with only a smattering knowledge of English, he didn't know what to do. Seeing his dilemma, Maia, in a friendly but no-nonsense manner, told them they were going with them. They were all taken directly to City of Paris department store for the women to purchase suitable attire for a wedding. They wondered why they were to attend but were pliant in the care of their new friends. And, after all, they had been promised assistance in locating Stephanie.

347

At Maia's spacious home, the new arrivals were taken on a house tour and assigned rooms. From the bay windows, they took in Elder's larger mansion across the way. Open to view were preparations for a wedding. There was also a construction crew on scaffolding working on room additions. Stephanie's mother, Gretchen, commented, "My goodness, many people must live there."

Maia gaily chuckled and said, "Not yet, but soon. The owner is David Elder. He's coming to meet you."

Elder did come. After 30 minutes of pleasant talk, he stood to leave. Gretchen extended her hand. Instead of shaking hands, he asked if she would mind if he hugged her. Gretchen, usually reticent with strangers, opened her arms. She liked this big man and his gentle manner. Upon leaving, he commented that he would see her the next day. "I'm the groom," he said. "I'm marrying a wonderful woman. Her hair and eyes are like yours. She's Jewish, so later we'll have another wedding, a proper Jewish wedding. My bride is a woman from. . . . " But Maia placed a finger on his lips, schussing him. Gretchen, amused, at his chastened look, gave him another hug. Maia said, "Elder, you better go." Gretchen wished him good fortune and commented to Maia, "He's a nice man."

Four days following the docking of the Morning Glory, on the day after Christmas, Stephanie was in the bridal room. A pervading air of excitement was prevalent. Many special, smiling looks had been cast her way. She wondered why, and if everyone, but she, was privy to something.

Sitting still, attired in her gown, Stephanie was thoughtful. Finally, looking at Abe pacing, she turned to Maia. She said, "Tell me!"

"All right," Maia replied and pulled a chair in front of Stephanie. Taking her hand, she said, "Elder has a surprise. You'll see It in the front, in the first row near the mayor. Since you're pregnant, it's been decided that a shock wouldn't be good for you and the babies."

348

Tears welled in Stephanie's eyes. She dropped her head, then raised her eyes to look at Abe and Maia. Fighting for emotional control, lips quivering, she swallowed and said again, "Tell me." But they insisted she would know soon enough. Hoping against hope what it might be but afraid to utter the words, she waited as if saying them would make it not come true.

It had been approximately one year since unique events had impacted the lives of San Franciscans, David Elder, and those close to him: labor strife, riots at the docks, attempts on his life and loved ones, the death of Caesar, new friends, and family, and the wedding of the former Father Raffael and Morgan. When it began, it was the Christmas season. A year later, with the city brightly decorated, he was to marry Stephanie Rosen.

Abe and Maia escorted Stephanie through the hall to the glass doors and the rear yard. In her father's absence, she had asked Abe to walk her down the aisle. She strived to see to the front, but it was futile with so many guests. The music of the wedding march began. The assembly rose and turned to see the bride. Three rows, four, five, six, seven, nine, 11, 15, and she saw the astonished face of her beloved mother, Gretchen, lifting her hands to her mouth. Stephanie's eyes jumped from her to Elder, grinning like a kid caught with his fingers in the cookie jar, and back to her mother. Rushing forward and shouting, "Mutter, mutter, mama, mama," and losing all decorum, she pulled Abe along, followed by bridesmaids and grooms—Maia with Matteo, Xavier with his mother, Aida, Kathy with Gus, Sam, Rachael, Morgan and Raffael—and fell into her mother's outstretched arms. If Stephanie was beautiful before, she was now radiant, her heart overflowing with happiness. Well, you can imagine. As the vows were recited, Stephanie's mother, sisters, and grandmother crowded with her and Elder in front of the officiating mayor, weeping and smiling. A beaming Gretchen kissed Elder so many times throughout the vows,

349

grabbing his face and planting kisses, that Mayor Rossi had to pause several times. Finally, he plowed through despite the kisses.

A woman sitting next to Father Raul exclaimed, "They have the best weddings! You never know what to expect." She had previously attended Raffael and Morgan's wedding.

The event was the talk of the town. As for Captain Ed Blodger, Elder was so grateful he bought him a mansion, and a flashy Merced-Benz convertible, and they went golfing. Not really. He and Sarah moved to Mendocino, California, and purchased a vineyard. They had four children, three girls, and a boy.

Jessica lived nearby in a two-story home overlooking the clean, clear ocean, with her husband and two children, Caesar Jr., and Georgia, Georgia, named after her maternal mother. The child had blue eyes after her mother. The boy, sometimes called Little Caesar, had brown eyes, like his father.

"Where's daddy," asked the child, Georgia. "Here he come," replied her brother. Jessica turned to see her husband, Caesar walking down from a sand dune, barefoot, grinning happily, and waving with his good arm.

Yes, Caesar lived, although the bullets Lugo shot into his shoulder shattered bones. But he was healthy, very content, and it remained to be seen if his shoulder could be repaired.

Sarah and the captain had invited Simon, the elderly gentleman, and his grandson to live with them, and they did. He still had his humor and wits about him; and having been an investment banker in Germany was a wealth of knowledge. His life with the Blodgers and his grandson is another story-- and that of Jessica and her son, Caesar—Caesar Elder O'Sullivan, my best friend. The last time I saw them, the whole clan was walking to the beach, chatting happily.

El Fin

350

Miscellaneous

On Wednesday, April 18, 1906, a devastating earthquake hit San Francisco at 5:12 a.m. with a magnitude of 7.9 (extreme). The earthquake lasted 45 seconds to two minutes [records are in dispute]. Destruction was Massive. Within approximately 45 minutes, the Southern Pacific began evacuating refugees to other cities in the bay area. With the resulting fires, three-quarters of the city was laid waste. Eighty percent of the city was destroyed, about 20 square miles. In a population of about 460,000 nearly 300,000 were left homeless. The fires destroyed all Banks with their records of deposits. Accounts were lost. Paper money burned; factories, commercial areas and homes were laid waste; government buildings, birth and death records were lost, as well as records of ownership.

It was said that only two percent of the destruction was directly the cause of the earthquake and the rest by fire. If a home was destroyed, but not by fire, the owners set it ablaze to collect on fire insurance, and the authorities looked the other way.

Trains, ferries, and the United States Navy evacuated about 320,000. Many trickled back within days. Horse soldiers arrived with pack saddles loaded with food and water. Wagons followed with shovels and gloves. Mayor Eugene Schmitz put out an edict authorizing Federal troops and police to kill any person found looting or in the commission of any other crime. Looters were to be shot forthwith.

A train loaded with provisions was sent from Los Angeles, and the U.S. Congress approved relief.

In some areas, fierce wind and gusts from the fires caused small tornados, ripping off roofs. Some poor souls were overtaken and killed by rolling fireballs. Never had the city experienced such a conflagration.

Initially, it was estimated 3,000 were killed. Later, it was revised to over 5,000. Not counted were those in the Chinese District, nor those in the cheap tenements near the docks housing illegal immigrants in the poverty area of Rincon Hill. In these areas, records were not kept by the city. Many were found crushed by falling debris. Also, during the conflagration, many were buried without being reported to the coroner or Department of Health. Some were buried in a trench at the military Presidio.

For four days, raging fires destroyed approximately 28,000 structures. In three years, they were replaced by 20,000.

Regarding opium, in the late 1880s and early 1900s, opium dens were common in San Francisco, just like houses of prostitution, so common that there were tour guides for paying customers. Opium dens were profitable, easily found in and outside Chinatown, and frequented mainly by the white population. Previously, in the 1880s, during a moral panic, San Francisco mapped every gambling parlor, every brothel, and every opium den.

During the labor strike of 1934, the ferries continued to run.

The 1934 labor strike that shook San Francisco closed all major west coast ports: San Diego, San Pedro, Stockton, Oakland, San Francisco; In Oregon: Portland and Astoria; and in Washington: Bellingham, Seattle, Tacoma, and Aberdeen. Although there was bloodshed in other ports, the strike culminated in San Francisco on Bloody Thursday, July 5, 1934. Near the end of the strike, there was a strike within the strike. It was the declared four-day city-wide "General Strike" affecting the whole city. It began on July 16th. Initially involving 14 unions, it expanded to about 63 and from 127,000 to 150,000 workers, depending on varying reports. It essentially shut down the city.

The larger strike began on May 9 and officially ended on July 31.

The longshoremen received .95 cents an hour ($18.16 in 2019 dollars) and unionization of all the West Coast ports. The Seaman's Union was left in the lurch and did not achieve its goals. Presently, the International Longshoremen's Association (ILA) is North America's largest union of maritime workers.

The luxury department store, City of Paris, closed in 1972. The old glass dome, and the rotunda were incorporated into a Neiman Marcus store.

Songs

"Wait till the sun shines, Nellie," 1905, by Harry Von Tilzer, lyrics by Andrew B. Sterling.

"Minnie the Moocher," Written and sung by Negro bandleader Cab Calloway, 1934.

"Just A Closer Walk With Thee," A Negro slavery gospel song, possibly pre-Civil War. Original author unknown.

"In the Sweet by and by." 1886, lyrics by S. Fillmore Bennett, music by Joseph P. Webster.

"Stormy Weather," By Harold Arlen and Ted Koehler, 1933.

"Cuddle Up a Little Closer," 1908, by Karl Hosch, and lyrics by Otto Harbach.

"The Old Rugged Cross," by George Bernard, 1912.

"Danny Boy," 1910, lyrics by Frederic Weatherly, music by unknown.

The Author

The author's career was in criminal justice on the Federal, county and State levels. Interface was with criminals, judges, attorneys, multiple police agencies: F.B.I., Secret Service, Immigration, etc; occasionally with foreign agencies. Experiences include presentations at prisons, the sole capture of a bank robber, threats to his life, offers of bribery, and sexual offers from females under investigation (none-accepted). He also served eight years in the California National Guard. He resides in a small beach town with his dog, Bradley. Contact: gonzaldacarp@gmail.com